The Reckoning

Set in South Park, Colorado in 1868, this fast-moving narrative is a blend of historical and mystery fiction. It's intriguing, and I got hooked from the first page. Every chapter was gripping. For certain, this narration will make a good script for a classic Western movie.

You can't guess what will happen next or how the story will end. Honestly, right now, this narration tops my list of the amazing books I've read recently.

Official review, Online Book Club

The Renewal

Great book! The descriptions of the land and mountains brought me into the location of the book. From that feeling it was easy to get involved with the characters and immersing yourself in the story. It had cowboys, beautiful ladies, horses, good guys and bad guys. I looked forward to finding out where the story would go every time I picked up the book. Loved it!

R. Robison

A Score to Settle

A Score to Settle is a classic historical western set in the 1870s. There are classic themes here which are well-presented with descriptive narration, gritty characters, and a historically accurate plot. Mike Torreano writes a compelling story with plenty of anguish. Every nuance is brilliantly detailed so the reader can escape into the rough landscape of the wild west. The plot moves at a good pace with tons of action scenes. My heart went out to poor Del time and again. I savored A Score to Settle and I look forward to reading more from Mike Torreano.

NN Light's Bookheaven Reviews

White Sands Gold
The elements we love in Westerns are all here, but they are tweaked in fresh ways that break stereotypes and surprise us! Though a treasure of hidden gold clearly is central, the addition of a priceless relic to this cache is both inventive and unexpected. 1890s New Mexico comes alive with multidimensional characters who breathe life into this compelling story. Torreano makes Lottie, Yancy, Lou, Twill, Ma Gilbert, and the others who drive the action totally believable. You'll be turning pages to know who gets to the treasure first? What price is exacted in personal loss? What is that relic? The answers make WHITE SANDS GOLD a Western you won't forget!

K. Ewig

Fireflies at Dusk

by

Mike Torreano

Fireflies at Dusk

Cover Art by *The Wild Rose Press, Inc.*

The Wild Rose Press, Inc.
PO Box 708
Adams Basin, NY 14410-0708
Visit us at www.thewildrosepress.com

Publishing History
First Edition, 2023
Trade Paperback ISBN 978-1-5092-5146-9
Digital ISBN 978-1-5092-5147-6

Published in the United States of America

Dedication

The men and women who fought our nation's Civil War ardently believed in their cause, both North and South. At the extraordinary cost of more than a half-million men and untold numbers of civilians, slavery in this country came to a long-overdue end. *Fireflies at Dusk* honors the bravery, valor, and sacrifice of these soldiers during the most tumultuous time in our history.

Acknowledgments

My author's journey hasn't been a solitary one—fortunately. I have been blessed with talented partners along the way, fellow wordsmiths who have helped me grow as a writer.

I'd especially like to thank my daughter, Lisa, for her support of and research on Fireflies. She uncovered many interesting historical tidbits, like the Sultana disaster, that I was able to weave into the story to make it richer.

My wife, Anne, has always been a valuable sounding board on my overall story arcs, and Fireflies is no exception.

I'm also privileged to be part of an outstanding critique group that helped me smooth the story and deepen my characters. Heartfelt thanks goes to Dr. John Andrews, Marilee Aufdenkamp, Rex Griffin (Moon of Black Hearts), Scott Hibbard (Beyond the Rio Gila) and Margaret Rodenberg (Finding Napoleon).

All talented writers in their own right.

My friend and fellow author, Gary Scheimer, has also been very helpful on the Fireflies journey.

Chapter One

Southwestern Ohio, Winter 1848

The front doors of the country meeting house burst inward. Windows rattled as the crash of splintering wood echoed throughout the small building. Jonathan ducked as four rough-looking men cradling long rifles stepped over the debris. He stared wide-eyed at men the likes of which he'd never seen before. Wild eyebrows, dirt in the creases of their weathered faces. Dusty, dirty brown overcoats.

His mother's trembling hand wrapped around his small one. She held the baby close and corralled her other son behind her skirt. When the intruders raised their guns, Jonathan cringed. His bundle of biscuits dropped to the floor. The bearded hunters looked around warily. Muddy boots thumped on loose planks as three of them strode up the middle of the circled benches. The stench of hard riding swept along behind them.

The man with the big black hat said, "Go on up there and raise that platform like I tol' you and start lookin'. That's where some of these places hide runaways, they dig cellars for 'em." Big Hat turned to the leader. "I know you're hidin' slaves here and we mean to find 'em. They're ours, right and proper, so stay out of our way."

"This is a place of worship. You can't just break in here and—"

Big Hat leveled his shotgun at the man. He said through a scarred mouth, "I just did. You Quakers ain't about to do nothin' to stop us, anyway. Now back up or get shot." The leader retreated, clasping his Bible to his chest, lips moving soundlessly. Pieces of broken door lay scattered at Big Hat's feet as he filled the doorway. A younger tough stood next to a small wooden table, waving his rifle at the congregation and laughing.

"Father, stop them," Jonathan implored, as they stood together in front of a worn oak bench. His shrill voice was a solitary echo in the still building. Tom Gray drew an arm tighter around his eight-year-old son's shaking shoulders. Jonathan's stomach jumped. He spun toward Belinda, his mother, tears winding down his face, sandy brown hair all askew. "Help them!" She stared at Big Hat as if frozen, Sunday bonnet framing a pale face. Jonathan flashed back to what his father said slave catchers do with runaways. *They drag them away. Sometimes they find who they're looking for, and sometimes they don't, but they always bring Negroes back south.* A murmur ran through the congregation. Jonathan thought of the little boy hiding in the cellar. He'd given him one of his best cats eyes after they'd shot marbles in the frozen dirt outside this morning. He couldn't make sense of men coming to take his friend away.

Jonathan trembled in the simple meeting house. He reached down to retrieve his precious bundle and pressed it tight against his chest. Biscuits his mother made just that morning for the runaway family. They were no longer warm against his overalls, but still smelled of fresh honey. The only sounds were low whispers as wives and husbands spoke in hushed tones. When his father moved to shield him, Jonathan peered around to watch the two intruders hard at work by the low platform.

Big Hat raised his shotgun. "Better stay right there, mister. And the rest of you, don't you move neither. Didn't come here to shoot no white folk, but I will if I have to. Just come to get them runaways. Once we find 'em, we'll be on our way. Then you can keep on prayin' to a God who ain't gonna save nobody here today." He fired a round of buckshot that tore into the low ceiling. Jonathan ducked back behind his father.

A scuffling noise rose as the bounty hunters scattered old furniture and tore up loose floorboards. One of them peered into a dark pit below the platform.

"Shine that lantern down there, Jacob. I see sumthin'. Yessiree, looks like we found ourselves a whole passel of 'em." He thrust his barrel into the pit. "Git on up here right now. Don't make me come down there, 'cause y'all don't want to see me mad. Now git!"

A family struggled one by one up a rickety ladder from the makeshift dirt refuge below. Father, mother, young girl, and a boy—the one Jonathan brought the biscuits for. They shielded their eyes from the light. Sweating. Shaking.

Jonathan stood wide-eyed behind his father, holding onto his pants, shivering.

"I got 'em, boss. Don't look like much. Can't see why anybody'd want 'em back."

"Don't matter what you think, now does it? It's enough for you to know you're gonna get paid once we march 'em back south. Now let's go."

Jonathan turned pleading eyes toward his father. "No! Don't let them take them!"

Tom stood mute like a statue. As Jonathan tried to move in front of him, his father held him back.

Big Hat and another slave catcher trained their guns on the worshippers. The other two pushed the family outside with their rifle barrels. The mother's mouth quivered as she held her little girl close. Jonathan rushed outside, followed by the rest of the people. He reached toward his friend, but his father held him fast.

Big Hat grabbed ropes off his horse and threw them to his henchmen. "Tie the big one's arms behind him, and throw a rope around his neck. Then rope the others to him."

Some of the women fell to their knees in the snow, hands clasped in low prayer. No one moved as the slave catchers bound the mother, then the two children to the husband and pulled them toward their horses.

Jonathan burst away from his father, screaming, "No! You can't take them away. They ain't yours. Let them go!" He clutched the bag of biscuits in his outstretched hand and sprinted toward the little boy.

Big Hat swung his shotgun and batted Jonathan's bundle away like he was swatting a fly. Jonathan scrambled to retrieve them, but the biscuits rolled away in the dirt, as if trying to flee the pitiful scene. He dashed toward the slaver, fists balled. Big Hat knocked Jonathan down with a swipe of his meaty hand and pulled out a whip. It uncoiled like a venomous snake searching for prey.

Tom stepped between the slave catcher and his son. Belinda tried to stop him. "Tom, please don't! Stay clear of the whip. Remember what your uncle—"

"My uncle ain't here."

Big Hat snapped the whip. The first blow knifed through Tom's shirt, but he didn't flinch. Infuriated, Big Hat swung again at the man who stood ramrod straight in front of him. A second blow and the lash cut into Tom's chest from shoulder to waist. He stared at Big Hat, the whip now lying limp at the man's side. The bounty hunter glared—when his gaze swung their way, his men looked away. He took a hesitant step backward, readying the whip to strike Tom again.

Jonathan leaped up, his throat filled with fury. "Leave him alone!" He started hitting Big Hat in the stomach, sobbing and red faced.

"This little boy's the only one of you that's worth a hoot." Big Hat spat black tobacco juice.

Tom staggered toward his son.

One of the other bounty hunters trained his rifle on him. "That's far enough."

Big Hat pushed Jonathan back to his father. Jonathan felt the wetness through his father's white shirt, now shredded and streaked with red. His eyes met the boy's, who reached a hand toward Jonathan with his marble in it. Big Hat yanked him back. The marble fell from his hand and disappeared in dirty snow.

The little boy yelled, "Help us!"

Jonathan strained to get free, screaming at the men as the four thugs mounted their horses. He collapsed to the ground in tears.

Big Hat turned in the saddle to the hushed worshippers. "Looks like your so-called 'underground railroad' just ran off the track." He sneered at the small crowd and raised his shotgun upright on his leg. "Don't nobody move till we're out of sight down this road. Ain't nobody here worth dyin' for." He started his horse off at a steady walk, leading the slumped family away. Just before the bend in the road, the boy turned back to Jonathan one last time, then disappeared.

Tom turned to his son. "Time to go home."

"No!" Jonathan had never yelled at his father before. Confusion tore at his soul. Why was his friend gone? Why didn't anyone stop them?

Tom lifted Jonathan up by the arms and stifled a groan. "Let's go home, son."

Jonathan glanced back at the horse tracks, then trudged behind his family to their wagon. The runaway boy's scared face haunted him as they rode away.

It was the heart of winter, so when the family reached home, Tom started a small fire which only took the edge off the chill in the cold, stone farmhouse. His mother asked her husband to sit so she could tend to his wounds, but he rose silently from the rock fireplace, his tattered shirt hanging loose.

"Tom Gray, come sit in this chair right now, or I'm leaving and walking into town in the snow." She motioned to an old wooden chair.

He pursed his lips and eased into it, his back clear of the chair's ladder back.

"Jonathan, run and get me washcloths and a pail of the cleanest water you can find."

Jonathan filled a dented tin pail and brought it back with rags and soap, paying no attention to the injuries his father suffered in his stead. His mother eased her husband's bloody shirt off and cleaned his wounds. When she'd finished dressing them, she handed him a clean shirt. "Why don't you stay here with us and rest up before supper, Tom?"

He grunted a "thanks," added wood to the reluctant fire, grabbed his weathered brown jacket and disappeared for the barn. Leaden clouds in a gray sky cast a gloomy light throughout the house.

Jonathan started for his room, his thoughts jumbled.

Belinda said, "Son, please come back here and sit down."

The last thing he wanted to do. Nothing made sense.

"Please."

What good was talk? Wouldn't save that family.

"Jonathan!"

Her forceful voice made him turn. Sadness roiled his insides.

She took him by the arm and steered him toward a chair. "Now sit. Please."

He'd never seen his mother so worked up before. Her hands pressed hard against his tear-stained face.

"You need to know why your father did what he did. And why no one lifted a hand to help the freedom seekers."

Jonathan stared at the floor, arms folded across his chest, heart pounding. He didn't want to hear anything more about what just happened. The little boy...no one helped.

"Jonathan, do you know what it means to be a Quaker? What we believe in?"

He lowered his gaze to the threadbare carpet. "It means we go to Sunday meeting, sometimes more than that. And it means we don't help people we ought to."

Belinda dropped her hands away. "No, honey,

that's not true. Do you know what we believe about slavery?"

His mother's intensity held Jonathan still. "I know it isn't right."

"We don't like it, either. But we're pacifists, we don't believe in fighting, even for freedom seekers. Even to end something we strongly disapprove of. So when those men burst in this morning, that's why no one helped them. We don't believe in taking matters into our own hands."

"But, Momma, they took that family away with ropes." His eyes blurred and his mother disappeared for a moment.

"There was nothing to be done about it. That's just our way."

"Well, that's not my way." He wiped at his face.

"Yes, it is. Someday you'll see that. Someday you *will*." She stared out the window toward the barn then pulled her chair closer. "I want to tell you something about your father. You know he doesn't like talking things out."

Jonathan knew that only too well. He rubbed his arms hard against the cold that still reached out from the corners of the house.

His mother draped an afghan from the cedar chest around his shoulders. "Years ago, your father felt just as angry as you do right now."

Jonathan stuck his chin out. "My father's *never* felt like I do."

"Yes, he has." With a hand to his face, she made him look at her. "Jonathan, listen to me, please. Just after your father was born, his father went off to fight the British in the War of 1812. Someday you'll learn about that in school."

"No, I won't." He didn't care about the British and didn't want to hear about anything else.

"Your grandfather went off to fight, even though your grandmother pleaded with him not to. And when your grandfather didn't come back home, your grandmother made your father promise he would never fight. And she cried and kept after him until he did. You see, your father never knew his father and it broke his mother's heart."

"But those ropes…the little boy was so scared." Jonathan's bottom lip quivered.

His mother held a hand up. "Your grandmother made your father promise, and he took that promise to heart. I tell you this so you will know why he didn't help the runaways today—he couldn't abandon his promise to his mother. And he would have put us and the rest of the people in danger."

"Wasn't there something…anything that could have…" His words drifted away in the still-chill air.

"No, honey."

"Why don't we fight, Mother?" His eyes brimmed.

"Because we don't take sides against any person or any people. We want to keep ourselves focused on God so we can honor Him."

"But God wants us to do what's right, doesn't He?"

"Yes. Even so, your father couldn't have overpowered those men, and I wouldn't have wanted him to try, because we believe God wants us to trust Him and not strike out against those who set against us. We live in America, but in a way, we've never been a part of this society—neither the North nor the South."

"Then why are we helping slaves? We've hidden

lots of them in the meeting house."

"Yes, we have, and I know that's hard to understand, but it's a stand we've taken as a faith community. We want to help them be free, not fight for them. We also help them with the quilts we all sew."

"You mean the quilts you put out on our fence?"

"Yes, those quilts. You're old enough to know the secret behind them. They're special. They tell the runaways things."

"Like what?"

"Like if it's safe to go north and the best way to get there."

"They're just quilts, though. How do they tell them anything?"

"Every square has a pattern and a color that tells the runaways something. Like where a safe house is, which direction to go next, or landmarks to look for. The different colors tell them whether they should travel or not. Even though we're against fighting, we feel it's God's will that we help the freedom seekers in this way."

"But Father's never said anything about that." He'd never said much about anything.

"Your father is a prideful man. It would never occur to him to share what he feels or thinks with his young son. And I want you to promise me you'll never mention this to him."

"Why?"

"Promise me."

Jonathan saw the urgency in his mother's face. He'd heard her words, but didn't understand them. The pain in his heart came from a realization that his father couldn't fix everything, but still wanting to believe he could. That's what Fathers did, didn't they? Set things right.

Chapter Two

Spring 1849

Jonathan and Sonny scampered to the Little Miami River to play the day away as spring made a fitful appearance. The nine-year-olds took their imaginary travels from Jonathan's tree fort to the nearby river. They raced across the newly-planted wheat field to see who could get there first.

Sonny slid on the muddy riverbank. "Beat ya! Beat ya!"

The two best friends skimmed stones across the rushing waters. Sonny flung a flat, light one that skipped eight times. He raised his arms in triumph then said, "My old man told me to be careful, like I was a kid or somethin'. Does yours do that, too?"

Jonathan shook his head. "No." He didn't know what his father thought about anything.

A thick black walnut reached for the sky beside the river and commanded the surroundings. Light green spring leaves covered sturdy branches that created a sprawling umbrella. The massive tree dwarfed everything and cast a protective canopy over both sides of the stream. Thick, barky grape vines curled up and around the trunk. Strong ropes that he and Sonny always used to climb the tree and swing out over the water. Sonny's dog, Sadie, lay nearby as the boys played on the wet riverbank.

Jonathan had never seen the river running this fast. He cast an eye on the darkening sky. At first clear, storm clouds had gathered and the wind picked up. Fat raindrops hit him as he climbed the walnut's vines. Steady rain punched new leaves and pinged off the river's surface. Maybe they should go home. The sun hid as if it didn't want to watch. Jonathan's first tentative swing landed him too close to the stony bank and he rubbed his bruised backside as he hopped out of the water. He'd push off harder next time. Sonny was already clambering back up the tree for another leap.

"Sonny, wait up!"

"No. This is gonna be the world's longest jump. Watch!" Sonny grabbed the wet vine and thrust away hard. His left hand slipped off first. Then his right. Jonathan watched in horror as Sonny tumbled backward to the earth, pierced the shallow water and slammed headfirst into the rocky riverbed. His limp body drifted out into the current. What?

Jonathan scrambled down the tree, heartbeat trip hammering in his ears. He'd pull Sonny out, he'd be okay. He just needed to get him out of the water. He'd be all right. The fast-moving waters had carried Sonny almost around a slight bend by the time Jonathan got down. His legs shook as he ran along the slippery bank trying to reach his friend.

"Sonny! Sonny! Lift your head up!"

The white body floated face down just under the water's surface. Jonathan lunged wildly for him time and again from the water's edge. Sadie dashed along, barking madly. Got to get him out. Jonathan sprinted and leaped into the water. The cold current shocked him as he grabbed Sonny's shirt and tried to pull him up. Ahead to his right, the rushing spring current had trapped a large log fast against jutting, round rocks. Thrashing furiously, he managed to steer them toward it.

With a soft *whump*, Sonny hit the sunken tree trunk headfirst.

Jonathan flung an arm atop the big spar and grasped Sonny with the other. If he could just get Sonny's head up. He strained again and again, but choppy waters pinned Sonny tight against the tree trunk. Soon, Jonathan could pull no more. He grabbed the log with both hands, sobbing. Sadie leaped in and swam to Sonny, pawing at him. When the current started to drag her away, Jonathan flung an arm around her neck. He stayed hard against the trunk a long time, hoping for a miracle. Rushing water swallowed his tears. How did this happen? They were just playing. He shielded his eyes as rain danced on top of the water.

Jonathan's arm shook. It went slack and slid off the wet log. He lost his grip on Sadie and slipped into the stream, his head barely above the water. As he started to drift, suddenly he and Sadie were being pushed toward shore. His feet touched the rocky river bottom and he dragged himself and Sadie up the bank, collapsing on the muddy ground. Gasping for breath, he glanced back, searching for his rescuer. No one. How?

Sadie paced the shore, whining. Jonathan staggered home through woods and fields, oblivious to the brambles that cut him as he stumbled by. He burst into the barn, shivering all the while.

"F—Father! Father! It's Sonny, he's in the water...he...he can't move! H—Hurry!" A vision of

Sonny face down filled his mind.

Tom yelled to Belinda to fetch the Walkers. He and Jonathan hurried to the river where Tom lifted Sonny away from the log and laid him on a grassy part of the riverbank. Pale, still body. Sightless eyes stared up at him. Sadie licked Sonny's colorless face, whimpering.

When Sonny's wailing mother arrived with Belinda, his father intercepted them. "Mother, please take Mrs. Walker over there." He pointed to a shady spot under a nearby cottonwood. Belinda wrapped her arms around her neighbor and moved away from the muddy scene. By the time Mr. Walker arrived, Tom had covered Sonny with the blanket the boys brought for a picnic they'd never have.

Jonathan stared unseeing at the guilty water, numb.

Sonny's father put his hands to his head and squeezed like he was trying to force the image of his dead son from his mind.

Jonathan couldn't take his eyes away from the lumpy, still blanket. How could that be Sonny? They were just...

Mr. Walker gathered the bundle in his arms and held Sonny tight against his chest. Tears streamed down his face. Mrs. Walker had stopped screaming and stood mumbling to herself. The hushed couple set out for the Walker farm. Sadie trailed the silent cortege, tail dragging on the ground.

Jonathan sank to the muddy shore. He shivered as the Walkers took Sonny away. Images raced through his mind. Sonny spinning off the rope. Limp against the log. Sadie whining. He couldn't be...gone...Jonathan's head dropped to this chest and tears spilled from his cheeks onto the riverbank. His fault...all his fault...

The sun faded behind the silent walnut tree. Clouds lengthened. Rain fled. Dusk crept over the churning river.

His father laid a hand on his shoulder.

"Come home now, son." Jonathan's head throbbed. "Now." He couldn't make his legs move. Tom helped him up.

Jonathan stumbled home in a sobbing fog. He stayed in his room three days, his mind filled with questions he had no answers to. Why had God taken his friend? If only they'd stopped when the rains came. He should have, he knew better. His mother left food on his bedside table but he had no appetite. The third day, she made him come into the kitchen to eat. He looked around for his father.

Belinda said, "He was in to see you, but you were sleeping, and now he's tied up with planting."

Jonathan walked down to the barn where his father worked away on a bridle bit. He sat nearby, getting his courage up. "Father, is Sonny in Heaven?"

Tom continued shaping the leather pieces without looking up. "Don't know, son. That's up to God."

After a long silence, Jonathan left the rest of his questions unspoken. The comfort he craved was nowhere to be found in the barn. He trudged back to the farmhouse, finding it harder to jam his guilt and conflicted feelings back in their dark hole.

Chapter Three

Belinda tended her vegetable garden by the side of the house. She'd planted a different type of tomato seed this year, hoping these wouldn't have the hard fleshy middle her husband didn't like. At a sound behind her, she turned to see the Walkers driving a wagon up the dirt drive with their two children and Sadie. She called to Jonathan. He came out of the farmhouse and sprinted toward the wagon. Sadie leaped out and dashed to Jonathan, licking him over and over and whining, nosing him backwards as the two tumbled to the grassy ground.

Belinda waved as they drew to a stop in the front circle. "It's so nice to see you all and Sadie."

Mrs. Walker said, "Thank you, Mrs. Gray. Sadie's actually the reason we came by today. Since Sonny's…well…since then, Sadie hasn't wanted to do much of anything. She mostly lies around with her head on her paws. At first we thought she'd perk up, but she hasn't. Mr. Walker and I decided to bring her over here to see if setting eyes on Jonathan would make any difference."

Belinda smiled. "Well, certainly looks like it has. She's perked Jonathan up, too."

"That's what we hoped for—that being with Jonathan would make her happy. So…we wondered…if Jonathan would like to have her?"

He sat with an arm draped around Sadie. "Can I, Mother? Can I keep her?"

"I'll have to ask your father—no...I'm not going to. Yes, Jonathan, you can keep Sadie."

Mrs. Walker beamed. "That's wonderful. Jonathan's the closest thing to Sonny that Sadie has now, and I know Sonny would want her to be with him. They were so...close." She fell silent, lower lip quivering.

When she came over to say goodbye to Sadie, Jonathan stood. The first time he'd seen them since... "I'm s-sorry...so sorry. It's all..."

Mrs. Walker hugged him and petted Sadie's head. "I know, Jonathan. Thank you."

Thank you? He didn't deserve to be thanked. It was his fault Sonny died. Sadie bumped a cool nose against his hand and he slumped to the ground as she laid her head in his lap.

Tom walked toward them from the barn, wiping dirty hands on a dirtier rag. He shook hands with Mr. Walker and nodded to Sonny's mother.

Belinda smiled. "The Walkers would like to give Sadie to Jonathan."

Tom rubbed his chin. "Don't know as we need a dog."

Jonathan drew Sadie close, his heart thumping. *He* needed her. Please let me keep her. Please.

Belinda glared. "The answer is yes, Tom. We're going to take Sadie. She's just what we need around here."

Jonathan let out a loud, "Yay!" She was Jonathan's dog now, and she seemed to know it as she danced around him in circles. "What kind of dog is Sadie,

Mother?"

"Well, if I had to guess, I'd say she's got a lot of blue tick hound in her."

Sadie chased Jonathan up and down the drive. From now on, it would be the two of them. She'd help him forget his gnawing hurt. His mother's words rang in his head. Sadie was just what he needed.

****

Belinda marched to the barn where Tom often holed up to sort things out. She found him hunched over his scarred workbench, pounding on an old iron horseshoe.

"Tom, I want to talk with you."

"What about?" His gaze never left the shoe.

"You know what about. Your son."

He stopped his battering and glanced sideways at her. "*My* son? He's always been a lot more your son than mine."

Belinda's heart skipped a beat. "Why do you say that? He's your son, too."

"All I know is, he don't seem to want to have much to do with me. He favors you in everything. He looks like you, thinks like you. There ain't much of me in him from what I see."

Sadness lay on her heart like an ache. "Is that what you really think?"

Tom's face reddened. "Sometimes." He shook his head. "Can't figure it out. Don't know why I have such a tough time gettin' on with him."

"For one thing, you're too harsh. Let up on him. He's just a boy trying to find his way. Like you were at his age. A boy who's just lost his best friend."

"He oughta know the world's a tough place. The

sooner he learns that the better. This farm is just as good a place for him to find that out as anywhere. Better'n some."

Belinda said, "That may be, but you don't have to be as hard on him as your uncle was on you."

"My uncle…" He trip hammered the horseshoe. The angry sound reverberated in the small space.

"And you have trouble with Jonathan because he loves you so much."

"That don't make no sense, woman." He flipped the hammer back onto the small workbench.

"Of course it does. He worships you, even though he doesn't understand you yet."

"Why? Because I couldn't stop them from taking that slave boy? That family?"

"That's only part of it. Most of all, it's because he wants to believe you can do no wrong. You're his father. His hero. So when he sees you can't make everything right, he's terribly hurt. And yet, in the midst of his disappointment, all he really wants is your approval, just an occasional 'well done, son.' He's still so young. He needs you to guide him, teach him. He's a good boy, Tom Gray. And you're a good man. I love you so much." She kissed him and stepped back. "Now, talk to him, please."

Tom stared at the gray metal horseshoe. "I just don't know the words. There's lots of times I wish I did. I see the good in him, I do." He picked up some shoe nails, ending the conversation.

****

Mornings, Jonathan snatched the kitchen lantern and ran out to the rickety wooden chicken coop in the dark. Always with Sadie. He'd reach under the hens, gather the warm brown eggs in his floppy hat, and place them in the little wire basket by the kitchen sink. Then it was down to the barn to help his father milk their cows. He tried to imitate Tom's frown as he pulled on the teats. Maybe if he worked even harder, he'd earn his father's approval. Fresh, foamy milk spilled from oaken buckets into the spring box to cool.

When weather permitted, he'd walk to school after a quick breakfast. His father silently wagoned him there when it wasn't. School was only open in winter and summer and let out just after midday, when he'd run home to help with chores. Jonathan looked forward to cold winter mornings the most. After bundling up, he'd rush to get to school early. He'd head straight for the schoolroom's black potbellied stove before the rest of the kids arrived. The teacher had let him fire it up ever since first grade.

Back then, Jonathan had asked, "Can I help you do that, Miss Shafter?" as she puzzled over the stove one cold morning.

"Do you know how, Jonathan?"

"Yes'm. Can I try? Please?"

"Certainly. Whatever I'm doing isn't working, that's for sure." She stepped back with a smile in her eyes while Jonathan settled in front of the old stove with the tall black pipe that disappeared at the ceiling.

He swung the cast iron door open wide. "All's wrong is that it wasn't getting enough air." He built a little stick house inside the stove, crumpled some loose paper underneath, and lit it with a match. "There. We just needed some more kindling, paper, and air. You were doing everything else just right." The fire blazed to life as they watched. He beamed at one of his small victories. There were few enough.

"How did you know how to do that?"

"Well, I've been doing it lots at home. Tomorrow, I'll bring in some candles my mother made and we can use them from now on, okay?"

He grinned when kids warmed their hands by "his" stove. He particularly looked for an approving smile from Barbra Carson, who sat across the room with the rest of the girls. She wore her auburn hair in long pigtails. He'd never pulled them, but he'd been tempted to. A little cloakroom to the side held coats and galoshes but otherwise the square schoolhouse was a large, open room with a few dirty windows. On cold mornings, it took until midday before his small stove's heat worked its way into the classroom's corners.

Jonathan was six years older than his brother, Peter, and eight older than his sister, Claire. He didn't mind helping take care of them, but they were too young to be real playmates. After Sonny died, he spent most of his time alone with Sadie.

Reading became his escape and replaced the tree fort of his youth. His mother spent hours teaching him to read before he even started school. When his folks wagoned into town, he'd rush inside the Cincinnati lending library and wander throughout the world with books that painted their own pictures. Each book created different rabbit trails that burrowed across the landscape of his mind.

When warm weather teased the land with spring, Jonathan went with his father into nearby Loveland to pick up seed and supplies. On the way back, he scanned the endless woods of big oaks that sat alongside fat, white-trunked beech. Lots of maples and towering elms. All sporting light-green leaves that summer's sun would darken.

At home, he hefted supplies from the wagon and carried them inside to his mother. As he walked back out of the kitchen, Jonathan lingered just outside.

"Don't know as we're goin' to make it this year, Mother. If there's bad weather, or bad luck, ain't much of a cushion to fall back on. None, in fact."

"We'll make it, Tom. You've always done for us, and with God's providence, we'll find a way this year, too. Together."

"I heard the Overstreets, two miles distant, are packin' up and movin' farther west."

"I am sorry to hear that," Belinda said, her hands fashioning a new quilt. "But that's not our concern. We're here and we're going to stay here."

"Lord willin'. Got a letter in town from my brother Charles today."

"How nice. Why don't you read it to all of us at dinner, dear?" That night, after Belinda finished serving, she raised an eyebrow at her husband.

Tom fished the letter out of a worn overalls pocket.

Jonathan leaned forward to hear news from the outside world. "What's your brother say, Father?"

"Well, he writes, *Things ain't good for us here in Maryland.*" Tom held the scant letter tightly. "Goes on to say, *We might have to pick up and come west like you and Abel and Sarah did. We don't have no money, but we ain't quite out of food yet because of what we put up last fall.* He asks if we've ever heard from—"

Belinda thumped a hand on the table. "I'm sure there wasn't anything else important in there, was there?" She sat upright, eyes flashing at her husband.

"Nope...I guess that's about it. Let's bow our heads."

After the blessing, Jonathan said, "What other things, Father?"

Belinda said, "Not your concern, son. Food's getting cold."

He scrunched his brow. "Mother, why don't we ever hear from your family?"

Belinda dropped her gaze to her plate. In a small voice, she said, "They're all dead." Her shoulders slumped as she walked back to the kitchen.

After dinner, Belinda shut the bedroom door behind her. She'd already checked to make sure Jonathan and the children were asleep.

She held a hand out. "Tom, let me see the letter, please."

"Ain't nothin' else in there worth seein', Mother," he said in mild protest.

"Tom. Give me the letter."

He slowly retrieved it from his overalls pocket.

Belinda skimmed the part she'd already heard, then pored over the last couple of paragraphs. "Why can't he just leave well enough alone? It's none of his business after all these years." She started crying softly.

In a gentle voice, her husband said, "He don't mean no harm. I'll write him back and let him know we're fine. It don't need no more talkin' about than that." Tom retrieved the letter from his wife and put it with the others in a small box on the closet shelf.

"And why in the world are you keeping those?" Belinda demanded. "At least throw away the one he wrote when we first came out here."

Tom's eyes widened. "I keep 'em 'cause they're

from my family, just like you'd keep letters from your family if they ever wrote you."

****

The Bible was always their common family bond. Around the fireplace at night, Jonathan read to Peter and Claire, explaining passages where he could. Belinda was a strong believer but it was Tom who took the spiritual lead. He launched into certain verses as he believed the occasion called for, mostly when he thought Jonathan wasn't measuring up in one area or the other.

Even though Jonathan was used to this scriptural finger pointing, inwardly he recoiled at Tom's heavy-handed manner. Among all the books he devoured, the Bible was the foundation of his education and the key to his soul. But, he guarded his relationship with the Almighty closely.

Chapter Four

1852

When he was twelve, Jonathan's long-simmering guilt boiled over. It was Thursday night—meatloaf, as usual.

"Mother, why don't you ever make anything else on Thursdays?" Jonathan pushed away from the table and stood. "We always have the same things every week. Why can't we ever have something different?" A confrontation was overdue.

His father pointed a finger at him. "You hold your tongue and apologize to your mother. I don't ever want to hear you—"

Jonathan snapped back before his father could finish. "Why do bad things happen? And no one ever does anything about 'em—just accepts them. What's your pacifism ever done that's any good?" He threw his napkin down, chin thrust out.

His father placed his on the table and rose, face reddening.

Jonathan had been angry with himself—and his father—for years. And he still blamed himself for Sonny's death. His ears rang and a familiar flush surged within him. Part of him knew that his father couldn't have stopped the slavers, but a bigger part wanted him to have tried. To have done something. He still hadn't figured how to live with a father who was so hard, who ignored his questions, who walked away instead of talking to him. Living with himself was bad enough.

"You were a coward!"

Tom's right hand flew. *Smack!*

Belinda gasped. The children stared wide-eyed.

Jonathan froze, the air ablaze between son and father. Tears welled and drops spilled down his face. He wanted to rub his reddening cheek but forced his hand away. The slap hurt, but he'd gotten a reaction. At least his father knew he was there.

"I ain't nothin' like you." Without a glance back, he rushed out of the farmhouse. "And I won't never be." Jonathan ran like he was punching holes in the ground. Every stride put more distance between him and his family.

His father hurried outside. "Jonathan, get back here. Jonathan!"

"Let him go, Tom." Belinda stared after her son.

"Dammit! I hit my own son. I ain't no better'n my uncle." He hurled a rock at a tree. All the air had gone out of him.

****

The next morning, Belinda answered a knock at the front door.

"Mrs. Gray, I'm Bea Shafter, Jonathan's teacher." Her brown hair was gathered and she wore a simple gingham dress with a bonnet that looked homemade.

"It's so nice to meet you, Miss Shafter. Jonathan has mentioned you. What brings you out all this way?" She peeked out at the front circle. "By buckboard, too."

"It's about Jonathan."

Belinda raised a hand to her mouth. "Oh my. Has

he done something wrong? He's not home right now."

"No, ma'am, just the opposite. That's what I'd like to talk with you and Mr. Gray about."

"Let me get him." She turned toward the barn, but her husband was already heading their way.

"Mr. Gray, I'm Jonathan's teacher, Bea Shafter. How are you, sir?"

"Fine, ma'am. What can we do for you?"

"There's a fine Cincinnati high school, called Woodward, with scholarships for bright students. I'd like to apply for one in Jonathan's name. I can't challenge him anymore."

Tom tipped his hat and turned back to the barn.

"Mr. Gray, don't you want to hear more about what that school could do for Jonathan?"

"Heard enough," he said, with a dismissive wave of his arm. He scattered the large white geese that always honked at him when he passed near their territory.

Belinda squeezed her hand towel tighter and tried to smile. "Can I get you some coffee, Miss Shafter?"

"No, thank you, I need to be getting back. Thank you…for seeing me."

That night in their bedroom, Belinda confronted her husband. "Why don't you want to hear about that school?"

"For one thing, he needs to do more around here, not less. Every day I fall further behind. Those fields don't plant themselves, and we're hangin' on by a thread as it is."

Belinda stood with arms crossed. "But that's not the real reason, is it?"

Tom fumbled with his shoes.

"You're afraid to let him go there, aren't you? I can tell. Aren't you?"

"All right, damn it. Yes!"

"For heaven's sakes, why?"

"You *know* why, woman. I'd think you of all people would be against it, too. Don't you remember what your fella said to me all those years ago? That he was going to be somebody important and you didn't figure in that. I don't want Jonathan turnin' out like him."

Belinda brought a hand to her mouth.

Tom heaved one of the shoes into their small closet. "And if Jonathan goes there, I'll likely have to ask my brother if he can stay with them while he's at that fancy school."

Belinda eased onto the bed. "What you're really afraid of is he'll learn about us from his Uncle Abel and Aunt Sarah, aren't you?"

Silence.

"You know that won't happen. I know you and your brother aren't real close, but I wouldn't worry about Jonathan staying with them. My guess is they don't even know." Belinda drew the bedcovers back, slipped into bed, and snuffed the oil lamp out. She stared at the darkened plaster ceiling long into the night.

****

When Jonathan returned home the next day, his mother said, "Thank heavens you're back. I've worried so. Are you all right?" She hugged him tight, then stood back. "I want you to apologize to him."

Jonathan pursed his lips, his emotions still raw.

She held him at arm's length. "Do it now, son."

As he walked to the barn, his heartbeat quickened.

He eased into the clammy lower level where they kept the cows. Damp stone that always smelled of manure. His father sat on his same old stool, almost as if he was part of it.

"Uh, Father…I'm sorry for…" The rest of the words wouldn't come. He stood trying to figure where to put his hands.

"I'm sorry too, son, but havin' more book learnin' never made nobody a better person."

"I'm sure that's true, Father." Jonathan steeled himself for another lecture.

Tom glanced up, and with a flip of a hand, muttered, "Do whatever you want about that school."

That was the longest conversation he'd had with his father in days. Later, when Miss Shafter told him he'd been accepted at Woodward, he didn't know how to feel. Excited for the opportunity, but a large part of him still didn't want to go against his father.

As they milked, he asked, "Father, could—"

Tom interrupted before he could finish. "Take the chestnut mare. She's old, but reliable—like your mother and me." He rose, poured his foamy bucket into the dented milk can and jammed the top on. Hard.

When Jonathan rode away his first week, he snuck a glance back. His father stood outside the barn, feet spread like a statue. He kicked the horse into a trot, tired of worrying about what the man was thinking. Going away to school would do him some good.

Once a week after Sunday services, Jonathan saddled his horse, Belle, got a small bundle of food from his mother, and headed the fifteen miles or so back to Cincinnati. Sadie ran alongside. His father didn't come out of the barn anymore.

Woodward gradually brought the larger world into sharper focus. Jonathan had never met anyone like the headmaster, Samuel Highwater. The teacher didn't even try to hide his disdain for the scholarship kids.

"Mr. Gray, have you heard of the Fugitive Slave Law?" Highwater rocked back and forth, hands clasped behind him as he was wont to do.

"No, sir, I haven't." The familiar feeling that he didn't belong here surged within him.

"Well," continued Highwater, crossing his arms, "then you don't even know what it's about, correct?"

"Yes, sir…I mean no, sir." A warm flush ran from his neck to his ears. He felt the stares from his classmates.

"What the law says is…runaway slaves are still owned by their masters and are to be returned to them."

"Yes, sir."

"Any idea what else it might have said?"

"No, sir." He slunk a bit lower into his seat.

"It says…" Highwater drew this out. "It says anyone helping a runaway slave can be put in prison and must pay a fine."

"Yes, sir."

"Mr. Gray, have you ever heard of something called the Underground Railroad?" Highwater preened as he walked, smirking at the ceiling.

"Yes, sir." The little boy all those years ago… "It helps slaves to freedom in the North."

"Correct…do you think it operates around here?"

"I've heard it does, sir, but I would have thought you already knew that."

The class tittered. He might not know a lot, but he wasn't stupid. This school would be his way off the farm.

Monday through Wednesday Jonathan stayed with his aunt and uncle, walking cobblestone streets to class now. The one-room City Library was close as well. With no chores, he spent most of his free time with his nose in a book and Sadie at his feet. Her unconditional affection broke up his occasional moments of homesickness.

One night he overheard Abel and Sarah talking downstairs. Unusual—they almost never stayed up as late as him. Theirs was a muffled conversation he wasn't paying much attention to, but when Sarah said, "Jonathan," he cocked an ear. He couldn't quite make out what they were saying, only snippets. When he heard his name again, he sat up in bed. "Don't know...told him...not our place...nothing gained...saying anything." That was all Jonathan could make out.

His uncle said, "Tom knows...but...discusses it...never ask."

What were they talking about? Their arrangement with his new school? Questions lingered until sleep drowsed him.

Wednesday afternoon Jonathan saddled the mare for home. Belle slowed when they approached the farm, as if she sensed Jonathan's ambivalence. He rubbed her down, filled her feed, and headed inside with an enthusiastic Sadie.

"Hello, Mother."

"Jonathan! It's so good to have you home." A quick hug. "Your father will be in from the fields soon. I'm fixing one of your favorite dishes for dinner. Tell me all about school." She flew around the kitchen, awash in her element.

His father came in as dusk claimed the land. He washed dark soil from his hands and acknowledged Jonathan with a grunt. Those familiar dirty, dusty bib overalls. Worn out work shoes. Tired stride. "What're you cookin', Ma?"

"You two sit. I'll call the children."

Peter and Claire hugged Jonathan, fluffed Sadie's ears, then dashed to their places. After Tom's prayer, the children passed the dishes and hogged the conversation. Jonathan caught up with their doings without saying a thing. As dinner wore on, he was reduced to an afterthought. The children still held some hero worship for him but tonight it had worn off by the time they passed the peas.

"How's my brother?" His father asked in between bites.

"He's fine, and so's Aunt Sarah. They said to say hello." Jonathan paused. "Why haven't we ever spent any time with them? They sure are nice people."

Tom glanced at Belinda for a moment, then nodded. "Yes, they are." He turned back to his food, leaving Jonathan waiting for more of an answer that never came.

After dinner, he found his father on the front porch where he usually rested in the humid late-summer air. He took the low chair next to his father's weathered wicker rocker that sagged around him. Tom was paying more attention to an appreciative Sadie than him.

Jonathan tried to engage him in conversation. "We're studying government in school, Father."

"Uh huh."

"I hear there's more trouble with slavery across the

33

country."

"Yup. Read something about a new law that lets settlers in Kansas and Nebraska territories decide whether they want slavery or not." He shook his head. "Likely just delaying the nation's day of reckoning."

How did his father know anything about what was happening around the country? Only thing he'd ever talked with him about was chores and Scripture. Jonathan continued some small talk about school but the more he tried to draw his father out, the quieter Tom got. An all-too-familiar disappointment filled Jonathan. He'd kidded himself thinking it might be different when he got older. He should know better by now.

Riding back to town Sunday afternoon, Jonathan pondered the two uncomfortable worlds he lived in. The farm didn't feel like home anymore and school never would feel like home.

Chapter Five

Wednesday afternoon and school was out. Jonathan saddled Belle for the long ride home and sweaty days of work in the fields. He and Sadie trotted down the main road east, at first cobblestone that soon gave way to well-traveled dirt. Dust kicked up as the sun warmed him. He settled the mare into a jog and wove in and out of a few wagons, horses, and people along the way. Sadie barked nonstop to be running free. Within a few miles, traffic thinned to nothing. Except for the occasional screech of a blue jay and the mare's hooves clip-clopping along, the muffled sounds of the surrounding thick woods left Jonathan alone with his thoughts.

As Belle rounded a curve, Jonathan saw two boys fighting. Ben Murphy was on top of a kid Jonathan recognized from his old school, pummeling him around the face and body. The fight was gone from him and he was covering up to deflect the blows.

Murphy was a bully, almost six feet and stocky, with a mean temper. Jonathan never had any trouble with him, though, because he'd always stayed away. That, plus Jonathan was close to Murphy's size, only leaner.

"Hey! Get off him." Jonathan spurred Belle straight toward the tough, who hovered atop his prey. Murphy raised up as the horse raced toward him, stopping within inches. He held his hands out and backed away. Jonathan kept Belle after him until the bully turned and ran. He helped the other boy to a stand while Sadie barked a steady, "And don't come back!"

The kid wiped dirt and blood from his face. "I'm…Andy Carson…I live not far from you, just down the—" He coughed several times.

Jonathan boosted him on his horse. "In another half mile we'll get to the Little Miami and I can wash you off." When they reached the river, he said, "Get down and let me clean you up some." Taking a wadded up hanky out of his pants pocket, Jonathan dipped it into the flowing cold water and wiped blood and dirt from Andy's head and face. After wrapping the cool, wet kerchief around his neck, Jonathan helped him back up on his horse. When they reached the Carson farm, Mrs. Carson was on the front porch rocking and knitting.

Jonathan reined the horses up in front and helped Andy down.

She stared at her son with a hand to her mouth in a silent scream.

Andy managed a soft, "I'm all right," as she hurried away into the house with him.

Back home, Jonathan expected his father to berate him for getting involved in the fight. He kept waiting for a lecture about why that's not their way, but Tom never said a thing, which was somehow worse. At least Jonathan could have reacted if he had laid into him. His emotions warred. Sometimes butting in was needed, but still, regret washed over him.

When Andy healed, he met Jonathan down by the river. "It was my belt he was after, you know."

Jonathan said, "Who?"

"Ben Murphy."

"Your belt?"

"This one." Andy pointed to his bright-looking belt made of thread covering rawhide straps. No one else in school had anything like it.

"You can wear that to school every day if you want to," Jonathan said.

"Why's that?"

"Because every time Ben Murphy sees that, it'll remind him of what happened when he tried to take it. Believe me, he doesn't want that memory or that belt."

Andy smiled and threw a six-skipper that Sadie chased partway into the river.

****

During Jonathan's second year of high school, he noticed a change in Sadie. The past summer she hadn't run as well as she used to. Her gait was stiffer, she moved slower, even limping a little. She'd always easily trotted back and forth with him, unless winter weather forced her to stay inside. But the trip back and forth to school was more than she could do anymore.

When the new term started, Jonathan sat and "told" her that. He'd developed his own hand language with Sadie over the years. He signed for her to stay at the farm. She laid a foot on his leg as they sat in the filtered sunlight of the apple orchard. He shook his head and told her again. She lowered her head to his lap. When the first faint stars appeared, the two trudged back to the farmhouse.

He found his mother in the kitchen and pursed his lips hard. "I'm not taking Sadie with me to school anymore, Mother. She deserves a rest, don't you think?" Jonathan stared at her, nodding.

Belinda cocked her head to one side, then looked from Sadie to Jonathan. "Oh…I agree. She'll be great company for me here during the week." She broke eye contact.

When Jonathan left for school, Sadie sat next to Belinda on the front porch, whining and barking her displeasure. Evenings, Sadie sat out front watching for him. But smart as she was, even she couldn't count days. Many times she patiently waited for a Jonathan who never came. Those days she'd pad back to the farmhouse at dark.

As spring neared, Jonathan rode home, ready for hard days tilling and planting. He led Belle into the barn and rubbed her down.

His father was inside as usual, but just stood looking at Jonathan. "How's school been, son?"

"Fine, Father. How are things here? Looks like you'll be getting ready to plant soon."

"Yup, gonna grow wheat this year, I think." He paused. "Uh…why don't we go on up to the house?"

Strange. His father looked like he was waiting for him. He always worked in the barn late into the evening but his small workbench was clear today. They walked silently toward the farmhouse. His mother stood on the front porch. She kissed him, then wrapped her arms around him. Hard.

"Jonathan, it's Sadie…"

Jonathan's stomach did a flip-flop. No. He wasn't ready. It wasn't time yet. No. But he'd seen the clouds that fogged Sadie's eyes; knew she couldn't hear him calling her. She didn't run out the door to greet him anymore, either. His mother led him into the kitchen where Sadie lay curled up in her favorite spot by the warm stove. She lifted her head when she saw Jonathan. He reached down and petted her. She licked his hand once and thumped her tail but didn't get up. Maybe she was just a little tired. Sadie looked fine. He'd take care of her. Stay home from school. She'd be all right.

His father cleared his throat. "She hasn't eaten in days and won't even take water anymore...I think she's got...the bloat."

The word punched him in the gut, almost doubling over as a gasp escaped him. No mistaking what that meant. He sat beside Sadie and stroked her, long caresses that travelled the length of her body. Her dark blue and white mottled fur stood, almost in a gesture of thanks. He gently felt her distended stomach and his heart rose in his throat. Sadie's tail lay flat. His parents stood by like statues.

Jonathan stared at his best friend, tears flowing freely. The thought of losing Sadie paralyzed him for a moment. He stood with a hand to his forehead. In a thick voice he said, "Would you bring me her blanket, please?"

His mother wiped at her face and hurried off. His father stood motionless, bottom lip quivering.

Jonathan carefully wrapped the faded red blanket around Sadie. Her favorite. He placed both hands gently underneath her and lifted. Silently, he walked out the side door. He eased Sadie down on the old wooden handcart that sat behind the house and...headed for the river. They trundled past the orchard, then the planting fields. Down the dirt path they'd taken so many times to the Little Miami. Jonathan talked to her all the way. She answered with feeble tail thumps. Slight perks of her ears. As they neared the river, he slowed. He wasn't ready. No. Not yet. His feet were lead. At the riverbank he stopped, tears streaming. His mind knew what he had to do but the rest of him screamed "No!" Sadie let out a low moan which tore his heart out. He eased his hands under and lifted her from the cart. His arms shook as he laid her on the grassy bank at a distance from the black walnut—Sonny's tree.

He sat beside her and looked out on a blurry river, reminiscing about their years together. About the first time he'd seen her with Sonny. How happy he'd been when the Walkers gave her to him. Traipsing around the farm together. Traveling to and from school.

She rested a paw on Jonathan's leg, eyes full of love. Dusk lay over the land when he finished recalling their special memories. Sadie blinked at him then closed her eyes. Her breathing grew more labored. He told her it's okay…even though it wasn't. Jonathan lightly stroked her, his tears wetting her fur. He placed his head next to hers and soothed her softly until she breathed her last.

Satin starlight shone from the heavens by the time he retrieved the shovel from the handcart. Jonathan buried her not far from where Sonny died.

When he got back to the farmhouse, his folks were waiting. His mother wrapped her arms around him tighter than he ever remembered. They both sobbed. Tears dripped from his father's cheeks. Peter and Claire rested their heads against his legs. Silent sobbing filled the living room.

His mother released Jonathan and looked up at him. "She…waited…for you, you know."

Jonathan nodded silently. He knew. Sadie told him.

Chapter Six

By his last year in high school, Jonathan's marks had attracted attention from colleges near and far. Some of the grants were for nearby schools, but two were to Ivy League colleges. Of those, Jonathan chose the College of New Jersey in Princeton over Williams College. He just liked the name "Princeton" better.

As springtime came to the Ohio River valley, Jonathan had a chance conversation with Andy down by the river.

"Heard you got lots of offers for college."

Jonathan flicked his fishing pole, and his line flew into the rushing waters. "Where'd you hear that?"

"It's all over school. Not many kids 'round here get scholarships. So yer gettin' a lot?"

Jonathan flushed. Never had liked attention. He reeled in slowly. "Not so many."

"Well, where do you wanna go? Somewhere near?"

"Nope, don't think so. Think I want to live and work in the East." Someplace where he'd be free to stand up for what he thought was right. The two young men dangled their feet in the water.

Andy said, "Hey, you know Loveland?"

"The town up the road a ways?"

"Yup. There's a spring festival there this weekend. Why don't you come?"

Jonathan chuckled. "I guess I won't. I don't know nobody there and nobody there knows me 'cept you, and I see you enough already."

"Hey, you don't hafta know anybody to have a good time." Andy tossed a five-skipper across the water.

"Well, what do you do there?" He'd never been to a festival and didn't know what the attraction was.

"Well, there's lots of good stuff to eat and there's a band and dancin'."

As far as Jonathan was concerned, Andy could have left that last part out. "Why are you going?"

"'Cause my folks are. So's my sister."

"Who's your sister?"

"Barbra Carson. You remember her, you used to go to school together."

Jonathan remembered her—he hadn't seen Barbra since he left to go to Woodward. He hesitated. "She's your sister?"

"Well, we got the same last name, don't we?"

"I guess you do. I just never put the two of you together." Had Andy picked up on the little note of excitement in his voice?

"We ain't together. She's my sister."

"You know what I mean." He eyed the calm, flowing waters and tried to imitate them.

"Well, just come on then."

"I don't know. We'll see." He gathered his line, grateful to end the conversation.

Jonathan grabbed Belle's saddle horn and hoisted himself up. "See ya later." He trotted alongside the river toward home, lost in thought. A couple of days later he mentioned it to his mother while she was making dinner. "Have you ever been to a spring festival, Mother?"

"Why, yes, sweetheart. I went to several when I was growing up. Haven't been to one in a long time, though." She broke into a smile.

"What do you do at them?"

"Well, mostly you see folks you haven't seen in a while or meet new people," she said. "There's usually music and food, too."

"Any dancing?"

"Sure, if you want. Sometimes couples like to get up and dance. There's always children running around and laughing. Why, honey?"

"No reason, I guess." Jonathan wavered. If he told her why he'd asked, she might make him go, and he didn't know if he wanted to or not. Before he knew it though, he blurted, "It's just I heard there's one up Loveland way this Saturday is all."

"Would you like to go to it?"

"I don't know, I've never been to one. Would you like to?"

"I'd have to talk to your father, but I'm pretty sure he wouldn't want to go."

Jonathan pursed his lips and let the matter drop. At breakfast the next morning, his mother said, "Your father said we should go if we want."

Jonathan brightened. "Go where?"

"To the festival, of course. And don't pretend you didn't know what I was talking about, Jonathan Gray," she teased.

Jonathan blushed. "You mean you and me go?"

"And Peter and Claire," she said.

"What about Father?" Mixed feelings of wanting

him to go—and not—warred inside him.

"He doesn't want to go."

"Well, all right, if you want to go." He tried not to sound too eager.

"I want to."

Friday, Andy came by the farmhouse with his ever-present grin. "You comin' to the festival?"

Jonathan decided to tease him. "Not sure yet."

"Well, go!"

"Don't know how to get there."

"All right, we'll come by tomorrow for you. We can go together."

"No, that won't work." Teasing Andy was a way of shifting his thoughts from Barbra.

"Why not?"

"'Cause we'll already be on our way!"

Saturday dawned with a hazy light gray sky, not unusual for a Cincinnati springtime morning. The ten-mile trip would take at least a couple of hours in the wagon, so they made plans to leave right after an early lunch.

Jonathan dispatched his chores in a hurry. He followed his father around like a puppy, asking what else he could do.

Tom glanced sideways at him. "Don't know as that iron pulley by the hay door has been checked lately."

"I'll take care of it." And Jonathan was off to the barn. The black hoist served to fetch hay in and out of the barn's open second story doors. The rope still looked strong as he rolled it. After scooting up the old ladder to the barn's upper level, he greased the pulley and tightened the bolts that held it fast against the barn's wooden side. Three times he hauled a bale of hay up and down. Satisfied, he hurried out of the barn to pronounce the pulley fit.

His father gave him a curt nod and hid a small smile.

"Anything else, Father?"

"Nope, reckon not."

Jonathan ran to change into his Sunday clothes. He hitched the horse and boosted his mother to the bouncy front seat. Peter and Claire scrambled into the wagon bed and Jonathan snapped the reins. With a rowdy goodbye to Tom, the family was off.

Soon, they neared the fork in the road to Cincinnati, a turnoff he'd taken countless times to school. As they passed, Jonathan watched it curve out of sight, surprised at his sudden wistfulness. In the distance ahead, he recognized the turnoff to Loveland by the solitary stand of cottonwood.

A few modest houses made up the outskirts of town, along with Mr. Ledbetter's mercantile, a stable, hotel/saloon, and a couple of other modest buildings. The closer they got to the crowd of people, the louder his brother and sister's nonstop chatter. His mother was also in a talkative mood. She remarked on just about everything she saw, from the weather to how green the spring fields were, to the color of the buildings and the looks of the buggies.

Jonathan slowed the buckboard. Music floated in the air and he allowed himself a quick grin. Peter and Claire whooped loudly. They jumped off and ran alongside the wagon until they got near the village square, then waited, almost bouncing with excitement. Jonathan brought the old buckboard to a halt in a bumpy field where other wagons and buggies were drawn up. He helped his mother down while she adjusted the yellow spring bonnet she wore for the first time. "Now stay nearby, please."

Peter yelled back, "We will, Momma." They disappeared.

Belinda strode toward the noise and the music and glanced back at Jonathan. "Hurry."

The festival was in a grassy square in the middle of town. According to Andy, it was an annual event. Jonathan wondered why his family hadn't been here before; it looked like fun. Sheer commotion. People of all ages were laughing, yelling, talking. Standing, sitting, running, walking. Tables labored under the weight of large dishes of food. A three-piece band played in the gazebo, which was garlanded with festive red, white, and blue bunting. The violin, mandolin, and trumpet made for an unusual combo but the music held up well.

Hundreds of people were enjoying a warm spring day and throwing the gray mantle of winter off. Jonathan and his mother circled the square, eyeing the different exhibits and homemade items for sale. They stopped at one table to admire smooth river stones painted with different woodland scenes. Jonathan harkened back to his stone-skipping days with Sonny. Now, Andy.

His mother roused him. "Let's go see those decorated wooden tops at the next table." As they walked over, someone yelled his name. He turned to see Andy coming toward him, waving. He was with two people Jonathan assumed were his mother and father. And a young woman he recognized as Andy's sister.

Jonathan couldn't take his eyes off her. She'd grown up. Filled out, too. Her dark jumper set off her pale skin, and her auburn hair was pulled back in a bun. He remembered the slight limp. She'd told him a fever left her with a weakened leg. But it was Barbra's light green eyes that held Jonathan's gaze. Everything and everyone else disappeared in that moment.

****

Belinda turned to see who was calling Jonathan. She turned her attention to the young woman right away, then glanced at her son as he stared at Barbra. Belinda put a hand out to greet the Carsons. "Well, hello, it's so nice to see you all again. It's been some time. Perhaps you remember my son, Jonathan." She wore a wide grin.

Jonathan hung back a bit. The two families knew each other somewhat due to their proximity, but this was the first social event they'd been to together. Belinda introduced herself to Barbra, who shook her hand. Andy grabbed Jonathan and pulled him forward as he stole a look at Barbra.

"Hello, Jonathan."

He shook her hand awkwardly, then nodded hello to the Carsons.

Mr. Carson said, "So you're the young man who saved my boy from a worse whuppin' a ways back."

Jonathan stood mute, his face flushed. He didn't know what to say.

His mother rescued him. "Any young man would have done the same," she said, all the while beaming at her son.

He avoided looking at Barbra and stood ill at ease as the parents made small talk about the day and the festival. Even now, he could see her warming her hands next to "his" stove in the old schoolhouse.

Andy said, "Let's get something to eat." He pulled Jonathan toward the food tables.

Jonathan tried not to look to see if Barbra was walking with them. She was. They neared the first table, full of meats.

Barbra came up beside him. "You know, it's been some time since I've seen you, Jonathan. It must have been several years now."

He mumbled, "Yes, it's been a while," then stuffed a chicken leg in his mouth.

"Andy says you're going to go to college in New Jersey. My, but that seems like a long way away."

"Oh, it's not that far," Jonathan mumbled, although distance from home was one of the reasons he'd picked it.

"What will you study?"

He fidgeted, his mouth a desert. "Don't know at this point. Guess I'll figure that out later on." He contented himself with carrying a plate of food around with her. She was even prettier than he remembered. Andy was already an afterthought.

As they walked, she glanced at him. "You've certainly grown up." Her face reddened and she waited for him to say something.

"So have you," he said, drowning in those green eyes.

"Your mother seems nice. I don't think I've ever met her before. Is your father here?"

"No, he's not." Jonathan left it at that. No sense in saying more. What would he say, anyway?

They walked and talked. Jonathan warmed to their

48

conversation as the afternoon wore on and the spring sun dipped in the western sky. He glanced around for his family, but they didn't need looking after. Andy buzzed around them, talking all the while. At first, Jonathan had been thankful to have him there.

Jonathan did indeed remember Barbra. He carried a picture of her in his head from when they were about twelve. She was walking toward him outside school, carrying some books. She wore a light blue top, her dark reddish hair trailing over her shoulders. No more pigtails. The scene was still as vivid today as if it had just happened. As she turned from the drink bowl toward him now, his heart raced.

Mrs. Carson called them over to the picnic table where she and Belinda were settled in. "Barbra Elizabeth, why don't you and Jonathan come sit with us?"

Jonathan said, "Elizabeth, huh... That's a pretty name. You know, I read about a girl named Elizabeth in a book a while back. Her family called her Lizzie."

"I've never heard that. You're making it up."

"No, really. It's in a book called *Pride and Prejudice*. You might enjoy it. I got it from the library in town. Anyone ever call you Lizzie?"

"No, and you better not be the first."

"Lizzie. Huh." Jonathan rubbed his chin and grinned. She scowled back but with the smallest of dimpled smiles. "How about you, Barbra? What would you like to do?"

"I'd like to be a nurse but I don't know how that could come about. We don't have money to send me to school."

"Maybe so, but wouldn't surprise me to see you

become one."

When dusk crept across the landscape, fireflies appeared as if from nowhere. They filled the air around their table. They were common this time of year, but to Jonathan, they seemed to be putting on a show just for them. His little brother, Peter, spun in the middle of the field, reaching for them. When one got caught in his curly hair, he looked like he had a blinking lantern perched on his head. Belinda called Peter over to the table and made him stand extra still. She worked through his curls, laying them aside so the firefly could find its way out.

Peter stared at it in her hands. "Momma, it's not lighting up anymore!"

"It won't, Peter, as long as I'm holding it. Fireflies only light when they're free." Belinda thrust her hand upward.

The firefly blinked away into the faint evening light. Jonathan watched Barbra smile as she followed the firefly, her head tilted slightly. He sat entranced by the curve of her neck. A moment he would never forget.

On the family's way back to the wagon, Belinda remarked it was about the nicest day she could remember. Peter and Claire chimed in with stories of sneaking desserts off tables, then climbing the big sycamore tree nearby and spying on everyone.

Jonathan smiled as he listened to their chatter, lost in his own pleasant thoughts. They climbed into the wagon, laughing. It had been a good day. He snapped the reins for home, green eyes filling his head.

Chapter Seven

Jonathan spent as much time as he could with Barbra the rest of that summer. As much time as she—and his father—would allow. His last day home he took her on a picnic down by the Little Miami. Jonathan brought their horses to a halt by the grassy riverbank.

"Andy says this is one of your favorite places."

He nodded. It was and it wasn't. Jonathan spread a homespun blanket under one of the ancient elms near the water—a distance away from the imposing black walnut that loomed over the land.

Barbra said, "I hear you two came here a lot over the last couple of years."

"Yup. Flinging stones, seeing who could skip the most. Eight's about the best I ever did. Andy could do ten or more. We'd lay here on the grass fishing. Never caught much. The fun part was just layin' there. Now, what I'll remember most about this place is you and me here."

Barbra fiddled with her food. "Thank you for bringing me to this special spot." She stared into the distance. "Do you have to leave tomorrow?"

Jonathan heard the crack in her voice. He leaned forward and gave her a quick peck on the cheek. With a big grin, he said, "I'll be back. Soon." They bundled what was left of the food and took their time riding back.

The next day, his family came to the new train station downtown to see him off to Princeton. Abel and Sarah smiled nearby. The buckboard horse neighed softly while Jonathan hugged his mother, Peter, then Claire. He turned to his father and shook his hand. What was that look? Sadness—or was he upset about something? A sharp longing for his father's approval washed over him. Would he ever outgrow that?

He tried to shake the feeling but a wave of melancholy tingled his nose. He wouldn't see his family again for some time. He'd wanted to leave the farm behind for years, but now happiness wrestled with nostalgia. Barbra said this was a family goodbye, so she'd stayed away. He missed her already. He lingered with his hand resting on the train's pull bar, gazing back as his family stood on the platform. With a wave, he hoisted himself into the passenger car. The train began a slow chug down the tracks, thick smoke hiding the station and his family, as he left.

****

Tom and Belinda talked long into the night in their bedroom. "You were very quiet when Jonathan left today," Belinda said.

"Reckon so."

"I know you well enough, Tom Gray, to know you have something on your mind. What is it?"

"Bah. You *know* what it is, woman. He's likely to get this fancy education, forget his upbringing, forget us. Get some hifalutin' job where he's more concerned with money than the people around him. He's going to college, for heaven's sake."

"That isn't what you're really afraid of, is it?"

Tom paused and shook his head. "You, of all

people, know how wealthy people are. They use others then discard them. He could grow up like—"

She stopped him, eyes flashing. "You know that won't happen. Don't even think it."

"Well, I do. I think on it all the time."

"You gonna hold that over me forever?" Belinda turned and stared out the window at the black night.

****

Trains had only reached Cincinnati from the East a few years ago, so Jonathan was taking his first train ride, his first journey away from the rolling hills where he grew up. The scenery along the way looked much like home, with forested hillsides of hardwoods cut by the occasional dirt road that disappeared into nothing in the distance. The landscape was dressed in early splashes of orange, yellow, and red. Hot and muggy air, just like home, rushed in through open windows.

Jonathan busied himself with his few books. With a long journey ahead, he had time to read them and more. But there weren't more. He'd packed everything in a worn feed bag that rested at his feet. Would he be able to keep up at Princeton? He rested a hand on his Bible.

The College of New Jersey, known as Princeton for the town that surrounded it, was far enough away to suit him. Stepping off the train, he was a little disappointed, though. The village was so small. Several rows of houses and small buildings lay scattered along the rolling hills of middle New Jersey. The town had a rural feel. Maybe the college would be more impressive.

Campus consisted of one main building which had recently burned. It was in the midst of being restored, but fire damage was evident everywhere. The college seemed no more grand than his high school. Still, it was college and far from home, two things he thought he wanted.

His scholarship required him to work on campus, which was fine. He was used to staying busy. No doubt Princeton would give him a window on a far larger world than local colleges could have. He walked into the charred building looking for someone in charge.

"You'll be living in a dormitory on campus," the proctor told him. "It used to be a feed warehouse but it has been cleaned up quite a bit since then. All the scholarship students live there. Nassau Hall—this building—is the center of the college. You understand that you are required to work?"

Jonathan nodded. "Yes, sir."

"Your job will be right here, where administration, academics, and activities take place. There is a little dining room off to the side in this building where everyone eats. It is rather small, so students and faculty eat in shifts."

"What's that big brick building, sir? Over there." Jonathan pointed out the window to the only other large building he'd seen. It sat grandly on a hilltop.

"That's the Princeton Seminary, a core part of campus life. This college was founded by Presbyterians, which you may or may not be familiar with. The seminary teaches students about the scriptures and the Presbyterian Church. Not necessarily in that order."

Jonathan walked the short distance to his dorm. Looked more like a barn. Faded gray wood. The roof sagged in the middle. At least he wouldn't have to ride hours to get to school anymore. Getting settled in didn't take long. He placed his few belongings on a shelf near the bed he'd picked out. The dorm was an open bay barracks, with simple cotton cots spread the length of the upper and lower floors. Ancient feed dust from harvests past played in shafts of sun shining through dingy windows. Warped, wooden floorboards groaned when he walked.

Didn't take long to figure his job out. He'd be responsible for keeping track of students, their academic standing, classes taken, monies paid, and church and school attendance. He'd gotten here a few days early to learn his job. When registration opened, students began to trickle by his desk.

As he was packing up one day, a voice behind him said, "So you're Jonathan Gray, the kid who took my job. Name's Charlie Williams. Just don't screw it up. Wouldn't look good to have my replacement fail. And I don't want to have to take it back." He laughed.

Jonathan allowed himself a small grin. "I'll try not to. Can I ask you something?" No doubt upperclassmen knew everything.

"Sure."

"What are classes like?"

"They're taught by professors but there's not that many. Sometimes upperclassmen teach, too."

"Kids here sure look different than back home."

"No doubt. Most belong to one of two societies on campus, Whigs or Clios. Unless you're a scholarship— like us. They let you eat with them and study with them, but you're not one of them. They don't have jobs, because they're rich enough that they don't have to work. 'Course, that's not us."

From the first day on campus, he could tell he was out of place. His clothes, too. Students dressed up here compared to back home. Didn't matter though, as he didn't have money for new clothes anyway. He'd make do with his two shirts and one pair of dark trousers. All he ever wore on the farm were old, stained cotton pants. Except to church. Then, his mother made him wear the trousers and a white shirt that was three sizes too big when she bought it. The next year it was two sizes too big, then one. By the time it fit, it was worn out. The only shoes he had were as old as they looked. Seeing the other scholarship kids' scruffy clothes didn't make him feel any better.

For the first time in his life, he felt a little shabby. Poor was poor, and was hard to hide. After the first few weeks of school, several of the scholarships were already gone. He never considered leaving, though. No way he was going to miss this first taste of life away from the farm. He had a freedom here he'd never experienced before. One he liked.

Jonathan was leaving Nassau Hall one afternoon when he heard his name called. The provost walked toward him with a smile. "Jonathan, you are doing a fine job. Do you think you could keep track of student grades as well?"

"Don't see why not, sir, if you can figure a way to get them to me."

"Very good. I'll have the teachers drop them off at my office, then you can pick them up, all right?"

"That'd be fine, sir."

On Sundays, students and faculty alike attended mandatory chapel at the seminary. The Presbyterians seemed to present a different gospel than the one he learned growing up. There wasn't anything said about accepting others, about kindness, or grace. Seminary sermons emphasized making sure you behaved the acceptable way, looked acceptable, and said acceptable things. If not, apparently it would go badly for you with God.

Jonathan decided to stop by the senior pastor's office one Sunday after services.

"Reverend Everhart, may I talk to you for a minute?"

"Certainly, son. Please come in."

"Thank you." The office was grander than anything he'd ever seen. Big mahogany desk, walls lined with full, wooden bookshelves. Thick carpeting. "My name is Jonathan Gray. I'm a freshman. Scholarship, sir."

"Nice to meet you, Jonathan. No need to call me sir. Reverend is fine. What can I help you with?"

"Something's been bothering me, sir. Every week it seems like the ministers present the same message with the same scripture, sing the same songs, and talk about the same damnation for sin in the same manner."

"Yes, well, Mr. Gray, there's a reason for that. There are certain things expected of us as Christians. We risk our eternal salvation if we fall short of performing those things."

"That's what confuses me, sir. I don't remember reading that we have to work for our salvation."

"Then you're not paying attention, son. There are standards we must live by and we must call out those who fall short."

"Is one of those standards grace, Reverend?"

"What does grace have to do with this?"

Jonathan hid his disbelief. He wasn't inclined to spend any more time with a senior pastor about something he should already know. "Thank you—sir."

The meeting prompted Jonathan to dig deeper into Scripture. The verses told him a different story—one of hope and assurance. That hope was what he carried with him when he laid his Bible next to his bed at night.

At Nassau Hall, he sought Charlie Williams out in the dining room. "Can I join you?"

"Hey, Jonathan. Siddown. How are things going? Haven't heard anything bad about you so far, so you must be doing okay."

"Things are pretty good but I was wondering about the Whigs and the Clios."

"Not much goodwill between them, huh? You know why?"

"No."

"The Whigs are monied kids from big eastern cities. Clios are southerners. Still wealthy, but from plantations for the most part, not cities. I was surprised when I first got here myself."

"About what?"

"That almost half the students are from the South. I guess they feel comfortable here, not like at some other eastern schools."

"Comfortable? What do you mean?"

"Because Princeton has never taken sides on slavery. But you don't have to worry about them, 'cause they don't have anything to do with us."

Jonathan sipped his coffee. Seemed like he was always on the outside looking in. He'd just heard where everyone fit. Or in his case, didn't fit.

At registration, Jonathan was checking students in when one of his classmates stood in front of him—someone he'd heard about. Robert Parker was from Philadelphia where his father had a thriving textile business. He was also the de facto leader of the freshman Whigs.

Parker stared at him. "I know you." He drew the words out like the slice of a knife. "I recognized you by your clothes, which don't seem to have been changed yet this year. Don't you have anything other than that brown shirt and black pants?" A smug smile.

"Just sign this. A receipt for the money your father paid for you this term." Jonathan emphasized "your father paid for you" a little more than necessary. Parker reminded him of Murphy, the bully back home.

Parker said, "I'll sign it if you change your clothes."

"Fine with me if you don't," Jonathan said. "I'll just tell the proctor you refused." But the last thing he wanted to do was get on this Whig's bad side.

"You trying to get me in trouble, kid?"

Jonathan said, "Nope. You're doing that all by yourself."

"Do you know who I am?"

"According to this piece of paper, you're Robert T. Parker. Is that you?"

"That's right. What's your name?"

"I'm just the guy they asked to get your signature," Jonathan said, trying to irritate Parker now.

"Gimme the paper, moron."

He handed Parker a pen with the slip of paper and watched him sign it. Parker started to give the pen back but pulled it away just as Jonathan reached for it.

"I'll keep it," he said. "And I hope they count these at the end of the day. Where'd you grow up, hayseed? On a farm that raised dirt?" He laughed and walked off, several other freshmen in tow.

Jonathan stared at Parker's back as he left. He *had* grown up on a farm with plenty of dirt—and he hadn't thought of home in a while. His mind drifted to the old tree in front of the farmhouse. A red maple that was a crimson harbinger of fall. The grass underneath it had been overtaken by shaded, dark brown ground some time ago. He'd spent hours in its limbs as a child, inventing games with Sonny. They'd take imaginary trips to lands across the sea, with the tree as their vessel. The two created a world of their own, one that transformed the Ohio farm they played on day after day.

Growing up, his father roused him every morning and then it was work, school, work. Free time if any was left. He'd always had boundaries on his childhood. His father laid out when, where, and what about his days.

"Jonathan, come down out of that tree now. And, Sonny, you need to be on your way." His father had a way of controlling Jonathan with his deep voice.

"Yes, sir."

"You haven't finished your chores yet, have you." It was not a question.

Jonathan sagged. "No, sir." Could he ever please the man?

"Well, get on out to the barn now and get them done."

"Hey, farmboy, I'm talking to you."

Jonathan snapped back from his daydream. An angry senior glared at him over the registration table. Parker was gone, like his childhood.

****

Jonathan ran afoul of Parker in Civics class during

a discussion about current events. The teacher was lecturing on what the Whig and Know-Nothing Parties stood for, when Parker chimed in. "I hear Jonathan Gray is a Know-Nothing. He really does know nothing!" He laughed and turned to the other Whigs who joined in.

Jonathan was surprised at Parker's outburst, not because of what he said, but because Parker knew his name. Even though he didn't want to be on Parker's bad side, he figured he already was, so he couldn't resist turning the tables.

"As I'm sure you're aware—" He glanced at Parker and paused. "—it's primarily because of the Know-Nothings that we're in this political tussle right now."

Parker squinted, like he was uncertain how to handle what he'd started.

Jonathan continued, "The Know-Nothing Party twisted the basic federal principles this nation was founded on, allowing the Whigs to eclipse them politically. Public opinion is favoring them as a result." His time in the little library was coming in handy. He'd find out soon enough if he'd pushed Parker too far.

The professor sat with his eyes trained on him while a lull descended over the classroom. Students looked from the teacher to Parker. Jonathan had put Parker in the difficult position of having to agree, or by his silence tacitly denounce the Whigs. And Jonathan guessed he wouldn't do that. Campus Whigs weren't the same as the national party, but the two had enough in common that Parker likely didn't want to publicly criticize them.

Parker scanned the room. "Hey, Gray finally got

something right. Let's make sure the teacher makes a note of it," he said with a forced laugh. A glare Jonathan's way.

The rest of that first year was a time of continual aggravation between him and Parker, along with his Whig minions. The novelty eventually wore off and Jonathan lost interest in trying to irritate him. He had daydreamed about escaping the farm to make something of himself, but this wasn't what he'd imagined. He wasn't fitting in anywhere and it began to chafe.

Chapter Eight

Jonathan didn't go home that first year. Something was keeping him away and he was getting used to being on his own. Out of his father's suffocating shadow. Besides, he couldn't afford the trip and neither could his folks. Writing them a couple of letters that just grazed the surface of his life would have to do.

Dear Mother and Father,

I'm sorry I haven't written more, I just seem to get so busy here. I hope this doesn't take too long to get to you. My classes are all right, but I like Civics the best. We're learning more about slavery. I don't know how we're going to fix that, but fix it we must.

I hope everyone is well. I'm fine here. The winter chill reminds me of home.

Your son,

Jonathan

He got several letters back from his mother filled with the banalities of life on the farm. Weather reports, garden reports, canning updates. He'd even written a couple of self-conscious letters to Barbra, which she'd been quick to answer. He'd taken to calling her Lizzie in them. When he was lonely, he reread them at night.

Dear Jonathan,

I love hearing from you. You are so far away but your letters make you sound close by. I wish I knew more about what you are studying.

*I have been looking forward to sharing some big
news with you. I just got a job with the railroad! I'm so
excited! It's not nursing, but it gets me off the farm. I'm
staying in town with my mother's best friend and her
family right now. I love being in the city and on my
own, most of the time.*

*How do you like college? I can just imagine you
there learning about all kinds of new things. I hope to
see you this summer.*

Your friend,

Barbra

*(And you can only call me Lizzie in your letters.
Nowhere else!)*

As the end of the school year neared, Jonathan
made plans for the trip back to Ohio. He couldn't afford
to stay in Princeton for the summer, although an ever-
increasing part of him wanted to. His father would need
help on the farm but separation from him had been a
salve for his heart. Would that vanish once he got
home?

The long, westbound train ride gave him time to
reflect on the past year. He wouldn't miss the Whigs,
and the Clios weren't any better. Both groups treated
him like white trash, but he knew one thing—neither
crowd was going to make him quit. In fact, if anything,
he'd stay just to annoy them, Parker in particular. He
didn't like to admit it, but Parker's comment about his
clothes stung a bit. Which led to buying a second pair
of pants with the little money he made from work—the
first time he ever bought anything. He smoothed at the
dark cotton material as he rode, then gazed at his worn
shoes. They'd be next.

After a day and night of cars and connections, he

was back in the Queen City. He'd written his folks, but wasn't sure anyone would be at the station to meet him. When the train rolled to a screeching stop, he grabbed his valise—an old one a Clio tossed out before going home. At nineteen, all his worldly possessions fit inside this little bag and the sides didn't begin to bulge. He scanned the small crowd hurrying along the platform. No familiar faces. How was he going to get home? As he trudged toward the little station house, he heard a shrill whistle.

"Jonathan!"

He turned to see Andy Carson running toward him. A little taller, but just as skinny. Hair just as red. Same freckles. Andy grabbed his hand and pumped it until Jonathan managed to extricate himself.

"How are ya? It's great to see you. I almost didn't make it, the noon shower muddied up the roads somethin' fierce."

"You've been here since noon?" At least he had one good friend.

Andy beamed. "Thereabouts. That's not so long."

"Are my folks here?" He was almost afraid to scan the crowd.

"Nope, they would've been, but I told 'em I'd come fetch you."

Jonathan felt a slight pang. If he'd been a better son, they'd have been here. "When did you see them?"

"I been seein' 'em pert regular." Wide smile.

"How's that?"

"I figured with you away and your brother still a kid, your pa might need some help with chores, so I stopped by every now and again. I think he was glad for it, but I couldn't really tell."

Jonathan frowned. "That's just his way." He knew his father's distant manner all too well.

"Come on, I've got the buckboard tied up right over there." Andy grabbed the valise and half sprinted to the wagon.

Jonathan took the sights in as they rode out of town. "The town looks bigger." He was surprised he'd forgotten much of what Cincinnati looked like.

"Must be. Seems like there's always more folks on the road every time I get to town."

He smiled. That couldn't have been very often. "How's our farm look?"

"Kinda okay. Spring weather's been too wet, so your father ain't been able to plant yet. I think he's worried about gettin' crops in too late."

Jonathan lapsed into silence. Had a year mellowed his father? Maybe not—his mood couldn't be too good if crops weren't in.

Andy rattled off rapid-fire questions about college. Jonathan patiently explained about his job and classes, about the large dorm, how his food was made for him, about chapel. He left out the part about how the Whigs and Clios couldn't stand him.

Andy's eyes grew wide. "I knew it! I just knew you'd come back knowin' about all kinds of things. There's nothin' happens here, just the same stuff every day."

Jonathan stifled a chuckle. He'd always enjoyed having Andy around and now he remembered why.

When they reached the Gray homestead, he hopped off. "Thanks, I'll come over to visit soon." Jonathan eyed the farmhouse. In the dim light, it still looked as well kept as he remembered. Barn seemed a little more tired.

He double stepped up the front porch. His mother burst out the door and hugged him hard. Peter and Claire wrapped around Jonathan's waist, yelling for his attention. His father stood to the side, but all in all a better welcome than it might have been.

Peter especially had shot up. His hand-me-down pants were inches short of the hand-me-down shoes he wore. A year had darkened his hair and rounded his face. Claire beamed up at her big brother. She had Belinda's straw-colored hair and tight ringlets that ran to her shoulders. Still small, she'd always been the sunshine branch of the family and had gotten all the curls he hadn't.

"How did you both get so tall?" Jonathan grinned while they giggled. He ruffled Peter's hair and turned to his father. "The place looks good," he said, already feeling a bit awkward as they shook hands. Strained feelings still lingered just below the surface. Would they always?

Tom looked out the window toward the fields. "We need a break from the rain so I can get the plantin' done." The worried expression Jonathan knew so well framed his father's face.

His mother had laid on a nice sideboard. Wonderful canned beets and green beans. Harvest bread still warm from the oven. Roast pig. Jonathan's throat seized. He pursed his lips hard. They only had two pigs.

The family stood at the table waiting while he pulled a chair out for his mother. After a blessing, Peter and Claire chattered away between bites and regaled Jonathan with their doings this past year. The way they'd grown was a raw reminder of how long he'd been away. Peter just turned twelve, the same age he was when he smarted off to his father.

As Tom rose from the table, Jonathan said, "Is there anything you need help with?"

"Nope." His father disappeared out the front door. Must be going to the barn. Jonathan's hand tightened around his napkin.

"How was your first year, Jonathan?" his mother asked. Before he could answer, she added, "I'm sorry we weren't better writers."

"Well, I wasn't very good, either. Seems like I never remembered to write when I had the time and only thought about it when I didn't. The year was good, though. It went pretty slowly while I was there but now it seems like it flew by. How have things been here?"

"Everything is fine. We've all missed you. A lot. The children have been so excited to see you."

While his mother readied dessert, Jonathan headed for the barn. His heart rate quickened as he pushed through the small wooden side door. His father sat on the familiar low stool, milking. Jonathan tried to think of something to say.

"Looks like school didn't hurt you none," Tom said without looking up.

"No, sir, it didn't." He fidgeted in place.

"Have any trouble gettin' home?"

"No, other than a few station changes. Princeton's pretty small but it's a nice place for the most part. Might be a good place to live."

His father's face furrowed and Jonathan berated himself. He hadn't meant that as a jab at his father or the farm. He rattled on, almost as if he couldn't control his mouth. Growing up, he never seemed to be able to get his father's attention. Now, the more he jabbered the worse he felt. Just shut up. He wanted to say he was sorry he hadn't been around to help but the words wouldn't come. Jonathan pulled a stool up beside a cow. He thought about how many times he'd sat here. The rhythm soon came back as his hands worked, his heartbeat slowed, and the warm flush left his face.

Barn cats gathered in a loose semicircle around him, tails twitching at a distance. Growing up, he would flick a teat in their direction every now and then, spraying them with fresh milk. They'd lick as much off as they could, then lick each other clean. Milking was the only time they'd come near. They spent most of their time hunting mice, or curled up in sun spots on the matted hay in the barn's second story.

One cat had taken a liking to him. After the milk spray, she'd rub against his leg purring. Then a quick jump up in his lap to get stroked. Rear end rising. She was a calico, a mix of orange, white, and black, as if the Lord couldn't decide on a color. He picked out the littlest cat and sprayed it as his thoughts drifted back to Princeton. He took his time wandering through some of the good memories. Classes had gone well, and he told himself he didn't care whether or not he was friends with the Whigs or Clios. Wasn't exactly true.

"Son!"

Jonathan snapped his father's way.

"You're daydreaming. Your ma wants you on up to the house. Claire says she's got a special dessert ready for you."

Jonathan turned in time to see his sister scampering back to the farmhouse on long, skinny legs. "Yes, sir, I'll just be another minute." When he was convinced his cow had no more to give, he poured the milk in the tin container, jammed the round top on the white foam, and started for the house.

He looked back. His father was milking another cow.

Chapter Nine

Late spring in southern Ohio is sometimes perfect, often with a lazy cloud cover giving way now and then to clear blue skies. Haze from the humidity covered everything with a light dampness as heat poured from the earth.

Every spring he followed behind as his father tilled the fields for planting, breaking the ground into rich, dark clods. He always planted two of the three fields and left the third fallow. Beets every year, and either green beans or corn. Sometimes wheat.

As he walked down to the barn at daybreak, Jonathan noticed a new tiller sitting outside. Shiny clean, it must have replaced the battered iron plow they'd had forever. The tiller resembled a large corkscrew lying on the ground. Circular metal blades rotated around an iron shaft heavy enough to chop up the packed dirt it passed over. As the morning sun peeked through a low-lying fog, Tom and Jonathan muscled the contraption away from the barn. They laid its gleaming discs on a hand cart they trundled to the south field. They'd use it for the first time today.

Dew clung to the grass as they led the workhorse out. They positioned the tiller on the ground behind the big animal. Long wooden rails extended from either side of the tiller's shaft. Jonathan tied them to the horse's harness with rawhide straps. He looped them through the iron rings then knotted and doused them with water. His father rode and he walked behind the horse, sod kicking up with every turn of the metal discs. With the reins in one hand, his father looked back to make sure the furrows were straight. As Jonathan scanned the rows, the horse veered slightly left, toward the old mulberry tree that stood like a lonely sentinel at the edge of the field.

Maybe his father hadn't cut it down because Jonathan and Sonny loved playing in it so much as children. Every summer, it produced plump, dark berries they jumped for on the bottommost limbs, dark juice staining their hands and mouths. When the lowest berries were gone, they'd shinny up the trunk for higher ones, skinning their knees in the process. Sometimes the tree doubled as a fort or a ship under attack by pirates, with berries perfect for bombarding foes into retreat.

The horse drifted. Dim morning light might have had something to do with it. As Tom looked back with a hand on the workhorse's rump, a large branch knocked him off backward. The iron tiller continued to turn, rolling on top of him as sharp blades slashed into his side and back.

"Aaahhhhyyy!"

All of Jonathan's strained feelings flew away when he saw his father being sliced up. He ran to the gelding, waving his arms. "Whoa! Whoa!"

The horse halted with the tiller still on top of Tom. He screamed while Jonathan tried to lift the shaft. It wouldn't budge and he couldn't untie the soaked rawhide straps. If the gelding moved, the blades would finish his father off. Jonathan steadied the horse again and yelled for his mother. She'd be readying breakfast by now. Morning wind must have carried his voice to the farmhouse because Belinda was soon running toward them.

She screamed. "Oh my God! Please help us, Jesus!"

A growing red stain spread over Tom's outer shirt in the cool morning mist.

Jonathan had to lift the tiller off his father—somehow. He gathered himself and squatted a second time. He dug his hands through the soil underneath the shaft, cradled the contraption with his arms in between the blades, and lifted for all he was worth. The tiller inched up, dirty, bloody blades slicing into Jonathan's stomach. Gored him. He struggled to a crouch with the blades still hugged to his middle.

Tom screamed as the tiller rose.

"Grab my hand! Quickly!" Belinda pulled her husband by the hand while he arm crawled toward her. Between their efforts, he inched out from under the merciless discs. Jonathan dropped the tiller and fell to his knees, gasping. Tears streamed down his face, adrenaline still surging. He carried his dazed father toward the farmhouse, bright red blood dripping from both into the dark soil. As he staggered forward, he was afraid to look down to see if his father was still breathing.

Jonathan shouted to his mother. "Run get the buckboard ready!" By the time he reached the farmhouse, he was barely moving.

Belinda had a horse hitched to the wagon. Peter and Claire ran out of the farmhouse, almost hidden by the mounds of towels and sheets they carried.

Jonathan hoisted a moaning Tom over the side rails and laid him on the wagon bed. He jumped in for a closer look at his father's wounds. Nasty cuts streamed red all along his left leg and arm, but the most serious wounds were to his torso. Blood was everywhere, but none spurted from the cuts Jonathan covered with blankets. Tom whimpered softly. His breathing came in gasps as Jonathan pressed towels over the deepest gashes.

Belinda grabbed the reins. With a yell and a snap of leather, the horse lurched away at a gallop. Tom screamed at every jolt as they careened down the dirt road. The nearest help was five miles away, not a doctor at all, just a neighbor with experience tending horses and cows. A real doctor would have meant a couple of hours into Cincinnati—time Jonathan didn't think his father had.

As the miles sped by, Tom's protests grew quieter and shorter. His eyes closed. When they didn't open again, Jonathan shook him by the shoulder. "Father, don't give up. We're almost there. Open your eyes!" They covered the distance in just under half an hour. At the Winfield place, Jonathan hurried to the front door.

"Mr. Winfield! Mr. Winfield!"

Mrs. Winfield rushed outside. She put a hand to her mouth and pointed to a field. Jonathan rushed that way on leaden legs. Back at the wagon, Winfield sized Tom's condition up, worry framing his face.

Jonathan tried to lift his father out of the wagon, but Winfield shouted, "Leave him be. Mother, get me some hot water, blankets, towels, and sewing material. Anything clean you can put your hands on. Hurry!" Blood trickled off the end of the bed.

Winfield splashed whiskey on Tom's lacerations, rousing him to feeble moans. For two hours, he cleaned, dressed, and stitched him as best he could. Belinda and Jonathan crouched close by, applying pressure with cloths. By now, Tom's bleeding had almost stopped. The alcohol's sting no longer stirred him. He lay unconscious, pale, his breathing shallow.

Jonathan tried praying for him, but his mind was a wall. He sagged against a tree and gazed straight ahead in blood-soaked clothes. His bleeding had also slowed but his wounds needed suturing and dressing as well.

"Go lay your son down on the ground, Mrs. Gray," Winfield said.

Beads of sweat no longer appeared on Jonathan's forehead or streamed down his chest. Belinda helped her dazed son onto the cool grass, shaded by a large silver maple newly leafed out. Winfield hurried down from the wagon and began to clean and rough stitch Jonathan's gashes.

Winfield wagoned them to what passed for a hospital in Cincinnati. A doctor cut Winfield's homemade stitches off and cleaned Tom's cuts with a white powder he called bromine. He loosely restitched the wounds so they could be washed more easily.

The doctor drew Belinda aside. "I don't know how he's still alive, but he is. Those blades couldn't have missed every vital organ, but seems like they did. Can't be sure about bleeding inside, though. Now we need to keep the wounds clean. We'll tend him here and hope for the best. And I've done all I can for your son. Take him home, but let me know if his cuts get deep red."

The next day Jonathan's head started to clear. The blades had opened sizeable slanting swaths across his stomach and arms that Belinda tended. His body screamed in protest every time he moved in bed. The pain almost doubled him over but he forced himself to get up and struggle around.

Barbra took leave from the railroad to help with his care. She read to him from the Bible when she wasn't changing his bandages or sheets. As she dabbed his forehead, he said, "Looks like you got your wish to be a nurse. Guess I can always say I was your first patient." A wan smile.

"Yes, but I wish you weren't, these cuts are so deep. This reminds me of when my mother cared for me as a child, though. Never did know what left me with this limp."

"I never knew you had a limp."

Barbra smiled. "You're a liar, Jonathan Gray. And a bad one at that."

He chuckled until pain overwhelmed him.

After a week, Jonathan was up and hobbling around. Barbra helped him shuffle to the barn where the guilty tiller lay off to the side. Dried blood had turned the shiny blades a rusty brown. He flashed back to that morning and a shiver ran through him.

Word of the accident spread to the other farms in the area—a scattered, but nonetheless tightknit community. Sonny's parents came by often, him to work the fields, her to bake food and tend the children. Jonathan struggled out to the fields daily, visiting with neighbors minding crops they'd planted for his family on their own. Some he knew, others he got to know.

His father came home a week later. Jonathan was working in the barn when his mother rushed in. "Your father's inside, snipping off the stitches on his chest and arms."

Jonathan hurried as best he could to the farmhouse and struggled up the stairs to his parents' bedroom.

His father lay in bed, scissors in hand. "Cut those stitches off my back, willya? Can't reach 'em."

Jonathan shook his head. "Those wounds aren't healed enough." His father protested but Jonathan stood firm. "In time," he said, "they'll disappear on their own." He hoped that was true. He'd never lied to his father before. Hard to see such a tough man laid so low.

When his father was able, Jonathan and Tom, slumped and with a cane, walked out to the mulberry tree with an axe. Tom said to fetch something they could stand on. Jonathan returned with an old wooden platform that once partly covered the abandoned cistern by the barn. He laid it at the base of the tree and painfully hacked away at the offending limb while Tom watched. They gave Jonathan's childhood fort, occasional sailing ship, its due and left the rest standing.

That night, Jonathan rocked along with his father on the front porch. How had he been able to lift that tiller? He couldn't have. Must have been God's subtle reminder that He was still in charge. He hadn't thought about God for a long time.

Chapter Ten

As August turned to fall, Jonathan said his goodbyes, lingered with Barbra at the station, and boarded the train back to Princeton. Walking from the station to the dorm, his thoughts kept returning to Barbra waving. He dropped his meager gear on a dirty, worn bed. Fewer scholarships this year. That first night they regaled each other with stories of their summers. Jonathan wasn't eager to talk about Barbra or his father's brush with death, but there was no hiding the angry red scars on his stomach when he took his shirt off for bed. The young men gathered around.

He said, "Just a farm accident. Wasn't much to it, really."

"You ain't gettin' off that easy, Gray."

Bloody images flashed in his head. His father's life pouring out bright red on the ground right in front of him. Still too soon to sort out mixed feelings of relief and regret, mingled with the stubborn hurt that had been his constant companion for so long. He'd never been able to figure the man out. He said a simple, "That'll have to do for now," and eased into his lumpy bed. Relief coursed through him as the oil lamps went out. His stomach muscles relaxed and his heartbeat slowed.

He had the same job again this year which was fine, but he wasn't looking forward to running into Robert Parker again. As he slipped behind the work desk the next day, the registration line in front of him lengthened. Then he heard a booming voice toward the back of it. Parker. He was telling everyone that upperclassman had line privileges as he moved past the freshmen ahead of him. The only ones he couldn't con were other upperclassmen, who told him in no uncertain terms what he could do with himself. But soon he stood in front of Jonathan, who gave him his class schedule and collected tuition money.

"Hey, Gray. Why'd you come back? I figured you had enough last year, but I'm glad to see you. You know why?" He didn't wait for an answer. "Because picking on you will give me something to do besides copying off everyone else." He laughed and turned to the freshmen behind him who stared wide-eyed.

"Just take the receipt and move on," Jonathan said, his stomach doing a little flip-flop. Nothing had changed. He hoped Parker had found someone else to make fun of. No such luck.

"See ya around, farmboy."

Sitting at his work table was a welcome relief. Stomach muscles that hadn't healed yet enjoyed a temporary reprieve. As the first few weeks unfolded, Jonathan endured more of Parker's badgering—even more personal this year. The Whigs picked on everyone, including laundry staff, dining room attendants, cooks, and anyone else who wasn't able to get them in trouble. But Parker reserved his best—or worst—for Jonathan. The nastiest times were right before class when Parker was together with other Whigs.

"Hey, hey, look at farmer Gray." Parker's patter was predictable. "Those are the same clothes you wore last year. Come over here and I'll give you a penny to get them washed."

Jonathan glared at Parker. "You seem to worry a lot about what I wear. Didn't know you cared that much."

"Just trying to raise standards around here." With that, Parker and his boys were off to class, laughing and glancing back. Jonathan stared at his retreating back. Sooner or later, he was going to have to fight him. Probably sooner than later and that time was closing in.

****

Halfway through the first term Jonathan had only written a single letter to his folks, but several to Barbra. He knew he should be writing home, but couldn't bring himself to do it. Something was different.

Dear Lizzie,

I hope you're not mad at me for not writing sooner. I got my old job back and it's keeping me pretty busy. My classes are okay, I'm not sure what I like best yet. Saying thanks for tending to me after the accident doesn't seem like near enough. Are you still with the railroad? They'd be crazy not to hire you again. It seems like a long time since I've seen you. Please let me know how you are. How's Andy? I miss (seeing) you.

Jonathan

Her letters back were newsy and upbeat. But there was something else that caught his eye. In the top right corner of each one, Barbra had drawn what looked like a flying bug. It must mean something, but he didn't know what. He wrote her a couple more letters after midterm and got several in return, each one with a drawing of that same little bug on it.

Dear Jonathan,

It's been so nice to get your letters. I look for them every day. I know you don't have much time to write, what with all your studies. How are your classes this year? I remember you said you were looking forward to Civics class. I don't get to see your folks anymore. How are they? I'm helping put together train schedules at the railroad but I'd still like to get into nursing. I spend as much time as I can at the library reading medical books. Some are very strange, but I'm learning a lot.

I look forward to seeing you over Christmas! I thought we might go for a sleigh ride.

Barbra

A wave of sadness hit him, knowing he didn't have the money to go home. He wanted to see Barbra, but whenever her smiling face flashed before his eyes, his father's stern visage usually followed. A lonely Christmas loomed, then came and went.

The first person Jonathan ran into after Christmas break was Parker. For someone who'd grown up in Philadelphia, the second largest city in the country, Parker didn't know much about current issues—like slavery. It was also clear he didn't care about them. He never paid attention in class, if he went at all. To pass tests he cheated and everyone knew it. Jonathan noticed that Parker picked his spots though, only palming notes in classes taught by upperclassmen. They had nothing to gain by reporting him and everything to lose, as any accusation would come down to his word against theirs.

But one day, Parker cheated in Civics, taught by a full professor. Jonathan sat in his assigned seat to Parker's right. He angled his body away, as usual, so Parker couldn't copy off him. A rustle of paper made

Jonathan look up. The professor was on the far side of the room looking the other way. Parker scanned some crib notes he had up his sleeve. He was getting away with it, too, until the professor turned around. Parker still had the piece of white paper in his hand. The teacher hurried to Parker's row with a scowl on his face. Parker let the paper slip from his hand and fall to the floor. It landed next to Jonathan's foot, where it stayed.

Until Jonathan moved his shoe on top of it.

The teacher stood over Parker and accused him of cheating. He searched Parker's shirt, sleeves, and surroundings, but came up with nothing. If he'd been caught, Parker could have been expelled, scandalizing his family and ruining any political prospects he might have had. The professor moved off, glowering.

"Pencils down."

Everyone passed their papers forward and collected belongings under the desks. Jonathan scooted his foot backward on the wood floor, leaned over for his books, and snatched the paper from under his shoe. He slipped it into his pants pocket and headed to work. As he left the classroom, Parker followed.

Jonathan sat at his desk, and out of earshot of everyone else, Parker leaned over him. "Why'd you do it?"

"Do what?" Jonathan twiddled with a pencil.

"You know what."

"Sorry, have to organize these papers." He was beginning to enjoy this now.

Parker stood with a blank look.

Jonathan kept working. Out of the corner of his eye, he could tell Parker was getting madder and madder by the way his fists clenched and unclenched.

Parker pinned one of Jonathan's hands under his. "What the hell are you up to, Gray?"

Jonathan glanced up at his nemesis. "Not sure what you mean." He yanked his hand free.

"You know what I mean. Why'd you hide the paper?"

"What paper?" Jonathan had him now.

"You know damn well what paper!"

Jonathan looked down at his notebook, scanning a list of things he needed to do. Parker was making it easy to drag this out.

"That paper I dropped and you covered with your foot. That's what paper."

"Huh. Under my foot you say?"

Parker hesitated. He stepped back and stared. Jonathan wondered if he was going to come at him, fists flying. But Parker just stood motionless for a moment, then left as other students trickled in.

The first thing Jonathan noticed over the next week was the now-silent stares of Parker and the other Whigs. But even that was better than the verbal harassment he'd been getting. Something was going on, he just didn't know what. The change was gradual but nonetheless real. Whigs were leaving him alone, although every now and again they still made fun of him loud enough to hear. Jonathan wondered what Parker's next move would be. Maybe he'd leave him alone. That's all he wanted. To be left alone.

Parker began to give him a wide berth. That's when Jonathan knew he wouldn't bother him anymore. His classroom surprise had turned out to be even better than fighting Parker. He'd gained the upper hand on his tormentor and it felt good.

****

The Civics professor flunked Parker on the test but couldn't pin cheating on him. The teacher didn't just stop at failing Parker, though. It made sense that someone nearby must have helped Parker get rid of the note, so the professor flunked the three students closest to Parker—including Jonathan.

When Jonathan saw his mark, he hung his head for a moment. His neck warmed as he dealt with the surprise of a failing grade. He could feel the professor watching him. A guilty person would take the grade in silence, an innocent one wouldn't. Jonathan hadn't cheated but he still kept quiet. Why, he wasn't sure. The other two reacted. A couple of "shits" and they fell silent. Complaining any more would be turning against Parker. But their outbursts were enough to shift the teacher's focus from them to Jonathan. How did the teacher guess he was involved?

He didn't have wealthy parents to give the school money like the Whigs and Clios, so he was in danger of getting expelled for cheating. That week he lost his job at school. All eyes shifted from Parker, who everyone knew was a cheat, to Jonathan, now tagged as a cheater's accomplice. And no one knew why. Jonathan wasn't even sure himself.

He had to find other work or leave school, so he walked into town to see what might be available. Because of all the writing he'd done growing up, he headed for the newspaper office first. The editor, Mr. Sampson, said he wasn't hiring but Jonathan said he'd work for free, so Sampson let him start on a trial basis.

Jonathan immersed himself in the workings of a

small-town paper, learning everything from setting type, to inking and using the hand-operated press. When he wasn't in class, he was at the newspaper. Mr. Sampson said his first attempts at writing were somewhat heavy-handed but told him there was potential in his prose. For the first time, Jonathan thought he might have found a way to confront some of the injustices that had rankled him forever. Maybe he'd even get his own column where he could hold forth on slavery.

With the newspaperman's help, it wasn't long before Jonathan got the opportunity to write a weekly column about some of the major problems facing the nation—slavery, temperance, abolition, women's rights. At school, Jonathan's disfavor eventually faded—some people even complimenting him on his pieces. In Civics, he sat in a different seat farther away from Parker. Still, tension with his classmate filled his days.

Jonathan's routine revolved around two things now—work and school. Three, if writing to Barbra counted. He'd said only a few words to Parker in the past two months. As he drew away, Parker seemed to try to draw closer. He sought Jonathan out at mealtimes and moved nearer in class. He even stopped by the newspaper office once.

When Jonathan's second year ended, he had scarcely more to stuff into the same worn valise. His Bible, another shirt. Second-hand books he'd bought in town added to his growing library. As the train home steamed toward Philadelphia, Parker maneuvered to sit in the seat next to him. Jonathan half listened to Parker describe high society events Jonathan knew he'd never be a part of. His summer would be taken up by chores.

At the Philadelphia station, Jonathan watched from a window as Parker found his parents in the crowd. Bear hugs all around and they were off in a grand buggy. What kind of reception would *he* get? Would anyone be at the station to meet him? Jonathan sat alone by a window as the train chugged on to Baltimore, then shot straight west to Ohio. As much as he liked Andy Carson, Jonathan hoped it would be Barbra there this year. When he glimpsed the familiar bends of the Ohio River, Jonathan peered out his window searching for the one face he wanted to see most.

The train steamed to a stop. He leaned out of a doorway, hanging onto a strap and scanning the platform. There! "Barbra!" He half ran, half walked to where she stood shielding her eyes from the sun. Beaming. She stuck out her hand. He ignored it and gave her a quick hug. In the buckboard, he chattered away like a jaybird, not stopping for more than an occasional breath. Glanced her way every now and then. Hard not to notice her figure. Her eyes the same light green that first penetrated his heart.

As they drew farther away from town, Jonathan leaned over and kissed her. He sat back mute as the horse's hooves thudded on the dirt road while a familiar flush warmed his neck. "I'm sorry. I didn't mean to do that. Well...I did...but it happened before I knew it!"

They rode in silence the rest of the way. Jonathan snuck glances at Barbra, trying to gauge her reaction. When she turned the wagon onto the dirt drive leading to the Gray farmhouse, he said, "You have to say something. Please."

She guided the horse to a stop. The bad-tempered geese that laid claim to the small green patch of ground out front scattered, honking their displeasure at the intrusion. She turned to him with a smile. "Will I see you tomorrow?"

Jonathan beamed. "You sure will." He jumped from the wagon with a big grin.

With the smallest of nods, Barbra snapped the reins and was gone.

Jonathan glanced around. The farm wasn't quite as well kept as he remembered. His father always maintained everything just so over the years. Andy's letter had set him on edge. Maybe just a hard winter. Still, it *was* mid May. Some of the barn's boards needed replacing. A rusted iron wagon seat lay to the side of it. The farmhouse could use a coat of paint, too.

He hurried into the house and surprised his mother, embracing her hard. Claire jumped on him but Peter was too big for that now, so the brothers hugged and laughed. He walked to the barn, slowing as he neared. Even the prospect of his father's dour personality couldn't entirely wipe the smile off his face.

"Welcome home, son." Tom was mending a worn-out harness. He didn't get up.

Jonathan jammed his hands deep in his pants pockets. "Thanks."

"I'd ask you how school was, but I can see you're happy about something."

"School was fine, Father. I got all top marks except in Civics."

"Sounds like you did well."

"I did all right but I should have had the top grade in that class, too," Jonathan said, frowning.

"Uh huh. Let's go on up to the house. Your mother will be wantin' to hear all about things."

"In a minute, Father." He caught Tom's eye. "How's things here?" Jonathan tried not to appear concerned, but the way things looked, there must not be any money to keep things up.

His father glanced at him sideways.

"It's just that I got a letter from Andy. Said crop prices were falling and everything hereabouts was dry as a desert. He said there was talk some of the local farms might go under."

"Farm's fine." His father squinted at Jonathan as he said it, meaning there would be no more discussion.

Jonathan hesitated, then walked back to the house.

At dinner, the family peppered him with questions about school, his job, and his studies. Peter and Claire had both grown, which he remarked on much to their delight. His brother in particular was changing from a young boy. This year, Peter would help plant for the first time. Backbreaking dawn-to-dusk work for grown men, much less a thirteen-year-old boy. He still looked up to Jonathan with the typical enthusiasm of a little brother.

The cozy days of summer slid by. During an August visit to the Carson farm, Jonathan grumbled to Barbra it had passed too fast, what with his work around the farm. What bothered him most, though, was he hadn't seen her enough. When he talked about what he was going to study this next year, Jonathan could tell Barbra was struggling with what she wanted to do.

"You've always said you want to be a nurse, Lizzie. Do you still?"

"Yes, but there aren't many opportunities for a country girl with only my education. Most of the women around here are either clerking or working as domestics."

"Do you really want to be on your own?" Part of him wanted her to say no.

"Yes, I do, and I need you to go back to school so I can do that. I need to stand on my own two feet." She set her jaw.

As fall approached, his feelings grew mixed. The farm was looking better, but how much trouble was the family in? His father would never say. He looked forward to working at the paper again but wasn't excited about much else at school. On his last day home, he rode Belle to Barbra's and they traveled the nearby hills for several hours. When Jonathan left, she gave him a light kiss and a long hug.

He traded heartfelt goodbyes with his family before heading to the train station. His mother embraced him then hurried back inside the house. His brother shook his hand for the first time ever, before giving way to Claire who wrapped her arms around his waist tightly. Jonathan turned to his father, who wore an expressionless face. Tom grasped his hand a little harder than he ever remembered. Jonathan watched him hitch his overalls up and turn away for the barn.

Chapter Eleven

Fall 1859

Starting his third year, Jonathan was asked to be an assistant professor for the introductory Civics class. By the same professor who flunked him last year. He was puzzled but pleased nonetheless. Time seemed to have smoothed the rough edges of unpleasantness.

Over the first few weeks, Jonathan noticed a difference. The Whigs weren't bothering him anymore. Parker kept trying to make friends, but Jonathan still held him at arm's length. As he was leaving Nassau Hall one day, he heard a shout.

"Gray! Wait up, willya?"

Parker was hurrying his way, not in the company of his usual Whig minions.

"What?"

"Just hold your horses for a minute, okay?" Parker stopped in front of him as red and gold fall leaves swirled in the air. "What's with you? I've been trying to be nice to you, but you won't have any of it. Are you just stuck up, or stupid?"

Jonathan chose to ignore that.

"Well, how come you're so stuck up?"

"Not stuck up. Just don't have anything to say to you." What was Parker up to?

"Well, I thought maybe if I started talkin' to you,

you'd start talkin' to me."

"Why would I? You've never cared a hoot about me before, why would you start now?"

"I don't...care about you...I only thought we might get to be...friends," Parker said.

An odd statement, but then he'd never understood Parker. "Fine. Let's just leave it at that."

Confusion stole across Parker's face. "Okay, I guess...see you around."

Jonathan hustled to the newspaper office to put his daily column together. He didn't make his usual stop at the library because new books were only delivered on Mondays and Thursdays. He greeted Mr. Sampson, who peered at him above his bifocals.

"Looks like you've got something on your mind."

"No, sir, just thinking about what I'm gonna write today."

"Well, you likely won't have trouble figuring that out because there's big news. An abolitionist named John Brown led a raid up the Potomac a few days ago. He and his followers killed some federal troops at a place called Harper's Ferry. There's going to be hell to pay for that."

"Harper's Ferry? Why?"

"It's a—was a—federal arsenal with troops, supplies, weapons, and ammo."

"Why'd he do that?"

"From what I've read, he thinks he can get nearby slaves to revolt. He's promised to arm them. Sounds like you'll be able to churn stories out on this for a long time. And you're starting to get a wider audience. A Philadelphia editor sent me a telegram this morning, asking to talk to you."

"What about?"

"Don't know. Are you going to keep writing about slavery?"

"Seems that's what most everyone's talking about."

"You mean at the school?"

"And around town."

"What are they saying over at the college?"

Jonathan paused for a moment. "Well there's some in favor of it; that's the southern kids—the Clios—and there's some who don't much care about it one way or the other—that's the Whigs. The professors talk about it in class sometimes, but I think they just do it to start conversation. Hard to tell what they think deep down. The seminary folks don't say much one way or the other either, according to the few conversations I've had with the pastors there. I think they pretty much accept slavery as just the way things are."

His columns almost seemed to write themselves. Sometimes he'd start with one point in mind, then the column would take off in a different direction. Whenever he started writing, he wasn't always sure where he'd end up, but that was half the intrigue of it.

Sampson rubbed his chin. "Son, I must say, there's always the same severe anti-slavery slant to your columns."

"Yes, sir, there is. Is that bad?"

"It's not bad but it can be tiresome. Look, readers want new material to read, different perspectives sometimes."

"So, are you saying I should change what I write?"

"No, not what you write—refine your style. Right now, your writing is more bombastic than reasoned.

That can put readers off. You're writing passionately, if not always well."

Jonathan's heartbeat quickened. "Well, I won't change my opinion on slavery, sir." His columns had become an outlet for the anger that had gnawed at his insides ever since childhood.

"Not asking you to. Wouldn't want you to. But, why don't we try to make your arguments a bit more persuasive? That's not a meat ax you're writing with, it's a pen."

In the midst of all that was going on, he kept up a steady correspondence with Barbra.

Dear Jonathan,

I hope you are well. I'm still enjoying my work at the railroad. It gets me off the farm and into the city. For the first time in my life I have some independence. I get home a couple of times a month, but beyond that, I'm on my own. And I'm meeting lots of new people.

I keep busy, mostly helping the schedulers build the railroad's routes and timetables. It's like piecing a puzzle together. I get to recommend what equipment goes where and how and when it gets there. Every night, I take the master schedule for the month home to study it. Then I write suggestions down and bring them back to my boss. He passes most of my ideas off like they were his, but that's all right. I enjoy the job and my freedom. I hope to move into my own room in a boarding house soon.

Write please!

Barbra

Jonathan pursed his lips. He supposed some of the people Barbra was meeting were men, drawn to her petite good looks and striking auburn hair. They would no doubt pay her lots of attention. You'd have to be blind not to notice her.

****

While Barbra was establishing herself on her own, a persistent Parker was wearing Jonathan's ambivalence away. He had never thought much of Parker, but now he began to reconsider. Even though Parker led the arrogant Whigs, he didn't seem to have any real friends. Maybe he and Parker needed each other. Him with the deep-seated hole in his heart and Parker with his false bravado. As the school year unfolded, Jonathan grew to accept, and even like Parker's company. He went with Parker to some high-society gatherings in Philadelphia that opened his eyes to a whole new lifestyle. One that intrigued him.

He looked forward to these new social affairs. He hadn't made any close friends at Princeton, so this friendship with Parker was new. Maybe someday he could have what the eastern boys all seemed to have—a promising future.

Halfway through the school year, Jonathan had only written Barbra a couple of letters. He hadn't responded to her last one and found himself making flimsy excuses for not writing. He didn't have time. There wasn't anything to say.

His columns were gaining popularity and he fancied himself a bit of a local celebrity. Even though he could afford to this year, he decided he wouldn't go home for Christmas. He convinced himself he needed to stay at Princeton and keep writing. This new life was exciting. And deep down, he really didn't want to go home.

****

Barbra grabbed Jonathan's letter from the letter drop at the boarding house and hurried to her room.

Dear Barbra,

I hope this finds you well. I have been so busy here, I just haven't had time to write. I'm now writing articles for the local paper, mostly still about slavery and why it's so wrong. I've been given a real column to write every week, which means I have to do a lot of research. So, I'll be staying here over Christmas. It'll be a good time to gather background material, since I won't have classes. Have a good Christmas and I hope to see you soon.

Jonathan

Dear Barbra? Not Lizzie? She dropped the letter on the bed and walked out front in a daze. A chill ran through her, but it wasn't the December cold that penetrated her winter coat. She drew the collar tighter. Andy would be here soon to take her home for Christmas break. When he drew the wagon up, Barbra didn't say anything as she got on. Sadness consumed her.

Andy frowned. "What's wrong?"

"Jonathan's…not coming home for Christmas."

"What? Why not?"

"Well if I knew, I'd tell you." A flush ran up her neck. She didn't mean to yell—but maybe she did.

"He didn't tell me he wasn't coming home."

"And why would he tell you if he was or wasn't, Andy Carson?"

"'Cause he's my friend…and…well…" His voice trailed off.

They traveled the rest of the way in silence, Barbra lost in her own unhappy thoughts.

****

Jonathan also wrote his parents he wasn't coming home. For the same reasons he'd told Barbra. Even as he wrote, the "whys" sounded hollow. Jonathan wasn't sure why he stayed at school over Christmas, he just felt different about things somehow. Different, and embarrassed by the difference, but not enough to go home. During the break, he busied himself with mundane tasks at the paper, but they served to validate in his own mind why he stayed. The start of classes came as a relief.

He got a letter from Barbra soon after the term started. She wrote about everyday things back home, but didn't mention his absence.

Dear Jonathan,

I hope you had a nice Christmas. I'm still enjoying my job and I like the people here. For a lot of them, this is their first job, too. I'm working with some of the engineers now. Andy says hello. He shot a turkey that we cooked for Christmas dinner. He was so proud.

We stopped to see your folks on the way home from the city a couple of weeks ago. They looked fine and the children are getting so tall. They had a nice big Christmas tree that almost filled the living room. Your father said he chopped it down over by where the two of you have gotten them in the past. They strung it with popcorn. It was so pretty.

I hope you'll write soon. I'd love to hear about your writing and your studies.

Fondly,

Barbra

The letter stung, but Jonathan pushed the feeling away. He didn't need to feel guilty about anything.

There was a good reason for staying at school. He threw himself into his studies, the paper, and social events with Parker. He was edging into wealthy Philadelphia circles now, attending elaborate events.

Despite this, Jonathan's opposition toward slavery remained white-hot. On campus, a natural tension developed between him and the Clios. He felt their animosity at every turn.

"Hey, cracker, keep your nose out of our business."

"Watch your back, poor trash."

"Keep writin' those lies and we'll teach you not to!"

The taunting followed him wherever he went. It grew bolder as the term unfolded.

At the paper, Sampson asked, "What's the matter? You've got a hang dog look about you."

Jonathan pursed his lips. "Doesn't look like there's any good way out of the coming trouble over slavery. And things are a muddle at school."

"You may be right. Princeton has never been particularly anti-slavery nor pro to this point—a neutrality that's getting trampled on by both sides now. Seems like the seminary is choosing to stay out of the fray, too. I interviewed one of the pastors last week. He said secular affairs didn't concern them."

Jonathan said, "But they're preaching to a secular world."

"Not sure they understand that. I've also heard church attendance is dropping, not among those who have to go to services, mind you, but among town folk. No doubt that worries those good Presbyterian pastors. They've always been secular enough to be concerned about their finances."

Jonathan shook his head. The seminary should be supporting abolition. Advocating for it. They were becoming irrelevant in the midst of the country's greatest moral dilemma. He sensed people's attitudes hardening on both sides. Wasn't hard to understand why the Clios were insulting him.

"I can take care of myself," he said as he walked to class one day with Parker and several Whigs. His big column of the week had just come out.

"No, you can't," Parker said, scanning the surroundings while Whigs formed a loose circle around him.

Jonathan said, "No one's gonna do anything stupid and you have better things to do than babysit me."

As they neared Nassau Hall, Clios surrounded the entryway. A big one stood directly in Jonathan's path. As Jonathan moved left, then right, the Clio did the same, until Parker shoved him out of the way. The two sides swarmed like a beehive knocked to the ground. Jonathan took a punch to the gut, but before he could respond, his father's image flashed through his head. Fine time for him to show up after all these years. He backed away.

After the fight, enrollment at Princeton quickly declined by a third as Clios quit to return home.

****

Jonathan's columns were being picked up by more New Jersey papers and in some neighboring states. In Civics class, students paid as much attention to him as the teacher. For the first time, he was enjoying Princeton. Weekends, he looked forward to staying with the Parkers and meeting influential new people. He'd never had a social circle, so he was proud of hobnobbing with Philadelphia's upper crust. He was having a hard time remembering where he came from after seeing firsthand how wealthy people lived and played.

By the end of the school year, he was still hearing from Barbra but hadn't responded to her letters. When Parker suggested he come to Philadelphia for the summer and look into a job with one of the local papers, he accepted without hesitation.

He told himself it didn't make sense to spend summers at the farm anymore. There was money to be made writing under the tutelage of Philadelphia editors. He penned a well-reasoned letter to his folks that took care of things back home—in his mind. He wrote a lighthearted and newsy letter to Barbra, in an attempt to erase the last vestige of guilt Philadelphia high society hadn't worn away yet. No more "Dear Lizzie." He held off mentioning he was staying in Philadelphia until the end of the letter. Should he add he'd see her soon? No. Even he didn't believe that anymore. Hopeful these two letters had taken care of "loose ends" back home, but knowing deep down they hadn't, he threw himself into his summer plans.

The first time he'd stayed at Parker House, Jonathan was amazed at how different his friend's world was. Imagine—a house with its own name. And all this opulence. A large crystal chandelier sparkled in the foyer. Real silverware. A servant to wash and lay out his worn clothes. Polish his scruffy shoes. A circular staircase. An elegant carriage with a hand-sewn leather interior. An atmosphere of genteel wealth filled the spacious house, and the grounds spread over a considerable area of the Society Hill section of town.

A new world.

Chapter Twelve

Summer 1860

Jonathan went with Robert to meet Samuel Hamilton, editor of the *Philadelphia Inquirer*, one of the leading papers in the country.

The newspaperman rose from his large, burled walnut desk. "Welcome, Jonathan. Mr. Parker sent me some of your columns from Princeton. Seems like you've got a passion for writing about slavery."

"Yes, sir."

"You like writing about anything else?"

"Sir, I like writing about whatever you want me to." By the look on Hamilton's face, that was a good answer.

"One more question. Why do you want to work here?"

"People all over the world read your paper, sir. Why wouldn't I want to work here?"

"Another good answer. How can I not hire you?" Hamilton shook Jonathan's hand. "You'll work on the opinion side of the paper with the editorial page writers. That should be a natural fit for you. Your job will be to research subjects, check facts, and review draft columns. You'll start immediately."

Considering the *Inquirer's* reputation, Jonathan pinched himself over his good fortune, even if he was an apprentice. Every week, Hamilton gave him new topics to ghost write articles on. Slavery, states' rights, politics. Jonathan didn't mind not getting credit for them—he was still astonished a big city paper would even consider printing anything he wrote.

As the months flew by, his style grew bolder. One of the editors approached him holding an anti-slavery column of his. "Say, Jonathan, aren't you staying with the Parkers this summer?"

Jonathan almost burst with pride. "Sure am." Upper class now.

"That seems kind of strange."

Jonathan cocked his head. "Not sure what you mean."

"Ironic, isn't it? You say you oppose slavery but you're staying at the home of a textile mill owner whose wealth depends on raw material harvested by slaves. I can't make heads nor tails of that. Can you?"

The irony never occurred to him before and he flushed at the contradiction. His long-standing hostility toward slavery was now playing second fiddle to the allure of the prosperous lifestyles that surrounded him. He pushed the paradox to the back of his mind. His time with the Parkers was passing well. The little bit of his upbringing left made him thankful for their hospitality.

But the copy editor's comment still gnawed at him.

****

Prominent Philadelphia families hosted socials during the summer—ideal ways to reinforce social, economic, and political connections. Each host tried to outdo the others at lavish parties in their highly decorated homes.

"You have to go to these things. It's required by the room and board contract you signed with my folks for the summer," Parker teased.

Jonathan had mixed feelings about the gatherings. He'd stand out like a sore thumb, but he also looked forward to spending more time among the wealthy. He finally had a presentable outfit to wear, Parker had made sure of that. No more crude repairs, no pins holding the seams of his pants together. New shoes, too. Most of what he made from writing had gone into his wardrobe. Memories of the farm, if he thought about home at all, grew more and more distant.

Parker House hosted one of the last events of the summer. As Philadelphia's social elite gathered, Jonathan felt more like he ought to be serving than mingling. He eyed his new clothes. The nicest he'd ever had, but even so, doubts about fitting in assaulted his confidence.

Parker shouted down the basement stairs. "Hey, you ready yet?"

"I'm about as ready as I'm ever gonna be, which isn't very. How much time do we have before people start arriving?"

"The wealthier you are, the later you arrive at these things. They'll be here soon enough, so get a move on."

"Coming up now." Jonathan climbed to the main level where staff was busy preparing food, setting plates, lighting candles, and arranging flowers just so. He forced himself to feign the same socially correct, somewhat aloof air of those around him.

A young woman came in with her parents about halfway through the social. She swept through the front door like a princess, breezing through the receiving line, and curtsying with a demure nod as she floated around the room.

Jonathan watched, transfixed. Rooted. With a glass of punch in hand, he rotated like a marionette as she paraded.

Parker sidled up next to him. "What's the matter, Gray, never seen a pretty girl before?"

Jonathan took a deep breath. "I've seen plenty…just never one like this."

"Want me to introduce you?"

"No! Don't you dare or I'll walk out."

Parker peered at him. "What are you talking about? I'll just take you over and you can say hello."

"No," he said a little too loudly. After slowing his heartbeat, he whispered, "I can't. Why haven't I seen her before?"

"'Cause she hasn't been here this summer. Spent the last few months on the continent. England, France, and Italy. Venice, I heard."

Jonathan stared at his new shoes for courage. Didn't help. There was no way he could he talk to a woman like that.

She wore her jet-black hair longer than most, not in a bob like so many young women her age. Her smile made her pale skin seem warmer. She was trim, but in a curvy sort of way, taller than Parker, though shorter than he was. Her dark eyes held him fast. Surely everyone in the room noticed him staring at her. As he glanced around, though, no one was paying him any mind at all.

Guests the Parkers introduced him to blended in a blur. He escaped to the punch bowl to relieve his cottony mouth while she strolled up beside him and flounced her green crinoline dress.

"I don't believe we've met yet. I'm Marion Harding."

He turned her way and his stomach jumped. "I'm...Jonathan Gray."

"I noticed you watching me. "

Jonathan's stomach continued its little flips. He stood mute. What could he say to that?

"I'm sure I would have remembered if I'd met you before. Who are you here with?"

His tongue reconnected with his brain. "Uh...I'm a guest for the summer with the Parkers. I have a writing internship with the *Inquirer*. I go to Princeton with Robert." He thought he sounded like a puppet. He did sound like a puppet.

"Princeton, is it? How did you happen to go there?"

In his nervousness, he shared more than he wanted about his scholarship and farm upbringing. His mouth wouldn't behave.

When he took a breath, she said, "My, you are a long way from home."

Jonathan nodded. Getting farther away all the time. He babbled on and on. Almost as if he stopped talking, some imaginary spell would break and poof, she'd be gone. At last he paused, his heart racing. "I've been monopolizing you. I need to let you get back to your visiting."

"Thank you but I'll stay right here a while longer." She curled a strand of black hair behind an ear.

Jonathan stood transfixed by her eyes. Were they black?

"Aren't you going to ask about me?" she said,

turning a beguiling smile on him.

"Well sure, I'd love to...I mean I'd like to...know all about you...I mean, where you're from, not where you're from because I'd guess you're from around here, just more about you...anything, really." He regained control of his wayward mouth as a flush rushed up his neck.

She laughed and told him about growing up in a wealthy Philadelphia family, in a household that had more servants than children. She batted long eyelashes. "Would you like to dance? They're playing one of my favorites Strauss waltzes."

Jonathan hesitated. "I don't know how."

"It's easy, I'll show you."

She led him to the dance floor and placed his arm on her waist. Delicate crinoline brushed against his arm as they moved together. The bewitching aroma of her exotic perfume filled his senses. By the end of the waltz, he was as aroused as he'd ever been in his life.

When they sat, he stared into her eyes, not really taking in anything she was saying.

She smiled as she talked, head tilted his way. He heard her ask, "Well?"

Jonathan had no idea what to say, he'd just been gawking. "Um...I have enjoyed meeting you...maybe I...ought to be getting back to...my writing." What a ridiculous thing to say. No doubt she was thinking the same thing. But it was out there now, so he stood from the ottoman. With a slight bow and a mumbled goodbye, he fled to the kitchen to recover his senses.

After everyone left, Parker found him back by the pantry with the help. "Jonathan, what are you doing?"

"Uh, helping clean up."

"Stop that!" Parker grabbed him by the arm and steered him to the study. He closed the door, poured two brandies, and handed one to him. "Don't ever do that again."

"What?" The liquor burned on the way down.

"Socialize with the staff."

"Why not?" The rules of the rich were so confusing.

"It's just not done. And don't ever let my folks see you doing that, either. All right?"

"Okay. I don't understand, but if that's the way you feel, all right."

"Okay. So what's up with you and Marion Harding?"

"Nothing." But Jonathan leaned toward his friend. "What's she like?"

"She's...well, she's one of the richest women around, besides having all the looks in the world."

"Were you ever...involved...with her?"

"No, she was never interested in me, although I've known her for years. Our families have been friends a long time."

At the next gathering, the last of the summer, Jonathan took a chance and asked if he could write her.

"Only if you send me some of those columns of yours, too. What were they about again?" She glanced sideways at him. Coy smile.

The small sliver of summer that remained was soon gone. As he packed to leave, Jonathan thanked the Parkers for their gracious hospitality.

"We have enjoyed having you here," Mrs. Parker said. "You are a good influence on Robert." She smiled at Jonathan, then at her son.

"You are welcome here anytime," Parker Senior sniffed, but Jonathan noticed Senior did seem more relaxed around him now. "I hear you've done some good work at the paper as well. Old man Hamilton tells me you have a future in the newspaper business. Keep it up. By the way, your articles about slavery have stirred some controversy around here. Did you know that?"

Jonathan nodded. Parker told him his father didn't care about slavery one way or the other, but he did need a continual flow of southern cotton for his mills. "Yes, sir, and thanks again for your help in getting me on with the paper. I've learned so much these last few months."

The two friends rode the train back to Princeton, Jonathan's belongings still in the same old valise. They gabbed the whole way, excited to start their last year.

A few weeks into the term, Jonathan sat to write a letter to his folks. He reddened as he searched for something to say. When had he last written and what had he said? What did they even have in common anymore?

Dear Mother and Father,

It sure was busy here the last few months in Philadelphia. As for news, I worked at the Philadelphia Inquirer *from June to September, mostly doing background work for other writers. I got to see my name on some articles, too! And I got paid a small stipend for doing it. The summer couldn't have gone any better.*

I'm sorry I didn't get to see you all before coming back to school. I'll be sure to see you at Christmas. I hope you get this letter soon.

Jonathan

Even as he wrote the part about seeing them at Christmas, he knew it was a lie. What he didn't say was that his stipend was already gone, spent on clothes and partying. He'd thought about sending some of it home, but the moment passed. No doubt his family was doing…fine without his help.

He didn't write Barbra because he didn't know what to say to her, either. But she still wrote him. He hadn't even opened her last few letters, just dropped them in his duffel. In the back of his mind, he knew the longer he waited the more difficult it would be to ever write her again. Barbra was just a childhood crush—his past, Marion his future.

Chapter Thirteen

Back at school, Jonathan took Marion up on her request to write.

Dear Marion,

I was pleased to find out I've been asked to take over the basic Civics course for incoming freshmen. I have an underclassman assisting me. My course is one of the most popular on campus. Even some of my professors crowd in to hear the give and take on slavery.

I prompt the students with questions like, 'Why shouldn't slaves remain slaves? They've been bought and paid for. Their owners own them right and proper.'

That last phrase still stuck in Jonathan's craw. An image of Big Hat dragging the runaway family away haunted his thoughts.

Then the class usually erupts. The southern kids as much as the northerners. They're talking about moving the class to a larger room soon. I don't understand why some people want to keep slavery just the way it is.

Please write,

Jonathan

He wrote Marion every week and even though he didn't get many letters in return, he told himself that didn't bother him.

Parker mentioned it. "I see you writing her all the time, but I don't see you getting many back. What gives?"

He wondered the same thing, but said, "W-Why do you care? She probably doesn't have time because she's too busy being gorgeous."

The two had become best friends. Weekends, Jonathan squired Marion to Philadelphia's social events. She was still the same highbrow, somewhat distant person Jonathan first met. On some level he guessed she was using him, but he didn't care. At first, he fended off Marion's coaxing to drink and gamble but she chided him until he bent to her will.

Parker noticed the change. "What are you doing? You're not like this." Jonathan hadn't come home until the wee hours that night.

Jonathan broke eye contact. "Whaddya mean?" As if he didn't know.

"I mean what you're doing with Marion these days. I don't even know where you go anymore."

"That's 'cause you're not invited." He reveled in being one-up on his friend.

"I'm not asking you to invite me. I'm just saying you're in over your head here."

"You're just jealous, my friend, 'cause you're not going out with a beautiful socialite." Something he could hardly believe himself.

Parker shook his head. "My guess is that lovely lady has some shady things in mind for you, *my friend*."

Jonathan had a vague sense Parker was keeping something about Marion from him, but he didn't really want to know what. His newfound prominence and the start of a heady romance was enough for now. With the money he made at the paper, he moved from the dorm to a boarding house not far from campus. He also spoke at several local political gatherings—rallies he looked forward to. He fancied himself the voice of abolition in middle New Jersey.

His relationship with Parker was also changing. Parker had always been the more dominant of the two with his wealth and connections but now Jonathan started treating his friend almost as if he were the poor farm boy.

A Friday afternoon and they trained to Philadelphia. Parker said, "What do you want to do this weekend?"

"Well, I don't want to spend it with you. I've got better things to do, like being with Marion."

"I just thought we could go to the Dock Club."

Jonathan replied with a small grin. "Maybe next time. Right now I'm docking with her."

"You're still going to stay with us, aren't you?"

"Sure, I wouldn't miss your chef's cooking for anything," he said with a flippant wave of his hand.

As Christmas break approached, Jonathan still hadn't written his parents—or Barbra. He pushed that slight guilt to the backroads of his mind. He'd stayed in touch with Mr. Hamilton, though, and confirmed he'd have his internship at the *Inquirer* during the break. He was looking forward to seeing Marion as much as she would allow. Lots of possibilities there.

"I wish you wouldn't spend so much time with her, she only thinks of herself," Parker said as they hurried up the front steps of Parker House.

Jonathan held a hand up. "No more. Please."

"Are you sure you don't want to go down to the Dock Club tonight?"

"Yup, I'm just going to head over to her house and

we'll see where things go from there," Jonathan said with a wink.

When he got to her house, Marion said she had something special in mind. She'd arranged a seat for him in a high stakes poker game in a downtown warehouse that evening. Jonathan pulled the buggy up at an old building in a decrepit part of town. Marion handed him a handful of paper money and gave him a glancing kiss on the cheek. "Good luck!" She smiled.

Jonathan joined the game with careless confidence. After all, he routinely bested Marion's friends. He fancied he had a natural talent for knowing when to bluff and when not to. He was the sixth player tonight. The others were older and seemed to know one another. One of them nodded his way as Jonathan sat. "Name's Easy Jack." The man introduced the other players around the rectangular green felt table. Dim lighting, grimy windows. He ordered Jonathan a whisky and started dealing. After a few hands, Jonathan noticed the deal wasn't rotating.

At first, the thick cigar smoke and fingers drumming on the table bothered him. But as the whiskies hit, his annoyance faded, replaced by mounting frustration. How did they always know when to fold and when to hold? That was his game.

Jonathan lost promising hand after hand. They kept filling his whiskey glass while his ever-dwindling stash of money mocked him. "Damn!" Wiped out in less than two hours, he'd lost Marion's money too. He looked her way as she sat to the side, smoking a thin cigarette. Was that a slight smirk?

Easy Jack expressed surprise at his bad luck. Jonathan yelled, "Give me shome money back. I'm broke!" He reached a hand across the table toward the man's stack. Jack jammed a knife in between Jonathan's two middle fingers. "Damn you all!" He'd been sure he couldn't lose. Jonathan grabbed the deck and hurled the cards across the room. Struggling to a stand, he stumbled from the table and staggered out into the street. Ribald laughter and curling wisps of cigar smoke trailed after him.

"Let's call it a night and go back to the Parkers," Marion said, grabbing his arm to help keep him upright.

He put a hand to his head to try to stop the spinning. "I losht all the money."

Marion grinned. "Didn't you notice the hidden cards? The drumming on the table? Those were all signals. Even I could tell that deck was marked."

Really? How come she'd noticed them and he hadn't? An image of his father, frowning, flashed in his head. After stumbling over a curb, Marion caught him before he pitched headfirst into the street. He said, "Robert wannd me to go to thuh Dock Club. Lesh go."

Marion said, "We can't. That's a private men's club. I'm not welcome."

"They can't keep ush out. Free…country."

At the Club, Parker moved to intercept a rowdy Jonathan. He stepped in front of him as he and Marion entered the drawing room. The place was filled with prosperous-looking men smoking, drinking, playing cards.

"You can't come in here with her," Parker whispered. He glanced around the room.

"Itsh time for that to…shange." He staggered slightly.

"Fine, but let's don't change things tonight."

Jonathan thrust his chin out. "We oughta be able to drink here, there'sh lots of booze."

Parker leaned close. "You already stink of whiskey, you don't need any more."

Marion wore the same small smile on her face as the scene unfolded.

Club stewards closed in on the pair. Jonathan put a hand up against them. They asked him and Marion to leave. Of all the nerve. He clenched a fist and shook his head.

The bigger one said, "Have it your way, son, but one way or the other, you're leaving."

Jonathan threw a few sloppy jabs at the big man, while the other bouncer moved behind him and circled an arm around his neck. Soon, he couldn't breathe. He swung wildly. A punch to his midsection and he was a rag doll. No air. The stewards picked him up, carried him out, and dropped him a block away. He lay sprawled on the street—sweating, vomiting, gasping for breath, Marion nowhere to be seen.

When he stumbled back to Parker House, he tried the front door. Locked. He staggered to the side of the house and found a partly-open window. Parker was sitting with a half-empty brandy in the darkened study when he finally managed to crawl in.

"Come here and be quiet about it," Parker whispered.

"I am quiet," Jonathan said, knocking a chair over. He put a finger to his lips and grinned. "Shssssh."

"Let's get you to bed. I won't even ask where you've been."

"I ain't been with Marion if thash what you mean. You seen her?" he said, reverting to his farm boy slang.

He shook his head. "She was with you at the club." Parker half dragged his friend downstairs to his small room. Jonathan collapsed on the bed—out as his head hit the pillow.

The next morning, Parker shook him awake. "Get up. My folks already know about what happened last night. Among other things, you're banned from the club."

Jonathan put a hand to his groggy head. "Was I that bad?"

"Worse." Parker headed upstairs.

At the last Christmas social, stares followed him as he walked in without Marion. He soon left. The next day, he visited her one last time before packing for school. Parker asked how things went.

"Fine, fine. She was glad to see me." Hardly. His words hid his confusion. If she was trying to shred his confidence, it was working. One final apology to the Parkers and Jonathan was on his way back to Princeton.

In between teaching class and writing for the paper, he spent almost no time in the boarding house. He wrote Marion several letters, but didn't get any back. Parker hadn't invited him home lately, either. Jonathan wrote Robert's parents another apology for his boorish behavior. Halfway through the semester Parker finally invited him to stay. When he arrived, he fell all over himself apologizing again. The Parkers were polite, but cool.

Marion also allowed him to visit. As he begged for her forgiveness, Jonathan noticed the same small grin, a smirk that was beginning to annoy him.

She sat on the couch like a queen, her dress a flowing royal blue, her mouth turned down in a stylish pout. "I wish you would have knocked those two bouncers off their pins. They dishonored me with their actions." But Jonathan was too caught up in his own remorse to reflect on her words.

The rest of that term she let him take her to some socials and smiled at the occasional wisps of gossip. As Jonathan drove her carriage home one night, she laid her hand on his thigh.

He wasn't sure if that meant what he thought it might. His confusion increased as her hand lay there. "What?…"

"I want you to do what I want you to do."

Still unsure, he steered the carriage off the road onto a deserted side path. Afterward, she smoothed her dress and hair, almost as if he weren't there. Confusion roiled his insides. They rode in strained silence to her house. What should he say to her? When Jonathan pulled up, she touched a finger to his mouth and was gone inside. He stared at the dark house for a few minutes and shook his head. Walking back to Parker House, he searched his soul. Did that really happen? Why didn't he feel better? He eased the front door closed behind him and headed downstairs to a fitful sleep.

****

Spring 1861

The national storm over slavery erupted just before Jonathan graduated when seven southern states seceded one by one.

War!

As they were packing to leave Princeton, the two friends talked about the future. Parker said, "Come to Philadelphia, Gray. You don't have anything else to do."

"I've been thinking on that. Maybe I will for a bit," he said, looking forward to spending time with Marion. "I probably need to head home sometime, too. I could try to get on with a paper back there, but likely I'll just end up joining the army."

Parker looked sideways at him. "What? Weren't you raised in a pacifist family. Quakers?"

Jonathan paused. His heart pounded at the thought of home. It had been so long. "Yes, but...my father...it was...he and I never got along."

"So what?"

"You wouldn't understand." He shook his head. "It's more complicated...he never tried...just forget it. It's not important anymore. I'm not like him anyway." Those last words came out louder than he intended. He hadn't thought about the family's pacifism in a long while, but he wasn't going to just stand by like his father always did. All this time away from home, all the time spent doing what he wanted hadn't purged his conflicted feelings.

Parker said, "Come to think of it, I've never heard you talk about him, just your mother. Anyway, why not stay here for a while? You could get on with the *Inquirer* or join the Tenth Pennsylvania with me."

"Why would I do that? You're the only one I know around here and you aren't gonna get me promoted anytime soon. With all your connections, I'd probably have to wait on making general until after you did and I couldn't stand that," he said, laughing his discomfort away.

"But you'd still be the second youngest general in the army. Right behind me."

"Well, I guess I'd like to be the youngest, so I'll just head back to Ohio and start my climb there." Jonathan chuckled again.

"What about Marion?"

"Guess I don't know." He squinted. "Don't have her figured out."

The next couple of weeks were a whirlwind of socials and more than a little bit of drinking. He spent as much time with Marion as she decided. She was a butterfly, flitting from place to place. He got just enough of her attention to keep him off balance.

As Jonathan readied for the trip home, Parker said, "You know you'll always have a place here, right?"

"Thanks, I know that. I hope we'll see each other again soon."

"Count on it. In the meantime, keep your head down."

"You, too." A quick hug as they separated at the platform.

Marion was nowhere in sight as his train left the station.

Chapter Fourteen

Before he left Philadephia, Jonathan finally wrote his folks he was coming home. He'd also written Barbra, hoping she might meet him at the Cincinnati station. Not likely. Not the way he'd ignored her. When his train pulled to a stop, he didn't see anyone he knew. Wasn't a surprise. He walked down the platform. Through the crowd, though, Andy Carson waved to him. Thank heavens someone came. Jonathan had learned how to push his guilt away for long spells, but that intruder always returned.

Andy was subdued on the ride home. Jonathan tried to draw him out but could only get one-word replies from him. He grabbed the reins from his friend and brought the horse to a halt.

"What's the matter with you? Aren't you glad to see me?" Anger had just trumped guilt.

"Why didn't you ever write us?" Andy shouted. "It's been a whole year since we've seen or heard from you. All you ever did was send some stupid things you wrote." His eyes blazed.

Heat rose in Jonathan's ears. "I guess I thought everyone would be interested in seeing those." How could Andy say they were stupid?

"It don't even seem like you care about us no more."

That hit home. "Sure I care. I've just been busy

getting ready to go off to war." Even he knew how lame that sounded. They rode the rest of the way in an uncomfortable silence and it was a relief when the Gray farmhouse came into view.

With a quiet "thank you," Jonathan hopped off at the front circle and looked around. Memories flooded through him. Barbra. Sonny. Sadie. His hard father, silent-suffering mother. He'd been away so long. He dreaded going through the front door.

Inside, his family greeted him with courteous welcomes, like they would a guest. No one rose except his mother. While everyone was polite enough, there was a distance he could feel. Even Peter and Claire, not small anymore, treated him like the visitor he was. After a few questions about school, silence suffocated the living room. Jonathan kept talking, as much to fill the strained hush as anything. He couldn't think of much to say so he blurted he was going to join the army. His father started to respond, but then left the room.

His mother put a hand to her mouth. "Jonathan, you can't! You can't do—"

"I'm going to, Mother. Nothing you can do about it." He stuck his chin out, but hadn't really meant to sound so harsh. He wished his father was still in the room to hear that declaration. The children ran outside and his mother turned away for the kitchen. As he sat in the living room, he'd never felt so alone in his life. That evening, he suffered through the most awkward dinner he'd ever had. In his own home. Or was it still? His father didn't look his way or say a word.

Belinda wore a wan smile and studied her husband as she cleared plates. "Tom, why don't we have a little gathering here to celebrate Jonathan's graduation?" The children perked up at the idea of having neighbors visit. A party.

Tom didn't respond.

His mother's eyes reflected her distress. "Well, good, it's settled then. We'll plan it for Saturday."

Jonathan hoped Barbra would be there. Part of him was looking forward to seeing her but another part wasn't. He'd ignored her for so long. What did they have in common anymore?

The party was a gathering of the few farm families nearby, most of whom Jonathan still remembered. The smallness of the group made Barbra's absence all the more noticeable.

"Hello, Jonathan." Andy loaded a plate with venison and canned beets at the sideboard.

"Hi, yourself. Thanks again for coming to pick me up."

Andy nodded. "How long you here for?"

"Just a little while, I guess. I'm going to join the army at Camp Dennison."

"That's what you said."

Jonathan struggled for something else to say. He tried to look interested as he said, "So, how are you?"'

"Fine. I just graduated from high school," Andy said with no enthusiasm.

"Yeah, I guess you would have, now that I think about it." Andy hadn't crossed his mind in a long while. "What are you going to do?"

"Well I don't have no money to go to college, so I'll likely stay here on the farm or look for work in town. Or maybe enlist."

"Aren't you too young?"

"You know how old I am. You sound just like my folks when I bring it up."

Just like my folks, too, Jonathan thought.

"Or maybe I'd work for the railroad, like Barbra did."

A stomach flutter took him by surprise and he tried to sound nonchalant. "Uh…how is Barbra, anyway?"

"She's fine. She said to say 'hello'."

That's all? "I thought she might be here." Part of him was glad she wasn't.

"Well, she couldn't make it."

Not surprising after how he'd treated her. "What's she doing these days?"

"She left the railroad when General McClellan went back in the army. He helped her get on with the sanitary girls."

"What's that?"

"I don't rightly know. I just know she helps out at Camp Dennison."

"Dennison?" That was right down the road.

"Yeah, it's a big mustering-in site for the army now."

"She's at Camp Dennison? Now?" Just a few miles away.

"Yup."

"Uh…what does she do there?" He didn't know if he wanted to run into her there or not.

"Takes care of soldiers, I guess."

"Well I remember she always wanted to be a nurse," Jonathan said.

"That's about all you remember, I'll wager."

"Whaddya mean?" But he flushed at the truth of it. Why did he even care? She had no place in his world

123

now.

"She thinks you've turned into a dandy. An eastern dandy." Andy's voice rose as he spoke.

"I ain't no dandy." Jonathan's heart pounded as a mix of anger and remorse swirled inside.

"That's why she's not here. That, and she has a fella."

"A fella! When did that happen?" He told himself *so what*?

"Some guy she met while she was at the railroad," Andy fibbed. Barbra did tell her brother that she thought Jonathan was a dandy, but he made the imaginary boyfriend up on his own.

Warmth ran up to his face. He'd never considered that Barbra would have suitors. Of course, she would. So what? He had his own girl now. "I'm sorry she's not here. I would have liked to see her. And you can tell her I'm no dandy." His voice caught—discomfort had become an all-too-familiar part of this visit.

"Well, that's what she thinks."

Jonathan spent the rest of the gathering talking with the other guests about his plans. He answered questions about everything from train rides to college, to newspaper writing and the army. He took extra time with Sonny's parents.

"Oh, Jonathan, you look so good," Mrs. Walker said. "And you just graduated from college. My oh my. A college graduate. Never known one of them before." A tear trickled down her right cheek. She wiped it away. "Will you stay here on the farm now to help your father?"

He searched for a way to say "no" without lying. "I guess I don't know for sure yet. I'm still getting used to being back." He thought of Sonny. They might have been joining the army together.

Mrs. Walker dabbed at her eyes.

Jonathan's gaze fell to the floor. Coming home had never felt so empty.

He spent the next few days helping his father around the farm. His brother and sister worked chores, too. Peter was about the same age he was when he went off to high school, and Claire wasn't a little girl anymore.

Nettled by the image Barbra had of him and wondering about her boyfriend, Jonathan made a trip to the Carson farm. He hoped at least one thing about this visit would go well. As he neared, guilt almost made him turn around. When he said hello, she smiled, but her eyes didn't. Jonathan sat on the porch in the double swing they used to sway on together. Barbra took a nearby chair.

"Congratulations on graduating from college. That must have been a lot of hard work. What will you do now?" She made only glancing eye contact.

"I think I'm going to join the army." Coming here was a mistake. He should go.

She looked a little surprised. "But, how could you? You're pacifists."

He pursed his lips. "My father is, my family is—I'm not." Had he ever been? He scuffed his shoe on the wooden porch. He wanted to ask what her plans were, but the words wouldn't come. As the conversation became more forced, he started to babble. "A friend and I are both joining up. He's in Philadelphia."

"A college friend?"

"Yes. We didn't like each other at first but now

he's my best friend." Calling her Lizzie was out of the question. Ages ago now. He prattled on about his writing, his opinions on the war, and where he thought he was going to be serving. Couldn't seem to stop himself, until embarrassment closed his mouth.

Barbra sat silently, hands folded in her lap.

He leaned forward. "Maybe I'll be at Camp Dennison. I hear lots of soldiers are signing up there. Isn't that where you're working? That's what Andy said."

Her face was expressionless. She said a simple, "Yes," and left it at that.

Nothing else to do but leave. Riding Belle away, he kicked himself. He hadn't the courage to ask about her boyfriend. But then, maybe he didn't want to know.

****

Jonathan brought an old issue of the *Philadelphia Inquirer* home to show his father. As they sat on the front porch watching the sunset, he pointed out a piece he'd written. Tom glanced at it and nodded.

Jonathan searched for a way to break the stony silence. He started to read from another article, "This one says seven southern states have already seceded from the Union, claiming they left to uphold states' rights, but I don't think anyone believes that."

Tom said, "I don't believe it, either."

"I saved a story about Ft. Sumter for you."

"The first battle, wasn't it? I hear Confederates took the fort. That's what they're calling themselves now, isn't it?" He puffed on his old pipe.

Jonathan sat speechless. He had no idea his father knew much of anything beyond the farm.

Tom said, "Heard another four states just seceded

in quick fashion, too."

Jonathan put the paper down. He stole a glance his father's way while the evening sky's pink rays faded. Crickets chirped as night descended. Silence reclaimed the porch. Tom rose and went back inside, leaving Jonathan alone with his thoughts. Why *was* he going to join the army instead of taking that job with the *Inquirer*? Mr. Hamilton said to come back when he graduated. And here, he hadn't even looked into a job with the *Cincinnati Enquirer*.

Before he came home, things he longed for had seemed to be in reach. He had a future, maybe the good life back in Philadelphia—perhaps a lucrative career, high society, Marion. Maybe Marion. Why hadn't he stayed there? There wasn't much to come back here for anymore.

The next day he rode Belle to nearby Camp Dennison and enlisted. A vision of his father floated through his head as he signed the papers.

Chapter Fifteen

Barbra was still working at the Ohio and Mississippi Railroad when she saw a circular about the newly-formed US Sanitary Commission. As she read, she immediately sensed that's where she was supposed to be. But with no connections to the organization, she figured she was a long shot to be hired. She did, however, have a link to George McClellan, the new commander of the Ohio militia, and she decided to use it. Her work at the railroad brought her into contact with General McClellan often enough that he had a nodding acquaintance of her. This was her opportunity to become a nurse. Although it was unlikely to happen, she was going to make the most of it.

There were no nursing schools and few nurses anywhere in the northern states. Even fewer in the South and they were almost all men. Nursing wasn't considered proper work for women. Still, she would try.

Barbra stood in front of the desk sergeant in McClellan's headquarters. "I would like to see the general, please."

"So would a lot of people," the sergeant said.

"But I must see him. He knows me."

"He knows a lot of people."

"Please," Barbara said.

The desk sergeant squinted. "Who are you and what do you want?"

"I worked for him at the railroad. I'd like to help in the war and I need his assistance to do that," Barbra said.

"Seems like he's already got plenty of help, don't you think?"

Barbra's heart sank. Just then, someone familiar walked by. "Mr. Thompson! It's me, Barbra Carson. I worked for you at the railroad." Thompson turned her way. Looked like he'd just joined McClellan's new staff as well. She waved.

"Why, hello...I remember you, Barbra. You were in the, uh...scheduling department. Well, it wasn't your department, but you did uh...a lot of first-rate work for us." A smile crossed his face. "And I remember that time your boss looked the fool for taking credit for your ideas." He broke out in a loud belly laugh. "What are you doing here? Not working for the railroad anymore?"

"No, I mean, yes, I'm still there but I want to join the Sanitary Commission. I wondered if the general might be able to help me do that."

"So you'd like General Mac to help you get on there?"

"If he could just put in a good word for me, that would mean so much. And I'd be helping our soldiers."

"Why don't you come with me and I'll see what we can do."

In McClellan's anteroom, Thompson scribbled a note that he gave to the Aide de camp, who took it in to the general. In a few minutes, the aide returned and asked Barbra to follow him. Inside, he whispered something in McClellan's ear and the general greeted Barbra with a resounding welcome.

"Nice to see you again, Miss Carson. I remember your fine work for us at the railroad."

"Thank you so much for seeing me, sir." A nice surprise, certainly.

"So you want to join the Sanitary Commission, is that it?"

"Very much, sir." She clasped her hands.

"What would you do there?"

"Well I'd help our soldiers with whatever they needed help with." She only knew what the skimpy flier had said.

McClellan drummed his fingers on the desk.

Barbra's heart jumped. Was he going to turn her down?

"Yes, I believe you would." He chuckled, put pen to paper, and gave the note to Barbra. "Take good care of my men." With that, he shook her hand and the aide ushered her out of the office.

Barbra was overjoyed. She headed straight for the small Commission tent pitched to the side of McClellan's headquarters building. A tiny, gray-haired woman with a determined air bustled about inside. She presented her note and the woman's eyebrows rose for a moment. Within twenty minutes, Barbra had completed all the paperwork necessary to join. As she finished her last form, the woman asked where she'd like to serve.

"Anywhere really," Barbra said.

"Well, if we had to get more precise about it, where would that be?"

"I guess I'd like to be a nurse if I could."

"We're sure gonna need plenty of them." The old woman directed Barbra to report to the Commission facility at Camp Dennison.

With the army's ranks growing by tens of thousands, Barbra found herself put to work right away. A little unsure at first, in a short time she mastered the basics of caring for all but the most seriously sick or injured men. She worked in a central nursing unit that served the entire camp complex, so soldiers streamed in and out of the treatment tents in a never-ending flow. By evening, Barbra's white smock was either dirty or bloody. Often both.

Most cases she saw involved minor injuries, but there were times men got shot in training or shot themselves. One of those casualties was a second lieutenant. He'd just returned to the Ohio camp from the medical tent and sat by the campfire, grinning.

Jonathan sat nearby, only half listening to their stories. One of the lieutenant's buddies said, "So, did you catch hell for being such an idiot?"

"I'll tell you what I caught. I caught sight of the prettiest girl I've ever seen. She's a nurse."

The other lieutenants nearby whooped it up. "She must have been impressed when you told her you shot your own thumb off. You did tell her that, right? You told her you dropped your sidearm and it went off, didn't you?" Guffaws around the circle.

"That must have slipped my mind," the young lieutenant said, laughing. "I did say something about shooting it out with a reb infiltrator. So don't any of you morons tell her any different."

Another voice chimed in, "What's she look like? Just so I'll know if I see her."

The lieutenant grinned. "She's got this auburn hair that comes down to here." He pointed to his chest.

"And I couldn't stop starin' at her eyes."

One of the others said, "Now, if you tell me what color they are, then I'd really be impressed, 'cause eyes ain't the first thing men usually notice on a woman." Loud hoots.

"Don't mind if I do. She has light green eyes that just swallowed me right up."

Jonathan peered over at them when he heard that.

"I asked her if she'd stop by camp to see how I'm doin'. Told her I've always needed a lot of checkin' on. She laughed and asked where our area was. When I said we're the Ohio boys, she kind of funnied up."

"Whattya mean, funnied up? What's that mean?"

"Well, she got quiet, then said I'd be just fine without her coming by. But she did say that if I ever shot myself again, I should come on back." A big smile crossed the lieutenant's face. "Guess I didn't fool her after all. Anyone got a gun? Go ahead and shoot me, 'cause I need to see her again."

The men exploded. "Well, what's her name?"

"Don't rightly know, she wouldn't tell me."

The young soldiers howled. All except Jonathan, who stared in the direction of the medical tents.

****

As a volunteer, Barbra received no pay and had only a stained canvas cot to her name. But her heart told her this was where she was meant to be. She didn't mind cleaning the common areas, nor cooking and serving in the mess tents. What she liked best though, was tending to soldiers' ailments as best she could. Putting to good use all those medical manuals she'd studied over the years. Sometimes she even took the place of a doctor in the short-staffed camp.

McClellan's note granted her complete access within the camp. She regularly visited the different state encampments, checking on the wounded and spending time talking with soldiers. Every day she marveled at the small canvas tents that spread farther and farther over the rolling green hills of southwestern Ohio. Barbra was on her way to the medical tent when a camp guard approached.

"Ma'am, would you stay right there, please?"

This wasn't the first time she'd been challenged. "May I help you, Corporal?"

"Yes, ma'am. Mind telling me your business?" He said it with a small hint of self importance, one hand resting on his sidearm.

"Will this satisfy your curiosity?" She showed the guard McClellan's letter of passage.

The corporal's face paled as he read. "Yes, ma'am, thank you. Sorry to trouble you. You see, it's just my job to...can I escort you anywhere, ma'am? Do you need any assistance?"

Barbra retrieved the paper. She gave the soldier her best smile. "No, I don't, but thank you. I understand you're just doing your job and you're doing it well."

The corporal brightened. "Thank you, ma'am." He fumbled with his hat and swept it off. A slight bow and he stepped aside.

Barbra stole a glance at the Ohio camp as she passed by. Her heartbeat quickened and she picked up her pace.

****

May 1861

When Jonathan rode into Camp Dennison, he was directed to General McClellan's adjutant. Soon, he was a new lieutenant in the 4th Ohio Infantry. Not long after, he took part in a pre-dawn attack on a small contingent of sleeping Confederates across the border in western Virginia. Greatly outnumbered, the rebels panicked and ran. Even though it was a minor engagement, it was his first taste of combat, and his adrenaline surged for hours afterward.

In his tent, he dashed off a quick note.

Hey, Parker!

I got the jump on you! Me and my platoon just busted up some Rebs across the way in Virginia! McClellan's likely a national hero now. Wouldn't surprise me if Lincoln called him to Washington to take command of the biggest Union army there is.

So, what have you been doing? Rolling maps up after the generals are finished with them?

Your combat-tested buddy,

Jonathan

Parker wrote back a couple weeks later.

Dear Johnny,

General McClellan just got here, like you thought he might. He's the new commander of The Army of the Potomac and I'm working directly for him! That's what I'm doing. All along the way to Washington, they say he was hailed as the savior of the North. I heard the crowds were so big and the cheering so loud, the Rebs could hear it all the way down in Richmond.

Since I'm on his staff, don't be surprised if I get promoted to general soon!

Your soon-to-be-captain friend,

Robert

Jonathan chuckled at that last part.

Fall 1861

Not long after, he received new orders for Washington. Jonathan was excited but he also kicked himself that he hadn't had the courage to speak with Barbra at the camp yet. He stopped by the Sanitary Commission tent where he was greeted by a short, middle-aged woman. "Ma'am, I'm looking for Barbra Carson, is she here?"

"Not right now, she's off tending to soldiers at one of the field camps."

"Do you know which one?"

"No, I don't. Can I tell her who asked for her?"

Jonathan stared at the woman, his insides a mess, his head jumbled. Didn't know whether to say he'd come by or not. "No...thank you." He turned to leave, then hesitated.

"Something wrong, Lieutenant?"

He nodded. "Yes, there is, but it's not something you can help me with. Please just tell her Jonathan said hello—and goodbye." He turned on his heel and walked away.

It didn't take long to gather his few belongings. Soon, he found himself on a train bound for his new assignment in McClellan's Quartermaster Corps.

Chapter Sixteen

The knock on the hotel door startled Jonathan. He slid his hand to the table where his holster lay and wrapped his fingers around the Colt's handle. Washington was filled with spies, sneaks, and scalawags.

A muffled voice said, "Lieutenant Gray?"

"Who is it?"

"Your bag, suh."

Jonathan hesitated, then opened the door. A hotel porter held his valise. He relaxed his grip on his pistol.

"Where should I put this, Lieutenant?"

"Uh, over by the window is fine." After the man set the bag down, he stood for a moment until Jonathan realized he needed to tip him. Jonathan pressed a nickel in his hand and asked what time dinner was served.

"About seven o'clock, suh, right downstairs. Should I knock on your door then?"

"No, thank you. I'll find my way." Jonathan dropped the valise on his bed, unsure how long he'd be staying. While he suspected how McClellan had come to select him, he wasn't certain. He'd been running the last couple of days over in his head. The message said to report as soon as possible, but his train ride had been a long series of stops and starts. The cars were filled with soldiers and civilians alike, all appearing to know where they were headed and why. That was more than he knew. The way ahead lay unclear as he unpacked.

The train trip had given him an opportunity to see a nation going to war firsthand. Men wore Union uniforms of all colors and styles, some exceptionally exotic with scarves, plumes, and dress hats. They could have been foreign regiments that had somehow strayed off course and ended up on a different continent. There was also a surprising number of women and children traveling. Most likely going to safer locales until the war was over.

He still knew little about the military and felt like a blank slate about to be written all over. Why would McClellan have asked for him, even if Parker *was* behind it? He was nobody. Most of his Princeton friends were monied easterners eager to get into the war, make their mark on some general's staff, and enter politics or take over the family business. Jonathan had none of those notions as he settled into his new surroundings.

He was buttoning the shiny gold buttons on his dress uniform when there came another knock on the door. "Who's there?"

"Who do you think? Open up!"

He pulled the door open. Parker. "I knew it had to be you."

"Of course it was me. I told you I wanted to stay ahead of you and the best way to do that is to have you nearby, under my thumb." They hugged and laughed as Parker ambled into the room. "You ready for dinner yet?"

"Just getting there." Jonathan adjusted his collar in the wavy mirror. "Hey, are my insignia on right?"

Parker pronounced his friend's braided gold bars

perfect.

Jonathan said, "Will McClellan be at dinner with us tonight?"

"Maybe. He's got good taste," Parker said, smiling.

"I've never seen him. What's he look like?"

"Don't worry. You'll know him when you see him."

"You know him some, right?"

"Yeah. Like I said, our families are acquainted. I'd see him off and on at different socials over the years in Philadelphia. That's how you got here."

Jonathan grinned. "Will he really be at dinner with us tonight with the war going on?"

"Who knows, he might prefer impressing us because he's pretty much got everything else taken care of."

"How's that?"

Parker said, "I mean he's written training manuals for the whole damn army. He's probably having trouble keeping busy."

Jonathan shook his head and smiled. Good to be with his friend again.

They walked down to the hotel's saloon where other staff officers gathered drinking whiskey and wine. One of the senior officers noticed them as the two lieutenants slipped into the cozy room.

"Parker!"

"Yes, sir, Second Lieutenant Parker at your service, sir."

The officer strolled over. "Where've you been, boy?"

"On an errand, sir. I'd like you to meet Second Lieutenant Jonathan Gray. He's the one I was telling you about. Just got here from Ohio. Lieutenant Gray, this is Lieutenant Colonel Stewart, General McClellan's executive. Also, one of this country's finest officers."

Stewart shook his head. "Welcome, son. Quartermaster Corps, right?"

Jonathan said, "Yes, sir!"

Stewart smiled at Parker. "I see you're still keeping an eye out for what's going on around you."

"I try to stay involved, sir."

"Stick with Parker, Gray, and you'll do well in this army."

"Yes, sir, thank you."

After a several-course dinner, Jonathan spent the rest of the evening meeting other staff officers, some of whom Parker said he'd be working for. As the alcohol hit, the group relaxed and clustered around Stewart, an outgoing, engaging storyteller. His tales of high adventure he'd shared with the general had no doubt helped create the sterling reputation McClellan enjoyed among his men.

Stewart raised a whiskey glass. "I predict this small skirmish of a war will be over soon, with General Mac standing on the throats of the Rebs. A toast, gentlemen. To General McClellan."

Everyone raised their glasses high. "To the general!"

Jonathan joined the rest of the staff in toasting a quick Union victory. Hard not to get caught up in the fervor of Stewart's enthusiasm.

"To the Union!" Stewart raised his glass.

The staff raised their glasses higher. "To the Union!"

After too many tales and too much whiskey,

Jonathan staggered up the stairs. In the morning, he shook the cobwebs away and shaved in the mirror, his reflection hopeful. If what he'd heard about McClellan so far was true, the war would be over soon.

****

As a quartermaster, Jonathan helped supervise the letting of contracts for food, weapons, and clothing. Whoever got those contracts was going to be rich. During his first few weeks, Jonathan saw occasional graft and bribery but steeled himself against it. As long as the men were getting what they needed, he'd look the other way. All that changed when a poorly-salted shipment of beef came in. Near rancid. Wasn't the first time this particular corrupt contractor had supplied the army with rotten food and gotten paid handsomely for it. Jonathan pulled another lieutenant off this contract so he could deal with the swindler personally. When the scoundrel finished his delivery, he strolled toward the Quartermaster General's tent. After inspecting the meat, Jonathan intercepted him.

"Ah'm here with the goods," he said, "so just make a requisition out for nine thousand, please, and I thank you."

Jonathan stared up at the big man. "Like hell."

"What? Say, you're new here aren't you, son? Why don't you just fetch me someone who can get me paid. Go on now," he said with a flick of his hand. The man's flabby neck jiggled when he talked.

Jonathan glared. "You'll deal with me from now on and you won't get paid until you supply this army with meat these men can eat!"

"Now, sonny, I don't have all day, so you just run along and get me your boss. You don't got to worry about this no more."

Jonathan moved in front of the fat cheat. The man was taller than Jonathan by several inches and outweighed him by maybe a hundred pounds. He had the appearance of someone who was used to getting his way. The vendor clenched a fist.

A guard asked Jonathan if he would like the man escorted from the campsite.

"Not yet." This wasn't over.

"You're damn right, not yet." The contractor pushed Jonathan aside with a meaty arm and strode for the quartermaster's tent. Jonathan hurried in front of him again, forcing the man to either stop or knock him down. With a whack to the face from a big bear paw, the vendor sent Jonathan sprawling.

The guards moved in, but as Jonathan sat on his duff in the dirt, he yelled, "Don't you dare touch him. Stay back. He's mine!" The guards backed off.

Jonathan grabbed the vendor's leg as he went by. The oaf turned. Jonathan took a kick to his gut but struggled to his feet and tackled the contractor. They went down in a heap and the big man went to work. He held Jonathan down with one hand and punched him again and again in the face. Jonathan was finally able to knee him in the groin and crawl out from under the fat man's grasp.

Wobbling to his feet and gasping for breath, he kicked the still-groaning brute as he lay curled on the ground. "Don't you *ever* show up here again!" Fearing Jonathan would kill the man, guards wrapped him in a big bear hug until he calmed down some.

They dragged the dazed crook to his feet and put him on his horse. A swift whack on the rump and the slumped man bounced away. They turned to Jonathan, chuckling about how riled he was and what he'd done to the grifter. They brushed the dust off him, but with lots of "sirs." A soldier took him by the arm to the dispensary to get checked.

That afternoon, the Judge Advocate called Jonathan in to hear his side of the story. Jonathan feared the worst. After listening, the judge sat with his fingers steepled, eyeing him from under bushy eyebrows. Jonathan stood ramrod straight, knowing this could mean a dishonorable discharge—and prison time. The lawyer came out from behind his massive mahogany desk, stood in front of Jonathan, and stuck his hand out. "Good work, son." The colonel left the room trailed by an aide, smiling. Jonathan stood dazed, unsure of what had just happened.

Back in camp, a horse pulled to a stop by his tent. "Lieutenant Gray!"

Startled, Jonathan popped outside. Parker. The first time he'd seem him in a couple of days. "Robert. You scared me for a second."

His friend dismounted and the two shook hands. "You should be scared, Mr. Gray, after what you did. I can't believe you kicked the crap out of that big old fat ass."

"Seemed like the right thing to do." At least he thought it was at the time.

Parker smiled. "Looks like he got a few licks in, too."

Jonathan's cheek was swollen and his nose red. He put a hand to his tender stomach. "I'll live."

Parker said, "Well, General McClellan thinks it was the right thing to do, too. He wants you to report around tomorrow morning."

"Am I in trouble?" He'd just gotten here and had already been in a scrap.

"Hell, no. You're the man of the hour. Come on by my tent in the morning and I'll take you to Colonel Stewart. Good work!" He grinned as he mounted up, flicked his horse's reins, and trotted off.

The next day Jonathan stood in front of the commanding general, absorbing his thanks and a lecture about the importance of taking care of the men. He felt inspired as he walked back to his tent. A strong desire to be back in the infantry rose in his heart. Leading troops. But that would likely have to wait.

He thought back to his short time leading an infantry platoon at Camp Dennison. His biggest concern then didn't have to do with soldiering. It was knowing Barbra was also there. He'd seen her in the distance a couple of times and dithered about whether to call out to her. Courage had failed him though, as guilt over shutting her out overpowered his desire to see her. Sadness ran through him as he pushed through his tent flaps.

He couldn't quite figure out how McClellan came to win such strong affection from his men. But the more he was around the man and his staff, the more he began to feel the same tug. A tug that was rooting out what little was left of his upbringing.

Chapter Seventeen

"Hey, Lieutenant, I just asked you a question. When's the general gonna go after them Rebs?" It was Joseph Anthony, a war correspondent for the *New York Tribune*, one of the most rabid abolitionist papers. Jonathan had also been assigned duties dealing with the press, which was fine with him.

"Not my place to say, Mr. Anthony. I just know that with all the preparation we're doing, when we do move, the enemy won't stand a chance." Jonathan was pleased with his answer.

"Fat lot of good these soldiers do just sittin' here." Anthony stomped off toward the mess tent.

As Jonathan watched the rotund reporter waddle away, he thought how appropriate Anthony's use of the words "fat lot" had been. After he'd fielded the last of the questions, Jonathan walked back to his tent, frowning. He hated to admit it, but he wondered the same thing. When were they going to move? He plopped on his cot.

Parker threw a dirty sock at him. "There's a rumor drifting through camp that the president and secretary of state went to McClellan's house to talk about his war plans. The story goes the president waited hours for him in the parlor. They say when the general did show up, he went straight upstairs to bed without speaking to them."

"Can that be true?" Jonathan asked.

"That's what I heard. He just walked on by as if they weren't even there."

"I guess I probably wouldn't have done that," Jonathan said.

"Serves the backwoods boy right."

Jonathan squinted. "Whaddya mean?"

"Lincoln and everyone else are pushing Little Mac to move but none of them are fighting men. They don't know how things are here in the field. The general knows what he's doing."

Jonathan nodded. He was becoming a McClellanite, shifting from tilting against society's injustices to defending his boss at all costs. He was part of McClellan's inner circle now but struggled with nagging doubts. "Why aren't we attacking Johnny Reb?"

Parker said, "I'm sure there's good reasons. There's probably a whole lot going on we don't know anything about."

"What's that mean? You're always nosing around, what are you hearing? Surely there couldn't be that many 'Clios' in front of us."

Parker laughed at the mention of their old Princeton nemeses.

Jonathan envied Parker's knack for working with the staff. Parker attached himself to those who could help him and skirted those who couldn't. He acted like he was one of them and not just a green pea second lieutenant. Parker told him he was rising among the senior staff. Jonathan didn't know how much of that was puffed up, although most of it probably was.

As they relaxed in their tent one evening, Parker

regaled him with more tall tales while Jonathan cleaned his boots and hung his socks to dry. Parker had a boy to keep his uniforms, socks, and boots—everything—clean and dry. Fit feet carried soldiers, and soldiers carried an army. A mass this size had plenty of civilian hangers-on, and Parker took advantage of them. The "train" consisted of not only supply wagons with all manner of provisions, but also sutlers of every stripe who supplied the men with everything the government didn't. Food, whiskey, women.

Jonathan didn't begrudge Parker his comfortable life—shades of his times in Philadelphia. He was an officer—entitled to live better than the enlisted who struggled daily with poor shelter, wet clothing, and bad food.

"Jonathan, will you teach me to ride better?"

He smiled. "Sure, if you get me a new pair of boots and socks." He was getting good at horse trading for what he wanted.

"Deal. How about going riding now? I don't want to die falling off my horse. If I get killed, I'd like to have a better story than that."

Jonathan laughed.

The two friends were used primarily as messengers, dispatched to carry correspondence from headquarters to the field. Couriers always ran the risk of being mistaken for rebels, or at least southern sympathizers. Union sentries were usually some of the youngest troops and nervous enough to be trigger happy. Jonathan had never had a mishap as he rode the environs of Washington, though, often navigating faint roads at night. But he didn't have much use for the monotonous work they were doing, either. His idea of a staff officer was someone with far grander duties.

As McClellan's influence seeped further into him, Jonathan's abolitionist bent began to fade. Word around camp was that they were fighting to preserve the Union, not freeing the slaves. Everyone repeated it so often that Jonathan started to believe it.

****

Fall 1861
Washington

McClellan came down with typhoid fever and was confined to bed for several weeks. The army lay stalled around the capital with little for Jonathan to do. Southern forces were in a holding pattern as well after their stunning victory at Bull Run. So the North dithered while the South dallied, all of which gave Jonathan and Parker the perfect excuse to get away. Putting in for leave, they traveled to Philadelphia to regale the locals with their derring-do. Jonathan was grateful for the Parkers' continued hospitality and spent as much time with Marion as she allowed.

By the time Jonathan returned to camp, Lincoln had removed McClellan as General in Chief, but at least he'd kept him as commander of the Army of the Potomac. At first, he was upset. But maybe that would finally motivate the general to move against the Confederates. Nonstop trains offloaded carloads of food, weapons, and ammunition. Formation drill increased. Quartermasters distributed equipment, powder, and bullets night and day. Jonathan labored long hours relaying orders from headquarters to the corps commanders. Riding through Union lines was proving to be almost as daunting as skirting the Rebs. No one knew who was who from a distance.

Jonathan was struck with a vague sense of guilt when he came in contact with the soldiers who would carry out the killing orders he brought. He spent extra time with the troops, eating with them, listening to them—in awe of their casual courage. Every time he left the field for headquarters, his discontent reared. He wanted to do the real work of the army. Fighting. Make amends for his runaway friend.

"Sir, may I speak with you a moment?" Jonathan corralled his boss, Lt. Col. Stewart, in the mess tent. "Sir, I want you to know how much I appreciate the opportunity to serve on the general's staff, but I'd like to go to the infantry, sir."

Stewart faked a look of shock. "Well I'll be— someone who's volunteering to get their butt shot up."

"Yessir, but I wouldn't want you to think I'm not grateful to have been assigned to staff. I am. Not that I would even be missed, I'm sure."

"Not true. We appreciate your good work, Lieutenant, and right now we can't spare you. We're going on the offensive and we'll need everyone we have to do that. But your request is noted. When the time's right, we'll get you over to the fightin' side of the army."

"Thank you, sir. Will you give the general my regards?"

"Yes, I will, son." Stewart smiled, shook his head, and walked away.

Chapter Eighteen

February 1862

As spring neared, McClellan moved his entire army by sea down to the Virginia peninsula. From there, the plan was to advance inland and seize Richmond, the rebel capital. Jonathan kept busy, sometimes writing the general's orders, sometimes riding them through federal lines. After one day-long mission, he flopped dog tired on his cot.

Parker said, "First town we're coming to is a place called Yorktown and I hear it's heavily fortified. Sounds like there's gonna be hell to pay to take it."

"Do you think that's true?" Jonathan said.

"Not sure. Doesn't seem like there'd be that many enemy dug in there, just waiting for us. If I were them, I'd be skedaddling."

Jonathan said, "That sounds like Pinkerton talking, the way he exaggerates everything we're up against. I hope there's someone else McClellan relies on besides him."

"Guess we'll find out soon enough."

As April faded into May, the "siege" of Yorktown came to an uncontested end. General Joe Johnston's Confederates had pulled out even before McClellan marched in. The army pushed toward Williamsburg and the vanguard tore into a rear echelon of retreating enemy. It began to look as if the war might soon be over.

After dinner in the sumptuous plantation house that was field headquarters, Jonathan waited just outside the commanders' dining room. Stewart's familiar voice interrupted his thoughts. He snapped to attention.

"Jonathan, General Marcy will be with you in a minute."

Marcy strode out of the dining room. "Jonathan, the commanding general needs you to take this to General Sumner. Do you know where his headquarters is?"

"Yes, sir, a couple of miles ahead, on the right, by a small rise."

"Very good. Get this to him within the next half hour. Can you do that?" He handed Jonathan a folded piece of smudged white paper.

"Yes, sir."

Jonathan saddled up and rode west as fast as he could. He stayed off the main road, fortunate to find a small path through the woods. As he rode along the edge of the trees, a meadow ringed by dark pines lay in dappled shadows before him. Somewhere beyond was Sumner's headquarters. Jonathan spurred his horse hard. Dusk was turning to darkness, the most dangerous time to ride. He heard voices off to his left, then glimpsed a picket line protecting Sumner's flanks. He and the horse came flying out of the trees into the narrow meadow in the dim light.

A voice carried to him on the night air. "Hey, lookee, must be a Reb, the way he's a-hightailin' it towards Richmond." Spooked now, the raw soldiers formed a skirmish line. Jonathan yanked his horse away from them. His heartbeat quickened and kept pace with his horse's hoof beats.

"That there Reb's gettin' away. Don't let him get to that tree line. Light 'im up, boys."

A cacophony of fire filled the dwindling dusk with puffs of smoke. Jonathan spurred hard. Just then, the horse jerked and its front legs buckled. Momentum carried him forward, the reins still wrapped around his right hand. As the horse tumbled, Jonathan catapulted through the air, then was snapped back and flung hard to the ground. He hit backside first and threw his other hand out to break the fall. Snap! His head hit the dirt and everything went black.

****

Pickets came yelling out of a thicket, scrambling over each other to claim their prize. "I got him, I knowed it!"

One raised his rifle high. Another said, "No! It was my bullet what put him down."

They gathered around the motionless courier as if he wasn't there, arguing about who'd knocked the Reb off his mount. The horse lay on its side, neighing and snorting. A soldier walked over, raised his rifle, and aimed at the horse's head.

"Whatchoo doin'?" another said.

The corporal said, "You can't leave a horse in a terrible hurt like this. It's best to put him down."

"Why would you do that? He ain't dead."

"You don't know nothin' about animals, that's for sure." The corporal fired a bullet square into the horse's head. The shot sobered the group some and the laughing and jabbering died down. They turned back to Jonathan and huddled over their unconscious prize.

151

"He ain't movin' none."

Another grinned and slapped his thigh. "That's 'cause he ain't never gonna move no more."

"Get back and let me have a look." The corporal shooed the privates out of the way. Kneeling, he put a hand on Jonathan's neck. "Still breathin'." He looked closer and saw the dusty blue uniform in the shadowy light. "Say, this here's one of our own. He's a dadblamed lieutenant, too!" The corporal rolled Jonathan onto his back and looked him over, the gold braid rank staring them all in the face. "Oh crap," he said, breathing hard. "We're in for it now for sure."

"What'll we do?"

A private said, "Just leave him here, somebody'll find him." He backed away.

"We can't do that, stupid," said another picket. "If'n he lives, he'll tell everybody we shot him and left him for dead."

The corporal busted in. "Enough of that talk. You, man there, grab him by the shoulders. And you. Grab his feet and follow me. And be quick about it."

The picket procession hurried back to the safety of the woods, then sent a runner for a wagon. By the time it came, Jonathan was regaining consciousness, babbling nonsense. They loaded him in and the driver hurried off in the direction of the field hospital.

****

Jonathan lay dazed in the back of the wagon. Everything was spinning. He slipped in and out of consciousness as he arrived at the medical tent.

The driver yelled, "Need a doctor here. Right now!"

An orderly ran to the back of the wagon. "Hold on,

Lieutenant." He helped a rubbery-legged Jonathan up and into the makeshift hospital.

"Message…" He pointed to his coat pocket, then passed out again.

The next evening, he woke up, still foggy, head throbbing. His arm and wrist were splinted. He played the events of last night over in his mind. Just his luck. Still, maybe he could return to duty. When he tried to sit up, his head wouldn't let him.

He recognized Sumner's executive officer standing by his cot.

Jonathan put a hand to his forehead. "Did the message reach General Sumner, sir?"

"Yes, it did. The general carried out the commander's orders and you played a big part in helping roust the rebels today, Lieutenant."

At least that had gone well. General Marcy sent a wagon for him, then sent him to Mower hospital in Philadelphia to recuperate. The doctor said his broken arm and wrist would heal, as would the concussion, but he'd be on bed rest a while.

As Jonathan regained his senses, a new arrival at Mower who'd lost a leg mid thigh occupied the bed across from him. He was a friendly, talkative type, despite the severity of his wound. The soldier was still getting oriented when the ward nurse came to check on him.

She glanced at a small scrap of paper in her hand. "And how are you today, Corporal…um…Billings?"

"Jest fine, ma'am." He laughed. "I been feelin' real good, but I been talkin' these boys' ears off around me."

Jonathan had to agree with that.

"Can I ask you a favor, ma'am?"

"What's that, Corporal?"

"Well, I'd like to let my family know I'm all right. Could you write 'em a letter for me? I don't write so good."

"Certainly. I've some paper and a pencil right here. What would you like to say?"

"Just tell my folks I been hurt but I'm doing okay now. Leave out the part about losing my leg if you would, please. And I thank you, ma'am." He gave the nurse an address and started telling everyone within earshot about his family. "They's got a little farm near Baltimore that's never done too good. That's why I joined the army—'cause I could get three meals a day and didn't have to work none." He looked toward Jonathan and laughed. "My pa don't read neither, but there's some can read the letter to him. If his sister was still around, she could. Papa always said she was real smart. Knows how to read and write."

Jonathan was half listening. His mother's maiden name was Billings, too. She'd never shared much of her background with him, but he knew that much. He wasn't sure where she was from, just that she was raised on a farm back east. The corporal kept entertaining the ward but Jonathan didn't need to hear anymore. His mother always said her family was dead.

****

Jonathan's splint had just come off when a voice behind him called, "Gray." He turned to see Parker grinning, walking toward his bed.

"What are you doing here? Did you win the war without me or something?"

Parker shook his head. "Nah, we just took

Williamsburg, so there's a standdown right now. Couldn't think of anything better to do, so thought I'd come see you."

Jonathan laughed and the two friends talked the afternoon away. After his release, he convalesced at Parker House. Sitting, shuffling, sitting. He sent word to Marion he was in town and eager to see her. She came by a couple of days later and joined him in the study, talking nonstop—sitting one minute, then springing up and swishing around the room the next.

"What's the matter with you?"

"I don't know, I just hate to see you so battered." She jumped up from her seat almost like an exclamation point.

"I'm fine, and it won't be much longer before I have to go back." He'd almost forgotten how pretty Marion was.

"Well, it's just…I can't take the worry of not knowing if you're all right or not, and here you are, all hurt, and now you're returning and I just don't know what to do." Her mouth drew down in a familiar pout.

"There's nothing you have to do. Just sit there and look beautiful."

"I can't. I just can't…stay any longer—see you like this. It's just too much."

Jonathan cocked his head as he sat on the couch. Why was she so jumpy? He tried some small talk. "You know I haven't heard much from you. I think I've written a lot more letters to you than you have to me."

"Oh no, that couldn't be true, it seems like I'm writing you all the time." She broke eye contact and edged toward the door.

"Come over here and let me kiss you."

Marion glanced around and inched farther away. "Why, I couldn't do that. What if someone should see us?"

"No one's going to come in here while the door's closed, so come here, will you?" He'd never seen her like this.

She hesitated, then came and gave him a peck on the cheek. As she leaned over him, Jonathan grabbed her around the waist and pulled her close. She felt good in his arms.

"Now stop that, I don't want you harming yourself. Why, whatever would you tell your doctor about how you got hurt again?"

"Give me another kiss. A real one this time." Why was she so skittish?

Marion kissed him on the lips, letting her mouth linger over his then pushed away. "I have to go now. I just have to…go!"

He'd never understood her moods. "All right, but be sure to write me, okay?"

As she hurried out of the room, she turned and blew him a kiss. "I will. I promise."

With a swish of her dress, she was gone. Jonathan stared at the empty doorway, which seemed to mock him.

Chapter Nineteen

Barbra had been serving as a nurse at Mower ever since the Camp Dennison surgeon recommended her. And she'd been quick to make the change. Helping the wounded brought a spring to her step every day. The morning briefing was just breaking up when she happened to glance at the patient list posted in her large ward. Jonathan's name! She stared at it, rooted, her stomach in her throat. My Jonathan? She stopped herself. Not really hers anymore. But still…

Another nurse walked up. "What's wrong?"

Barbra tore her eyes away from the roster. "What?"

"You're staring at that as if you've never seen one of those before."

She shook her head. "I'm sorry, I'll be back." She hurried away, list in hand, searching for the head nurse. When she found her, she said, "Ma'am, what can you tell me about Jonathan Gray? He's on this list."

The nurse checked her notes. "Gray, Gray, yes. He's gone. Just this morning."

Her heart caught in her throat. "He's gone? What do you mean, he's gone?"

"He was discharged this morning. What did you think I meant?"

"Oh, thank heavens. He left, he's not gone," Barbra said.

"That's what I said." She walked away, leaving

Barbra to read Jonathan's scant medical notes with relief. Nothing life-threatening. He'd been in another part of her ward for almost a week. What would she have done had she known? Part of her was glad she didn't, part still wished she had.

****

When Jonathan returned to camp with Parker, they were new first lieutenants. A celebration in their tent followed, with some rum Parker had stashed. He said, "Here's to Little Mac, the new mayor of Richmond."

Jonathan shook his head. "We've been close before, let's don't celebrate too soon. They aren't going to give up Richmond without a tough fight. This isn't Yorktown. Wretched weather's on their side, too."

"Don't be so doubtful, my pessimistic, newly-promoted friend. Surely, the end of the Confederacy is near. I say, here's to that." He raised his tin cup.

Jonathan raised his as well. It did seem like a quick blow would end the war. He wasn't up to riding again yet, so he worked a desk, overseeing the flow of communications in and out of headquarters.

He'd just finished his daily briefing to General Marcy when he blurted, "There's nowhere they can run, is there, sir."

"No, there's not, unless they want to give up their capital. We've hemmed them in pretty well. Hopefully, one more big push will finish them off."

Parker chimed in, "I can see us now." He waved his arm in a big arc. "Marching down Richmond's main street, horses frisky, flags waving, pretty girls swarming us, glad there's some Yankee blood in town. I already know what I'm going to do after the war. I'll be an aide at first, for the senator who lives right near us in

Philadelphia. Think I'll write him tonight about taking me on. Then later I'll take his job."

Marcy sported a wry smile. "Hold on, *boys*. We aren't there quite yet."

"Glad we won't have to do this any longer," Parker said as he and Jonathan walked back from the mess tent.

"All this talent wasted on messengering, but no more," Jonathan said with a chuckle. "Getting promoted hasn't made any difference in getting paid, though. The pay wagon must be stuck in the mud along with everything else. It's been three months now. And with us on the march, it's likely to be even longer than that."

Jonathan reveled in his silver first lieutenant insignia. He adopted more of Parker's airs in dealing with the enlisted—like making them stand at attention while they repeated orders he'd just given them. Directing them to set up headquarters war rooms, having them fetch him coffee. Whatever was left of his desire to join the infantry he'd pushed to the backroads of his mind. Staff duties were more in line with his new status. Even though he was still taking notes for the generals, Jonathan fancied himself an important cog in the army's juggernaut. A juggernaut that was encircling Richmond now.

Jonathan woke to the sounds of battle. What was happening? He hadn't heard anything about going on the attack this morning. The artillery booms left no doubt, though. He glanced at Parker just waking up on the other cot, too.

"What's going on?"

Jonathan shook his head. "Don't know." He threw

his uniform on and ducked out of the tent. The terrain was filled with black smoke and hellish fire. Bedlam. The Union wasn't attacking the Confederates, it was the other way around! Soldiers scurried to form up. Jonathan sprinted to headquarters where McClellan and staff were in a panic. No one seemed in charge.

Someone shouted, "Secure the documents, the battle plans!"

That could only mean one thing. Retreat! He looked around for something to grab.

The next several days were a blur. Jonathan was pressed back into courier duty amid near-constant riding. The huge Union army was withdrawing from Mechanicsville, just north of Richmond. A flood of blue backtracked away along the James River. Days later, McClellan's army finally secured a small, last-stand position on the river's banks at a place called Harrison's Landing. Behind this behemoth was nothing but water and in front lay annihilation.

The two friends huddled over a cold dinner of jerky. Parker said, "How did this happen?" The entire camp seemed like it was on sentry duty, watching the enemy gather to their front. They'd been whupped. Was capture—or worse—next? He scanned their surroundings warily. "We had them and then we didn't."

Jonathan was bone-weary, hungry, and scared. He looked up from the first food he'd had in more than a day. "Washington shouldn't have stripped all those men away right before we came down here." It was easier to blame Lincoln than his commander.

"How are we gonna get out of this fix?" Parker chain puffed a hastily-rolled cigarette. "What do you think happens next?"

"I'm not even sure what just happened, much less what happens next." Jonathan stared out at the largest Union army ever assembled, languishing on the lowlands of tidewater Virginia. Frustrated faces, sullen officers, darting glances everywhere.

"If McClellan gets fired, where does that leave us?"

"Don't know," said Jonathan, "and right now I don't even care. Let's just work on getting out of this mess." For the first time in a long time, he felt rudderless. Nothing was as it should be. He couldn't count on much anymore. Except Parker.

His tentmate said, "I wish it was Joe Johnston we were still up against." Lee had replaced an ailing Johnston.

"And I wish we were marching down Richmond's streets right now." Jonathan stared at Parker through weary, bloodshot eyes. They slumped around a flickering fire that seemed as glum as they did. Tension in camp was as suffocating as the enemy artillery that hammered their little salient.

Jonathan hurled a stick into the flames. "Someone said we're gonna go back on the attack. Do you think that's true? Do you think we can still whip Lee?" He was hoping Parker would say yes.

"Of course we can. What kind of talk is that? You know Little Mac can beat anyone if Washington would just leave him alone." Parker even sounded like he believed that.

"I know, but…" Jonathan's words trailed away amid his unspoken misgivings. He stared at the flames that only took the edge off the cool evening air. Fire

161

devils danced in the dusk, laughing at him.

****

Jonathan read the message and his heart sank. He didn't want to give it to General Marcy, but he did. Lincoln had just relieved McClellan. The army had managed to hold Lee off at the river, but the failed peninsula campaign was over, and a flotilla was evacuating what was left of McClellan's forces. Jonathan said, "How could Lincoln fire the best general we have, sir?" He was staring at the prospect of being a backwater lieutenant on a discredited general's staff. His grim prospects matched his mood.

Marcy pursed his lips. "That's *President* Lincoln, Lieutenant."

Parker spoke up. "Does this mean we need to find another post, sir?"

"That will all sort itself out soon enough."

The two friends wandered back to their makeshift tent. Jonathan scuffed at rocks on the way. "How could things turn so fast? We were right there at Richmond. They were ready to surrender. Then…everything fell apart."

Like his life was doing.

Chapter Twenty

With the army in limbo, Jonathan took a short furlough to Philadelphia with Parker, unsure of what lay ahead. Staying there was a good way of avoiding going home. Writing Barbra was something he'd pushed to the back of his mind. Sadness choked his thoughts. His folks wouldn't understand anything he wrote—fighting wasn't his father's way. Jonathan wasn't sure he understood the war anymore, either. But he still had Philadelphia. Leave couldn't come too soon.

The two traveled north on trains full of troops whose pristine blue uniforms marked them as raw recruits. Wide-eyed stares also gave the greenhorns away. Some played with their hats, others shifted on their feet, a few gawked. Jonathan stood out like a grizzled veteran in his faded blues. He rubbed a hand across his scruffy beard as he watched them fidget.

The second lieutenant seated across from him spoke up. "Hey, where you comin' from? How's it goin'?"

Jonathan didn't look his way.

The greenpea said, "Say, you weren't part of McClellan's mess, were you?"

Jonathan sprang to a stand and leaned forward, chin thrust only inches from the youth's face."Shut up, butterbar. And start 'sir-ing' me!" Parker tugged on his sleeve. Jonathan's simmering, grim mood had bubbled to the surface. Soldiers stared his direction, but he wasn't about to let criticism of his commander pass. He clenched his fists. "Anybody else got anything to say?" His challenge hung unanswered in the packed train car.

As the train rolled along, Jonathan's fury faded and his mood lightened. By the time they left Washington for Philadelphia, the two best friends were already shaking their heads about some of the follies of an army camp. Their laughter was a welcome break from the tension they'd been surrounded with for months.

Parker had telegraphed his folks they were coming, so someone would likely meet them when they arrived about midday. At the station, hundreds of soldiers milled about on the platform, so it took a while to link up with the family coachman. When the carriage drew up at Parker House, Parker double stepped up the front stairs and breezed inside as if he'd just been to town and back. Jonathan stood outside a moment and gazed at the house that had become his second home. Maybe his only home now. He pushed back a twinge of regret as he followed his friend. The two stripped off their uniform coats and headed to the kitchen for a home-cooked meal.

Mrs. Parker invited several guests for dinner that evening to celebrate, Marion among them. She swept in wearing a revealing green satin dress. Captivating as always. After a five-course formal meal, Jonathan waited for a chance to squire her outside to the back terrace but was buttonholed in the library. The men surrounding him were too old to fight and too rich to have to, but they all wanted to know how the war was going. Jonathan tried to excuse himself time and again. He nursed a whiskey and spouted clichéd optimism.

Through the open library doors he kept tabs on Marion, who was holding court with the ladies in the hall.

She sashayed into the library to take her leave, offering her hand to Mr. Parker, then sallying out with a coy smile Jonathan's way. Jonathan freed himself and hurried out. He caught up to her in the front portico. "Walk outside with me. We could hide behind those trees over there and no one would ever know." He wore a lopsided grin.

Marion's eyebrows arched. "Now, why would I ever do that? You know someone might see us and that would just be the biggest scandal ever and my parents certainly wouldn't understand. You've already gotten me in enough trouble as it is, what with that scene at the Dock Club." She smoothed her black hair back with a flourish. "You wouldn't want to cause me more difficulties, would you?" She flashed the same half smile that had so beguiled him when they first met.

"All right, then. I'll come see you tomorrow, okay?" The words almost bounced off her back as she strolled away. He scanned the other guests quickly. Had anyone else heard their exchange? He wasn't even sure he wanted to see Marion again, but part of him still did. He pushed his uncertainty back until it was no more than a faint whisper in his head. He couldn't put his finger on what was bothering him, but it was there.

The next day, Jonathan drove one of the Parkers' coaches on the short trip to Marion's. He could have walked but driving the buggy would give him a good excuse to take her for a ride. When he pulled up to the house, another coach was drawn up out front. The maid ushered Jonathan into the foyer to await Marion. She soon appeared in the company of a Union captain.

"Hello, Jonathan. I'd like you to meet Captain Stephen Caldwell," she said with a fanciful wave of her hand. "Stephen, this is Lieutenant Jonathan Gray." Jonathan nodded at Caldwell. "Stephen, Jonathan is the one I was telling you about who came from some little farm in Ohio and did so well at Princeton and is now on General McClellan's staff." She sniffed. "Or was."

Caldwell looked Jonathan up and down. "Too bad about how he failed in Virginia." Caldwell emphasized *failed* a little too much. "I guess you're looking for a new job now?"

Jonathan stiffened. "And why would that be, Captain?" What an ass.

"Because you all got whupped so bad at Richmond." He turned to Marion with a smile.

Jonathan stared at them, a familiar flush warming his neck.

Caldwell said, "We're building up our army now. You might want to try to get on with General Pope. He's getting ready to thrash the Rebs and end this war."

The heat rose to his face. He straightened as tall as he could. "Don't think I will, because I hear General McClellan may have a whole new campaign soon." A lie, but Jonathan said it with more hope than conviction.

"Word is the only campaign he might be in is the next election against Lincoln. No doubt he'll lose that, too." Caldwell broke into an insulting laugh.

Jonathan balled his fists and forced himself to look Marion's way. "I'll be leaving now. Thank you for seeing me." With a short bow, he turned to walk away.

Caldwell called after him, "Aren't you going to address your goodbyes to a superior officer as well, Gray?"

"No, I'm not." He spat the words out and strode toward the front door.

Caldwell continued, "Hey, I think I've heard of you, Gray. Weren't you a writer for the *Philadelphia Inquirer* a while back? At least that's what Marion said. Can't say I care much for your point of view about the darkies."

"Can't say I care much whether you like what I wrote or not."

"Watch your tongue, Lieutenant, or I'll have you brought up on charges of insubordination."

Marion stood to one side, watching, that familiar strange smile playing over her face.

Jonathan stared eye to eye with Caldwell. "I can't imagine anyone being subordinate to you."

Caldwell grabbed his gloves from his uniform belt, took two quick strides, and slapped Jonathan across the face. "You, sir, are no gentleman, and I will have my satisfaction, either with pistols or sabers."

Jonathan flashed back to the time his father slapped him as a boy. His cheek stung the same way. He wanted to rub it but didn't, just like then. He looked from his antagonist to Marion and back. She stood smiling at Caldwell.

Jonathan cocked his head. "Are you challenging me to a duel?" His adrenaline was up and he was egging Caldwell on now. He added his own little smile, too.

"Sure am, Lieutenant bumpkin. Meet me tomorrow morning at the downtown stables and that'll be the last time you ever sass a superior officer."

Jonathan fixed Caldwell with a stare. "Pistols." He walked out. Bigger smile. A picture of Barbra flashed through his head. What brought her to mind? The smile faded and regret coursed through him.

The next morning, Parker pleaded with Jonathan as they rode to the stables. "You don't have to do this. You don't have to prove anything to anyone. Just let it be. They deserve each other."

"Yes, they do. But Caldwell made it personal and I *will* respond."

Jonathan got down from the buggy and walked to the barn where Caldwell and another officer stood. Marion was nearby with her handmaid, along with a coterie of the curious who had heard about the challenge. As the sun burrowed into the morning fog, a small man in a tall black hat and coat and tails called to him and Parker. Jonathan strode over. He eyed Caldwell, who wore a smug expression.

"You come over too, Captain Caldwell," the little man said. He cleared his throat. "I'm Colonel Malcolm Stanley, US Army, retired. I would ask you both to reconsider this affair." No response. "So be it. I'm here to see that this duel is properly conducted. This will be a contest of Colt .44 pistols, the standard sidearm for officers, so the both of you should be familiar with the weapon. Each weapon has one bullet." Jonathan carried the same gun but couldn't remember the last time he'd fired his. The colonel looked at Jonathan and motioned toward Parker. "Is he your second?"

"Yes."

To Caldwell. "And this one yours?"

"Yes."

He turned to the seconds."Do you understand that if these duelists fail to comply with my instructions, you, as seconds, will be required to replace them?"

They nodded.

Jonathan glanced at Marion. She stood to the side with just the hint of a stricken look on her face. Was she just now realizing the seriousness of what she'd set in motion? This was no parlor game. It was likely he or Caldwell would soon be carried lifeless from the field. Jonathan had grown up shooting rifles but he'd fired the Colt enough to be comfortable with the handgun. But how good was Caldwell?

Stanley eyed them both. "Any questions? Fine. You will stand back to back and listen to my voice. As I count off, you step. When I get to ten, stop in place and turn toward each other, then aim your pistol. Fire when told. Not before. Now come here." They each reached into the open case he held out and took a gleaming pistol. Stanley lined them up back to back.

"One!"

Jonathan stepped with his pistol pointed skyward. In a few minutes, he'd either kill a man or be killed. Perhaps both. He forced himself to slow his breathing.

"Two!"

Fog swirled around Marion's billowing skirt in the morning breeze. How had he fallen so far under her sway that he was ready to kill for her? Union officers were supposed to shoot Confederates, not each other. Out of the corner of his eye, he saw her put a hand to her mouth as he stepped. Her parasol umbrella looked ridiculous in the gloom.

"Three!"

Jonathan was dressed in the only suit he had. A brown tweed he'd gotten second hand in Princeton right before graduation. It wasn't the first time he'd worn it, but today might be the last.

"Four!"

How ironic. He was dueling with an idiot who accused him of being anti-slavery, as if that was a bad thing. He did feel a tinge of regret about the ego that propelled him to be here this morning, though.

"Five!"

Jonathan stepped again. And again.

When the colonel shouted "ten," Jonathan stopped and turned. Caldwell already faced him, his pistol pointed straight at his chest. Before Stanley could stop him, Caldwell fired. A bullet ripped into Jonathan's left arm, knocking him sideways, but not off his feet. With his right arm, he slowly leveled his pistol at Caldwell, who stood helpless, his gun falling from a shaking hand. Jonathan waited. And waited. He wanted the arrogant officer's fear to last as long as possible. He saw the pleading look, the outstretched palms. Not so smug anymore. He fired.

The bullet cut a small furrow along the side of Caldwell's face and slammed into the barn behind him. Jonathan dropped his pistol and grabbed his shoulder. He leaned against Parker, who'd come up behind him.

Marion dashed to Caldwell with a fervent, "Are you all right?" Caldwell held a bloody hand to his face, staring wide-eyed at Jonathan. Stanley stood red faced, inches from Caldwell, cursing him.

Jonathan watched Marion fawn over Caldwell. He turned to Parker. "Let's go."

Parker supported his friend back to the buggy and helped him inside. With one hand on Jonathan's collar, he snapped the reins and the horse jumped into a gallop.

"Thanks for being there for me," Jonathan said through clenched teeth.

"I'm your second, I had to be there," Parker joked, hoping humor would mask his concern.

As they neared Parker House, Jonathan closed his eyes. Robert yelled to his mother to get the doctor, and half carried, half dragged him down to his room. The Parkers ran after him. Parker laid Jonathan on the bed.

"Go get the doctor, I said!"

After the elderly doctor cleaned and bandaged Jonathan's wound, he turned to the Parkers. "I gave him a sedative. He's lucky. The bullet went right through the fleshy part of his upper arm and didn't hit anything major. He should be fine in time. Keep changing the bandage and cleaning the wound, though. And keep him quiet this week." The man rubbed his chin. "Anyone have any idea how he got those big scars on his stomach?" Those were the last words Jonathan heard before he passed out.

Jonathan soon recovered enough to be up and around. Parker shuffled with him along the front of the house as Jonathan regained strength.

Parker looked at him. "You missed him on purpose, didn't you?"

"I didn't miss him."

"But you didn't kill him, for sure."

"No, I didn't. I did something worse. I humiliated him."

"Why?"

"Let's just leave it that I didn't kill him, okay?" He didn't want to think about the duel anymore.

"But the way he shot you...he cheated. He deserved to die."

"Never met a man I thought deserved to die. Yet. Why don't we leave it alone, okay?" Jonathan leaned on Parker as they hobbled up the avenue.

"Well, he's still a jackass."

"Agreed." He shook his head. "Now Caldwell has Marion's love, or what passes for love with her."

During his convalescence, Jonathan thought about how different his life had turned out than the way he'd imagined it would. He wondered what his father would think of him now. It galled him that he still wanted his approval. Growing up on the farm had been simple, but seemed like another lifetime ago. Scenes from his childhood flashed through his head. That special spring festival with Barbra. Skipping rocks with Sonny. Happy days with Sadie. Where had they all gone?

He wandered around Parker House getting his legs back, and came across a family Bible in the library. Picking it off the shelf, he carried it down to his room. Later that night he opened it. He couldn't remember the last time he'd spent time in Scripture. The verse, "For God so loved the world" stayed with him. Could God still love him after all he'd done?

When Jonathan returned from leave, the army was still outraged at their commander's dismissal. Meanwhile, Lee's forces had been on the move, routing another Union army again in northern Virginia at Bull Run.

After reading a new headquarters message, Jonathan ran to find Parker. "Good news! McClellan's been restored to command. Now, the country will see a quick end to this war." Jonathan grinned from ear to ear.

Parker beamed. "About time. No doubt Lincoln knew he made a mistake and Bull Run showed him how big a one." Within weeks, McClellan resurrected the demoralized Union army. Ample supplies laid in, morale restored, troops readied for hard combat.

Jonathan felt a surge of redemption at this turn of events. All had been set right, but when nothing happened, he said, "I wish we'd get moving. I can't stand this sitting." He paced in the small canvas tent he shared with Parker. "Seems like something always happens to trip us up."

"Just hold your horses. Little Mac's got things under control. You'll see; this time we'll whip 'em, whip Lee good." Parker whittled a small piece of wood with a knife from the Gaines Mill battlefield.

"You say that like you're sure," Jonathan said.

Parker continued to shape the wood. "I'm sure. I've always been sure."

"What's that you're making?" Jonathan hoped against hope his friend was right as he watched Parker bring a small wooden horse to life. He was tired of hearing the same old complaints about the general. But when Lee made the first move again, he was crushed. Confederates streamed across the Potomac. Into Maryland. Union territory.

He stormed out of the tent and heaved his tin coffee cup into the woods.

Damn!

Chapter Twenty-One

Summer 1862

Parker rushed into their tent and handed Jonathan a telegram. "Take a look at this. Little Mac's givin' Lincoln an earful. About time, I'd say."

Jonathan scanned it. He shook his head. He didn't think a military commander had any business advising the president on politics. "I can't see anything in here that's going to help us beat Lee." He handed the message back to Parker. "Has this been sent yet?"

"Yup, sent it a while ago myself," Parker said with a self-satisfied smile.

Jonathan said, "Then there's been no response from the president, yet?"

"No, and my guess is he won't answer it. He's probably trying to figure out how to get out of the fix he's put himself in."

"What fix?"

Parker waggled a finger. "Well, Lincoln must know he's wrong. Surely, he won't issue anything about freeing slaves now."

"I don't think a letter from McClellan is going to stop him from doing that, do you?"

"Little Mac's the most powerful man in the country right now. Lincoln better listen to him."

Parker always sounded so sure. Jonathan's insides

filled with familiar qualms. He tossed and turned well into the night.

****

Parker Senior needed southern raw materials, especially cotton, but the war had dried the supply up. His textile mills ground to a near halt. Desperate, he took a train to Washington and met with his son over bourbons at the plush Washington Union Club.

"Son, you probably have an idea why I'm here, other than just to say 'hello', right?"

"Why don't you tell me, Father?" Truth be told, he had no idea.

"It's this damn war, it's no good for anyone," he said, slamming his glass on the polished wooden table so hard the noise reverberated inside the staid, paneled room. Men in coats and ties peered over reading glasses.

"Everyone knows that."

"But not everyone knows how much it's hurting businesses. I can't get raw cotton anymore, and a cotton mill without cotton isn't a mill, it's just an expensive, empty pile of bricks."

"So, how bad is it, Father?"

"Bad enough that I've had to let several servants go. Your mother is doing some of the cooking, and you know how awful that is." With the tension broken, Senior asked Robert to talk to McClellan—try to get him to force peace.

"But…that's the president's job."

"Oh hell, all the president's hopes ride on McClellan, even if the man does have suspect loyalties." Senior took a large gulp. "This whole army could turn around, march on Washington, and force the government to negotiate peace with Lee."

Robert shuddered at the very thought, but there was some truth to it. He stared silently at his father.

Senior continued, "Lincoln ought to cut a deal now. Get the North and South to stop killing each other and get on with recognizing the South so I can get my cotton. He'll be a one-term president anyway. He's in way over his head."

This was dangerous talk—his father had never said anything like this. "Is that what you want?"

"What I want is for this damn war to stop interfering with my business. That's what I want. I'm going broke!" Heads turned.

"What makes you think I can do anything about it?"

"Hell, I don't know. You—or someone you know—must have McClellan's ear. The Democrats all want peace, too. There must be others on his staff who feel the same as me. Talk to some of them. Talk to all of them."

Parker stared at his father, shaken. His stomach churned and he downed the rest of his bourbon. Fire rose in his throat. He took his time riding back to headquarters. After guiding his horse to the stable, he walked to his tent, oblivious to the stable hand's greeting. He flipped the flap up and dropped on his cot. What should he do?

****

Jonathan looked up from reading his Bible. "How's your father?"

"Fine."

"He must have had something important to talk with you about for him to come all the way to

176

Washington."

Silence.

"You weren't gone very long. You couldn't have had dinner and cards there."

"No, we didn't." Parker stared straight ahead.

"Why don't we head over to the staff tent and see who's playing? I'll bet everyone's still celebrating Mac's reinstatement."

"You go ahead. I'm a little tired from my trip...think I'll turn in early."

Jonathan glanced sideways at him as he left.

The next morning, Parker jostled him awake. "Come on, let's grab some grub."

Jonathan shook the cobwebs away and sat up. "Guess I must've drunk too much last night, but everyone was in such a great mood. It was crazy. You missed it."

"That's okay, another time. Let's head to the mess."

Something was eating at Parker, but Jonathan figured he'd hear about it sooner or later. They finished their meal in silence. At headquarters, officers were in constant motion, organizing for a new campaign. The staff beamed, in contrast to Parker's sour expression. Later that night, Jonathan walked with him through camp, reveling in their new circumstances.

Parker shook his head. "Do you think this war will ever end?"

Jonathan eyed his friend. Where did that come from? "Of course it will. And soon. Why do you ask such a ridiculous question?"

"I don't know, it just seems like it's dragging on and on. I'd like to get this over with so we can get back to living again."

"All of us would like to get the war over. And we are living."

"You know what I mean—get on with our lives, our careers."

"Well, I've been thinking about maybe making the army a career."

"You can't mean that. You've got more talent than that, Gray," Parker said.

"What's wrong with staying in the army?"

"Well, I'm done with the army after the war. I'm gonna go back to Philadelphia and go into politics or join my father's business."

"Well, you got me there, 'cause I'm not going back home to the farm."

"What would you do?"

"Maybe I'll go into the newspaper business, in Philadelphia, maybe covering politics."

"That's all right I guess, but wouldn't you rather go into politics, instead of just covering it?"

"Why would I do that? I don't even know which party I'd belong to." McClellan's tug was warring with Jonathan's abolitionism.

"Of course you do. You'd be a Democrat because you don't want the country torn apart anymore."

"Well, I am in favor of that."

"Sure you are. You'd be a natural for public office."

"Never thought anything about it."

"With your Princeton background, you could be a senator from New Jersey."

"A senator?" Jonathan laughed. "Me?"

"Sure, you'd have to meet the right people and

spend time with them so they get comfortable with you. But, hey, my family could help you do that."

"Whoa, we're getting ahead of ourselves, aren't we?"

"I can see it now. Jonathan Gray, Democrat senator from the great state of New Jersey."

"Tell me again why I'd be a Democrat?"

"'Cause you want this war over. Don't you?"

"Sure, but the war's gonna play out in its own way."

"McClellan's the one man who could end this right here and now."

"Whaddya mean, end it now?"

Parker paused for a moment. "He could take this army, march on Washington, and force Lincoln to make peace with the South."

Jonathan stared wide-eyed. "What? You're talking treason here."

"Is it treason to save lives? How many thousands of lives would be saved if the war ended now? On both sides."

"Yes, but that's not for us to decide."

"Maybe so, but McClellan could do it with a little prompting."

"What are you suggesting?" Jonathan couldn't believe what he was hearing.

"If the war ended now, we'd all be the better for it."

"Do you realize what you're saying?"

"Someone would just have to put a bug in Mac's ear."

Jonathan's jaw dropped. Robert wouldn't really do that, would he? And where had he come up with such a notion?

Parker began planting the seed of the idea among his closest confidants on staff. He said if McClellan had an opportunity for a private audience with Lincoln, he could push for a ceasefire in place, with a return to each side's original boundaries under the terms of a peace agreement. If the senior staff joined in the effort, the argument would be persuasive indeed.

Parker took key members of the staff aside one by one. He suggested they arrange a meeting with the president where the army was camped. Here, where the impact of the idea would have the most effect. Here, where the president would see firsthand how devoted the army was to their commander. How a bloodless coup could occur if he didn't agree to the plan. The Confederates certainly wouldn't object, and Union armies in the western theater wouldn't be able to stop the plot before McClellan forced the government to capitulate, surrounded by the largest army in the land. One that was loyal to him through and through. Soldiers in the West probably didn't like the war any more than those in the East did.

No one on staff was saying "no."

****

Parker hadn't mentioned the idea again, so Jonathan assumed it had been just idle conversation. Dangerous, but idle. That's when Colonel Stewart asked to speak with him. He took Jonathan aside and laid out the details of Parker's plan.

"I don't want any p-part of this," Jonathan stammered. "I'll go to the general and reveal what's being suggested if anyone pursues this any further."

Stewart said, "The general has already been

informed, along with select corps commanders as well. A brief is being prepared right now that is going to be presented to the president when he comes here in two days."

"The president is coming here?"

"Yes."

"For what purpose?" He hoped he didn't already know the answer.

"The general will give the president the option of approaching the Confederacy through back channels himself, or he'll do it for him. If Lincoln objects, he'll be threatened with a march on Washington."

"General McClellan actually said he'd do that?"

Stewart didn't answer, he just suggested Jonathan go along with the plan.

That night Jonathan tossed and turned. He couldn't get the conversation he'd had with one of the senior military officials in America out of his head. The next morning, he ignored Parker, who sat on his cot staring at him. Jonathan knew what he had to do. Deep down, his whole life, he'd always known what was right. Hadn't always done it, especially lately, but had always known. But this could mean the end of his dreams. It might also mean the stockade. He needed to do it now before he lost his nerve.

Jonathan marched into the headquarters building, the grand Washington mansion of a southern sympathizer. Strode past protesting aides and a startled secretary into McClellan's inner office. He burst in upon several senior commanders in huddled conversation. McClellan sat at the end of a long dining room table, the room dimly lit.

"Sir, I must speak with you."

General Hancock put his hand out to intercept Jonathan. "What do you mean by barging in here, Lieutenant?"

"I must speak with the general, sir, and I must do it now."

The senior staff rose as one, their faces etched with disapproval.

Jonathan had just committed an unforgivable breach of protocol, but he didn't care. He would not be deterred. This plot had to be stopped. If it was ever discovered, all of them would go to prison, anyway—or worse.

McClellan waved the staff off. "Let Lieutenant Gray have his say."

"Sir, there's a rumor afoot this army might attempt to force President Lincoln to sue for peace with the South and might threaten to march on Washington to make that happen."

The room took on a stillness as if it was empty. Jonathan stood at attention, afraid to even twitch.

McClellan stared at him, silently drumming fingers on the polished table. After an interminable pause, he said, "Nothing like that is going to happen, Lieutenant." Another long pause as he rose. "The only reason we're here is to win this war, and that's what we're going to do." He maintained eye contact with Jonathan, who stood ramrod straight. No one spoke. Jonathan's gaze shifted around the room, his mouth full of cotton.

"Is there anything else, Lieutenant?"

Jonathan stood in stunned silence, trying to make sense out of what he'd just heard. "No, sir...nothing else, sir...by your leave, sir." Jonathan saluted, did a slow about face, and left the room, as confused as he'd ever been in his life.

Walking back through camp, he gazed at the tens of thousands of soldiers spread out in makeshift shelters on the rolling hills of Virginia. He was shaken, knowing if they had been asked to advance on nearby Washington, most would have done so without hesitation. In his tent, he searched for his Bible, pulled it from his knapsack, and placed it on his cot. With a hand lingering on the cover, he breathed deeply and lay down. Sleep would come hard again tonight.

Tension with Parker remained high. Jonathan removed his few belongings from their tent. He slept near his work desk, lying on what passed for a thin mattress on the floor. He guessed everyone must have heard about the scene in the staff meeting.

Parker kept trying to engage him in conversation over the next few days but Jonathan was having none of it. His relations with the senior staff were strained as well, their disdain thinly masked. As uncomfortable as he still was with the idea of a coup d'état, he also thought he might have had a hand in stopping it.

How much McClellan bought into the idea, he didn't know. But Jonathan wondered. Surely the plan would have become widely known, owing to the number of people who had firsthand knowledge of it.

His distance from Parker wasn't all that was gnawing at him, though. Ever since the conversation he'd overhead from that corporal during his hospital stay, he'd felt a tug to find out more about his mother.

And his father.

Chapter Twenty-Two

September 1862

After dusting the Federals at Bull Run, Lee set his army in motion again, crossing the Potomac River west of Washington. Word was he was marching north into Maryland, still a Union state. Jonathan had heard speculation that if the South could bruise the Federals in their own backyard, England or France might recognize the Confederacy and pressure the North to agree to peace talks.

No one was more surprised than Jonathan when McClellan set off in quick pursuit. Union forces flowed into Frederick, Maryland only days after the Confederates wound north and west out of town. Soldiers lounging in a recently-abandoned Confederate campsite found some cigars wrapped in a piece of paper with writing on it. A sergeant brought it to Jonathan, who rushed it into the general's staff meeting and hurried the note to McClellan. Some of the senior commanders, already leery of Jonathan, rebuked him for his temerity. McClellan was engrossed in reading it, however. Soon, murmurs died out and silence reclaimed the room. All eyes fastened on the general.

McClellan rose. "I now know the routes the Confederates are going to take over the next several weeks. Lee and his army are within our grasp. Here is a paper with which if I cannot whip Bobbie Lee, I will be willing to go home."

That evening, over dinner, Jonathan shared the discovery with Parker. "Even though I'm not speaking to you right now, I've got some great news." Parker looked up from his plate with a confused look. Jonathan leaned close. "McClellan just got hold of Lee's whole strategy. He knows right where he's headed."

Parker's eyes widened. "What? How'd that happen?" When Jonathan told him, Parker said, "If we can trap Lee now, the war could be over soon. That might be quick enough to save my father's mills."

Jonathan didn't know what that meant, so he let it go.

The next morning, much to Jonathan's surprise, the Army of the Potomac was up and winding like a long, lethal snake toward western Maryland. Lee was falling back toward Sharpsburg, a small town which lay alongside fast-moving Antietam Creek. By nightfall, his army was hemmed in. Jonathan warmed himself around one of hundreds of Union campfires that flickered into the night, eager for the morning.

When the army didn't fall on the enemy the next day, Jonathan hurled his hat in his tent. "We didn't do nothin'! Nothin'!" When he was mad, he had a way of talking like the farmboy he used to be. "What's the sense of knowin' what the enemy's gonna do, if you don't do nothin' about it. All this sittin' here is just helpin' Lee."

Parker said, "Whoa there, Johnny boy. Our commander knows what he's doing. He's probably got Lee thinking all kinds of things. Like maybe we're getting reinforcements. I bet Lee's wondering if he should make a run for it."

Jonathan frowned. "There's no other Yankee army near us and Lee knows it. And he's got even better cavalry than we do. He knows McClellan, too. The only thing we did today was give the enemy more time to get ready for whatever we might throw at him."

The next day turned out to be more of the same, only a cautious feeling out of rebel positions. Jonathan yelled, "Damn it!" He spotted Colonel Stewart coming toward him outside the headquarters tent. "Sorry, sir." A swift salute.

"What's the matter, Jonathan?"

"Uh...nothing, sir, It's late. Just coming from a staff meeting?"

"No, that was over a while back. Was just going over some battle maps."

"For tomorrow?" Please say yes.

"Yup. We're gonna hit 'em in the morning."

"Yes, sir! I sure do like hearing that." His words sounded more optimistic than he felt. All their hopes had been dashed before. Would tomorrow really be any different?

Jonathan moved back into the tent with Parker. He had to work with him during the duty day, but he still kept his distance, speaking with his former friend only as the occasion demanded.

Parker tried to draw Jonathan out as they sat after dinner. "Seems like we've got old Bobbie Lee bottled up good this time."

Jonathan grunted without looking up from his cot. "Heard that before. We just better strike hard tomorrow." He took a deep breath and tried to reconcile himself to what the morning would bring. Or wouldn't bring.

"Do you think he will? I mean, we will?" Parker asked.

"Don't know, but please, dear Lord, let this be where we finally make a stand." Jonathan yawned. He'd been in the saddle couriering for two days straight. The cot promised precious rest. He'd just begun drifting off when Parker broke the still night's silence in their darkened tent.

"You still awake?"

Jonathan blinked his eyes open. "I am now."

"Remember what I said a while back about trying to get McClellan to stop the war?"

"Yup." It was not something Jonathan could forget.

"Sorry if you thought I was being...disloyal. I just couldn't stand to see my folks suffer."

"What do you mean?"

"My father's going bankrupt because of the southern blockades. He can't get any cotton for his mills."

Jonathan let that sink in. "So *that's* why you wanted McClellan to sue for peace." They lay in silence again, Jonathan a mixture of emotions. He didn't want the Parkers hurt but he badly wanted to hit Lee.

"I didn't know what else to do. My father asked me if I could talk with McClellan before he lost everything."

Jonathan mulled that over. "I'm not sure what I would have done in your place, but I'd like to think I wouldn't have done that."

"No, I don't suppose you would have," said Parker. "You've always had strong character. That was something I admired, even when I was picking on you at Princeton."

Laughter filled the darkness.

"Speaking of that, why *did* you pick on me?"

"Because you were different, you were smart, and I was neither of those."

Jonathan said, "You were smart enough. And you had all the Whigs following you, leading those fellas around by their noses." He stretched a hand out and laid it on his Bible.

"Yeah, that was fun. But I only picked on you when I had other guys around 'cause I had no doubt you could take me easy."

"I didn't want to take you. I just wanted to be left alone."

"That's what I mean. You were different. You weren't part of the crowd, didn't want to be. Part of me wanted to be like you. Strong and smart."

A short silence.

"I was jealous of you, too." Jonathan's voice was barely above a whisper.

"Me? Why would you envy me?"

"You had everything. Money, friends, girls—other guys followed your lead. Why wouldn't I envy you?"

"Huh. You know…I've always wondered something. Remember when I cheated in that Civics class?"

Jonathan smiled at the memory. "How could I forget?"

"Why'd you cover my crib sheet with your foot? Never could figure that out. I was always needling you, making fun of you."

"And my clothes!"

"Yeah, you had no reason to want to do anything to

help me. Why'd you do it?"

"Don't know. My foot was over it before I knew it."

Parker paused for a moment. "I don't believe that. You did it on purpose. Why?"

Jonathan raised his arms over his head as he lay there. "Guess I never wanted anyone to get in trouble if they didn't have to. If I could help somebody, I did it. Just like you helped me at the duel that morning. I never needed any more reason than that."

Parker looked toward Jonathan in the dark and smiled. Then laughed. "That was *so* great, you just slid your shoe right on top of it without moving, neat as anything. The teacher never knew."

"Well, he knew there was a cheat sheet somewhere near you, he just couldn't find it. So he failed me too." Darkness hid the big smile on Jonathan's face but couldn't hide the chuckle in his voice.

And they were boys again, snickering into the night.

Chapter Twenty-Three

At dawn, Jonathan's hopes were answered when the Union right swung into action. Lt. Col. Stewart said he'd be riding to and from General Burnside's headquarters on the southern end of the battlefield, Parker the northern end. Three hours into the battle, McClellan crafted an order for General Sumner.

Stewart whirled around. "Lieutenant Parker!"

"Here, sir!"

"Report to the commanding general."

"Yessir!"

McClellan returned a salute. "Robert, I need you to take this to General Sumner. See that patch of trees down there on the left? He's just beyond them. Damn! Can hardly see anything with all the smoke and fires. Can you get this to him?"

Parker folded the piece of paper and tucked it into his coat. "Yes, sir. Right away, sir!"

"Good, now go."

Parker set off at a fast gallop toward the fighting below.

General Marcy rubbed his chin. "I hope he gets through. That's a furious melée down there."

McClellan focused his eyeglass on Parker as he galloped into a haze of tangled battle. When Parker reached the stand of trees, the young man tumbled from his horse. McClellan shook his head. "Damn! Almost

190

like they were waiting for him. Damn! Get me another courier."

Marcy took him aside. "George, why don't you *tell* this one what you want Sumner to do, instead of writing it down? Remember how Lee's battle plan fell into our hands? Let's don't take another chance with this message. We already have one courier down. If they knock this one off his horse and search him, they'll know what your intentions are."

McClellan motioned to a sergeant. "Come here, son, don't be nervous." He gave the soldier verbal orders and had him repeat them back. As he shooed the horseman on his way, McClellan yelled, "And steer clear of those woods there on the left!"

****

Jonathan had been riding back and forth all morning between Burnside's location and headquarters. The acrid smoke from countless roaring batteries burnt his eyes. *Whumps* of artillery shells assaulted his hearing. He'd given up worrying about the withering fire coming his way. If it was his time, it was his time. Nothing he could do about it. That's what his father always said. A vision of an expressionless Tom flashed through his mind. He wished it away and whispered small prayers as he tried to skirt the maelstrom. He dodged bodies both writhing and still. So much death. There had to be a purpose in it—didn't there?

When he returned to headquarters after yet another harrowing ride, he brushed dirt off his uniform and reported in.

Marcy nodded his way, then turned to McClellan. "Sir, this is perhaps the critical moment in the whole battle, perhaps the entire war. If you send your reserves in now, we could likely split Lee's army in half. Then you could wheel in either direction and roll their flanks up."

McClellan shook his head. "No, no. I can't do that, wouldn't be smart. It would leave me with no rear guard if Lee attacked again. He likes surprise attacks. Send couriers out to tell my commanders not to expect help."

Jonathan stood stupefied. He couldn't believe they weren't going to hit the enemy with everything they had. The biggest battle of the war. His heart sunk. What good was a reserve if you never used it?

Stewart shouted his name, "Lieutenant Gray!"

"Here, sir!"

"Report to General McClellan."

Jonathan hurried over as McClellan glassed the battlefield.

"Jonathan, I need you to ride to General Burnside again. Tell him to secure that stone bridge to his front. Now." McClellan pointed toward a small span that crossed Antietam Creek. Burnside's troops were massed just this side of it, waiting for the order to attack.

"Yes, sir!"

"One more thing. Watch out for that artillery fire coming from the heights beyond. Now go with all dispatch!"

Jonathan swung up and was off. Burnside was little more than a mile away over battle-ravaged earth. A gray pall hugged the ground as Jonathan rode south along the ridge line. Soon, he angled to his right and descended from the wooded heights in a fast gallop. Fires formed rings around him as if he were riding in the depths of hell. He couldn't see Burnside's headquarters through the dense smoke, but knew the way by heart by now.

The nearer he got, the louder the screams, moans, and cries for help. Federal skirmishers lined the outskirts of Burnside's army. Jonathan flashed back to the Yankee pickets on the peninsula who'd knocked him off his horse. This time he carried a US flag with him, letting it flap freely in the breeze as he galloped. Hopefully, they could see it through all the smoke—he wasn't keen on getting unhorsed again.

As he neared Burnside's sentries, Jonathan's mount skidded to a halt as if she had run into a wall, nearly pitching him off headfirst. Jonathan reared back in his saddle as far as he could. The horse's legs splayed straight out front, her ears perked. What just happened? She stamped her feet in place, as if she couldn't or wouldn't move. The mare snorted and tossed her head rapidly.

The whistle of an incoming artillery shell reached him just before it hurtled to earth not twenty yards in front of him. The concussion knocked him from the mare. Iron debris rained everywhere. He sat dazed, then struggled to a knee, covered in dirt and blood.

Even through the billowing smoke, some of the skirmishers to his front had vanished. Others lay on the ground moaning or scrambling back to the shelter of the woods. He searched himself for wounds but found none. Where did all the blood come from? He gazed around the battlefield as if outside his body. The horse lay nearby, legs flailing. Staggering to her, he saw the big hole in her chest where she'd taken a large piece of shrapnel. He stroked her neck for a moment, then unholstered his Colt. One shot put her out of her misery. He wobbled to the shell's still-smoking crater. It hit right where he would have been if the mare hadn't stopped. She shielded him from certain death.

He retrieved what remained of his flag, lurched in front of a riderless animal and after two attempts, struggled up into the saddle, headed toward the woods ahead. When he reached Burnside's headquarters, soldiers were speaking to him, but he couldn't make out what they were saying. His head was a beehive.

Still stunned in the saddle, he heard a faint, "Sir...down...the...please." A soldier motioned for him to dismount. Gripping Jonathan by an arm, another tipped him over like a pitcher and caught him with both hands as he toppled off the horse.

Jonathan tried to get his body to cooperate as he stood on suspect legs. He shouted, "I have to see General Burnside." He brushed at the dust and dirt that covered him and stood tilted to one side. He spit debris out and tried to work saliva into his mouth without success.

A soldier escorted him to Burnside's command post where the commanding general stood surrounded by staff. He saluted on rubbery legs. In a distant, muffled voice he said, "Lieutenant Gray reporting, sir."

A quick return salute. "What do you have for me, Lieutenant?"

"Sir, orders from the commanding general." Jonathan sensed he was yelling but he could barely hear himself. His head pounded and his ears buzzed.

Burnside arched his eyebrows while Jonathan shouted the message. "Thank you, Lieutenant. That'll be all." The general spoke faintly to one of his officers.

"Captain...care...lieutenant...rough...of it." Jonathan watched as Burnside rode with his staff to the side of his waiting columns. The southernmost of the three narrow bridges spanning Antietam Creek lay to their front, the enemy massed on the other side. Waiting.

Burnside's regimental flags rose, then fell. Thousands of screaming soldiers rushed the stone bridge. Jonathan shook his head. So many men struggling to cross something so small. Mounds of motionless blue and gray-clad bodies soon hid the arched structure from sight.

Jonathan turned away from the devastation. He looked skyward and raised a prayer, his nose full of the smell of death.

Chapter Twenty-Four

Jonathan's hearing began to return as he turned away from the fury on the bridge. He cut out a chestnut mare from Burnside's corral; one that reminded him of Belle back home. So far away now. Another lifetime. Easing into the saddle, he aimed the horse toward the heights he'd come from. His head throbbed as he fought to keep his balance, settling the mare into a slow trot over tangled ground tortured by enemy artillery. Strewn with so many still bodies. Angling to his right put him out of range of Confederate shells and in a few minutes, he was well clear. The *whump, whump* of black falling death grew fainter as he neared headquarters. He reined his horse to a slow halt and hurried as well as he could to where McClellan's staff watched the battle play out below.

"Lieutenant Gray reporting, sir." A quick salute.

"Where've you been, boy?" Lt. Col. Stewart rested a hand on Jonathan's shoulder with a worried look.

Jonathan stood with dried blood spattered on his face and uniform. "Sorry for my appearance, sir."

Stewart said something and Jonathan cupped a hand behind an ear. "Sir?"

"Where...have...you...been?"

"Had a little trouble on the way to see General Burnside, sir."

"Well I guess you did, from the looks of you.

Anyway, glad you're back. You sure you're all right?"

Jonathan got the gist of what Stewart said. "Yes, sir. What do you need me to do?"

"Stay close by, please."

Jonathan took a position to the rear of the staff.

McClellan's eyes grew wide when he saw him. "Jonathan! How are you? I was beginning to worry about you, son."

"I'm fine, sir. Just ran into a little difficulty."

"Just like Bobby Lee's butternuts down there." McClellan pointed at Confederates retreating now in front of Burnside.

"Sir?"

"See them drawing back now as we advance on Sharpsburg?"

Jonathan had regained his hearing for the most part but was still shouting. "Yes, sir, they're definitely retreating." Suddenly, a mass of soldiers rushed in from the south, tearing into the Union forces. Thousands of them. Where did they come from? Their battle flags were Confederate, but were those blue uniforms they wore? Jonathan couldn't be sure from this distance. The firing intensified and Burnside's soldiers started to flee. Just then, one of Burnside's couriers reported in with a petition for more men.

As McClellan read Burnside's request, Marcy said, "You're going to reinforce him, aren't you, George? They're being routed."

"I can't. Can't risk it. Our reserves are our last line of defense."

Jonathan turned away in disgust, insides boiling. Was McClellan ever going to act like a battlefield commander? He looked for Parker. "Colonel Stewart, have you seen Lieutenant Parker, sir?"

"Not…for a while, son. The general sent him out some time ago." Stewart turned away.

Jonathan strode to where another courier held a horse. "Have you seen Lieutenant Parker?"

"I seen him," the sergeant said, shifting from one foot to the other.

Jonathan nodded. "Where is he?"

"Uh…that's not what I mean, sir." He stole a sideways glance at Stewart. The colonel's eyes were fixed on the battle.

"Whaddya mean?"

"I mean I seen him go down." The sergeant's voice trailed away. He broke eye contact.

"Whaddya mean, go down?"

"Got knocked off his horse, he did."

Jonathan's stomach stuck in his throat. What? Knocked off his horse? Couldn't be. Must be another courier. Robert's okay. He had to be. "Where?"

"Yonder that way." The courier pointed toward Sumner's troops who were pulling back from the center bridge amid horrific fighting.

"Show me!"

"It ain't gonna do no good, sir. He's down and he ain't moved since, from what I done seen."

"Show me where he is!" His heart raced and his legs nearly gave out as he pulled the sergeant forward for a better view.

The courier pointed to a stand of trees about a half mile below to their right. "Went down just by those oaks. I reckon that's where he still is."

No! Jonathan passed a hand over his eyes and said a little prayer. His head swirled as he wobbled to his horse. Robert couldn't be down—they had too many plans. He grabbed the mare's reins, worked himself up into the saddle, and spurred her hard. As the horse bounded down the hill, he heard Marcy shout, "Jonathan! Jonathan!" but he didn't break stride. A smoky gray cloud gobbled him up on the shredded plain this side of the woods. He took pains to dodge the fallen along the way.

Bodies increased as he neared the trees, but he ignored the artillery shells heaving the ground up ahead. His hearing faded again as concussions continued to shake him. Squinting through the haze, he glimpsed distant Federals deployed in a defensive perimeter. He slowed, scanning left and right as he rode, sidestepping still soldiers on his way toward the woods. Minié bullets buzzed by his head. Where was Robert? He tried to swallow but couldn't. Heartwrenching screams from broken blue rag dolls rose to meet him as he trotted back and forth. He searched the injured and the dead, soul aflame.

"Robert!" And again. "Robert!" Hoping to hear his friend's voice call out to him. "Tell me where you are!" Agonizing minutes passed as he worked his way over the bloody field.

There.

Face down.

His best friend.

From the way Robert lay, Jonathan knew he was dead. Part of him wouldn't believe it, though. He shouted, "Robert! Robert!" He stared at the motionless body, unaware anymore of the battle raging around him. His vision blurred and a rapid pulse pounded in his ears. Artillery shells burst in his head. He wanted to shut everything out—the thunder of the shelling, the moans of the dying, the acrid smell of gunpowder, the pitiful sight of his friend. Dismounting, he knelt and ran his hand along Robert's back, the dusty uniform warm from the midday sun. As Jonathan stared, Sonny's face flashed through his mind. He shook his head. None of this was real. A bad dream.

He stood immobilized, hands to his head, scanning the tortured field for someone. Anyone. It looked like Robert tried to crawl away from the trees. He laid on his stomach, one arm stretched above his head, as if in supplication. Jonathan's surroundings spun. Laid a hand on his horse to steady himself.

And wept.

Details would be sent out to gather the wounded, then the dead, when the battle was over. But when would that be? Jonathan recoiled at the thought of his best friend laying here all alone, perhaps for days, under the hot sun.

He turned Robert over. The wound gaped in the side of his chest. There wasn't enough blood for him to be dead. Sightless eyes stared up at him. Guilt surged in Jonathan from the feeling he had somehow abandoned Robert when he needed him the most. He bent and gagged, wiped at his mouth, and folded Robert's arms across his chest. He opened his bandana and laid it over Robert's face. What else could he cover him with? Jonathan stood, searching for what, he didn't know. He gathered himself again and knelt. Taking Robert's pale hand in his, he recited the Lord's Prayer over and over. His tears fell freely onto Robert's dusty, dirty uniform.

He looked back up the hill toward McClellan's headquarters. Didn't they know he needed a wagon?

Weren't they watching? Didn't they care? The moans of the dying floated up to him as the shelling paused. He bent over Robert and whispered goodbyes. Shells shook the earth underneath him again.

Wiping his eyes, he stood and steadied his horse. Then, placing his arms underneath Robert, he hugged his friend's body to him for a moment. The same way he'd held his father's bloodied body close all those years ago. Jonathan gently draped Robert crosswise over the mare's saddle. The horse had a wild look in her eyes, but Jonathan kept a tight grip on her reins. With one hand grasping the bridle and the other on his friend's back, he started back up the hill, oblivious to the violence still swirling around him.

Up top, Jonathan cleared a wagon bed and laid Robert's body on it. He cleaned his face and uniform as best he could, then trundled him to a mass burial site. He prayed for Robert's soul, that God would take him into His presence. Resting a hand on his friend's chest, he rendered a slow salute. Godspeed. His vision clouded and he turned away as a burial detail approached. He'd never felt so alone among so many people. After another short prayer, he looked skyward. How could this have happened?

The sun would set soon on this most terrible of days.

Chapter Twenty-Five

Jonathan missed Robert the most at meals. He'd grab food from the mess and usually eat alone in his tent. Often he glanced at the empty space where Robert's cot had been. No doubt some new unfortunate inherited it. Was that soldier gone already, too? Col. Stewart hadn't put anyone else in his tent and tapped him to take over Robert's position as McClellan's junior aide. Jonathan tried to settle into the position, but it didn't feel right. Wasn't comfortable with it. Wasn't comfortable with much of anything these days.

One thing he was put off by was McClellan's gloating manner after Antietam. The commander showed no urgency to catch Lee, but Jonathan forced himself to swallow his frustration. The longer the army idled in place, the more he sensed malaise creeping throughout the ranks. Hadn't they just bested Lee at Antietam? Why did it feel like a defeat? Why weren't they chasing the enemy?

He received a letter from his mother, one of the few he'd had since joining the army. Dated several months ago. He opened it on his cot.

Dear Jonathan,

We hope you are well. We're concerned that we haven't heard from you in a while.

Your father used to look forward to his trips to Loveland because sometimes there would be some news from you. But there hasn't been for quite some time. Now, he doesn't even like going into town anymore.

I do hope you will write and let us know how you are. He worries so, but doesn't show it. I hear Barbra's a nurse now at a Philadelphia hospital.

Love,
Mother

He read and reread her words and cursed himself for being so callous. He sat down to write them, running the events of the past few months over and over in his head. Nothing of any substance came to mind, as there was little substance left in him these days. His thoughts were a scattered mess but he felt obliged to write back. All he could do was fill part of a page with generalities that only skimmed the surface of his world. It would have to do—he didn't have any more. What else had they heard about Barbra? He shook his head. Mower. Right where he'd been a patient not long ago. His eyes misted, knowing how he'd hurt his folks and realizing how close he'd been to Barbra.

He didn't mention Parker. That was still too personal. Too raw. For the first time since Robert's death, tears wracked his body and he cried alone in his tent.

****

Jonathan knew he had to call on the Parkers with Robert's personal effects. Part of him wanted to, but a bigger part didn't. Why was he hesitating? Surely he should bring his best friend's belongings back to his parents. Sorrow choked him as he wrestled with regret. He should have been there with Robert. Maybe he could have done something to keep him from being killed.

Mike Torreano

McClellan's inertia after Antietam gave Jonathan time to make the somber trip to Philadelphia. He couldn't delay any longer. He gathered Robert's few things in his friend's brown haversack. Money clip, gold family ring, the lieutenant insignia he'd retrieved from his uniform. Gray Colt 44. A faded, grainy picture of his parents. He'd leave the blood-soaked bandana behind.

Jonathan took his Bible and headed for the train station. From Harper's Ferry, he boarded an eastbound train to Washington. He rode with his head in his hands, knowing the Parkers would want him to relate Robert's last moments. As he stared out the window, he wondered what he would say. The words wouldn't come. His stomach was a knot.

Washington station was near calamitous as soldiers and civilians swarmed the terminal. Jonathan stood in a ticket line for Philadelphia, clutching Robert's effects. His thoughts drifted back to some of their exploits. He smiled as he rummaged through the better memories. He'd let the Parkers know he was coming. His feet were lead as he walked toward the train, fingering the message he'd gotten in response. Mr. Parker was brief.

We'll meet you at the station.

Perhaps too brief. Senior almost sounded angry. Did they blame him, too?

An unusual buzz in the station surrounded him. Snippets of conversations drifted his way. McClellan's name came up again and again as soldiers passed by. He overheard two well-dressed men talking about McClellan—being fired. Was that possible? Again?

"McClellan's been relieved?" Jonathan said, putting a softer edge on it.

One of the middle-aged men puffed himself up in front of him. "That's right, Captain; about time that southern sympathizer got let go. He never intended to whip Lee, he just wanted to nibble at him until we all got tired of the nibbling."

Frustration momentarily replaced Jonathan's grief, but he was tired of defending McClellan, so he let the comment pass. Maybe his expectations of the man had been too high. He thought of his father. Had his expectations of him been too high, too? He took a deep breath and strode to a small group of soldiers. "So it's true, then? General Mac's been removed?"

One of them nodded. "Yeah, sounds like Lincoln's had enough. And good riddance I say, sir. We've missed too many chances to beat Lee. About time we got somebody who fights."

Jonathan shook his head. The staff would probably already be stirring up the troops, stoking their anger. Jonathan passed the leg to Philadelphia in a fog. Disconnected thoughts raced through his mind. What did this mean for the army? For him? The future? A momentary vision of Barbra interrupted his reflections.

When the train pulled into Philadelphia, he snapped out of his daze. Through a window, he scoured the crowd for the Parkers. As he stepped off toward the station house, from somewhere ahead he heard, "Jonathan! Jonathan!" His heart thumped in his chest. He drew a big breath and wrestled the frown from his face. Mrs. Parker. She broke through the swarm hurrying his way, then wrapped her arms around him, sobbing. Tears streamed down his face. He stood mute as Robert's mother held him tight. Tears raced along Parker Senior's cheeks, too, as he patted Jonathan's shoulder.

Mrs. Parker stood back and brushed Jonathan's uniform off. She wound an arm in his and led him to their carriage. Jonathan couldn't speak. Inside, she regained her poise and chattered on with small talk that meant nothing.

"You look wonderful, Jonathan. It's so nice to see you." She paused to compose herself.

Mr. Parker broke his silence. "Yes, it is good to see you, Jonathan. We have been looking forward to your visit."

Jonathan knew there was only a kernel of truth in that. Robert should have been right here beside him. It still didn't seem possible.

"Thank you for coming. It's…" Senior stopped.

Jonathan's voice caught in his throat. He swiped at his face as the carriage clattered over the cobblestone road. Choking up wasn't going to help anything. Stop it.

When they arrived at Parker House, there was an initial awkward spell. Mrs. Parker said, "I'm sorry everything isn't just so for your visit." No staff flitted around. The house had a dreariness he'd never seen—or felt—before. "Why don't you drop your things in your room and freshen up before dinner?"

The meal was somber. No one mentioned Robert, and Jonathan still didn't know how to. Later they all retired to the study, even though women didn't usually sit with the men after dinner. His heartbeat quickened.

"Please tell us everything," Mrs. Parker said.

The stuffy room closed in on him.

She leaned forward in her chair, pale hands clutching a whiter hanky. Drawn face and hair mussed.

Eyes red.

Jonathan hesitated. He searched for the right words, knowing anything he said would be upsetting. "I'm sorry to tell you about Robert's last moments. I wish it was him sitting here and not me." A powerful wave of grief shook him. He wiped at his nose. "I know how much you loved him and how much he loved you."

"You are the very one we want to tell us...about Robert."

Mrs. Parker laid a hand on his arm. It felt as heavy as his heart. Jonathan shook his head, his gaze falling to the floor for a moment, his throat thick. What should he say?

Mr. Parker stared silently out a window, hands clasped behind his back.

Jonathan pursed his lips and cleared his throat. "You know...from the letter I wrote...that Robert was...struck...during the battle of Antietam."

Mrs. Parker's eyes widened. She held the embroidered handkerchief in splotchy white hands.

"Robert...was riding to one of the corps commanders, carrying a crucial message from General McClellan." He took a slow sip of sherry, brushed at his nose, and cleared his throat again. "The general tended to trust Robert with the most important messages...because he knew he could always count on him. This was the most important one General McClellan sent that day. He asked for Robert personally. I remember...Robert had a very determined look on his face, knowing how vital the message was." Nothing he'd said was true, but he hoped his version would bring the Parkers some comfort.

"Robert was a hero, riding through that awful

chaos. He was almost to General Sumner when he went down. As Robert lay there, other soldiers told me they came to his aid." Jonathan pursed his lips and took another sip. "Robert handed them the message and said to make sure it got to the general. They carried him to the shade of a nearby tree and gave him a drink. They told me he passed with a peaceful look on his face." Jonathan stared at the floor, tears falling to the carpet. A hanky to his nose. That was the version he wanted to believe, too.

It wouldn't do to tell them Robert died alone from his awful wound and his message was never delivered. Jonathan's vision clouded as he looked up at Mrs. Parker. She dabbed her eyes. Mr. Parker wiped at his face with a big brawny hand and turned away.

"Thank you...so much, Jonathan, for sharing Robert's...passing...with us." She swept a hand through her hair and looked more at peace now. Senior stared at a nearly empty bookcase on the wall.

"Do you know what his last words were?" She squeezed his hand, bottom lip trembling.

"No, ma'am, I don't," telling the truth for the first time.

"Is there anything else important we should know?"

Jonathan paused. No sense in mentioning the falling out they'd had before that. "Well...maybe only that the evening before the battle, Robert and I talked in our tent well into the night. We shared some very good memories. I'll always remember that as such a special time. A very...special time. We laughed..." His voice caught. That much *was* true. He downed the rest of the sherry and asked Mr. Parker, "Can I answer any questions for you, sir?"

"No, I don't think I want to know any more. Thank you." He lapsed back into stony reserve.

Silence reined as they finished their drinks. Jonathan's emotions swirled. Had he said the right things to honor Robert—to comfort his folks? Did he do him justice? How did he come to be sitting here today, mourning the death of his best friend? Nothing was as it was supposed to be.

Senior said, "Caroline, I'm retiring for the evening. Would you join me, please?"

"In a minute, dear." She leaned toward Jonathan, eyes fastened on the last link to her fallen son.

"Please come to bed, Caroline." Senior nodded to Jonathan once more before leaving the room. When they'd gone, he poured himself another sherry and drained it, alone in the dark.

In the morning, no one mentioned Robert, although his unseen presence dominated everything. Parker House wasn't as well kept as Jonathan remembered it. At dinner the night before, Mr. Parker had alluded to how difficult things had become. The southern boycott was ruining his business. Jonathan thought back to Senior's request of Robert. The start of their rift.

After breakfast, Jonathan said, "If it's all right with you, Mrs. Parker, I'd like to go into the city." With Robert gone, he had to know if Barbra still cared. If anyone still cared about him. Didn't know why anyone would. He didn't much care for himself.

"Certainly, Jonathan. You must take the buggy."

As he rode away, he glanced back. She stood on the front veranda waving a white hanky with a hand to her mouth. She looked so lonely standing there by herself. Jonathan clip-clopped over the cobblestones toward town, lost in his regrets. So many—they were piling up like the dead in this war. He asked people where Mower Hospital was. After a series of twists and turns, he arrived in a part of the city called Chestnut Hill.

The building resembled a large wheel laid on its side with wards radiating out from the center like spokes. Buggies and wagons were drawn up in a front circle. People streamed in and out of the large off-white complex. Bandaged men hobbled silently about the grounds, or sat in rickety chairs, or stared from wooden benches. A dreary sky set the mood. Jonathan wanted to turn around and leave. Even if he could find her, what would he say? What could he? How could he make it right with her? He'd been so self-centered, ignoring her for so long. Hurrying by the wounded outside, he slowed as he passed through the main entrance. His eyes adjusted to the dim light while crowds of people hurried to and fro. Hard to tell who was who as there were few uniforms. He stopped the nearest person walking by.

"Do you work here?"

"Yassir."

"Do you know where can I find a nurse?" His heart pounded. He was here where Barbra was.

"Whut's wrong wit' you?" the man said.

"Nothing's wrong with me. I'm just looking for a nurse I know." Maybe he should look around on his own.

"Oh, then you gots to go find somebody with a white cock hat, they knows who's who 'round here."

"Thank you." Jonathan gazed around the teeming

front lobby.

Wounded men lay on stretchers, others sprawled on the dirty wooden floor. Midday heat poured through open doors and windows. A pervasive, fetid smell filled the air as if the odor was coming from the plaster walls and wooden floorboards themselves. Heat blended with the groans of the wounded and dying as the drama of life and death played out in front of him.

Everyone Jonathan saw wore the same blank expression, lips pursed as if to keep their worry from escaping. He was embarrassed to be among all this misery and pain, but his discomfort wasn't physical. Guilt dogged him as he moved among these valorous men. But he pressed on and stopped at a nearby table.

"Excuse me, ma'am, but I'm looking for someone. Could you help me? …Ma'am?"

Behind the small desk, a woman's head jerked up. She squinted at him. "What do you need, sir?"

"I don't need anything, I'm just trying to find someone."

"Who's that?" said the frazzled-looking woman as she shouted a request at another coworker. "Blast, I can't get anyone to help around here. What is it you want again?"

"Ma'am, I'm looking for a nurse named Barbra Carson. She's supposed to be working here."

"Son, do you see anyone around here who's not working?"

"No, ma'am, I don't. In fact, you look very busy yourself. Are things always this hectic?"

"Yes they are, Captain."

She thawed some as Jonathan talked with her. "What you'll need to do is visit the nursing stations in every ward. Heaven only knows where she might be. She might not even be here today, or she might have gotten moved closer to the fighting near Harper's Ferry. They do that, you know."

"Do what, ma'am?"

"Move doctors and nurses closer to battlefields after a big battle. Could be she's not even here."

"Yes, ma'am. Thank you anyway for your help." His heart fell to his feet. Was he going to miss her again?

"What did you say her name was?"

"Barbra Carson, she's in her early twenties, auburn hair, pretty as anything, has a wonderful way about her, and a smile that—"

"That describes a lot of the nurses here. I don't know her. Good luck."

"Thank you." Jonathan turned and took the first hallway he came to.

The ward consisted of a long open bay arrangement with cots full of wounded men in varying stages of distress, lined up next to each other by the walls. These men were all amputees, and there weren't enough beds. Some lay curled up shivering on the floor. Others had stubs for arms or were missing legs, most often amputated just above the knee. So many lifeless eyes, like whatever flicker of hope they had was gone with their limbs.

Jonathan tried not to stare when a one-legged soldier nearby propped himself up on his cot. "That's right, Captain. Take a good look. Ain't many who's been hit above the knee still here. Nurse said I'm one of the lucky few. Don't feel so lucky." Jonathan forced himself to maintain eye contact. "Damn minié balls.

They hit you, you'll die, unless it's an arm or a leg. Even then, your chances ain't good. If the bullet don't get you, gangrene likely will."

Jonathan shook the maimed soldier's hand. A large lump in his throat kept him from saying anything. His troubles weren't anything compared to what these men were facing. He walked through the wards, searching the faces of the ladies in white he passed. In the fourth ward, he got lucky.

"Oh, Barbra, yes, I know her," said the nurse. " She works on this ward but she's not due for several hours. Are you a friend?"

"Yes, an old friend. Do you know where I can find her?"

"Well, she's normally right here, except when the surgeons need her. She's so very good at helping the doctors, but I'm sure you already know that."

"Actually…I don't," Jonathan said.

The nurse gave him a strange look. "Well, I'm sorry, but she's not here yet."

Jonathan couldn't mask his disappointment. He just wanted to see her. His heart thumped in his chest. He'd come all this way…for nothing. Frustration and guilt sparred inside him along with some relief at not having to face her. He wanted to bolt. Instead, he pushed his gloom back. "Any idea when she might be in?"

"Like I said, maybe a couple of hours but I'm not sure. Sorry, Captain. Anything else I can help you with?"

"No thanks." He paused. "Yes…would you please tell her Jonathan stopped by?"

"That's all? Will she know you?"

"She used to…but I'm not sure she'd recognize me

now." He shook his head and headed toward the front entrance. As he maneuvered through the crowd, suddenly there she was, coming toward him.

He waved an arm wildly back and forth. "Barbra! Barbra!"

She broke into a wide smile. Jonathan pushed his way forward until he stood only a couple of steps in front of her. Just as he was about to say "hello," she threw her arms around him and hugged him hard. His body, stiff at first, relaxed and he held her back. She felt so good in his arms. Barbra pushed away to look at him. Green eyes bored into his soul. His ears warmed.

"Jonathan, what are you doing here? Are you hurt?"

"No, I'm okay." For the first time in a long while, he allowed himself a small smile. She was so pretty. He wanted to reach out and hold her again.

"Why are you here, then?"

Her directness threw him off. He'd been so intent on finding her, he hadn't thought about what he was going to say when he did. He gathered his wits about him. "I brought someone back here from a battle we were in together." An image of Robert lying on the battlefield flew through his head.

"Where is he? Maybe I can look after him."

"No, that's not what I mean." He paused. His sorrow surged, as if it had been just waiting, searching for a way out. "I mean...I brought his personal effects back to his parents here in town. Robert was my best friend...he went down at Antietam."

"I'm so sorry, Jonathan." She put a soft hand to his cheek. "I've heard awful stories about that battle. So you were there?"

Her touch was electric. He forced himself to focus on her. "Yes, but I was just riding back and forth carrying messages."

"Sounds like they could have gotten you, too."

"I wasn't in any real danger. I was lucky. Lots of our soldiers weren't, but you already know that from the look of things around here." The swirl around them disappeared. All he saw was Barbra and those beautiful eyes.

"There are so many here from Antietam," she said. "We're overflowing. Some don't last long. Every day we lose so many, but they're still grateful for whatever we're able do for them. Even the ones near death."

"All I know is they're lucky to have you to care for them. I always knew you'd be a wonderful nurse." Jonathan pushed his sadness back. Maybe this visit would turn out all right after all. He needed it to.

"Yes, but this wasn't how I thought it would be. I didn't think war would be this horrible, but I'm glad to be here, helping."

Jonathan started to say something just as another nurse called to Barbra.

"Barbra, we need you *now*, there's more wounded just came in. Most look like they'll end up on our ward, too."

Barbra frowned. "I'm so sorry, Jonathan. I'd like to stay and talk but I'm afraid I have to get back to work. Every minute counts with some of these soldiers."

"Sure…I understand." A lie. Before he could say goodbye, Barbra reached up and kissed him on the lips. His insides burned as he watched her hurry away down the hallway.

She stopped and looked back. "Be careful." There

was something else, but he couldn't hear what it was with all the commotion. Greeting people as she passed, she disappeared into the thick of the crowd.

How he wished she could have stayed. There was so much he needed her to forgive him for. His eyes filled. Had she really just been here? He gazed down the hall where she'd vanished—everything he wanted to say running through his head. All the things he wanted to tell her. The things he'd seen and done. To share all of that with her. To explain. Most of all, to apologize...to tell her he was sorry. Now, his chance had disappeared.

Emptiness claimed his soul as he realized he might not ever see her again.

Everything he once held dear seemed gone.

Chapter Twenty-Six

The visit also served to remind him of when he was a patient here a few months ago.

And the soldier he'd overheard.

And what he'd said about his family.

He made a last-minute decision to stop through Cincinnati on his way back to the army. Going home would get him some answers. He'd make his folks tell him what they'd been hiding. But as the train to Washington rattled on, doubts crept in. Questions swirled in his head that he couldn't, or didn't want to ask his parents—yet. Prying information out of Abel and Sarah was the next best thing. Surely, they'd know if there was a family secret. They'd tell him what he wanted to know. That way his heart wouldn't be laid bare in front of his folks. He thought back to the night he'd overheard his aunt and uncle talking in their living room. Was that what they were discussing? His family?

He'd telegraphed from Washington and asked them not to tell his parents he was coming. When he arrived in Cincinnati, Jonathan walked to their house in the dark and knocked on their door. As he took his coat off inside, Sarah blurted, "How did you find out?" Jonathan was at a loss for words. Before he could say anything, she said, "Did your folks tell you?"

Jonathan's mind raced. "About what?"

Her eyes grew big. "About your mother. We

thought that's why you came. Isn't it?"

"What about my mother?" What was it that everyone seemed to know but him? His aunt's face paled. From the looks of her, she'd likely tell him anything now.

"When we got your telegram we were sure...what did you think I meant?"

Abel jumped in. "That's enough, Sarah. Let Jonathan talk."

"What *about* her?" Jonathan's heart thumped. He wasn't sure he wanted to hear more but he couldn't up and leave now. His life was filled with too many regrets already.

Shock shone in her eyes. "You mean you don't know? Lord amighty. You really *don't*, do you?"

Jonathan squinted. "Tell me what I don't know, Aunt Sarah."

"It's...it's not my place to say." She looked toward her husband, stricken.

He stared at his uncle. "Then *you* tell me, Abel—what have my folks been hiding?"

Abel glared at Sarah. "Why'd you say anything? He didn't even know."

Jonathan raised his voice. "Tell me. I'm not leaving this house until you do. And I mean it!"

His uncle's shoulders slumped. "Jonathan, please sit down." When they were seated, Abel asked, "What do you know about your mother?"

"All I know is what she's said. That she's from a farm back east and her family's dead."

Abel and Sarah exchanged glances. His uncle pursed his lips. "Not exactly. The truth is—" He rubbed his forehead. "—when your mother was a young woman, she worked as a housekeeper for a wealthy family in Baltimore. Her family had a little farm outside of town, and they sent her to the city to be a maid when she was sixteen."

Jonathan interrupted, "Would their name be Billings? The soldier next to me in Mower Hospital was named Billings. He said his father and his aunt were from a small farm near Baltimore."

"Yes," Abel said, running his hand back and forth through thinning hair. "Billings."

Sarah leaned forward. "These were not nice people. They treated their staff very poorly. Their son was the only one who showed your mother any kindness. He was handsome and charming, smart and educated. Your mother had never met anyone like him."

Abel continued, "He got her in a...family way. As you can imagine, it was a scandal. His family was able to keep it secret, but they turned your mother out all the same."

Part of Jonathan didn't want to hear the rest, but he didn't stop them, his throat dry.

Sarah said, "On top of that, her family disowned her and she was on her own. A baby due and all. Your father, Tom Gray, had always loved your mother. He came from a farm not far from hers and they'd known each other since they were kids. He was a little older than she was. When he found out what had happened, he sought her out and asked her to marry him, knowing her...condition."

Jonathan's head spun. He pushed up out of his chair but didn't seem to be able to form a coherent thought. He wanted to yell and scream. Throw something. Bile rose in his throat. His whole life had been a lie! He sat with a *thunk* and rubbed a hand over his eyes.

"So, Tom married your mother and brought her to Ohio for a fresh start. Where no one knew them. A few years later, we moved here from Baltimore, too. I don't think your father was very happy to see us. I'm sure he worried you might find something out with us being here."

"Like he just *did*," Abel said, glaring at Sarah.

Jonathan stared at her. "She was pregnant with me, wasn't she?" He knew the answer before he asked the question.

"Yes...but your father has always considered you to be his own natural-born son."

Jonathan's ears rang. How could his mother keep such a secret from him? And Tom Gray. He wasn't even his father. That man had played an even bigger part in the charade.

He was adrift, alone in a boat with no oars. Wind howled and waves washed over him, but the dampness on his forehead was only his own beads of sweat. He was capsizing.

"Thank you for telling me. I...I just—" In his shame, he cast his eyes to the floor. He donned his coat without looking up. With a cheerless, "Thank you," he left, headed for the train station. Wasn't about to go home. He'd take the next one straight back to camp. No wonder he'd never gotten along with his father. He wasn't even blood kin. There was nothing of Tom Gray in him after all. Now it all made sense. Maybe that was best. And how could he call him father anymore?

When Jonathan returned, the Army of the Potomac was in mourning. The men had just fought the biggest, bloodiest battle ever on the North American continent, forced the enemy to retreat, and their commander had just been relieved. A gloom hung over the camp that matched Jonathan's mood.

He sat immobile in his tent. His whole world had spun out of control. His parents weren't even his parents, he hadn't been able to reconcile with Barbra, his best friend had just been killed, his commander fired. He couldn't remember when he'd last prayed to God to sustain him. He wondered if there was even a place in Heaven for someone like him.

He fell to his knees, clasped his hands together, and prayed. "My Lord, please forgive me my many shortcomings, my thoughtless behavior, my selfishness, and my pride. And come by my side now. Grant my soul some peace, Lord." He grabbed his Bible, sprawled on his cot, and slept the sleep of the dead.

****

Word was, with McClellan relieved, the staff was to be dispersed. Jonathan wasn't surprised when he was summoned a few days later. He rode to headquarters, wondering where he would be going.

General Marcy greeted him with his usual reassuring smile. "Jonathan, you are being reassigned to Major General Sherman's army. You are to take a troop train west to join Sherman near Memphis, where General Grant is getting ready to advance on Vicksburg, Mississippi."

Jonathan stood mute. He'd heard the words but hadn't taken them in.

"Do you understand, son?"

"Yes, sir." No.

Marcy draped an arm around Jonathan's shoulder.

He spoke as a father would to a son. "You have done a fine job for us here, Jonathan. The general thanks you for that. I thank you for that. Now, you hold your destiny in your hands. What becomes of you will be up to you." He added a cryptic, "Welcome to the fighting side of the army, son."

Jonathan took a step back. "Sir, yes, sir! Thank you for your guidance." He saluted, did an about face, and walked away into a haze of uncertainty.

Chapter Twenty-Seven

December 1862

Sherman.

From all Jonathan had heard, William Tecumseh Sherman was an irascible, hot-tempered redhead who seemed to want nothing more than to pick a fight with someone. With his fiery eyes and passionate behavior, he had the reputation of being a bit unbalanced. Although Jonathan hadn't known what to expect in a new assignment, he didn't expect Sherman. The posting almost felt like punishment for being associated with McClellan, now in disgrace among everyone except his troops. "Lost" wasn't a big enough description for how he felt.

Jonathan gathered his small bundle of worldly possessions and saddled his horse for the train station. He was joining Sherman, but no longer as a staff officer—he'd be infantry. Something he'd always thought he wanted. Now that it was staring him in the face, he wasn't sure anymore. As his train lumbered west, he dithered back and forth. Doubts about his ability to lead men tore at his confidence. All the anchors in his life that he'd cut loose over the years left him drifting.

The route would take him through Cincinnati. Should he visit? He hadn't been home in more than a year but as he thought about them, anger at his parents—mixed with guilt—surged within him. He decided to pass through without stopping.

When the train eased into the terminal, though, Jonathan found himself up and out of his seat—almost as if his legs had a mind of their own. As the cars belched to a stop, he stood in an open door. Stepping off, he scanned the platform for a contractor with a wagon or horse to rent, settling on an old gelding that looked like its hurrying days were over.

Jonathan strapped his brown haversack on and pulled his collar tighter against a winter wind that pummeled him. He rode east along the Ohio River, now tamed by winter, then turned north along hard dirt roads with barren trees he remembered from childhood. After three hours of encouraging his horse along, he came to the turnoff to the farm. He sat for a moment taking in the wintry surroundings and the dusky sky filled with early evening stars. Nudging the horse into a half trot, the old farmhouse soon came into view. Lazy gray smoke rose from the chimney against a darkening background. Even in the dim light, he could tell the place needed a coat of paint. Dull, faded gray. He guided the horse down the path toward the barn. After caring for his mount, he walked to the house.

His first visit home since he found out about his father.

And his mother.

And himself.

He eased the front door open. The whole family sat around the fireplace, singing. They looked at him like he was a ghost. Claire bounded off the floor and threw her arms around his waist.

"Jonathan!"

Peter charged him with a big smile. His father rose out of his chair.

His mother sat where she was. Immobile. She put her hands to her face and began to cry, softly at first, then with big sobs mingled with fat tears. Jonathan took her gently by the hands and lifted her out of the chair. He hugged her in a light embrace until she wrapped her arms around him in a tight bear hug. She wouldn't let go. When he finally extricated himself, he eyed everyone with a sheepish grin, humbled and embarrassed by their warm welcome. Tears clouded his vision. How poorly he'd treated his family. The prodigal son come home to a welcome he didn't deserve.

His father broke in with a hearty, "Good to see you, son!"

Claire bounced around the room laughing and Peter grinned at him. Jonathan slipped his coat off and his mother brought a hand to her mouth again. "You're so thin! Stay right there, I'll fix you something." She rushed to the kitchen.

"Come sit by the fire, son." Tom pulled another chair up.

Son? Jonathan stared at the man who'd masqueraded as his father. Memories flooded his senses. The tiny fireplace in the little living room that roared throughout winter. The small dining room sandwiched between it and the kitchen. The winter evenings he'd spent in front of the fire or by the cast iron stove in the kitchen, where his mother always kept a plate of cookies. When wintry nights were coldest, the oven doubled as a second fireplace. He'd taken his first breaths in this house.

When Claire was born, she was tinged bluish gray and struggled for breath. Tom wrapped her in a blanket, lit the oven, and placed her in a roasting pan on the open door until she pinked up.

Jonathan warmed his hands by the fireplace and fielded questions. Yes, he was fine, and, no, he couldn't stay long. Yes, he was still in the army, and, no, he wasn't with McClellan anymore. Yes, the bars meant he was a captain, and, no, the war wasn't near over. He told himself to be patient, his hands wrapped tight around a steaming mug of coffee his mother brought. How could he have ignored them like he'd done? The warm flush he felt wasn't from the fire.

He described where he'd been and some of what he'd been doing, with no embellishment or particular pride. He left out the parts about his injuries. And Robert's death. They didn't know Robert, and he didn't feel like sharing his friend with them yet. Maybe he never would. Bonds formed in war aren't something easily shared with people you haven't gone into battle with. Even family. He kept his conversation general in nature. Too soon to go any deeper.

Before long, it was Peter and Claire's bedtime. They hugged Jonathan then scurried out of the room. Scuffling noises on the stairs followed their exit.

Tom asked, "What are you doing here, son?"

"I'm on my way to Memphis to join General Sherman's army."

"Sherman, huh? You've been near Washington up to now, haven't you?"

"Yes. I was back in Virginia after a battle across the Potomac in Maryland."

"Antietam?"

Jonathan nodded. The man was still full of surprises. He responded with brief answers to Tom's questions, his insides at war. The man wasn't really his father, but he was the only father he'd ever known. His mother sat with an arm around him, staring up as if examining him for bedbugs, oblivious to what he was saying, and never taking her eyes off him. The room seemed smaller than he remembered.

"Please excuse me, but I'm a little tired. Is there somewhere I can sleep?"

Belinda snapped out of her reverie. "Of course. You'll have your brother's room tonight, I'll just go tidy it up." She headed for the stairs where she found the children spying. Claire jumped up and ran to her room giggling. When Belinda told Peter he'd be sleeping with his sister tonight, disappointment framed his brother's face.

In the morning, Jonathan was up almost as early as Tom. Out of habit, he threw on an old cloak and poured a cup of hot coffee. He started to leave to gather eggs in the chicken coop but Peter stopped him with, "My job now." Tom was already at the barn milking one of the dairy cows when he got there. Jonathan took a stool. They worked in silent rhythm, Jonathan's fingers cramping some.

Tom asked about the fighting he'd seen.

"I reckon I haven't been around as much as most," Jonathan said. "Spent nearly all my time in safer areas behind the front lines." Tom had told Jonathan since childhood that his life was the Lord's province.

Tom grunted. "So, how's the war going? We don't hear much around here. I only get to read the papers every now and then."

He was surprised at Tom's interest, being a pacifist. Jonathan paused. "Hard to say. I'm not sure I rightly know." The closer he was to the fighting, the less Jonathan seemed to know about how the war itself was playing out. Ironic.

"How long you gonna be with us?"

"Have to leave tomorrow." A bit of wistfulness hit him. When would he be back? Would he ever?

"Too bad." Pause. "You know, I've heard about Sherman some. I've also heard he might be a little off."

"Don't know. Guess I'll find out." Jonathan had heard the same thing.

"He's an Ohio boy, so he can't be too bad. From somewhere north of here, around Columbus."

"Didn't know that." His father always seemed to know more than he ever let on.

As Jonathan finished the morning tasks, Tom asked him to take a ride. "Let's don't take the wagon; let's just saddle a couple of horses." Jonathan glanced sideways at the man. It was unusual for him to attend to anything besides chores before breakfast.

"Belle looks like she's still in good shape," Jonathan said. He had her bridled and saddled in no time. They were up in the stirrups trotting as the sun peeked over the horizon. A well-worn dirt path wound between the pasture and the orchard. As he passed the bare fruit trees, Jonathan's thoughts drifted. He and Sonny would jump for apples dangling from the lowest limbs then shinny up the tree trunks. They'd grab one or two on the way and sit in the crook of a limb. Not all the apples got eaten though. Some were so tart, their mouths almost puckered shut at the first bite. They saved these to heave at the bull in the pasture below. They could never throw far enough to hit him, but it wasn't the hitting that was the most fun, it was the throwing.

Everything was a dormant brown. The morning wind whistled through Jonathan's light clothing. He drew gloves on, wondering where they were going. Not far ahead, the land rose to a round, piney hilltop. He'd been out here a few times as a child but it was a long way for a young boy's short legs.

They started up the rise. Tom said, "Look around, son," as if there was something in particular to see. They crested the small hill ringed with evergreens. A wintry landscape spread before them. "I figure this would be as good as spot as any and better'n most."

"What for?" He couldn't remember anything special out here.

"For you and your family."

"For me? Not sure what you mean."

"I been thinkin' about buildin' a new house here when you're back from this damn war. Make it big enough for you and a wife and kids when they come. Maybe Barbra?"

Jonathan smiled at the thought in spite of himself. He sat for a moment taking it all in. "It's a pretty spot, all right." He took a deep breath. "But I don't think I'm coming back here after the war's over." Didn't the man already know that? Still, his stomach churned at the thought of how Tom would react. And how did he even remember Barbra?

"I reckoned you'd take the farm over when I get too old to handle it."

He took his time before responding. "I appreciate

that, but I'm not planning on living here." Never had. And he was having trouble thinking of the man as his father. Why was he feeling like a little kid again?

The vein on Tom's neck pulsed. For a moment, Jonathan thought he was about to launch into a lecture, but instead, he sat silently. Then, "Well…this will give you a reason to come back, and something to think about as you figure out what you want to do."

They rode back to the farmhouse amid a few forced words that didn't knock the tension back. By the time he reached the barn, Jonathan was almost warm. He was surprised Tom seemed to take the news fairly well. A change. After unsaddling the horses and rubbing them down, they headed to the house. Jonathan spent the rest of the day helping his mother inside, playing games with his brother and sister by the fireplace, gazing now and then in the direction of Barbra's farm.

That evening Belinda prepared a special dinner. They didn't normally have fresh food this time of year, but she went all out with what she did have. Jonathan especially appreciated the canned beans she served. They were a treat, as army fare was long on potatoes and short on greens. After dinner, they gathered around the fireplace and sang the night away. There used to be a small piano, but when he asked about it, his mother said they didn't have it anymore. Didn't say why.

He silently scolded himself. If he ever got paid, he'd send money home.

The next morning Jonathan took his time saying goodbye. He hugged Claire and shook hands with Peter before hugging him, too. Tom grasped his hand and laid his other hand on Jonathan's arm. Jonathan thought about hugging him but didn't. Just couldn't. Maybe wouldn't ever again.

He hugged his mother though—not that he had much choice. Before he could give her a goodbye kiss, she wrapped her arms around him. As she slowly released him, she looked up. "You be careful, Jonathan. We'll see you again soon. I'm sure of it." Tears ran down her cheeks. She let them fall, not bothering to wipe them away.

"I'm sure of it too, Mother." His eyes filled and he pursed his lips.

Tom gathered the family around Jonathan. While they held hands, Tom prayed over him. "Lord God, please continue to protect our Jonathan and return him safely to us when this damn war is over. Pardon my language, Lord."

He promised to write, then was off to the train terminal and the way west. As the forested seven hills of Cincinnati receded in the distance, he wondered when—or if—he would ever see them again.

Chapter Twenty-Eight

December 1862

Winding south across the Ohio River, Jonathan's train chugged west to Louisville. There, it angled down to Nashville before turning west for Memphis. The wooded rolling hills of Tennessee reminded him of home. Maples and oaks were barren, but clusters of evergreens still spread a light emerald blanket to the horizon.

The troop train overflowed with soldiers, most so very young. Clean blue uniforms. Their wide eyes darted around the car, a dead giveaway that few had ever faced the enemy. Enlisted stood while officers sat. As the miles clattered by, Jonathan's thoughts drifted to his family. The visit had been far too short. He'd get back again. Soon, he hoped.

As the December landscape rattled by, he wandered back to snippets of childhood winters. Toward Christmas, the family would hang bells on horses' harnesses, then bundle up for frosty wagon rides in the early evening. They'd feast on canned goods his mother put up earlier that fall. Pickled beets were his favorite. He'd ride with his father to cut an evergreen down and fashion boughs for the mantle. He even missed the cold morning chores.

Jonathan thought about the man he'd always called

father. Did he really know him? Bottled up feelings resurfaced. Sentiments he hadn't sorted out yet. Would he ever?

The train rocked along, almost in a rhythmic manner over the iron rails. Hard to believe he was headed west to join another army. What would his new unit be like? He lifted a quiet prayer. "Lord, please let me fit in." He'd never led men before, aside from that short foray into western Virginia that didn't really count.

As the train travelled the last leg to Memphis, someone called his name.

"Lieutenant Gray! Lieutenant Gray!"

He turned. A sergeant maneuvered toward him through the crowded car.

"Lieutenant."

He didn't remember the sergeant but the soldier apparently knew him.

"I thought that was you, sir."

Jonathan rose slowly and stood mute.

"Oh...sorry, sir, I didn't know you'd been promoted to captain. Congratulations."

"Excuse me, Sergeant, but I don't—"

"You goin' to join Sherman too, sir?"

"Yes...I am." Where did the man know him from?

"Me too. I heerd it's different than our old outfit."

Who was this?

"You don't remember me, do you, sir?"

"No, I'm afraid not."

"Hey, that's okay. I'm Staff Sergeant August Hargrove. I was on General Mac's quartermaster staff. With you."

"Um, Sergeant Hargrove. I remember you now."

He didn't.

"Boy, that was an outfit, wasn't it, sir?"

"Yes, it was. How did you get assigned to Sherman?"

"Same way you did. Guess they wanted to clean us out."

"Why, what did you hear?" Jonathan thought he knew what Hargrove was about to say.

"Well I heerd tell that Washington told the new commander to scatter the general's staff, and so here we are." Wide smile.

"Why would Washington care about breaking up General McClellan's staff after they fired him?" He wanted to hear the scuttlebutt.

"Ain't you heerd what they're saying about the general?"

Jonathan had heard some whispers, but still said, "What's that?"

"Well I been runnin' into these soldiers on the way out here and we get to talkin' 'cause I like to talk. When they find out I was with McClellan, they either start laughin' or poking their finger in my chest tellin' me what they think of him."

"I take it they don't think much of him, right?" A reflection of his own thoughts now.

"Right as rain, sir."

How times had changed. "What does anybody have against him?"

"From what I hear tell, they think McClellan is a traitor."

"But that's not true." The man was far too cautious, but he wasn't a traitor.

"Well, it was all over the papers back east. Some of

these writers and politicians thought the general was trying to make peace with the South. That mebbe he was even going to march on Washington."

"Where would an idea like that get started?" Jonathan knew exactly where it got started. He was afraid this might happen. Secrets had a way of worming their way into the light of day.

"Don't know, and don't matter if it's true or not; only matters if people pay it any mind. Seems like a lot of people are."

Jonathan scowled. "We need to stop that kind of talk when we hear it, Sergeant Hargrove."

"Reckon we got our work cut out for us then, sir."

He and Hargrove stood squeezed between two beefy corporals. Jonathan glanced around the car. Soldiers listened with silent contempt on their faces.

"I'm just telling you, sir, that's what I've been runnin' into. Don't know if you will or not."

Jonathan rode the rest of the way in silence. As the train neared Memphis, he pulled out paper and pen to write Barbra for the first time in—he couldn't remember when. He wanted to start the letter with "Dear Lizzie" but didn't feel like he had the right to anymore.

Dear Barbra,

I was so glad to see you at the Hospital, even if it was only for a few minutes. I didn't get to share something with you that's been weighing heavy on my heart. I need to apologize for ignoring you the last couple of years. I've done some bad things, things I'm not proud of, and I hope you have it in your heart to forgive me.

Please.

It would mean so much.
Jonathan

He didn't share what he'd found out about his parents. Still too raw. At Memphis, he addressed the letter to Barbra at Mower Hospital and hoped it would find its way to her.

Uncertainty reigned when Jonathan arrived at Sherman's headquarters. Word around camp was the commanding general was on a leave of absence due to "stress." Some said Sherman had been relieved of command. Some said he was crazy. The few articles Jonathan had read assailed Sherman for what they called his erratic behavior. But they also said he was bold, rash, quick. General Grant's strong right arm. The men called him "Uncle Billy." Apparently, they liked and respected him. Sounded a little like McClellan.

Grant commanded the largest western army, the Army of the Tennessee. His scattered forces were converging south of Memphis, preparing for a push against Vicksburg, the biggest Confederate city in the West. On the Mississippi.

When Sherman returned, Jonathan watched him ride by for the first time. Not even an escort. The general was short like McClellan, but unlike McClellan, he apparently didn't care a hoot about his appearance. Scruffy, soiled uniform, short stogie stuffed in his mouth. Wild, uncombed hair that gave the impression he was a bit off kilter. Intense, penetrating eyes, even from a distance.

Jonathan was assigned to Sherman's XV Corps. He didn't know much about XV but they had a reputation for toughness. His regiment was the 76th Ohio, and within the 76th, he was deputy commander of C

Company, one of the regiment's ten companies. Although Jonathan had the rank to command the company, his regimental commander, Colonel Austin Hays, thought he needed some experience first. Fine by him.

"Welcome to the 76th, Captain."

"Thank you, Colonel Hays." Jonathan stood at attention. The colonel's tent was well ordered. Papers just so on his desk. Books lined up by height.

"Coming to us from the East, right? McClellan?" Hays paused, as if he were chewing on something sour. "Tell me a little about your duties with the general."

"Yes, sir. I was part of the Quartermaster Corps at first, sir. Then the general made me one of his couriers and I also handled the press. Later...I was his junior aide."

"Any infantry?"

"No, sir."

Hays leaned over and spit tobacco juice into his brass spittoon. "What did you think of General McClellan?"

It was such a direct question, it threw Jonathan off. He chose his words with care. "Sir, General McClellan had the respect and admiration of his men."

Hays stared at Jonathan a long moment. "I'm sure he did, Captain. That'll be all."

Hays had made it clear without saying so that he didn't think much of McClellan and by association, him as well. As he left Hays' tent, someone called to him.

"Captain Gray. Oh, sir, might I have a moment?" He recognized First Sergeant Owens, C Company's top enlisted soldier. A big man who was hard to miss.

"Yes, Sergeant Owens?"

Owens' thick reddish eyebrows arched. "Sir, that's *First Sergeant* Owens."

"Sorry, my mistake, Serg—I mean First Sergeant." Not off to a good start.

"Sir, officers never say 'sorry' to enlisted men. Welcome to C Company, the fightingest company hereabouts."

"Than—er—very good, First Sergeant." What did Owens want?

"Sir, if you have any questions about the troops, just let me know. You can go to the commander, Captain Thompson, for everything else. All right, sir?"

Jonathan squinted. What? He had to go through Owens? He paused. "Fine, I'll let you know if I need anything, First Sergeant."

"Good. I'll be getting back to the men, sir. Call on me if I can do anything for you." Owens saluted and walked off, yelling for his platoon sergeants.

Jonathan stared at Owens' retreating back. Who did he think he was? An image of Colonel Hays spitting into the spittoon appeared.

The men of C Company were a hard lot, having proven themselves in hard combat at places like Shiloh over the last year and a half. It quickly became clear they had no use for Jonathan and they let him know it. Casual, half-salutes as they passed. Glancing contact. He thought back to what Sergeant Hargrove said. The taint of McClellan must still cover him.

****

C Company marched to Chickasaw Bluffs, just north of Vicksburg. Jonathan tried to prepare for his first action, but wasn't sure how to. As the men formed, Captain Thompson gave the order to advance at the rout step. Jonathan moved forward toward rocky heights, over forested terrain that was dangerous, dark, and dense. Turns out there weren't any reliable maps of this mossy-treed, humid swamp. He slogged blindly ahead into fetid bogs that wound around clumps of strange-looking trees.

As he climbed out of the swamp, Jonathan toiled through soggy terrain. Thick, brown southern mud seeped into his boots. Branches pulled at his uniform. Black flies stung him. He shadowed the company commander. The men held Captain Harry Thompson in high regard. Thompson came from a modest background but had a straightforward way about him the men responded to. He'd been elected commander when the regiment was still a volunteer outfit.

He turned to Jonathan as they pushed forward. "Stay close. Watch, listen, learn."

At first, only an occasional artillery shell thudded nearby. As they advanced, canister sounded from cannons commanding the heights ahead. Soon, whistling minié balls sliced the air as enemy skirmishers made their presence known. Units became separated, fronts disappeared. Jonathan turned just as the corporal next to him dropped like a stone. He reached to cradle the man's head, felt the wetness on his hand and drew it back. Bloody, pinkish. The man lay with sightless eyes. Jonathan gagged as he covered the soldier with his coat. Robert.

Still, blue-clad bodies dotted the upslope ahead. Jonathan stayed low as he climbed out from the thick, choking smoke at the bottom of the barren hill. A private went down as he sprinted to a rock formation ahead. He yelled for help. Thompson dashed forward.

Thompson grabbed the private by the arm and was hit in the leg. Another soldier raced from behind a rock and made it to his downed mates. He put a hand to the private's neck, then hoisted Thompson up to a crouch. They zigzagged back under covering fire. Jonathan had seen firsthand why the men respected Thompson the way they did.

The first sergeant made Thompson sit on a rock while he tended to his leg. "Sir, the bullet's taken a nice little chunk out of your calf, so I'd suggest—"

"I'm staying on the field, First Sergeant. Dress it as best you can. Let's get off this flat ground and up that rise." He grimaced as Owens tightened a bandana around his leg. "Ready the men."

The advance started well, but slowed as enemy fire grew hotter, then forced a halt altogether. Thompson yelled, "Take cover!"

The earth shook as artillerists above weighed in. *Boom, Boom, Boom* echoed all around them.

Jonathan squinted at the heights from behind a small rock. How could they possibly scale that? He kept his thoughts to himself as he sheltered.

Thompson waved his sidearm high. "Fall back!"

Jonathan crept away from his cover, at first backtracking from the enemy and firing, then sprinting headlong down the hill. At the bottom, with his hands on his knees, his heart thumped like he was still sprinting. Had he measured up? He'd seen Thompson's leadership firsthand, saw the respect the men had for him. In the aftermath of this advance, the brutality of war struck him hard. He'd been part of gruesome engagements before—mostly from an antiseptic distance—but here he was in the midst of the fighting.

Dried blood covered his hands and uniform. He unlaced his boots, made a pillow out of his bedroll, and laid down. His heartbeat slowed. Despite the ringing in his ears, he drifted off to sleep. Someone shook him awake.

"Sir, it's time for us to head back and rejoin the rest of the regiment."

He stared up at August Hargrove. "Sergeant Hargrove. What're you doing here?"

"I'm in the seventy-sixth too, sir, just not your company. I'm with Bravo. We saw you all take it pretty bad up that hill. They kept us down here to plug holes in the lines. Saw you hightailin' it our way. Sorry we couldn't help you none."

Jonathan glanced around. Charlie Company was gone. "I'll head back with you." He shook his head. They'd let him sleep while they moved off. Anger and embarrassment surged.

They crossed two bogs before Hargrove pointed in the distance. "There's your outfit, sir. I'll be gettin' back to mine now. Sir."

Jonathan returned Hargrove's salute and headed toward the white flag with the big red C. The rest of the company milled around it.

"Where've you been?" asked Thompson. "We're ordered back to the Yazoo and I'm not sure what's next."

Jonathan wanted to ask why they left him but let it pass. Still, he knew he wasn't the only member of the company who'd taken advantage of a few minutes' rest to grab some sleep. "I'm here now, sir. What would you like me to do?"

"Just follow me and don't get lost again." Jonathan wanted to look around to see if anyone else had heard the rebuke, but didn't. Damn! Thompson limped off. The regiment moved back the way they'd come that morning, over swampy terrain that only frogs and flies could find attractive.

Thompson had been dead calm during battle. So had the rest of C Company. This was the nature of the soldiers Jonathan joined and they'd let him know—just as if they'd shouted it—he didn't belong.

He'd never measure up to Thompson.

After dinner, the commander called Jonathan over. "Captain Gray, come sit with me, please." The two sat on a fallen log under an overcast evening sky a short distance away from the campsite. Feeble warmth radiated from a sorry excuse for a campfire. A chill ran up Jonathan's back.

"You're not fitting in, Gray. You're smart enough to know that."

"Yes, sir, it doesn't feel like I am. It seems—"

Thompson cut him off. "Give the men time. Give us all time. This is a tight-knit group. We've formed deep ties with each other. You're an outsider to the men, but I need you to start earning their respect. This company needs you to step up and take your place alongside us. Right now, that's your job. Work on it and you'll be fine. That's all." Thompson looked away and lifted a tin coffee cup to his mouth.

The meeting, such as it was, was over. As he walked back to his tent, Jonathan prayed in the darkness, "Lord, please guide my way. I will leave this in Your hands."

He was drained. Disconnected thoughts flew through his mind. Barbra. Measuring up. Robert. War's senselessness. Reaching in his duffel for his Bible, he found the stack of Barbra's unopened letters he'd stuffed in there another lifetime ago. His vision blurred as he read them one by one. He reached for paper and pen but still couldn't call her Lizzie. He'd surely squandered that privilege. She hadn't replied to his last letter, but then, where would she have sent one?

Dear Barbra,

I hope this finds you well. I'm with my new outfit in General Sherman's army. We're moving against Vicksburg, Mississippi, a big Confederate city on the Mississippi River. It's even bigger than the Ohio. I'm trying to fit in but the men in my company don't seem to like me. I don't know how to change that.

Something else has happened that I haven't told you about. It's my parents. They've been hiding a secret from me for years. Turns out my father's not my father!

His pen strokes almost punched through the paper.

He's just someone who married my mother when she was pregnant with me. All my life, they let me believe he was my father. Every day I seem to feel angrier and angrier. And hollow at the same time.

I used to think I knew who I was.

I have to go, but I'd sure like to hear from you. I surely would.

Please.

Jonathan

Jonathan had never opened up like that before to her or anyone else. He wrote Barbra's name and the same simple address, Mower Hospital, on the envelope and gave it to the company clerk. In his tent he slumped on his cot, dealing with one of the hardest days of his life. As if by themselves, his hands came together. He

fell to his knees and prayed for peace. For the country.
And himself.

Chapter Twenty-Nine

Winter 1862-1863

Captain Thompson pulled Jonathan aside. "You will handle this action."

"You mean lead the company?"

"Yes."

XV Corps was ordered up against Fort Hindman, an enemy garrison upriver from where the Arkansas joined the Mississippi.

"I'm not sure I'm ready to lead the men yet. I don't think I know what needs to be done."

Thompson squinted. "Then that puts you squarely in the ranks of most company commanders. Listen to regimental staff. Do what they tell you until they tell you different. Right now they told us to be here, ready to advance on the fort." He raised an eyebrow. "Can you handle that?"

"Yes, sir." Could he?

"One more thing, Captain. Take heed of what the sergeants tell you."

"Yes, sir."

Jonathan sent the company clerk in search of his platoon leaders. He guessed this was either Thompson's way of teaching him how to lead the men or throwing him to the wolves. Right now he wasn't sure which, but that was secondary to getting ready to fight.

Company leadership gathered around. He wasn't sure what to say. "So, I'll be in charge today, men." No reaction. "Uh, most of you don't know me. I'm Captain Gray and I came from back east. I've only been here for…" He stopped. What the hell was he saying? Just tell them what the orders are. "We are to be ready to attack today, when the order's given." That sounded so dimwitted. Of course, when the order's given. "So, be ready to move. On my command. Any questions?"

Expressionless stares.

"Uh…that's all, then." He stared at the backs of the men as they moved off. What kind of a briefing was that? They must think he's an idiot. He was an idiot.

As they staged at a distance from the fort, the hours dragged by, punctuated by never-ending artillery shells arcing overhead both directions. The order to advance came midafternoon as the defenders fell back into the fort's low structure. Jonathan led the men forward, rifles at the ready, marching in rout step. The stronghold, ringed by formidable earthwork battlements, loomed on a grassy plain ahead. As they neared, grape shot tore holes in their lines. Screams mixed with the *zing* of small arms fire.

Jonathan yelled, "Advance at the double quick!" The men ran to get underneath a hail of fire. They wavered as they took casualties under the command of someone with almost no combat experience. Jonathan ran in a crouch along his lines encouraging the men to stand fast. His "Hold! Hold!" was swallowed by the constant roar of battle.

They stared at him—doubt flickering in their eyes as they hunkered down behind whatever protection they could. After almost two hours of exchanging fire, the men were still sulking under cover when white flags appeared on the battlements.

Jonathan's heart raced twice as fast as normal. He couldn't catch his breath. Where was Thompson? He wondered if he'd done all right—if he'd embarrassed himself.

****

After the skirmish at Hindman, C Company went into winter camp. A tense mood permeated the men and an undercurrent of disrespect flowed his way. He didn't know what to do about it.

He approached Thompson. "Sir, have I done something to offend the men?"

"Just a natural reaction to a new officer, Gray. Guess they still associate you with McClellan."

Sounded like Thompson did, too.

He stared at Jonathan. "Anything else?"

"No, sir."

During the malaise of winter camp, he got his first letter from Barbra in over a year. From the date, it had taken more than a month to find him. He tore it open.

Dear Jonathan,

I so appreciated getting your letter. Thank you for the apology, I needed to hear that from you. We've all done things we're not proud of. You need to forgive yourself as much as anything. I'm not sure where you are, so I addressed this to you at General Sherman's army. I hope you are well. I'm still here at Mower, helping the wounded. More and more arrive every day. Will this war never end?

Please be safe.

Barbra

Jonathan folded the letter with care. Instead of in

the trunk by his cot, he put it inside his uniform blouse. Any way to keep her close.

He'd seen men garrisoning in a dreary winter camp before. McClellan's were filled with combat veterans with no more to do than busy work. Endless firewood details. Sickness. Wounds that wouldn't heal. Teeth so bad soldiers were relieved when they fell out. Cold tents and wet socks that never dried out. A steady diet heavy on beans and bread that did its part in bringing the men's spirits down further.

The men's contempt for Jonathan continued, especially from one of his platoon sergeants, Henry French. Jonathan had to work with French, so it was hard to ignore his disrespect. Nothing Jonathan did worked with this man. Not professionalism, not taking him into his counsel, not ignoring him.

Things came to a head when Jonathan overheard French talking loudly in his tent. "Don't know why the commander keeps that pretend captain around. He ain't nothin' but extra baggage. Gonna get us killed."

Jonathan had had enough. Instinct took over from reason. He yelled, "French, get out here!" The sergeant glowered as he came out of his makeshift shelter. Jonathan dropped any pretense of decorum. "Follow me. Now!" Jonathan stomped to a secluded spot in the piney woods out of sight and sound of the men. He practically ripped his uniform top off in the cold.

French glared down at Jonathan. "What're you doin'?" No "sir" with it.

Jonathan ignored the question. "I don't know why you hate me so much, but I'm through putting up with your crap."

The sergeant squinted.

"It's just you and me now, French. No rank, no nothin', just you and me, so let's go." He raised his arms and balled his fists, looking up at the big man.

French's eyes widened. A quizzical look spread over his face.

"Put 'em up, you bastard!" Jonathan was in a fury, his ears pounding with every heartbeat.

All the starch went out of French. He opened his palms and kept his arms at his sides.

Jonathan yelled, "Fight, you yellow dog! It's just the two of us. This never happened, so no punishment, no rules. Man to man."

French pursed his lips. "Uh…I don't know what you're talking about…sir. I've never had a problem with you."

Jonathan leaned forward, inches away from the sergeant's face. The man was lying through his teeth. "Bullshit! You've been on my ass ever since I got here. Here's your chance to take me down, face to face."

French brought his hands up, palms still open, facing toward Jonathan. "No, sir, I never meant…no harm." His voice trailed away.

Jonathan saw red. "The hell you didn't. You either fight me here and now or I'll make you a by-God solemn promise. If I ever hear *any* more crap about me, I'll come and kick your ass, and this time I won't drag you away from everyone. I don't care if it didn't come from you, I'm coming for you, personally. Understand?"

The sergeant nodded a quick, "Yes, sir!"

"Don't 'sir' me! It's just you and me here. No captain. No sergeant."

"Yessir!"

Jonathan glared at a bewildered-looking French for another moment, then grabbed a rock and hurled it out of sight. He swept his shirt up and stormed back to camp, leaving the sergeant standing there alone.

Jonathan never heard French utter a bad word about him again. French even began to seek Jonathan out on problems that rear their heads in any military camp—issues that arise from too much pent-up energy and time. Jonathan knew he still had a lot to prove to the other men, though, who clearly still regarded him with skepticism.

He was surprised at how cold southern winters were. The men were fighting a losing battle to stay warm, even in Mississippi. Buttoning up coats and stomping feet did little to overcome threadbare blankets and holey mittens. Flimsy tents of canvas, wood, and cotton were easy pickings for the raw winter wind. Worn, dirty uniforms cracked as men donned them in the morning's chill. At meals, soldiers hunched over plates of never-warm food to shelter them from constant cold gusts.

As winter slowly lost its grudging grip, Jonathan heard a knock on his front tent pole. First Sergeant Owens said in a booming voice, "Sir, the commander's called a meeting."

"Thank you, First Sergeant. I'll be—" but Owens was already walking away.

Thompson said, "Gather 'round, men. We're to march south tomorrow, then our navy will ferry us across the Mississippi. Finally, we'll be out of this damn swamp. Once across, we'll head northwest for Vicksburg. Get your men and your gear ready to move out."

Jonathan was glad to be leaving this sodden camp but had a bad feeling about the coming campaign. He wrote Barbra as he sat in his tent. "Lizzie" felt a little more comfortable this time.

Dear Lizzie,

Thank you for writing back, it meant so much when I seem to have so little. I mean of the important things in life, like self-respect.

I can't understand why my mother hid the truth from me. She should have told me, not let me find out from someone else. And my father. Who's my father? The one I never knew or the one I know but don't understand?

I wish you were here to help me sort things out. The only times I think about you are day and night. I hope this letter reaches you and I hope to see you again sometime. Soon.

Write please.

Jonathan

Chapter Thirty

Grant's behemoth was across the Mississippi after months of trying. Marching north, the troops brushed aside a Confederate assault at Jackson, Mississippi, east of Vicksburg. Grant pivoted his army west toward the Confederate citadel, hounding a retreating enemy. As they neared the rocky fortress, C Company prepared to attack over ragged, choppy earth while defenders rained deadly fire from high bluffs. The company hugged the very ground, pinned down by another earthwork-hidden enemy.

Jonathan shadowed Captain Thompson, whose "Charge!" echoed through the ranks. C Company double quicked up the incline to their front. Heads low, dodging shell and shot. Round after enemy round poured into the company's advancing ranks. Minié balls flew through clouds of thick smoke that obscured Jonathan's vision.

He heard the bullet thud into Thompson. The captain grabbed at his neck and crumpled to the ground. Jonathan shouted, "Medic!" and knelt by the commander. No! His throat tightened as he stared. Robert's pale face flickered in his head. Thompson's neck lay ripped open. Blood spurted from a gaping wound. A crimson circle widened on the grass around his head. Jonathan pressed his hand over the gash to try to stop the bleeding.

Thompson grasped Jonathan by the collar. Pulled him close. "Gray...take...care of...my men."

Jonathan nodded, unable to speak.

"They're your...men...now." Thompson's eyes grew distant. They rolled back almost white. The gushing stopped.

The first sergeant checked for a pulse. He paused for a moment, then pressed his hat against his chest. "Shit!" He turned slowly to Jonathan. "He's done for, sir. You've got to make the best of a bad situation now." He raised his eyes to the heavens and crossed himself. "Lord, help us."

Jonathan backed away. That can't have just happened. Thompson can't be gone. But the battle still raged, nonetheless.

Owens yelled, "Sir! What are your orders? Sir!"

"What?" His head spun.

"We need to continue the attack. Those are our orders."

"Yes...First Sergeant. Of course." Jonathan windmilled for the platoon leaders to join him. As they circled around and crouched, they kept a wary eye out for rebel infantry. The men stared at their commander, a small red C Company bandana covering his face. That incriminating dark patch of still-wet dirt. Jonathan had a detail move him to a sheltered spot farther down the slope. As word spread, more and more men angled back Jonathan's way.

The shock of Thompson's death shook him, but he stood and said, "Men, nothing's changed. Captain Thompson ordered us to take that hill and drive the enemy from their entrenchments. That's what we're going to do." Jonathan grabbed the guidon bearer by the arm. "Private, shake this flag for all it's worth. Get up that hill. On the double!" Amid a cacophony of death and destruction, C Company renewed the advance. Jonathan dashed up the slope, yelling, "Charge!"

The higher they went, the hotter the fire and the more casualties the company suffered. When they couldn't advance farther into the withering onslaught, Jonathan motioned for the men to take cover. Shelling and small arms fire continued throughout the morning and into the stifling afternoon. Bullets pinged off Jonathan's rocky cover. Smoke colored the air gray.

The Mississippi spring day was heavy with humidity and C Company suffered under a hot sun with parched throats. Scattered fires blazed. Black, biting flies stung. At dusk, the firing finally died away. Jonathan ordered the men to fall back. Blue-clad bodies littered the field, but Jonathan had just one soldier in mind. He ordered a squad to find Thompson in the dim light. When they recovered him back to their line, one of his new lieutenants stared at the body. "Looks like he's sleepin', 'ceptin' for that big hole in his neck."

Jonathan glared at him.

The lieutenant said, "So, Cap'n Gray, you're in command now?"

"I am until someone with more rank tells me different."

"Well…okay, sir, what do we do next?"

"We wait. We wait right here."

The next two days were spent preparing for a second general assault on Vicksburg. Jonathan sensed the company's loyalties were still divided. Some accepted him as a matter of course, while others didn't trust him for any number of imaginary reasons.

Fortunately, Jonathan had inherited a demanding first sergeant. Rupert Owens was a no-nonsense noncom who treated the men as his personal property and kept officers out of his business. Owens sat in, uninvited, at every officer staff meeting Jonathan called. He had a flippant way about him, but he could get the men to do what Jonathan wanted, so he gave Owens some leeway. All that really mattered was that C Company had confidence in him. It was clear Owens knew the business of combat. It was also clear to Jonathan the men looked to Owens more than their new commander.

Jonathan's relationship with the first sergeant evolved as he got to know Owens' mannerisms. He wasn't put off by Owens' brash ways, though. Owens had accepted Jonathan immediately after Thompson's death. He stood no chance with the men, and the company stood no chance of success in battle, if the first sergeant turned his back on Jonathan. If the commander didn't succeed, the company didn't succeed. So Jonathan had been gifted with a first sergeant who would do everything in his power to ensure C Company's success.

Jonathan didn't know how to ready the men for another major assault, so he let Owens handle the planning. The senior NCOs all looked to Owens for direction, anyway. The lieutenants just stayed away to avoid embarrassment. The next attack promised to be as difficult as the last, but Jonathan was confident his battle-tested veterans, regardless of what they thought of him, would perform well.

Thompson's words echoed in his head. *Listen to your sergeants.*

Mail call usually came and went with nothing, but today Jonathan got a letter from Barbra. He carried it back to his tent as if it were breakable, then carefully opened it.

Dear Jonathan,

Thank you for writing. I look forward to your letters so. I sympathize with the anger you're feeling toward your parents. I do. But I marvel at the nobility of what your father did. Your father's compassion is a wonderful example of God's grace. I cannot imagine any greater love than the love a parent has for a child. Your father rescued your mother when no one else cared about her. His love gave your mother a future when she had none, and gave a sense of belonging to a young boy who had to grow up too fast. It's a wonderful love story and you are the good man you are because of their love.

I must go now, please stay safe and write me! I so love hearing from you.

Yours,

Barbra

The words blurred. His tears fell freely into the dark brown Mississippi dirt. He read one of Barbra's sentences again and again. *Your father rescued your mother when no one else cared about her.* The words seemed to jump off the page at him. He wrote back, this time with a milder protest about his parents. Resentment still swirled inside him, though, tempered for the first time by a grudging appreciation for what Tom did.

"Captain! O, Captain!" Owens' jocular voice jolted Jonathan out of his reverie. First Sergeant Owens rapped on the tent pole, then burst in.

Jonathan swept Barbra's letter aside.

"A word if you please, sir. If I might go over a few things, all right?"

"Certainly, First Sergeant."

"I thought I'd be letting you know how matters might unfold tomorrow when we kick this little party off."

Jonathan was getting used to Owens' way of talking—part impertinent, part amusing. He hid a small smile.

"So, when the sun comes up, we're gonna head up yonder hill again if I don't miss my guess. Right, sir?" It was more of a statement than a question.

"That's right, First Sergeant." Where was this going?

"So we'll be askin' the boys to get up and join us for the day's festivities around oh, say four thirty, sir?"

"That sounds about right."

"Then we'll be having our ham and eggs and toast and butter, served on fine china by waiters, followed by sipping grand coffee for a decent amount of time, all right?" Another question in the form of a statement.

Jonathan smiled and played along. "Fine."

"And after we finish breakfast and relax a bit, followed by hot showers and smooth shaves, we should be in line ready to roll just the other side of five?" Owens had a habit of smacking his open palm with one finger to emphasize his points.

"Again, that sounds like good timing."

"And C Company will be at the head of the party line, I'm sure. Can't let those sorry SOBs in the other companies have all the fun now, can we?"

"Well, I don't know if we get to be first or not.

257

We'll find out tomorrow."

Owens glowered. "Well now, sir,"—his face reddening—"in the morning why don't we just file in line *ahead* of those other fellows and act like we were born to be there." Another question that wasn't a question.

"I suppose we could do that…see to it, First Sergeant."

"Yes, sir!" Owens' eyes twinkled.

Jonathan's insides smiled as he returned Owens' salute. He watched the man walk away with his purposeful stride, already yelling for his sergeants. The chicks flocked around the hen. Jonathan shook his head. Morning would come soon enough.

For some reason, he got a good night's sleep, letting his worries about leading the men disappear with the setting sun. The next morning after he finished praying, he placed Barbra's letter in his tunic. True to form, he heard the first sergeant before he saw him.

Owens announced his presence from a distance. "And a lovely morning it is to be having tea and crumpets with our friends across the way. O, Captain, I hope you're dressed decent, as your manservant is here with your warm muffins." Owens' voice was loud enough to wake anyone who might have still been sleeping. No one was.

"I've come with your favorite breakfast this morning, sir—sizzling bacon with buttered toast, fluffy scrambled eggs, and coffee made from pampered beans." He pushed the tent flap aside and entered, then glanced at the plate in mock horror. "Who put this rubbish in my hand? Where's my feast for the captain? This coffee smells awful. Sir, please excuse this. It's so hard to get good help around here. I've requisitioned a new chef but this will have to do in the meantime."

Jonathan chuckled. "First Sergeant, I'm hardly dressed to receive visitors."

Owens put the meager rations on a stool and whistled his way out.

As dawn streaked the sky, C Company sprinted into position, the other companies falling in behind. Owens was in his element. Everyone deferred to the man with the thundering voice and take-no-prisoners manner.

When the sun snuck above the horizon, Jonathan got a clear look at the heights they'd be assaulting again. The ground was still littered with debris from two days ago, although details had recovered the dead and wounded. He felt compelled to address the men as they stood waiting for the order to advance. He gathered them around.

"Men, I have an idea what Captain Thompson might say if he were here with us this morning. He'd say he was never prouder of a group of men than he was of you. He'd say you have served this nation with honor and courage—that you saw your duty and did it without fail. He might also say this battle to seize Vicksburg is one of the most important of the war and you were not put here this morning by chance. He'd say you were here because the country needed their best men right here, right now, to help end this. So, men...let's do Captain Thompson proud as he watches us go about our work."

Jonathan glanced around the silent gathering. Men stood with their hats off, eyes downcast. First Sergeant Owens nodded, eyes filling in the waking light.

"That is all," Jonathan said.

Owens cleared his throat. With a swipe at his cheek, he bellowed, "You heard the commander! Fall in, you shirkers. Slackers in front!"

Men *raced* to the front of the company's ranks.

Chapter Thirty-One

Union batteries had lobbed artillery shells overhead since dawn, softening the enemy for the infantry charge to follow. A major from regiment galloped up as sun began to light the heavens. "Captain Gray, you and C Company weren't supposed to lead the charge today, but…since you've taken the forward position, you now have the honor of spearheading the way for the rest of the regiment. Good luck!"

Jonathan saluted as the major rode away.

Owens shouted, "C Company, form up! Load! Fix bayonets!"

Jonathan turned to his troops. "Men, I'll see you on top of that ridge. Hold fire until we close with the enemy." He waved his hat in the air. "At the quick step—march!"

The company hurried forward. Rebel artillery to their front came alive, spraying the ground with death and debris. Left and right, C Company moved through a hail of shot and shell. Morning fog mingled with smoke to cast a thick haze over the field. Jonathan's eyes stung. He wanted to get well up the slope before the enemy came crashing down on them. In the early light, he couldn't tell if he was still in front of the men or not. Every now and then he glimpsed a familiar face alongside him. Their advance slowed as they came within small arms range. Jonathan crouched lower as bullets whined around him. He held his fire. No enemy to shoot at yet.

When he reached the first rock outcropping partway up the hill, intense fire from above forced him to take cover. A cry for help came from his right. He couldn't see the man through the smoke, but he moved toward the voice, stumbling low over a rock field on the way. The soldier lay on his back with an ugly wound to the right side of his chest. Didn't look like he was going to make it. Jonathan tore the bandana from around his neck and pressed on the fresh wound. The man was in shock.

"Keep your hand here until help arrives. Understand?"

A slight nod of the head. Glassy eyes.

Just then, a shell hit about fifteen yards away but felt like it exploded on top of Jonathan, knocking him sideways and deafening him. Antietam again. Stunned, he struggled to a stand. Three of his men lay nearby, motionless. He lurched to each one. All dead. A groan ahead caught his attention. He crept to a soldier lying in a fetal position. Not one of his. One arm was gone, a tattered sleeve the only evidence it ever existed. Taking the man's cartridge sling off, Jonathan cinched it around the bloody stump. The soldier neither whimpered nor cried but lay with a faraway look.

Jonathan continued uphill. In front of him somewhere, First Sergeant Owens bellowed orders and kicked up a general fuss. He sounded enraged. Moving toward him through the dense smoke, Jonathan saw the reason for the commotion. Owens had been hit in the lower leg and was leaning on the other leg, using his rifle as a crutch and shouting, "Spread out as you climb." Soldier after soldier was drawn toward his voice through the dense haze, but he waved them away and threatened to kick them in the "arse" with his good leg if they didn't scatter.

"Get up that hill, you slackers," he roared, like the wounded animal he was.

Jonathan rushed up in a stoop. "First Sergeant, are you all right? Why don't you sit down?" From the look on Owens' face, it was the wrong thing to say.

Owens' eyes blazed. "Sit down? Sit down? I'll sit down all right, sir! I'll sit on those Rebs' pointy heads soon enough. I'll sit on top of this ridge sipping a gentleman's fine whisky when we're done with our business. That's when I'll sit down. Sir!"

Jonathan helped him sit.

He knew better than to suggest some of the men help him off the incline. The only way Owens would ever leave an active battlefield was if he were dead. Jonathan tended to the leg wound while Owens protested so much his ears hurt.

"Shut up, First Sergeant." He cleaned the wound as best he could. He took Owens' belt off under protest and twisted it around the leg, telling him to hold it just so. Not more than a minute later, another shell shook the earth nearby. Those who hadn't already been knocked off their feet flattened themselves against the ground. Owens berated them again. "I said, get up that hill!"

Jonathan took a private aside. "Son, you stay near the first sergeant. Help him if he needs it. Don't let him know you're staying behind, though. If he stops yelling, that's a bad sign. You get him down off this rise. Got it?"

"Yessir!" the wide-eyed private said.

Jonathan started back up the slope. Owens' voice receded in the distance, but he was still swearing up a storm. Jonathan kept moving.

Confederate Infantry stayed under cover while their artillery punched holes in the 76th's lines. When C Company neared the top of the ridge, the enemy charged from their fortifications like wild men, screaming their eerie rebel yell, a high-pitched wail—akin to banshees shrieking. They ran firing and attacking with fixed bayonets, halting the company's advance.

Jonathan caught up with his lead soldiers as the bayonet attack began. "Make a stand! Right here!" They did. Several soon crumpled, shot dead in their tracks, or bayoneted before taking their final breath. He whirled to a blood-curdling yell from behind. A manic Confederate charged, bayonet fixed. He sidestepped just in time as the soldier thrust. No time to draw his Colt. Jonathan punched him in the face. The man's rifle flew away in the dirt. They grappled and fell. The rebel pulled a knife. Jonathan slapped his hand on an empty holster. Damn! He sprang to his feet, dodged lunges, and tripped the soldier as he charged. They spun to the ground together—Jonathan was pinned. The soldier had one hand on his throat, the other held high, ready to plunge a knife. A shot rang out. The Confederate crumpled on top of him, shock filling his face. Jonathan felt the man breathe his last. He jumped up, heart trip hammering. No way to discover who his rescuer was—there were so many shooting, fighting, dying. His men had to be running low on ammunition. He was. He motioned to whoever could see him to pull back, his

264

sidearm still missing in the chaos.

Jonathan led an orderly withdrawal in the midst of the most awful tempest he had ever seen, much less been a part of. Shells, minié balls, bayonets—a hellhole of death, noise, and smoke. Stinging eyes. Reddish pools in brown dirt. Detached limbs. Spent soldiers. Bodies that didn't resemble men. The company collected at the bottom of the hill. They gathered around Jonathan. Legs gave way. Most dropped to a knee. Shaking hands lit dirty cigarettes. Grimy faces warily scanned their surroundings. A powerful wind cleared enough smoke for Jonathan to glimpse the mayhem that swirled around him.

No more Owens' bellowing. A sound he'd hoped he would still hear. "You four men, back up the hill. Find the first sergeant." After an anxious wait, the gray haze parted. Four soldiers appeared carrying an unconscious Owens, his head lolling with each step they took. The private Jonathan left with Owens trailed behind, shaking and stuttering.

Jonathan couldn't hide his worry. He grabbed one of his lieutenants. "Get a wagon and take the first sergeant to that makeshift field hospital we saw over there this morning." He pointed east. "And hurry!" He turned to one of the bearers. "Was the private with the first sergeant?"

"Yes, sir. Curled up next to him."

The youngster looked pale and shocky. "Better take him with you, too."

Jonathan said a quick prayer of thanks that most of his men had gotten off the hill alive. Still, he knew some wanted nothing to do with him. Was he ever going to measure up in their eyes? A thin line of C

Company provided a rear guard while weary men straggled back to camp. As he watched the first sergeant disappear down the road, he wondered if he'd ever see him again.

Jonathan gathered his lieutenants and senior NCOs together that afternoon for an accounting of casualties. A preliminary count totaled ten dead, and another eleven wounded or missing. Jonathan held a hand to his forehead as if to push his grief away. C Company had under sixty effectives, when there were eighty a few weeks ago. A far cry from the almost one hundred they'd started the war with.

Jonathan rode back to the field hospital to check on Owens. A harried doctor said he'd likely live but might lose his leg. He turned away to saw on another unfortunate.

****

After attacking Vicksburg with no success, Grant settled in for a siege, throwing up a ring of entrenchments around the beleaguered city. Nothing went in or out as he clamped down on the trapped inhabitants.

Jonathan and his men were forced to live together in close quarters during the blockade. This gave him more time with his soldiers. He circulated in the trenches among the men. Ate with them. All things Thompson likely would have done. Two months later when they marched into a surrendered Vicksburg, he sensed most, if not all, had accepted him as their commander. They greeted him with salutes, instead of sulks. Stayed close by, seeking his guidance. Inside the shattered city, Jonathan reeled at the devastation, the empty stares of starving citizens, the hollow eyes, dirty clothes, widespread rubble. How had they lasted this long?

After Vicksburg capitulated, the company went into bivouac. Jonathan heard a knock on his tent pole the next morning. A grinning Sergeant French stood outside. "Happy Fourth of July, sir. We did it! We took Vicksburg."

Jonathan stooped coming out of the tent. "Yes, we did, Sergeant French. And we couldn't have done it without the leadership you showed in your platoon. Well done, soldier." They locked eyes.

"Thank you, sir. I…I just…wanted…" He snapped to attention, boots heels clicking. "Sir!" He snapped a salute.

Jonathan returned it with a smile. "I heard we also just won a great victory at a place called Gettysburg back east."

"Yes, sir, I heard that, too. Rumor is General Grant's been put in charge of the entire western army. Must mean General Sherman's gonna take over from him here, don't you think, sir?"

"I'd bet on it. He has the rank for it." He chatted with French as they walked to the small mess.

****

Jonathan wrote Barbra another letter while the army stood down. He said nothing about the horrific fighting he'd just been in. Too hard. Besides, no way to describe it.

Dear Lizzie,

Your last letter was like an arrow aimed right at my heart. I have been struggling with how I feel. What you said about my father, his noble act, made me stop and think, something I've not done a lot of lately. I've

267

had unrealistic expectations of my parents, like most kids probably do. But really, they're just people. People who make mistakes. People who have a son who's not smart enough to see all the good things about them, and let the rest blow away in the wind. Thank you for helping me see what I'd chosen to ignore.

I wish you were right here, right now, so I could see your pretty face, look into your smiling eyes, see the breeze blowing through your hair. Thank you for being there for me when I wasn't there for myself.

Yours,

Jonathan

That night, Jonathan was in a fierce battle. Soldiers ran at him from every direction, screaming his name. "Gray! Gray!" Bayonets gleamed in daunting sunlight. Thrusting. He scrambled for his rifle but couldn't find it. The rebel yell rang out. They were on him. Jonathan wrested a rifle away from an enemy soldier and turned it back on him. The soldier had crazy eyes and a grubby beard. He kept shouting, "I got 'em, boss, I got them slaves," but Jonathan couldn't see his face. He raised the bayonet and plunged but didn't feel it hit anything. The soldier yelped, then was silent, falling on his stomach. Jonathan stood over him, afraid to look. But he had to. He knelt and turned the body over. Robert! Jonathan screamed a blood-curdling *Ahhhhhhhhh!*

He bolted upright on his cot, sweating, heart pounding like it would burst out of his chest. Took him a second to recognize the familiar surroundings of his tent. Just a dream—that's all. He sat shaking, sweating. Footsteps ran toward him from outside.

"Sir, you all right?"

"Who's there?"

"It's Corporal Carter, sir. Are you okay?"

"What...time is it, Carter?" Jonathan eased up, brushed at his face and swept the tent flap open.

"Must be nigh on to one a.m., sir."

"What are you doing up this time of night?" Jonathan tried to slow his heart rate with deep breaths. He wiped more sweat from his brow. An awful dream. That's all it was.

"Sentry duty, sir. I wuz nearby and I heard you scream. Sir?"

"I'm fine, Carter." The cool night air chilled Jonathan through his soaked sleep shirt. Heads peeked out from other tents.

"Would you like a chaw, sir? Might calm your nerves."

"I don't chew...but thanks, anyway." Jonathan returned Carter's salute and disappeared back into his tent. He scavenged under his cot. His hand wrapped around a new bottle of whiskey. Something he'd been saving for a special occasion. He poured a short glass and drained it in one gulp. Fire spread down his throat and produced several hacking coughs. He wiped at his mouth and stuffed the bottle back under the cot. Not the occasion he'd imagined, but anything to help him get through the night.

A hellish day.

Chapter Thirty-Two

September 1863

Jonathan mounted up. He was leaving the company campsite when he heard someone call his name. He turned to see Sergeant Hargrove.

"Hello, sir. You goin' to regiment to find out where we're headin'?"

"What makes you think I'm going to regiment? And what makes you think we're going somewhere, Gus?"

"Oh, I hear things off and on."

Seemed like the enlisted always knew what was happening before officers did. "So, what are you hearing?"

"Well, sir, there's heavy traffic in and out of General Sherman's headquarters house."

That might not mean anything. "More than usual?"

"Yup, lots."

All that time as a courier told him something probably *was* up. "Meaning?"

"Well, and this is just a guess, mind you, sir, but if I was a bettin' man, I'd wager we're about to head up east a ways."

"So if you had to venture another guess, where do you think we'd wind up?"

Gus smiled. "I hear Chattanooga's real pretty this

time of year. But I also hear we better bring our own rations, because they're all out over there."

"Well, if that's where we're headed, I guess I'll find out soon enough." A quick salute. He nudged his horse and trotted off.

Col. Hays scanned his company commanders. "Men, there's been a terrible battle just south of Chattanooga, Tennessee. A place called Chickamauga. Our boys got whipped. Almost thirty-five thousand casualties on both sides. The army's retreated back to Chattanooga and that's where they are right now. Surrounded by the enemy. No food and no way out."

Someone spoke up. "Sounds like they're in need of rescuin', sir."

Hays said, "Turns out that's what General Grant thinks, too. Get your men ready. We leave tomorrow for Tennessee. Let's see if we can't give the Rebs a taste of their own medicine."

When Jonathan arrived in Chattanooga, Colonel Hays told him C Company would be part of Sherman's left flank in relief of the Confederate siege. He eyed a brooding Missionary Ridge that loomed east of town, where the enemy already held the high ground. Securing those rocky heights was the key to breaking the trap.

That evening, C Company waded across the nearby Tennessee River fronting the heights. As day broke, they helped drive the enemy back from the base of the ridge up toward the summit. The top showed full of battle-hardened Confederates. Jonathan had no doubt they were as desperate for victory as Sherman was. As the sun of noon looked down, a courier from the 76th found him.

"Captain Gray, sir," said the lieutenant, "Col. Hays requests you form your men and advance to the summit of that rise." He pointed a saber at the northern part of Missionary Ridge.

Jonathan wondered if he ever looked that young. "Thank you, Lieutenant."

The steep terrain in front of them promised nothing but heartache and death. Weren't they ever going to fight on level ground? Another attack over a fearsome bit of jumbled terrain that would slow them enough to make good targets. Jutting rocks, scrambly gravel, loose clay.

One of the corporals hollered, "Here's another fine piece of Johnny Reb ground we have to get to the top of." Jonathan eyed the man, and the soldier fell silent. Men checked and rechecked their bullet bags, copper caps, gunpowder.

Jonathan led his men forward but his commands were drowned out by the din of the shells crisscrossing overhead. He resorted to hand signals. As C Company pushed through the scant first defensive line, Jonathan waved his sword high over his head with a flourish and pointed up the hill. His men charged into a horrendous fusillade of bullets, smoke, bedlam, and fire. The company's ranks had thinned by the time they reached the enemy's mid-rise breastworks.

Shot poured into their midst. Shells flung huge mounds of earth in the air and hurled deadly shrapnel and rocks everywhere. A constant roar drowned out voices. Jonathan signaled to take cover. He crouched behind a rock outcropping, checking to see how his men were faring. Blue-clad bodies sprawled in cratered dirt the length and breadth of the field of fire. Some crawled, some groaned. Some didn't do either. Survivors hunkered down behind rocks, trees, or bushes.

Jonathan spied one of his sergeants lying nearby. He jumped out from behind cover and ran in a zigzagging crouch as sharpshooters let loose from above. Something punched him in the side. He staggered for a moment, then regained his footing and hurried toward his man. Grabbing him by the blouse, he dragged him back to cover and checked the wound. Dark red blood surged from his chest—the bad kind that comes from deep within the body. Foamy pink bubbles rose from his mouth.

The soldier's voice was raspy. "Will I be okay, sir? I'll be okay, won't I?"

"Yes, you will. I'm sure of it."

His face changed from a grimace to a peaceful look. "That's good. Do you think I could have a drink, sir?"

"Sure." Jonathan asked him his name.

"Arnold, sir…George Arnold."

"Fine, George."

Jonathan reached for his canteen, but the bullet that wobbled him had punched through the edge and emptied it. They stayed put, parched, and waiting for the sun to disappear. Jonathan kept pressure on the wound and kept talking, trying to keep Arnold awake. They were stuck, unable to back away from the onslaught. The sun hung low and lower in the early winter sky. When it disappeared, shelling faded away to nothing except the occasional report of a sharpshooter. Lazy smoke still hugged dim ground.

As dusk claimed the land, Jonathan hefted the man

over his shoulder and struggled off the rise with him. Most of his troops had already dragged themselves off the killing field and set up a makeshift camp out of small arms range. Waiting for him. No shelter. Cold rations. Near enough to hear doctors sawing off arms and legs amid screams. Jonathan had two privates carry Arnold toward the field hospital. The pitiful noises coming from there were worse than being pinned down all day.

Later that night, Jonathan found Sergeant Arnold laying among the casualties. Orderlies had deposited him on the cooling ground. Jonathan spoke with the surgeon who removed the bullet from his upper chest. "Will he live, Doc?"

"Don't know. Either he will or he won't," he said with no enthusiasm. Jonathan knelt by his side, recited the Lord's Prayer, then checked on the rest of his wounded one by one.

As daylight faded, he gathered his staff together. The field they'd just retreated from still smoked. He gazed at grimy faces with grim stares. Men with dried spittle around chapped mouths. A sputtering campfire threw off scant heat. Chill winds had already turned the scalding day into just a memory. Intermittent distant *pop, pop, pops* split the otherwise still night air.

One of the NCOs stared at the ground. "Sir...we took a beating today. It was *real* hard out there." His voice died away.

Jonathan eyed his men, slumped around him. "Yes...it was hard. Very hard. But...I want you to hold your heads up. I want you to know...how proud...I am of you. You did more than your share of knocking the enemy back today." He threw a small piece of wood on the fire, his face framed in the flames. "General Sherman must have known this ground would be the toughest to take, so he put his best men here. He put you here. He put C Company here. Men who know the meaning of courage. Of honor. Men who willingly put their lives in each other's hands for safekeeping. Men who see their duty and do it. The best men Sherman has. The best men this country has. That's who C Company was today. And I know the first sergeant would feel the same way."

The men sat in silence for a moment, then glanced at each other. One soldier tipped his cap to his buddy next to him with an almost-shy smile. Soon, the whole campfire had done the same, men nodding to each other. They rose to go back to their own campfires, arms over one another's shoulders, supporting each other. A certain peace claimed the camp.

Jonathan stared at the company's casualty list in the flickering light and pursed his lips hard. They'd depended on him. He'd let them down. They deserved better than dying on some distant field in a battle soon forgotten. Damn war.

A courier brought his mount to a halt nearby. "Captain Gray, where's Captain Gray?"

A listless, "Over here."

"Colonel Hays requests the pleasure of your company, sir."

"Right now, Lieutenant?" Whatever it was, didn't sound good.

"Yes, sir," he said, still sitting his horse.

Jonathan mounted up. When he reached Hays' tent, the lieutenant announced him.

"Come in, Captain Gray. Please take a seat."

Jonathan remained standing. Hays said, "How are you, Jonathan?"

"All right, sir."

"Do you know how the day turned out?"

"No, sir, other than we lost a lot of good soldiers." His nose tingled and his voice caught in his throat. He hoped the colonel didn't notice the quaver.

"Well, I have good news. General Thomas has the enemy on the run. When he hit them in the middle of the ridge, they turned tail. So tomorrow when the sun comes up, we're hard after them. Good job today." A pause. He stood ramrod straight. "I know how difficult the fighting was in your sector. Please give my respects to your men."

The news was the only bright spot in Jonathan's day. Back at camp, he called his staff together. Shocked stares greeted him as he told them of the Confederates' retreat. "Men, it's simple. We are to attack first thing tomorrow morning and chase the Rebs wherever we can find them." Just like that, C Company's grim mood changed to one of hot eagerness. The lieutenants scattered to tell their men the good news.

After a meager dinner, Jonathan walked among the company's flickering campsites. He passed a small group and nodded. One of the soldiers called out to him.

"Captain Gray, could I have a word, sir?"

"Certainly. What's on your mind?" He peered into the darkness. It was one of his platoon sergeants, Charles Borden. The man rose, facing him.

"I just want to apologize, sir."

"What for, Sergeant Borden?"

"I been givin' you a hard time here with the men,

sir, and I'm sorry for it."

"Not sure what you mean."

"Wellsir," he said all in one word, "I didn't think much of you when you first showed up here. Nosir, I sure didn't."

"Sergeant, no need—"

"Sir, if you don't mind. I want to get this off my chest and I want to do it in front of my slacker buddies here. I didn't care for you a lick, 'specially when I heard some of the things the boys were sayin' about you. They said you wanted to kiss them Johnny Rebs, not kill 'em."

Jonathan shifted from one foot to the other.

"We heard you wuzn't a real officer, just some dandy on somebody's staff. So I sez I don't care as long as we got Captain Thompson, but you know what happened to him. And then the first sergeant went down and we wuz stuck with you. So we're sittin' here thinkin' we got the short end of the stick on this one. But you done good, sir, you done real good, and so I'm the first to apologize for sellin' you short and I want you and these slackers around me here to know how I feel."

Jonathan flushed in the cool evening air. He took a quick swipe at his cheek.

"When we wuz up against it at Vicksburg, you wuz there fightin' with us and takin' care of us. We all seen you carin' for the captain and lookin' out for the other boys who got hit. You took over right away and kept us all from gettin' killed. And here today, same thing. Don't nobody forget somethin' like that—how men act in combat when they're up against it. And I'm proud, sir, to serve with you. You just tell me what you want me to do. By God, I'll do it."

Jonathan blinked hard. "Well…uh…I guess the first thing I'd like is for you to stop, Sergeant Borden," he said, feeling more than a little sheepish.

The sergeant said, "Yessir, I will, but I just wanted you to know the way it is, sir. The way it is."

Jonathan's vision clouded in the darkening light. "Well then…umm…fine. Just…carry on, men." They were all standing now. As Jonathan started to leave, they saluted him. He rendered a quick salute and was gone.

He wandered around more campsites amid the small fires that couldn't quite take the chill out of the November evening air. Men rose as he neared.

The occasional, "Captain." A nod.

"Evenin', sir." A nod in that direction.

He was at home now among his men. He wouldn't have guessed it a year ago, but this was where he belonged, his soul at rest. For the first time in—he couldn't remember how long—he'd found some peace. In war, of all things.

McClellan's firing was the best thing that could have happened to him. As he stood out of sight of the men that evening, he said a quiet prayer for their safety and for wisdom in leading them. He thanked the Lord for sending him here. Thanked Him for bringing Barbra back in his life. Asked for forgiveness for how he'd treated his father. Walked back to his bedroll and said a prayer for his mother and the first sergeant. As stars twinkled overhead, he was asleep as soon as his head hit the makeshift pillow.

In the morning, the remaining rebels fled from Missionary Ridge south into northern Georgia.

Jonathan had C Company up before dawn and scrambling over the summit after them. His men's pride was bruised—his too. A renewed spirit carried them this morning. The outfit covering the Confederate retreat was the same one that bloodied them yesterday. When his men saw them, they broke into an all-out sprint. For the first time since he'd joined XV Corps, Jonathan saw the backs of the enemy.

After days of punishing retreating Confederates, Jonathan had to halt his men and tell them they were turning back to go into winter camp. On the march back to Chattanooga, he looked northeast, the direction he imagined Mower Hospital was. What was Barbra doing? Was she thinking of him like he was thinking of her? He longed to be with her. Sometime soon, he hoped.

He walked alongside his men with a steady stride. Winter would give him time to ready them for the tough fighting come spring.

Chapter Thirty-Three

Winter 1863-1864

Jonathan gazed around the company campsite. Truth be told, he missed First Sergeant Owens' big presence. While he maintained a professional relationship with the senior enlisted men, he ate with them and spent time with his NCOs, sitting and listening more than anything. The backbone of the company.

He made sure the men had proper training, rations, and shelter for winter's short days and long nights. Most of the work involved folding greenhorn replacements into platoons. The encampment consisted of small, haphazard shelters built with pieces of wood scavenged or chopped from surrounding pine forests. Tennessee's chill winds blew through them the same as Mississippi's had.

A soldier approached as Jonathan sat at his campfire's meager embers one night. A quick salute. "Sir, Private Morrison. May I join the captain?"

"Sit down, Morrison. You must feel like a real veteran among all these new recruits."

"Yes, sir." Morrison glanced up at the starry heavens. "It gets real dark early here in winter, don't it, sir?

Jonathan nodded.

"Uh...you ever have women problems, sir, like with a sweetheart?"

Jonathan paused for a second. Barbra's face shone in the glowing embers. The problems were his, not hers, but she'd forgiven him.

"The thing is, I don't think I'm ever gonna see my girl again."

"Why's that?"

"I don't know; I just got a feelin'. I never told her I love her but I think she loves me and we ought to get married when I get back home. I don't know why I ain't asked her; I guess I wuz just scared she might say no."

"Sounds about right." Near to how he felt about Barbra.

"I just hope she ain't taken up with some no account rich boy who paid somebody to take his place so's he could be with my girl. She wouldn't do that, I know she wouldn't, but I still think about it."

"Have you written her?" He needed to write Barbra. And his parents.

"I wrote her a bunch but it's just that you know we don't get letters much these days bein' on the march and all and so I ain't heard from her and it's drivin' me crazy not knowin' what's goin' on and there's nothin' I can do about it."

"You'll be home soon, son." Jonathan wondered if that was true.

"You think so, sir? That sure has a nice sound to it. I can't remember the last time I was home. It was maybe last year about this time when it gets dark early and the wind chills up. I can't even remember my girl's face and I don't got a drawing of her 'cause I couldn't afford one before I left. I should've got one anyway."

He smacked himself on the forehead.

"I'm sure you will be." He wanted to sound sure, if nothing else. Home had a nice feel to it again. So did the image of Barbra's flowing auburn hair and green eyes that held his heart like a vise.

"Guess I'll be headin' back about now, sir."

"Goodnight, son, get some rest."

"Sir?" Morrison saluted, a flicker of hope in his eyes. "Thank you."

Jonathan disappeared into his tent and pulled out pen and paper.

Dear Lizzie,

Thank you for writing me, and listening to me grumble about my life. I really don't have much to complain about, do I? Not compared to some of the men you see every day, I'm sure.

I think about you, especially on cold, windy nights when the stars come out clear as anything. I always stare at the North Star because I know that same star is shining down on you, and it brings me some peace.

Come spring, we're off after the enemy, and I don't think they can last much longer. Thank you for taking care of our men. They are lucky if they have you as their nurse. I hope you think of me half as much as I think of you. Guess I better go now. Write me please, your letters mean so much.

Jonathan

This time, the letter wasn't all about him. He lifted a prayer and a certain calm came over him. The ire that always seemed to be his constant companion was fading. He penned a note to his folks for the first time in a long while. The words still didn't flow, but came more easily now.

Dear Mother and Father,

I'm sorry I haven't been a better letter writer. Please forgive me for that. We are in winter camp in Chattanooga until spring comes. It's very different here, but the piney hills circling the town remind me of home.

How's the farm? Have you eaten all of those beets you canned, Mother, or did you save some for me? Father, how's that pulley on the outside of the barn? Checked it lately?

Jonathan hoped Tom remembered him working on it before that spring festival years ago.

I'm fine and the war should be over soon, so don't worry about me. The worst thing that could happen is I get an upset stomach from the food they feed us. Write please.

Your son,

Jonathan

He hoped his mother believed the part about the worst thing that could happen.

****

Days dragged on for C Company. There wasn't any real work to do other than guard duty, and you could only read the few letters that found their way here so many times. A camp this size had its share of talent, though, so at night there were any number of banjos strumming, voices singing, and stories floating around. Men spoke in hushed tones around small campfires. Most just stared into the reddish-gold flames, lost in their own thoughts. There was almost no mention of army things. The talk was about families, girlfriends, and what they were going to do when the war was over. During these chill months, Jonathan came to know

283

more about how his men felt than perhaps the women in their lives did.

His men had seen Jonathan openly pray ever since he joined C Company. They came to him with spiritual issues as much as they went to the regimental chaplain. They shared doubts and failings as if they were talking to their parish priest and he let them talk. He had a way of listening that seemed to make them feel better.

One of his platoon sergeants, Louie Addams, approached him at his campfire. A quick salute. He rubbed his hands together over the flickering fire. "Sir, it sure can get cold here in the winter, can't it? I thought the South stayed warm year 'round."

Jonathan smiled. "I thought so too, but not so much, huh, Louie? Won't you sit?"

Addams nodded. "Thank you, sir." A pause as he eased onto a felled log. "Sir, may I ask you a question?"

"Sure."

"I don't think I'm good enough to get into Heaven. Seems like I do more bad things than good."

"Good thing the Lord doesn't have a scale. He welcomes everyone who believes in Him."

"But I'm just a shiftless drifter. Somebody paid me to join up. I didn't even have the guts to enlist on my own."

"What you just said about how you got here may be true, but what you said about your courage isn't. I've seen you in combat, seen your steady hand, how the men look to you. You're a good soldier and a good man. And I'm proud to serve with you."

Addams wiped at his nose.

Jonathan continued, "Have you ever heard of grace, Louie?"

The sergeant cleared his throat. "Yes, sir. When I was growing up, we'd say grace before every meal."

Jonathan smiled. "No, I meant God's grace. Did you know He makes it available to everyone? It's a free gift. It's His promise we'll live with Him if we believe in Him. None of us deserve it, we can't earn it. God doesn't keep a scorecard on you and me. If he did, there's no way either of us could ever be good enough to be with Him. He loves us just like we are. Like you are."

"You mean there's hope for someone like me?"

"Yup. For both of us." Jonathan thought about Barbra's last letter. Full of grace he didn't deserve.

"But you don't need it, sir."

"We all need hope."

****

Jonathan was in his tent when a sentry yelled for him. He burst out, "What's the matter, Corporal?" The guard pointed to a lone horseman coming in the morning light. The first sergeant! Word spread like wildfire. Grizzled men ran after his horse like kids. A circle of troops had him surrounded by the time he dismounted near Jonathan's campfire.

Owens walked toward him with a pronounced limp, leaning on a cane and frowning. Bigger than life he still was. Beefy-red face that matched his rust-red beard. Familiar scowl. Jonathan stood stunned. He'd had no way of knowing where Owens was or even if he was still alive.

The first sergeant drew up in front of him. Snapped off a smart salute. "First Sergeant Owens reporting for duty. Sir!"

Jonathan returned a crisp salute. "Glad to have you

back, First Sergeant."

"Well, it's a good thing I am back, sir." He glanced around. "Looks like the place has gone to hell," he said, in a voice loud enough for all to hear, near and far.

"Yes, well, I'm sure you'll have us all back up to snuff again in no time."

"I can see I have my work cut out for me, sir. I'll be going now to check on the men. Let me know if you need anything."

"Will do," Jonathan said, trying to hide a grin. The day seemed brighter and the winter sun warmer.

"And, sir."

"Yes, First Sergeant?"

"Thank you for taking care of my boys so well." Owens saluted and Jonathan returned same. He lingered a moment, squinting at Jonathan. Was the first sergeant's bottom lip quivering? He stood ramrod straight as a small smile crept over his face.

Jonathan cleared his throat and blinked rapidly. "Anything else, First Sergeant?"

With a twinkle in his eyes, he said, "No, sir." Owens wheeled about, using his cane as he limped away, shouting orders as he went.

Jonathan smiled as that gravelly voice faded away. He wouldn't have wanted to be Owens' doctor. Or nurse. The man must have been a terrible patient. What if Lizzie had to take care of him? Jonathan chuckled at the thought.

The war became a little more distant with Owens back. The men put more energy into their daily routines. They couldn't wait to be yelled at by the first sergeant, who couldn't wait to yell at them. It was a badge of honor for Owens to call you a slacker.

Jonathan was chewing hardtack and sipping coffee by his campfire when a new recruit passed by with his platoon sergeant. "What's a slacker, Sergeant?"

"If you have to ask what one is, you ain't one."

"That don't make no sense, Sarge."

Jonathan pretended not to be listening but bent an ear that way.

The sergeant fixed the recruit with a stare. "Slackers are soldiers who always do their damnedest. They figure out what needs to be done without being told and they do it before anyone else. They're first in line for the hardest duty in battle and they do their jobs in camp without whinin'. And they shut up about things they cain't do nothin' about. We'll find out if you're slacker material soon enough."

As spring approached, the company was as combat ready as it had ever been.

Camp had given Jonathan time to catch up on his writing. He received several heartfelt letters from his folks in return, most written some time ago. His mother thanked him again and again for letting them know he was all right. Barbra wrote newsy letters where she responded with the same tender tone Jonathan wrote to her with. She told him about wintertime in Philadelphia and asked about the war but didn't mention the carnage she saw every day. Most nights he read and reread them before turning in. Same bug up top. She asked if he was going to visit home any time soon.

Maybe he would. Why not? Winter bivouac was the best time to take leave. He approached Colonel Hays.

Seven days!

He dashed a telegram off to his folks and one to

Mower Hospital. As he packed his few belongings, the first sergeant stopped by his tent.

"So I'm hearing you're going to give those Johnny Rebs a break now, are ya, sir?"

"I think they'll still be here when I get back. How's the leg feel, First Sergeant?" Wrong thing to say.

"And what leg would that be, sir?"

"Right." When would he learn?

"You just have a good time, sir, and come back to us all fat and happy."

"I'll do that, First Sergeant. I'm going to lend the company to you for a few days. Please see that no one swipes it from you." He missed the men already.

"Right as rain, sir."

"Oh, and First Sergeant, let the lieutenants think they're in charge while I'm gone, will you?"

"I'll behave myself, sir. You just go on and go. Skedaddle!"

Chapter Thirty-Four

After several train stops, Jonathan arrived in Cincinnati. Disembarking in the city's small terminal, he searched for a nearby stable. He hadn't gone far when he squinted in the distance. Was that? Yes. Barbra was walking his way! His stomach jumped. Same smiling eyes, pale skin, shining auburn hair.

He broke into a trot. "Barbra! What are you doing here?"

A radiant smile from under her bonnet. "I thought it would be a nice day for a ride to the train station and look who I found!"

Jonathan gave her an awkward hug, then stepped back to say a proper hello. She linked an arm in his as they walked to her wagon. He drove while she peppered him with questions but stayed away from asking about the fighting he'd seen. "How do you think the war's going?"

"I guess I don't know. I hear things about how we have them on the run, but I think that's mostly just army talk."

Jonathan snuck glances her way as they rode. Even the overcast winter sky couldn't dim her beauty. For some reason, he'd always thought of her as younger, although they were the same age. Maybe because he'd always felt older than his years.

"How's Mower?"

"Most of the time very rewarding, but it's painful to see our boys so injured. Still, I wouldn't be anywhere else. The men are so appreciative, even when they've suffered so much."

He shook his head. He couldn't do the kind of work she was doing. Wouldn't have had the stomach for it.

She smiled. "When I got your telegram, I decided to take some time off."

They rode by familiar city landscapes. Barbra reminisced about some of her favorite memories—working at the railroad, stopping by the small library, visiting the tidy little German eatery in the center of town. As they approached the outskirts of the city, traffic on the dirt road dwindled to nothing. Barbra asked him to stop the wagon.

A strange request. He pulled on the reins and the horse slowed to a halt.

She turned to him in a commanding voice, "Jonathan Gray, I want you to tell me you love me. Right now."

"What?" he said, startled by her outburst. "Why'd you have me stop the wagon?"

"You know very well 'why'." He tried to slap the reins, but Barbra grabbed them. The horses started, jerking Jonathan back in his seat. She jumped down and started striding away.

Jonathan didn't know what to think. He got down, too. "Barbra, wait. Come back." Seeing her leaving tore at his heart.

She looked back. "I mean it. Tell me you love me!"

He put his hands up. "Just wait a minute, will you? Hold on. Please." He couldn't let her walk out of his life again. An image of her disappearing in the crowds at Mower raced through his head. She was all he thought about these days.

She stuck her chin out.

Those eyes. Melting his heart. "All right."

"Say it."

Jonathan scuffed at the dirt road. "All right, I love you."

Barbra beamed. "I knew it. I love you, too!"

Jonathan held his arms out. She hurried toward him and he drew her close. His hard kisses gave way to soft ones all over her face. Barbra's legs weakened in his tight embrace. "Now, back up on the wagon, ma'am," he said, smiling.

A soft, "Yes, sir," was all she managed.

****

It had taken time, but Jonathan had come to terms with the secret his parents hid all those years. He was undecided about whether to tell them he'd learned the truth. For some reason, he didn't feel a need to tell his mother. It was different with his father, though—he'd grown so distant from him growing up. What could he say? How to start? He'd had time to reflect on the love the man showed his mother and almost felt self-conscious around him now. The two emotional strangers rocked on the veranda one chilly evening after dinner. Tom whittled on a small piece of wood as Jonathan wrestled with the regret that had replaced his anger. The dark silence was only broken by the rhythmic singing of nearby whip-poor-wills.

"Father, thank you..." He fell silent, embarrassed to look his way, even in the dim light. The night wind picked up and Jonathan tried again. "I just wanted to say…" Again he stopped. He put a hand on Tom's sleeve. "Thank you…for being my…father." As stars glittered in the black canvas overhead, Jonathan sat motionless on the porch, eyes glistening. He was almost afraid to move, to even have the rockers creak on the wooden planks.

His father cleared his throat.

Jonathan let his hand lay there.

****

Leave was passing as well as Jonathan hoped it would. He was enjoying this visit more than any he could remember. Perhaps because he'd released the hurt and anger that had scarred his soul for so long. Maybe because he felt more relaxed with Barbra at his side. Days, they rode the surrounding fields and woods, Jonathan pointing out childhood haunts, and Barbra doing the same. Down by the Little Miami, he made a wide path around the commanding black walnut. Thick vines still hung down. They looked so innocent.

Leave was almost gone. He and Barbra bundled up after dinner and hitched the wagon. As they trundled along, they marveled at the black winter sky, its endless white diamonds muted by a slight evening haze.

"See that bright star overhead?" Jonathan pointed to the North Star. "I used to look at it, wishing its light could send my love to you." Sadness overwhelmed him. Damp winter air crept through his heavy coat. A biting wind swirled around him and his pensiveness. He was sweating despite the chill.

Barbra put an arm through his. "What's wrong, Jonathan?"

"I just don't want to leave you and go back to war."

"I can understand that, but—"

Before she could finish, Jonathan's feelings erupted like water bursting through a dam. "No, you *don't* understand. *I* don't even understand. Just about every friend I've ever had except you is gone and I never got to say goodbye to any of them. They were gone just like that. And I couldn't help any of them! Part of me has always felt helpless. And I took it out on my father. I've been so foolish. All those years…"

Barbra stared wide-eyed.

"Now I have to go back to my unit and I won't see you again for who knows how long. I just wish I could come back here and start my life with you right now."

"Is that a proposal, Jonathan Gray?" Barbra's frown turned into a smile.

"Yes, I suppose it is. Yes!"

"Well…my answer is yes. I'll marry you. But you already knew that, didn't you?" Her face shone even in the darkness.

"All I know is we're supposed to be together and I say the sooner the better."

"But you have to go back, Jonathan."

"The only reason I'll go back is for my men. I'm not even sure I know what we're fighting for anymore. But I'll go back for them. I wouldn't let them down for anything. I love my men almost as much as I love you. And when this damn war is over, I'll come back to you."

"I'm not sure if I'll be here or still at Mower. Will you write me often? Every day? Or at least every other? You write so well."

She was flattering him so he'd write, but he didn't mind. "Yes, I promise I will. But now that you mention it, there *is* something I've been meaning to ask about. On every one of your letters, you always draw a little bug at the top. Why?"

Barbra feigned a hurt look. "Those are fireflies, silly."

What did that mean? He waited for Barbra to say more, but she didn't. "Am I supposed to know something about fireflies?"

Barbra's pout turned to a smile. "Do you remember that spring festival in Loveland we went to years ago?"

How could he forget that day? Even now, he saw her turning toward him from the food table, eyes smiling. "Yes…what about it?"

"When the sun went down, faint stars came out at dusk. You and I were sitting at a table with our mothers. Your brother, Peter, came running up from some mischief. A firefly blinked off and on in his curly hair. It was the most adorable thing. I don't know why, but that's always been my strongest memory of us when we were growing up. I think that's when I started to fall in love with you."

Jonathan laughed. "So you fell in love with me because there was a firefly caught in my brother's hair?"

That teased a smile from Barbra. "No, they just remind me of the first time I thought you might be the one."

Jonathan said, "So you drew those fireflies on your letters to me as…love bugs? You know, I thought those were crickets or maybe ladybugs but now that you mention it, they could be fireflies—if you don't look too close."

Barbra hauled off and hit him on the arm. "Don't

you ever tell anyone else about them, Jonathan Gray. Ever! That's our secret."

Jonathan could see she was serious. "Okay, they'll have to boil me in oil to get me to talk." As they rode, he said, "It looks like when spring hits, we'll be up after the enemy, chasing them into Georgia. Hopefully, they'll surrender soon and this damn war will be over."

Barbra paused. "From what I read, it does seem like the southerners are on the run almost everywhere, so perhaps the war *will* end soon. And then you'll come home to me."

Jonathan's emotions churned. He wanted to hold her and never let go. He slowed the wagon to a stop. "Lizzie, will you marry me before I go back?"

Barbra nodded. "Yes, I'll marry you, but not before you go back. When you come home, we'll do it properly. That means letting our parents know, finding a place to live, and you getting a job."

Jonathan bowed his head for a moment. He couldn't wait any longer, he'd waited too long already. "Marry me tomorrow. Here! Let's don't wait. Will you marry me now, Lizzie Carson?"

Barbra was surprised, yet delighted by the urgency in his voice. From all she'd seen of war, she knew only too well God doesn't guarantee tomorrow. She'd come face to face with death and dying so many times. Folding her hands in her lap, she hesitated. "Yes!" She leaned forward and kissed him.

Jonathan belted out a "Yahoo!" that bounced off nearby treetops.

As they rode back, the muted glow of oil lamps in the Gray farmhouse beckoned to them. Wisps of white smoke rose from the chimney against the dark blue night. They climbed the front steps, Barbra clutching his arm. Jonathan burst into the bright living room with a big smile. "We're going to have a wedding tomorrow!"

Belinda put a hand to her mouth and hurried over to hug them. Peter and Claire laughed and clapped. Tom rocked in his chair, smiling, puffing on his pipe.

His mother was a blur. "How wonderful! I'll go to the meeting house in the morning and start preparing. Oh, we need to let everyone know. Tom, you go and ring the bell. I'll start baking, or maybe I should go there with Jonathan. No, I want Barbra here with me, but then I'm sure she's got things to do at her house, so I'll just…" She prattled on as she left for the kitchen, a spring in her step.

Jonathan wagoned Barbra home and followed her into the Carson farmhouse. He gave a surprised Andy a big hug, then sat with Barbra's parents in the small living room. "Mr. and Mrs. Carson, I'd like permission to marry your daughter."

Mrs. Carson looked toward her husband who studied his daughter. "Barbra, what do you have to say about this?"

"Father, this is the man I want to spend the rest of my life with."

Mr. Carson nodded. "Jonathan, Barbra has loved you for a long time. The Good Book says a man shall leave his parents and be united with a wife. And they shall become one flesh. One flesh. Jonathan, will you keep that command?"

"Yes, sir, I will."

"Then you have my blessing."

The next day, Jonathan and Barbra exchanged

vows in front of family and a few friends. The leader prayed over them, asking God to bless their union with children. They exchanged vows of love while staring into each other's shining eyes. The short ceremony was performed near the place where the slave boy was dragged away so long ago but Jonathan pushed that memory away. It couldn't compete with his happiness today. He wore a wide smile, unable to take his eyes off a radiant Barbra, her hair done up in a becoming bun. She glowed in the blue jumper he liked so much. He couldn't believe such a blessing—to share his life with this beautiful woman. The leader finished with a nod at them both.

Belinda nudged Tom on the bench and they stood. He said to the small crowd, "You all are invited to stay and break bread with us in God's name as we honor this new family."

His mother was in her element. She prepared Jonathan's favorite dishes for the reception. Pickled beets she'd canned, fresh corn, roast pig—their last. A large cake festooned with homemade vanilla frosting that Claire helped her bake sat on a table. Claire and Peter had cut one of her best sheets into strips they fashioned into bows tied around the room. Belinda beamed throughout the wedding and the simple reception that followed.

Back at the farmhouse, she spruced up Jonathan's old room for the newlyweds. Jonathan was a mix of nerves and eagerness as he closed the bedroom door behind them.

The first light of morning peeked over the horizon. Tom knocked on their door, then walked away. Soon, they all chatted in the kitchen, enjoying Belinda's large breakfast of pancakes and eggs. Leftover pork, too. Afterward, the newlyweds came outside for goodbyes.

Barbra reached for Jonathan, tears falling as she wrapped her arms around him and gave him a long kiss. Whispered for him to be careful. She turned to Belinda. "Mrs. Gray, I'm so happy to be a small part of your family now."

Belinda took her by the hand. "Why, Barbra, I couldn't ask for a better new daughter."

She held her hand out to Tom. He stood still for a moment, then hugged her lightly, patting her on the back. "You are the newest Gray and our family is all the better for it."

Barbra wiped tears away. She hugged Peter and Claire, then climbed up on the wagon. With a wave, she started for the Carson farm.

Jonathan watched her disappear in the distance. A longing ran through him. When would he see his wife again? Would he ever? His father prayed over him while everyone held hands. He hugged them all one last time, then the two of them climbed onto the wagon.

Tom said, "You want to drive?"

"Yes, sir. Thanks." Jonathan snapped the reins and the horse started for the train station.

"I've always liked Barbra," Tom said. Jonathan sat in surprised silence. It was unusual for his father to start a conversation anywhere, at any time. "I'll bet she'd love that acreage out to the east I showed you last visit."

"Which was that?" Jonathan said, his mind still focused on his new wife.

"The patch of land atop that little hillock. Remember? The one I said would be a good spot for a new house."

"Yes, I remember it. What are you planning on doing with it?"

"You're not listening, son. It's still there, waiting for you to build on it."

Now was not the time to remind his father he wasn't coming back after the war. No sense spoiling a great visit. "That's good land, Father. Any idea what a house there might look like?"

"Well, I do have an idea, and I might tag a little note about that on one of the letters your mother writes. You should show that land to Barbra and see how she likes it." They rode a ways farther in silence. Tom said, "You still with Fifteenth Corps?"

"I am."

"The Seventy-sixth and C Company?" His father was full of surprises this morning.

"Yup."

"Good outfit?"

"Yes. A good outfit. I miss the men."

"Good."

Jonathan hesitated. His heart told him he still needed to ask his father's forgiveness. He wiped at his dry mouth. Wrapping his hands tightly around the reins, he stared straight ahead. "Father...I need you to...forgive me." Pause. "For the way I've treated you." He white-knuckled the reins.

"There's no forgiving needed, son. We've both already been forgiven all we need to be."

"But I've blamed you for bad things all my life. Things you had nothing to do with. Couldn't have done anything about." Silence. He dared not look over. "Blamed you for things I thought you should've done different."

"There's lots of things I *should've* done different." He cleared his throat. "I was too hard on you, Jonathan. Didn't let you have much of a childhood."

"I didn't want to be anything like you, wanted to get as far away from you as I could."

A soft, "I know."

"It was just me being stupid. All these years."

As they rode farther, Tom said, "I remember feelin' the same way about my father. I was so angry he left me and my mother all alone. I never knew him. If I had, maybe I'd have known how to be the father I meant to be. Wanted to be."

Jonathan knew to be quiet.

"Wasn't my father's fault, of course. The war took him. But I still blamed him. For years. I let go of that when I fell in love with your mother. Had to. Had to make room in my heart for her. Best thing I ever did was marrying her and having you for a son. You've got yourself something special in Barbra now. Your mother's gonna be wantin' a grandchild soon. A little girl, I'll bet."

"Yes, sir. Thanks…Father."

Chapter Thirty-Five

Jonathan watched the small buildings of Nashville disappear behind him through the train window. He slumped into his seat, a mix of sad and happy swirling inside. He couldn't believe he was married to Barbra! His heart danced at the thought. The wedding and wedding night had gone so well. He glanced around, grinning. A car full of troops stood wedged next to each other, the smell of dried sweat filling the air. The rocking train had almost lulled him to sleep when a soft voice called his name.

"Captain Gray, you awake, sir?" Jonathan opened his eyes. August Hargrove stood in front of him. "Didn't mean to bother you none, sir. I wuz just surprised to see you here. Remember me? August Hargrove? Seems like we see each other mostly on trains comin' or goin', don't it?"

"Hello, Sergeant Hargrove. Yes, it does. Where you coming from, August?"

"My people are from up Columbus way near where the general's from. I never knew him or nuthin', I just know he's from there. How about you, sir?"

"A little farm just outside of Cincinnati."

"Is that good farmland?"

"It's good. We raise corn and beets, sometimes wheat, depending on how much rain we get in the spring. How you holding up, August?"

"Call me Gus, if you would, sir. My friends all do. I mean, I ain't your friend or nothin', but I'd just like it if you'd call me Gus. Looks like we both got that old McClellan thing off our backs with all the fightin' we been doin', huh, sir?"

Jonathan didn't know what to say to that.

Hargrove continued, "I been hearin' 'bout you some in the regiment. 'Course I ain't in your company, but I been hearin' some all the same."

Jonathan sat mute.

"I heerd you done good with your boys after your captain got killed. That you been takin' care of them and just doin' good as an officer."

"I don't know about that, Gus. The fighting's been pretty hard, as you know. Sherman's led us all fairly well, I think," Jonathan said, trying to divert the focus.

"Still, good for you, sir."

"Thanks, Gus. I hope you stay well."

Jonathan leaned back in his seat and closed his eyes. Spring would come soon enough. He didn't look forward to the rough fighting it would bring, but the scuttlebutt was winter had been hard on the Confederates, too. Talk was their boots were moldy and full of holes—maybe worse than the Union's. Tattered clothes. Meager rations. But no doubt they still had fierce fight in them, so the coming battles would likely be brutal as the weather warmed. Life on the farm had taught him a cornered animal is the most dangerous kind.

When Jonathan stepped off the train in Chattanooga, someone called his name right away. "Cap'n Gray!" A private hurried his way through the crowd, holding a long salute. "Sir! First Sergeant

Owens said I'm to fetch you up and hurry back to camp before anything happens to you. So would you come with me right now, sir, so's I don't get in no trouble and I thank you."

Jonathan chuckled to himself. "Sure, son. Been here long?"

"No, sir, just since yesterday."

Jonathan's horse was saddled and waiting at a hitching post nearby. "Looks like you've got everything under control here, Private. Thank you."

The youth beamed as they rode off toward camp.

As Jonathan dismounted, Owens greeted him with his usual gusto. "Top o' the morning to you, sir, and welcome back to our little home away from home." He rendered a smart salute that Jonathan returned along with a smile. "I expect my man here took good care of you."

"He couldn't have done a better job, First Sergeant." The private grinned and rode off.

"How've the men been?"

He smacked a finger on his palm. "Itching to go, sir. Just waiting for you to get back."

"Aren't you going to take any leave before spring?"

"Nope. I'm too good-looking for just one woman. Besides, I can't leave these chicks to fend for themselves. No telling what trouble they'd get into. Sir!" And the first sergeant was off, shooing the men back to work as they greeted their captain with salutes and smiles.

****

There were different ways of coping with winter's cold. Rubbing arms, blowing on hands, stretching a second pair of socks over holey boots. Jonathan endured it, waiting for the calendar to turn to March. Trees were leafing out and grass had greened up all around Chattanooga. Early spring rains had already rendered the area's dirt roads almost impassable. When they dried, the regiment would be on the march again. Okay with him. The sooner they got after the enemy, the sooner the war would end.

He'd received several letters during camp. All of Barbra's had that little bug at the top. He allowed as how it could have been a firefly but it still also could have been a cricket. No matter. Barbra wasn't the best artist, but she did stir his heart.

The army was readying to march south into Georgia when a letter arrived from his father. Unusual. The first one he'd ever gotten from him. He opened it slowly, wondering.

Dear Jonathan,

I hope you are well. About a month after you left, the whole family came down with typhoid fever. Claire got it first, then the sickness spread to Peter, then your mother, and then me. It hit your sister and mother hardest, and for weeks they suffered high fevers, chills, and wracking coughs. It was just too much for your mother. She passed after lingering in pain for too long. Claire hovered between life and death for weeks, but survived, as did Peter and me.

Your mother wanted me to tell you she loved you very much, and she's so sorry to leave you this soon.

There's a big hole in our hearts now, son. We need you to stay safe. Please.

Father

Jonathan let the letter fall to the cold ground. His

vision blurred. He sat with his head bowed, lost in memories of his gentle mother. Her tender words when he was sick. Gentle care every day as he grew. Smiling face, full of love. He was roused from his grief by the company clerk rapping on his tent pole.

"Sir, dinner's being served in the mess."

"Thank you, Sergeant Locke." Jonathan still didn't move, weighted down by a heavy sadness.

The clerk said, "Uh…are you all right, sir?"

"Uh…fine, Sergeant…I'll be along directly. Thank you." Jonathan fell to his knees, weeping. Arms lifted high. "Thank you, Lord, for sparing the rest of my family." He prayed for his mother's soul. She'd seen too little joy in this life. His Bible lay on the small wooden table next to his bed. He rested his hand on it a long while and gathered himself. With a swipe at his eyes, he headed to the mess tent.

Jonathan threw himself into his work—anything to channel his thoughts away from the hurt. Waves of sadness hit him day and night as his mother's sweet face came and went. They'd always shared a special closeness. She'd been the go-between between him and his father. A feeling he hadn't treated her well gnawed at him. Her life had been so hard. No doubt, he made it harder. She never complained, even though she endured so many disappointments. He was sure he had been one of them. Grief wrapped around his soul like a suffocating blanket, but preparing for what he hoped would be the war's final push couldn't be delayed.

He wrote his father, thanking him for being there for his mother, and thanking the Lord for sparing him, Peter, and Claire. He was so grateful she had been able to plan his wedding. She looked so happy. One of the shining moments of her life—he'd seen it in her eyes.

****

May 1864
Northern Georgia

As the spring campaign began, Sherman aimed to attack, attack, attack, over the hundred miles between Chattanooga and the southern prize, Atlanta.

Jonathan's men formed part of Sherman's right as the sixty-thousand-man behemoth flooded south. Outside the little village of Resaca, the enemy withdrew to protective breastworks. Jonathan gathered his troops as night fell. "The fighting will be hard here on out, maybe harder than any we've faced so far. We are to press them everywhere, all the time. Men"—he gazed around—"we're headed to Atlanta and the end of the war." Nods from grim faces were the only response.

When morning dawned, Union artillery was already pummeling the enemy spread around the small town. C Company sprinted through gaps in enemy lines over rough, torn-up ground. Jonathan paused in the woods to catch his breath as a hail of bullets cut the air. *Zip, zip, zip.* Still blue and gray bodies littered the field. He checked to see if any were his men. Pine trees burst into flames around him as shells struck nearby. A light wind failed to sweep acrid smoke away. Artillery and small arms fire pummeled what little cover there was. Jonathan couldn't be heard, so he waved the men to keep bearing south. He bypassed frontal attacks, intent on rolling up the enemy's flank while Federal artillery pounded them. Combat so close that burning gunpowder sparked flames as the two sides exchanged fire. The Confederates initially held, then pulled back before cobbling together a shaky stand farther south.

Jonathan called a halt under cover of what was left of a small collection of pine trees. Grimy men with frozen expressions dropped to a knee, holding rifles still sizzling in the blazing sun. Daylight dimmed. Jonathan grabbed a stale biscuit from his haversack and gathered his staff around a feeble fire.

The first sergeant pursed his lips. "Sir, we've sustained some precious losses. Four dead, six wounded, two missing."

Jonathan bowed his head in silent prayer. "Platoon leaders, please re-form your squads. Consolidate as necessary. Men, our orders are to continue to flank the enemy. We'll be moving south after them again tomorrow." The rest of C Company gathered on the outskirts of the campfire, standing shoulder to shoulder in the cool evening air.

One of the platoon sergeants spoke up, "Captain, how'd we do today?"

It was clear to Jonathan what he needed to say. What they needed to hear. His throat tightened in the smoky air and his eyes filled. "Men, I couldn't have been prouder of anyone than I was of you today. And there's nowhere I'd rather be than with you right here, right now." His stare held them hard as he gazed around the circle of soldiers. "And tomorrow, if the Rebs are still there, I know you'll make them wish they weren't. Those that survive the morrow will remember the valor of C Company the rest of their lives." The men nodded. "First Sergeant."

Owens pushed up off a log and drew himself to his full height. "This company earned its pay today, sir. I have to hand it to these slackers. They looked Johnny Reb right in the eye, and Johnny blinked." His booming voice drew men from other fires. "It's as fine a whuppin' of the Rebs as I've seen to date." He hitched his pants up and stuck his chin out. "The most surprising thing was, these ne'er-do-wells were the ones doin' it!"

The men roared. With a slight smile, Owens shook his head and sat down, bad leg stretched straight out front again.

Jonathan doused the small fire with a fling of his cold coffee. Steam sizzled as it rose, disappearing into the black night air. "Get a good night's sleep, men. Tomorrow's not going to be any easier."

The next day mirrored the first. The enemy fell back under the company's steady advance. Two of Jonathan's officers were hit—how bad, he didn't know. The platoon sergeants kept everyone pressing forward. No rebel yell split the air, the battlefield strangely muted. A steamy sun burned in the clear sky.

Jonathan called a halt about noon to give the men a breather, and a chance to reload. One of his soldiers rushed forward and knelt by a downed Confederate to their front. His platoon leader started for him, but stopped. The corporal carried the body back to C Company's line while the Confederate rear guard held their fire. Jonathan hurried over to the man. "You could have been killed, all alone on that field."

Louie Addams looked up. Tears streaked his dirty face.

"Addams, what is it?"

"This here's my brother, sir. My momma's favorite child."

Jonathan rested a hand on his shoulder. "I'm sorry, Louie."

Addams stared at his commander. "I hope what you said about Heaven is true, sir. I just hope that's where my brother is now."

Jonathan thought back to their campfire conversation. He hoped so, too. "Why don't you go back to regiment? Rest a spell. We'll see to your brother's care."

"Thank you, sir. I guess...I will." He rose, staring at his brother's still form. "No...I won't. I'll stay right here with the men. Where I'm supposed to be. Bart would want me to...I'd want the same for him."

Jonathan nodded and glanced the first sergeant's way.

Owens yelled for the men to continue the advance. While daylight held, they chased a fleeing enemy beating a fast retreat south, Addams quick-stepping at the front. As dusk descended, the two sides began to break off. Firing died down. Addams squeezed off a shot, reloaded, then fired another before turning away. An enemy round knocked him off his feet. Jonathan sprinted to him. The man was facedown with a bloody hole in his back. Jonathan turned him over. He gazed at a peaceful, still face. And almost retched.

His lips moved in silent prayer.

When they returned, C Company dropped dead tired onto one less, ratty bedroll.

Resaca was part of the Union once more.

Chapter Thirty-Six

Outside Atlanta, July 1864

The first sergeant strode to Jonathan's tent. "Oh, sir, it's time for our morning hike." Faint pink colored the early dawn sky.

Jonathan was already up, pulling on his boots. "Form the men, First Sergeant." He tied his meager bedroll and scanned the burgeoning city of Atlanta to the south.

Owens strode among the company's dead campfires. He roared, "You slackers in C Company fall out. Now!" A flurry of activity followed as veterans and recruits filed into formation. "Our commander would like to say a few words. Some of you won't understand him because you don't know the English language, so just nod your heads like you know what's going on." Turning to Jonathan, he saluted. "Sir, all present and accounted for."

Jonathan stood in front of a semicircle of his soldiers. "Men, we're getting closer to finishing off the Confederates. All we need are a few more good pushes and the job will be finished. We are to hold a railroad cut today. We expect stiff attacks as the day goes on, but we're going to hold that ground. We're going to make Johnny Reb wish he'd never been ordered up against us. Today, men who aren't C Company will see your bravery and wish they were part of this outfit. When your grandchildren ask you about the war, you can tell them what we did here. How we punished the enemy amid acts of heroism too numerous to count. Today, we live or die right here. Here we stand!"

Jonathan doffed his hat in an uncharacteristic display of bravado. He swirled it high above his head. The first sergeant took his cap off and swung it, too. The men joined in, cheering and whooping.

"Godspeed!"

Owens began kicking some of the men near him softly in the rear. "You won't be able to slack off today!" They beamed at him, others asking him to kick them, too.

Jonathan took Owens aside as the men moved into formation. "First Sergeant, we're part of the middle of the Federal line. We're to protect an earthen cut that a railroad passes through." The channel bisected nearly-barren, ten-foot-high walls of red Georgia clay on either side. "We will hold position on the south edge, while Companies A and B hold the northern side. Regiment says this railroad line is crucial, so I expect the fighting will be hard. I'm sure the Rebs want this patch of land back as bad as we want to keep it."

By sunrise, C Company was in position behind earthworks. The *pop-pop-pop* of small arms fire sounded to the south. An eerie noise split the air. The high-pitched scream of the rebel yell had unnerved him more than once.

"Here they come!"

C Company crouched low behind hastily thrown up log entrenchments. The Confederates slammed into them, screaming as they ran from the outer defenses of

Atlanta. Jonathan's men held their ground only with the help of Federal artillerists behind them who rained death on the fanatical enemy.

Withering small arms fire pinned C Company down. Confederate batteries kept up a relentless *boom, boom, boom*. The ground writhed with a life of its own as shells pummeled the earth. A hot sun showed no mercy. The enemy came in streams. Some fell in their tracks, soon replaced. Still coming. Near now. Bayonets soon. Blinding smoke. Had he ever been in a more horrific fight? There seemed to be no end to the enemy. The corporal next to Jonathan crumpled with a neat hole in his forehead. The dreaded rebel yell came from everywhere. Were they surrounded? The company teetered on breaking in the man-made smoky inferno.

Jonathan wavered. Should they stay in place and be sliced up, or give ground and try to regain it before nightfall? He yelled, "Hold the line! Steady!" Again and again, Confederates hurled themselves against his men. Rebels poured through a gap in the company's fortifications, bayonets fixed, finally overwhelming the position. He windmilled to withdraw while batteries rained destruction on both sides.

Jonathan was dazed by the repeated concussions. He formed the men again, at some distance from the cut and ran along his line in a crouch, pistol high. "Hold position, men!" Thunderous Federal shelling began to take effect, which slowed the enemy advance and threw them into confusion. The enemy slowly gave way back toward the cut. Small arms fire died down.

"First Sergeant," Jonathan yelled.

"At your service, sir!" Owens was not five feet away. "Sir, you know I'm right by your side when we're fighting."

Jonathan nodded. "Right now, we need to make a push to recapture that cut we just came off of."

Owens' eyes grew wide.

"Gather the staff. Hurry!"

The first sergeant hobbled off at a run, yelling at the top of his lungs.

Company leadership crouched around Jonathan. "Men, in every battle there's a point where the outcome hangs in the balance. This is that point. We win or lose right now. I want us to attack with everything we have left. Let's hit the enemy that's come between us and the cut, then retake it. Any questions?"

Owens said, "Sir, do I understand you want us to not only charge them Rebs that was just chargin' us, but plow through 'em back to the cut we just left?"

"That's right, First Sergeant. That cut is ours! If we don't attack right now, we'll lose any chance of getting it back. Prepare for a bayonet charge."

Platoons formed for the counterattack while small arms fire sliced the air around them. A haze hung between them and the enemy infantry. Maybe it would hide their charge. The first sergeant yelled, "Fix bayonets!" Men hurried to attach their last bit of weaponry.

Jonathan waved his pistol. "Charge!" He ran in a stoop. Blue and gray soldiers melted into a swirling mass. Acrid gunpowder assaulted Jonathan's senses. He stabbed at gray uniforms through watery eyes.

C Company smashed into a thin line of rag-tag Confederates, yelling, thrusting, then ran by them. Surprised looks on the rebels' faces told the story. Jonathan led them back to their morning position—the ground littered with still bodies. C Company held the southern side of the cut again.

Jonathan yelled to Owens, "Have the men form a defensive perimeter and go to ground behind whatever cover they can."

Even Owens' booming voice couldn't be heard above the fray, but his arm waving served the purpose. When more Union troops reinforced the south side of the railroad cut at a distance, a body of Confederates was trapped in between. They turned and ran, firing, trying to break out back toward Atlanta.

Jonathan dropped to the ground behind a shredded tree. A startling sight unfolded in front of his eyes in the haze. About twenty of his men, along with some from A and B Company, were still chasing the rebels, now streaming back toward the city. They disobeyed his orders to halt at the cut, but their blood was up. Jonathan watched with dread as his men raced farther into the salient created by the fleeing enemy.

"Come back! Stop!"

But there was no halting them. Jonathan leaped up and sprinted their direction. He raced with pistol drawn, glancing left and right. As he half ran, half crouched, he heard a soft, "sir" to his left. A soldier lay on his back on the smoky, tumbled ground. Oh no! Sergeant Hargrove.

Jonathan ran to him. "Gus! Where are you hit?"

In a whisper, Hargrove said, "I guess I'm done for, sir."

Jonathan knelt. A wheezing noise came from Gus's gaping, bloody chest as he breathed. "Don't talk. I'll get help."

"No…sir, please don't leave me. If I have to…die

in someone's company, I'm glad it's you."

"You're gonna be fine, Gus, just let me get some help." He placed his hand over the wound to stop the sucking sound.

"Sir…somethin'…I wanna say," he said in between raspy breaths.

"No need. Just rest until a litter-bearer comes. Medic!"

But Gus shook his head. "Couldn't stand you at first. You was…all full of yourself. Didn't care…nothin' about nobody…you and that lieutenant. All the men…felt the same way." He paused to catch his breath.

"You just save your energy, Gus. We can talk about this after I get help."

A coughing fit doubled Gus over. Foamy pink bubbles spread down his chin from the corner of his mouth. His face paled and he laid a hand on Jonathan's.

Jonathan's bottom lip trembled. He had no words.

"But you started to change…and before I pass…I want you to know how…proud…I am to have served with you… sir!" Deep, racking coughs. Gus drew long, labored breaths. A smile broke out on his pinched face and his dark eyes grew distant.

Jonathan's tears made fat, dark splotches in the red Georgia dirt. "Thank you, Gus. Thank you."

A peaceful look came over him as he breathed his last.

Jonathan swept a hand over Gus's eyes and prayed. Owens stood behind him, cap to his chest. As Jonathan stood, something struck his arm and spun him to the ground. He lay splayed on his back, not sure what had just happened.

The first sergeant crouched over him. Owens yelled, "Stay down, sir! Stay down." He knelt beside Jonathan and examined the wound, a worried look on his face. "Sir, the Rebs running away from us got reinforced. And the Rebs we just fought past came back up behind us. Looks like we're cut off." The enemy circled them. Owens signaled the men to lay down their arms. "We're not going to die here today with red Georgia dirt on our bellies!"

The Confederates poked and prodded their new prisoners. Jonathan yelled as loud as he could for the men not to resist.

The first sergeant straddled him. "Sir, there's about twenty of us that's been taken prisoner."

"Anyone else wounded? Anyone else need medical attention?"

"Don't know yet. We'll check everyone in a minute." Owens raised his arms over his head in surrender. Several Confederates taunted him as he strode toward them. The red-faced first sergeant yelled, "My captain is in need of medical attention. Now!"

A Confederate trooper blocked his way. "I'm sure he is, Sergeant, but our docs are busy sawin' away on our own troops right now."

Jonathan was feeling around his wound when Owens returned. He had to survive to see Barbra again.

"Sir, there's apparently no litter-bearers right now, so can you stand up with my help?"

Jonathan struggled to his feet and took stock of his men. They surrounded him, looking to him for what to do next. Two blue-clad bodies with red homemade XV patches lay in death poses nearby. Artillery whistled overhead. A Confederate captain gestured for the prisoners to move out toward Atlanta.

Jonathan's legs buckled. Owens grabbed him and yelled at two privates to carry him the rest of the way. He lost consciousness as they marched, only to be prodded awake by the barrel of a Confederate captor.

"You so much as touch him again, and I'll kick your arse," yelled Owens at a rebel youth who couldn't have been much more than sixteen. The private looked at his corporal, who had the good sense to tell him to move away.

The captors marched C Company into Atlanta to a rail yard where trains fanned out in all directions. They were herded away from the station to a side rail where several busted-up, rusted cars sat alone.

"This here's gonna be your new home for a while, bluebellies," a Confederate sergeant snorted. "Your car ain't leavin' 'til tonight, so better get yourself some rest."

The first sergeant started to shift Jonathan to a small piece of shade.

"You, man, halt!" The captain of the guard raised a rifle. "Get back here where I can see you."

Owens kept walking. He said over his shoulder, "Shoot me in the back if you will, but I'm moving our commander out of the sun. Steady on, men."

The guard hesitated, then told his soldiers to lower their rifles. "Stay right there, or you'll be shot."

After laying Jonathan down in the dappled shade of an old elm, Owens said, "Get his shirt off." He got his first look at Jonathan's wound. Hard to tell, but it looked like the bullet might have hit bone in the upper arm. He saw the old scars that covered Jonathan's stomach. "Lordy, who did this to my captain? He's all

Mike Torreano

torn up." He splashed precious water on the ragged red bullet hole, frowning.

Chapter Thirty-Seven

That night, Jonathan and his men loaded onto dilapidated cattle cars, headed for Andersonville prison. The sickening stench was only somewhat dulled by air rushing through the open slats of the rolling car. His men laid Jonathan in a corner, covered with a moth-eaten blanket. The train's screeching rattle brought no comfort in the stifling August heat.

Owens stared at his commander. Pasty face. Dull eyes. Shock. The bandana the first sergeant tied above the wound was covered with blood, so he replaced it with another. The bleeding was slowing. Maybe the bullet hadn't hit any major blood vessels.

He called for the men's canteens. Everyone held theirs out, even though they were all parched by the hot Georgia sun. When Owens cleaned the wound, Jonathan didn't react, responding to questions with only a nod or shake. The first sergeant placed a knapsack under his head. There was nothing more to be done for his commander right now.

As the creaky train groaned to a stop the next morning, Owens surveyed the surroundings. Andersonville—the war's largest prison camp. The compound sat on a cleared field of red clay ringed by Georgia pines. A hellish-looking place.

Jonathan was semiconscious. His men carried him through Andersonville's massive iron gates that stood apart as if waiting to swallow them whole. Armed guards kept vigil on either side. A suffocating stench of sweat, urine, and filth hit as they walked in. Fifteen-foot-tall timbers ringed the stockade inside, with another row of wooden fencing outside of that. Prisoners jeered their arrival.

Two guards who looked to be fourteen marched them to a crowded, clay-baked area. His men set Jonathan down gently. Shabby, tent-like shelters surrounded them, scant relief from the boiling summer sun. Owens dropped his gear on the soiled ground and gathered the men from A and B Company who'd been captured along with them. "You soldiers are now part of C Company, provisional. You'll be under Captain Gray's command as long as you're here." He bellowed to the two guards, "My captain needs a doctor immediately!"

They ignored him until Owens rushed them, followed by the men. One of the guards stumbled backward. The other swung his rifle upward and fired wildly into the air. The sound attracted the attention of a roving guard detail that hurried to the scene.

"What the hell is going on here?" The staff sergeant eyed his two corporals. His men trained their rifles on the new prisoners.

"These men wuz chargin' us, Sergeant, and I guess I'd a shot 'em all if'n you hadn't showed up just now," one of them said.

"You'd have shot them all, Corporal?" The sergeant eyed other prisoners clustered nearby. "You men stand back." He spotted Owens. "What's the problem, First Sergeant?"

Owens was in a fury, his uniform top drenched by

the stifling humidity. "My captain needs a doctor. He was shot yesterday and needs his wound looked at."

One of the guards raised his voice. "They was attacking us, Sergeant. Tell 'em they can't do that here."

The staff sergeant ignored him. Jonathan lay pale against the red dirt. "Take your captain to the hospital. Over there." He pointed toward several white tents in the distance, then turned to the corporals. "Can you two nitwits escort these prisoners to the hospital tent without shooting them or yourselves?"

After seeing Jonathan to the infirmary, one of the guards turned to Owens with a sneer. "I'll see you again, Yankee Doodle."

Owens stepped toward him, his face inches away. "I'll count on it, sonny."

C Company put up makeshift shelters and established camp as best they could in their squalid new home. Not much more than skimpy lean-tos. The first sergeant stayed with Jonathan. It was another several hours before he was seen by the doctor.

Jonathan was delirious. He mumbled, "Barbra...write you...couldn't get my hand...pocket."

The doctor glanced at Owens. "This arm's got to come off. Even so, I'm not sure he'll live. Should have gotten him here earlier. Help me hold him down."

Owens rested a hand on Jonathan's shoulder. "Doctor, can't you give him something to knock him out?"

"Don't have anything, Sergeant, but I doubt anything's needed. He likely can't even feel pain right now."

As Owens held Jonathan down, the doctor sawed

his left arm off below the shoulder. Jonathan screamed once, then was silent. He lay as if dead.

"Thank the Lord he's unconscious." Owens crossed himself.

The doctor cauterized the stump with a hot steel blade that stemmed most of the bleeding. He poured a white solution on it and wrapped the end with a dirty piece of cloth. "I don't give him much hope. Bring him back tomorrow if he's still alive." With the same bloody saw in hand, he turned away to work on another soldier.

The men carried Jonathan to their makeshift camp and laid him in one of the shelters they'd set up. A torn blanket draped over wooden poles. Other "tents" were uniform coats slung over dead branches, or ragged sheets of canvas.

Owens eyed the sluggish stream running through camp, polluted by urine and feces. "Get me some clean water from your canteens."

Among them, the men had enough water to last about a day. The first sergeant dribbled some over Jonathan's unresponsive lips. The next day he regained a groggy consciousness.

"Where are we, First Sergeant?"

"We're in a prison camp and not a good one neither, sir."

Jonathan grimaced as he tried to move. He looked down. "What happened to my arm?"

"You got shot. They took it off to save your life."

Jonathan stared at him for a moment, then nodded. Nothing to be done about that. "Where are the men? How are they?"

"They're around. They'll be mighty glad to see

you're awake, sir."

"I'm so thirsty. Can I have a drink?"

"Yes, but just one. We're saving the rest for the dancing girls coming over tonight."

Jonathan smiled wanly at the thought. "Will you do something for me, Rupert?"

Shock played over Owens' face. "Well now, sir, I didn't know you even knew my first name, much less that you'd use it."

"That's just between you and me. Will you—"

Owens cut in, "It's just that I don't want the men knowing—"

"Knowing what, Rupert?"

"I just don't want the men knowing my first—"

"Knowing what?"

Owens caught on. "Ah…thank you, sir."

"I need you to help me write a letter."

"And who might that be to?"

"My wife. I didn't get to tell you I got married last visit home."

Owens put his hands on his hips in mock anger. "No, you didn't!"

Jonathan tried to say something but only waved his hand before passing out again. Owens lingered a moment and rubbed his chin. He covered Jonathan with the threadbare blanket and limped to the mess tent.

Next day, Jonathan woke up in a daze, hallucinating and calling for Jesus. His men found him in his shelter, slumped on the ground and mumbling into space.

Owens yelled, "Get him to the doctor, now!"

The camp only had two doctors and a couple of nurses—male prisoners who'd been paroled to help care for the men. Owens stormed into the medical tent and found a doctor working on another soldier. Over his objections, Owens steered him to where Jonathan lay nearby. The doctor took his bloody dressing off and grimaced. An ominous bright redness surrounded the festering stump.

"I'll have to cut his shoulder open. His chances aren't good. Hold him."

With that, the doctor took a large knife and wiped it on his bloody smock. He sliced into what was left of Jonathan's upper arm, following an angry line of infection. As the flesh opened, a putrid smell filled the air. Blood mingled with yellow pus oozed onto the table. The doctor cleaned out as much of it as he could, then poured more of the white powder on the gaping wound. Jonathan was unconscious the whole time.

"Keep this open so it can drain. Wash it out every now and then. There's a little bit of clean water over there but I have no bandages. You'll have to do the best you can. He may not live to see the morning."

The first sergeant organized an around-the-clock vigil. C Company took turns cleaning Jonathan's wound and dabbing their commander's hot forehead. Jonathan mumbled through the night and by morning fell into a fitful sleep. Two more days passed the same way as he clung to life. The third morning he rallied somewhat, eyes fluttering and nodding in response to Owens. The area around the wound was no longer as bright red. Jonathan became more alert as the day passed. By nightfall, he was asking about the men.

Owens brought his first food in several days. "Sir, the Confederates have gone to almost no trouble to supply us with this feast tonight. What's your pleasure,

Captain? How 'bout a nice steak?" He held a tin cup up to Jonathan's mouth filled with a sorry liquid that passed for soup. Jonathan swallowed some along with sips of water before falling back into a deep sleep.

Owens bartered for a bar of soap and washed a tattered shirt to cover Jonathan's shoulder with. He sent a private to the hospital tent to buy a bottle of the white powder from one of the nurses. The doctor wouldn't give him anymore.

Jonathan awoke again two days later.

"Welcome back, sir." Owens smiled, but worry still etched his face.

"Hello, Rupert." Jonathan paused. "Do I look as bad as your face says I do?"

"You're back with us, now. That's the only thing that matters."

"How long have I been out?"

"Long time, sir. When you passed out, I didn't have this beard." Owens grinned.

Jonathan's eyes crinkled. "Would you write a letter for me?"

"Already done."

"What do you mean, already done? I haven't even told you who I want to write to."

"Barbra Carson Gray, a nurse at Mower Hospital in Philadelphia."

"How'd you know that?"

"You told me," said Owens, smiling.

Jonathan shook his head to try to sweep his confusion away.

"When you were crazy with fever, you kept calling her name, so I just asked you about her and you told me. I wrote her a letter to say you'd been wounded and captured and were here. Hopefully, we'll hear back from her soon."

Jonathan stared in amazement at this big bear of a man. "Thank you, Rupert."

"Sir, you ain't out of the woods yet, so don't go getting any ideas about starting to order us around, hear? In fact, I think we'll just keep you sick a while longer so's you can't be telling us what to do and spoil our vacation in this here garden spot. Yessir, I think that's what we'll do—keep you feverish till we've had our fill of letting loose. What do you think of that, sir?"

But Jonathan had already lapsed into another deep sleep.

Chapter Thirty-Eight

Summer 1864

Barbra stared at the envelope she'd just been handed. Addressed to her, but whose handwriting was this? Not Jonathan's. Was it about him? Her hands trembled as she drew the letter out and opened it.

Dear Mrs. Captain Gray,

My name is R. Owens. I'm your husband's first sergeant. He's been wounded and we've been taken prisoner here at Andersonville prison in Georgia. Captain Gray is fighting for his life but he asked me to write you, so you would know where he is.

She struggled to make sense of the words on the page. Jonathan's been wounded? Where? How bad?

I want you to know I'll do everything I can to see that he gets well. Don't you worry about him none. He's strong. And we all know about Mower Hospital. I'm sure you're giving our men great care there.

Respectfully,

R. Owens

"Dear God!" Barbra grabbed her coat. "I have to go now, Ruth."

"Go where, Barbra?"

"Georgia. Andersonville prison camp. My husband is being held there. He's been badly wounded!"

"Oh, my. I hear that's a dreadful place. The worst.

But you can't go, they don't allow northern women there."

"How do you know?"

"Because other nurses have tried to get in."

"What can I do?"

"Not much, I don't think. Pray."

"But I must see him; I could tend to him there. Surely, they'd let me do that."

The nurse shook her head. "Barbra, you're not thinking clearly. No, they wouldn't. All the newspapers are saying we should destroy the South for what they're doing to our men there. There's hardly any care...uh..." She stopped.

"Is there any hope they'll release Jonathan because he's injured?"

"I don't think so. Remember when they stopped prisoner exchanges a while back? My guess is it was helping the South more than the North. And I've never heard of anyone escaping from there."

"What if he dies? He could be dead now! That letter is a month old." Barbra dropped her coat and sagged to the floor.

****

Owens sought out one of the Union nurses he'd become friends with. "My captain's been here almost two weeks and isn't getting any better. If he doesn't start improving soon, he'll go downhill again. And in his condition, there likely won't be another rally. I need some more medicine. What should I get?"

"Well, for starters, you oughta get some of this bromine. Also, some medicinal herbs and tinctures. And some decent food...meat, or at least soup with some meat in it."

"Can you get those for me?" Owens asked.

"Yup, probably."

"Don't give me, 'yup, probably'. Yes or no?"

"Yes, but it'll cost you."

"Stay right here, I'll be back." Owens double timed in a limping run back to their camp. As dusk fell, he dug up the men's money. Prisoner gangs roamed different areas of the compound, so Owens squirreled his men's money away in a sock he buried inside his so-called tent. He dug it up and took the money back to what passed for the hospital.

He haggled with the nurse. "I'll give you a dollar for the bromine and that carbolic acid, too, and another for that other stuff there." The nurse disappeared into the hospital tent and returned with a cartridge sack containing the medicines. The first sergeant had a similar exchange with the mess sergeant.

Over the next couple of weeks, Jonathan's condition stabilized. He was more alert, no longer sleeping most of the day away. The first sergeant was getting some food in him, too. The company's kitty was almost empty by the time Jonathan rallied enough to get up and gimp around his shelter, sweating, shaking—Owens his constant shadow.

Jonathan said, "I'm so weak and thin there's no way Barbra would even recognize me."

Owens laughed. "I don't even recognize you." As they ate what passed for a meal, he said, "Looks like we hit the jackpot today, sir. At least most of the maggots in my...what is this...meat?...are dead." He held his potato up. "Damn, these are still plenty alive, though."

When Jonathan was able to be up and out, Owens had the men clean his shelter as best they could. The putrid smell was overpowering but keeping clean was the best way to stay alive. As he regained strength, Jonathan began to form the men up before breakfast, checking on their physical condition. He hoped this would restore some of the pride stolen from them when they were captured. The guards didn't like it but didn't interfere.

Another group that didn't like it was the prisoner gang that operated in this section of camp. Called "Raiders", they taunted C Company whenever they formed up, ridiculing them in front of the rest of the stockade.

"You sorry yokels. With all that marchin', whaddya think yer gonna do? March right out of camp?" They laughed and carried on. Jonathan had to restrain Owens. Being ridiculed by your own was almost worse than being shot. The two guards who'd had the confrontation with Owens the first day stood watching. Smiling.

C Company clashed with the Raiders daily as the criminals worked to keep control of this sector of the stockade. They shook prisoners down for money and controlled commerce in camp. Jonathan ignored them until they hurled rotten garbage at his men in formation. Food so foul not even starving prisoners would eat it. That evening, he and Owens sat in Jonathan's "tent" to plan how best to respond.

"We've got to hurt them somehow, Jonathan."

Whoa. Owens used his first name? That startled him, but then he'd sprung the same thing on Rupert. The tone the first sergeant used was one of respect, so Jonathan let it go—he had bigger things to worry about. "Yes, but how? We're outnumbered and the guards give the Raiders free rein because they're being paid off."

"Why don't we just surround them and beat them silly?"

Jonathan shook his head. "No, there's too many and they stay together. Besides, some have wooden knives."

"Well, we can't do nothing, sir. They'll just keep harassing us."

"I agree...here's an idea." And Jonathan laid out his strategy.

The next afternoon C Company gathered around Jonathan's shelter. He went over the plan. The men headed toward the "dead line" to scout the sentries. It was a simple post and rail fence almost twenty feet inside the stockade's timber walls. Towers spaced nearly a hundred feet apart dominated the camp perimeter. Guards manning these "pigeon roosts" shot anyone who dared cross the dead line.

As the day turned to dusk, Jonathan's men found two Raiders who roamed their sector together. One of his corporals taunted them, then backed away toward the perimeter. "You two ain't nothin'. My sister's tougher'n you! Ain't you scared to be out here all by yourself? Where's the rest of you cowards?"

One of the Raiders yelled, "Your sister's *uglier* than us, too." They howled and started after the man. The rest of C Company materialized from behind the guards.

Jonathan watched the plot unfold. This needed to be done. He asked the Lord to please forgive him.

As the corporal backed up, C Company grabbed the two Raiders from behind and hefted them up and over the dead line railing—screaming. Three shots rang out and C Company melted back into the crowd.

Jonathan's men searched for more Raiders over the next several nights. They found another two and disposed of them in the same way. Jonathan figured the guards, both the honest and corrupt ones, would do nothing to stop them. Corrupt guards would be scared something like that could happen to them. Honest guards would silently applaud this long overdue reckoning and look the other way.

Several nights later, Raiders pounced on some of C Company and beat them bloody. In turn, Jonathan's men took out another Raider, but this time other prisoners joined in. Several more Raiders ended up over the dead line. No longer just up against C Company, the criminals in Jonathan's sector melted away. After that, extortion and robbery within the camp dropped to nothing.

After C Company scattered the Raiders, the guards left Jonathan alone as he set about restoring military order in his area. He and Owens rebuilt morale by forming the men, even in their very confined quarters and weakened condition. He had them dig out the downstream end of the choked creek that bred dysentery throughout the camp until it ran faster, cleaner. But he couldn't increase the food supply. The saying went that it took seven prisoners to make one shadow. Camp officials allowed Jonathan the run of the stockade. Still, he was always accompanied by a small coterie of his men.

The first sergeant started a bank with Jonathan's help, and security provided by the company. Owens took money in from prisoners in exchange for credit. He spent it on medicine, food, socks, and boots—precious items he spread around camp. None of these made much of a dent in the nearly hundred deaths every day, though. Wagons brought food in the morning and trundled the dead out as they left, often stacked high.

The camp had its own economy. Most prisoners came to Andersonville still with some money in their pockets. With the camp's large numbers, hundreds of dollars changed hands every day. The day they arrived, the first sergeant had the men empty their money on his blanket, declaring he'd be their banker for the duration of camp. He doled money out to buy occasional privileges from guards, for extra food rations, or to bribe nurses for medicine.

A welcome August storm brought a hard, cleansing rain. The men caught everything they could in filthy hats, cups, shoes. They stripped and washed themselves in it, reveling in clean water. As the storm continued, a private pointed to the sky. "Lordy, Captain, what is that? I ain't never seen nothin' that scary-lookin' before. Somethin' that bad can't be good."

Jonathan eyed a solitary, dark, billowing cloud that appeared in an otherwise crystal-clear blue sky. The ominous formation moved toward camp, then hovered overhead. Suddenly, it unleashed a terrifying bolt of lightning which struck a fouled bank of the camp's stream. A strong flow of clean water sprung from the scorched earth and washed down the slope to the creek. Prisoners named it Providence Spring. For Jonathan, it was an answer to prayer.

Recent prisoners brought news of the outside world. Sherman had burned most of Atlanta to the ground and was on a march to the ocean. Word was he'd pass close by on the way. There were also rumors of a prisoner exchange, perhaps even of a mass release.

C Company was rounded up and loaded on a boxcar, amid fervent hopes the exchange rumors were true. The car's clattering reminded Jonathan of his train trips home. Home. That sounded so good, yet so far away. He yearned to see his wife and her smiling face. Hold her again.

There was no exchange. Jonathan sagged as the train pulled up at yet another prison camp, far away from Sherman. C Company languished for two weeks at this overcrowded stockade in eastern Georgia until the Union army passed by. The sick and infirm remained at Andersonville, Sherman could have them. Jonathan's heart sank as he and his men were herded on a train back to their same nightmare. False hope was as deadly a killer as dysentery. Sherman was so close. Why didn't he send soldiers to free them?

Chapter Thirty-Nine

The Raiders still operated in other sectors of the stockade while bribed guards turned a blind eye. Jonathan kept order in his area, so the commandant left him and his men alone. As a favor for keeping the peace, honest guards snuck him an occasional extra ration or fresh water when one of the men was sick. Clean water was the camp's most precious commodity.

Jonathan warmed a hand with his soldiers around a pitiful fire of bits of wood and scraps of paper. Sergeant Joe Evans was holding sway. "I'd even prefer gettin' shot at to being here, sir. Rather be dodgin' Reb bullets than just sittin' here idle, wastin' away. Not knowin' if we're ever gonna leave this hellhole alive. That's the worst part. I don't even look like myself anymore and neither do any of you."

Jonathan wanted to offer encouragement but words failed him. He'd seen men lose hope and when they gave up, they died. Despair was a relentless predator.

He asked the commandant if his men could man some details to break up the dreary daily routine. Soon, they were serving at the mess tent and gathering what little firewood was left from nearby woods. Firewood details gave C Company their only chance to leave the stockade, even if for just a short time. Jonathan cautioned the men to be on their best behavior, though. Other prisoners had been cut down trying to escape while on that same detail.

He'd written his father but hadn't heard back, not even sure the letter ever got to him. He wrote Barbra whenever he could find some paper, but guessed most of those letters never reached her, either. He feigned a cheery tone in them, not mentioning his health. One thing he didn't hold back on was telling her how much he loved her.

One letter from Barbra did make its way through, though, bringing the best news he'd ever heard.

Dear Jonathan,

I hope your health is better. I pray that prayer every day. Tell First Sergeant Owens I'm holding him to his promise to take care of you, because I have some wonderful news. You are going to be a father! Yes, it's true. I don't have a feeling yet if the baby's going to be a boy or girl, but I'll let you know when I do. This baby needs a father, so please be safe. I love you so much!

Yours,

Lizzie

Jonathan stared at the letter. A baby! He was going to be a father! He rushed to find Rupert and tell him the good news.

After exchanging a hug with his captain, Owens arranged a ceremonial toast with the men. Whiskey somehow turned up for the occasion. Spirits lifted their moods, if just for a while.

Fall replaced summer's burning scorch. Jonathan received another letter from Barbra updating him as she grew larger.

Dear Jonathan,

I think it might be a girl, so I thought of some names. Let me know if you like any of them. Belinda, certainly. Elizabeth? And I've always liked the name Claire. Wouldn't your sister like that!

I love you!

Lizzie

More than ever before, he looked forward to seeing her fireflies. But worries battered his confidence. How would he be able to hold his son when he got home? If he got home.

The promise of fatherhood kept Jonathan going—until dysentery felled him. The camp's abysmal sanitation spawned this dreaded killer. Nearly every prisoner had it at some point. Most hoped it wouldn't kill them. Some hoped it would.

At first, Jonathan thought his would be manageable. But the scourge was relentless. He'd eat, feel better, feel awful, then terrible. The cycle repeated itself until Jonathan grew so weak he couldn't get up. Owens tried taking care of him, but he was battling a milder version himself.

Jonathan was failing.

Owens called on Major Wirz, the camp commandant.

"Sir, you must help save my captain. If he dies, your hopes for a peaceful camp die with him. Those Raiders aren't gone yet. They know he's got dysentery and they're just waiting for him to die. If you lose him, you'll have nothing but trouble on your hands again."

The commandant had a doctor tend Jonathan directly. He gradually recovered but the disease left its mark on his insides. When he was strong enough, Owens got him up and around with a wooden cane he fashioned from firewood.

"Thank you, Rupert. This cane'll come in handy

when I walk out of here with you."

"That'll be soon enough, sir. I feel it in my bones."

"Funny you should say that." Jonathan gripped the gnarled cane in his right hand. A familiar pain ran all the way down his missing left arm. "Every now and then, it almost feels like I still have both arms. When the pain hits my left hand, sometimes I glance down to see if it's there. But every time I look, it's still gone." Jonathan managed a weak grin as they walked to the mess line.

Fall gave way to winter. Suffering increased. What scarce scraps there were, weren't fit to eat. And no more firewood. Sherman was long gone, along with all hope of being freed before the war ended. When would that be? And would they live to see it? How much longer could they hold on?

Winter skies brightened when Jonathan received the news from Barbra he'd been waiting for—hanging on for. He was a father! He hurried, as well as he could, for Owens.

"Rupert, I have a son!"

"Congratulations, Jonathan! You have started a new generation of Grays."

Jonathan beamed. "And I won't let him get involved in any damn wars like this one." The first sergeant had squirreled some cigars away just for the occasion. Smoke soon curled in the air around them, momentarily displacing the persistent stench. Jonathan talked the first sergeant's ear off well into the night.

By December, C Company had only scraps of clothing left to ward off the harsh elements. The only good thing cold southern evenings did was kill the mosquitoes that sickened everyone.

The bleakness of winter lingered. Jonathan could tell the South was teetering on collapse. The guards' sunken eyes gave them away. They looked as broken as he did, just not as skinny. Their mumbled conversations carried a hopeless tone. They grew distracted and there weren't enough of them to do even a poor job of running the camp anymore.

As spring peeked around the corner, the commandant approached a weak Jonathan. "Captain Gray, would you and your men like to form a standing detail to offload the trains? Your men will receive the cargo onto wagons. The guards are needed elsewhere now." Southern manpower dwindled daily.

"Yes, sir, we'll do that for you." Jonathan would have shaken hands but Wirz lost the use of his right arm in battle. Jonathan his left. A fine pair. "Might there be extra food for helping out?"

"That can be arranged, Captain. Please start with the next train."

The first sergeant formed teams to receive cargo and trundle it into camp. Large wooden crates contained everything from medicines to foodstuffs to clothing. Still, the trains never held enough to make much of a dent in the shortages.

While Jonathan and Owens were organizing the teamster detail, Raiders crept in. Everyone knew C Company had scattered them before. A guard alerted Jonathan to the danger, who went over things with Owens. They talked as they walked toward the train that had just whistled to a stop.

C Company maneuvered a wagon into position next to the open train car door. The cargo being offloaded by prisoners on the train, none of whom he recognized. They manhandled a heavy wooden pallet onto the wagon and jumped on while Jonathan's men drove it to the camp entrance. Two strangers moved in alongside Jonathan's men on the ground. Prisoners nudged the large crate to the edge of the wagon, while men on the ground positioned themselves at the crate's corners.

As the load cleared the wagon, the prisoners on the corners appeared to be having trouble holding it up. Several C Company men jumped in to lend a hand. Jonathan started forward but was stopped by the big arm the first sergeant flung across his chest. The prisoners pushed the crate off the final few feet and the corner prisoners let go. The crate crashed to the ground, on top of two of Jonathan's men. Where Jonathan would have been. The four phony prisoners backed away, trying to melt into the crowd that always gathered to watch offloadings.

Owens yelled, "Those are Raiders. Stop those devils before they get away or I'll guarantee you all hell will break loose in this prison!"

The guards shouted for the running prisoners to halt. They shot two dead. The other two were cut down by tower guards who continued to pour fire into the lifeless bodies as if taking target practice.

Owens grabbed a still-startled Jonathan while his men surrounded their commander. "Let's get you back to camp, sir." Others hurried to help their injured comrades.

Jonathan stared at the billowing cloud of red dust rising from the pallet. "My men—"

"I'll make sure they're cared for, sir, but right now we need to get you out of here."

Jonathan glanced back as they rushed him away. Damn this senseless war. Two more of his men had died under his command. His heart ached as he lifted a prayer for their souls.

The captain of the guard came to see Jonathan that afternoon. "Those Raiders bribed two of my so-called guards to get on the train. You may remember them. They're the ones your first sergeant tangled with that first day in camp. Long gone now, disappeared into the countryside."

Southern desertions were increasing daily. Jonathan stared at apparitions impersonating men as they staggered around the stockade. The dead lay where they fell. Prisoners shuffled around the bodies. Guards ignored the fallen as long as they could, the putrid stench overpowering. Fat rats scurried around the compound, always just out of reach. Black flies nearly covered everyone, both alive and dead.

Jonathan kept a close watch on his men as conditions deteriorated and spring approached. He wasn't sure he'd live to see war's end. As February ended, he was down to willing the company to survive. He had run out of ways to keep morale up when wonderful news came. The captain of the guard approached with a big grin. "Grant has authorized exchanges again and Major Wirz has already manifested you and your men on one of the first trains out."

Jonathan wanted so much to believe him. He prayed, "Please, Lord, let this be true. We couldn't take getting our hopes dashed again." Jonathan, who had worked so hard to keep his men's spirits up, was on the hoping end of things now.

341

Chapter Forty

March 1865

Union trains cued up outside the prison—the prospect of freedom almost too much to comprehend. Jonathan gathered Barbra's letters and the one from his father. Nothing else mattered. He didn't look back as he leaned on Rupert's cane and struggled to the train with him. He said a prayer for the souls of his eight men who would stay behind forever.

Their boxcar was another filthy, smelly cattle car but he was beyond caring. There was no jubilation, no yelling, no laughing. Jonathan gazed out the open car door in apathetic silence as Andersonville disappeared from view.

They'd be exchanged at Vicksburg, four hundred miles west, a trip that would take several days. When he arrived, Jonathan leaned on Owens as they hobbled over the Big Black River bridge. They'd board a boat here for the last leg of their journey home. That word never sounded so good. To be this close, but still so far away was almost worse than the hellhole they just left.

They sat down to their first good meal in—forever. The mood was subdued. Vicksburg was the site of some of the company's fiercest fighting. Several of their comrades, including Captain Thompson, breathed their last here almost two years ago. Jonathan led a prayer service for them that first night. There was no interest in visiting those wretched battlegrounds again.

An army exchange lieutenant approached Jonathan in the mess line. "Captain Gray, you and your men will be here until the war is officially over and proper transport can be arranged."

"How long might that be?"

"Dunno, sir. As soon as Lee surrenders, I guess." The lieutenant stared wide-eyed at the skeletons of C Company.

Jonathan noticed. "You think we look bad, Lieutenant? Well, we feel just as bad."

"Sir, if you would, please take your men to the quartermaster's tent, where you'll be outfitted with new uniforms. I took the liberty of drawing a sidearm for you, along with a new holster." The lieutenant smiled as he thrust the gleaming Colt toward Jonathan.

Jonathan stared at the gun. In a quiet voice, he said, "I won't be needing that anymore."

"But...sir. Officers have sidearms—it's part of the uniform."

"I said, no thank you, Lieutenant."

The lieutenant stared at Jonathan, confusion etched on his face.

The first sergeant stepped forward. "Didn't you hear the captain, Lieutenant? He said that'll be all." Owens grasped the Colt. Jonathan returned the man's salute.

The first sergeant took Jonathan aside. "Sir— Captain Gray, sir—might I suggest wearing the pistol?" He glanced at C Company lounging nearby under a live oak tree. "The men will wonder, sir, if they see you without a weapon. They expect you to wear one.

You're an officer, but you're more than that to them—you're their commander."

Jonathan hesitated. "Give it to me, Rupert." He took the pistol, checked to make sure it wasn't loaded, had Owens help him strap the holster on in the skinniest notch, and stuck the weapon in it. With a hand on the first sergeant's shoulder, he said, "Now let's see about some of that cornbread they're so fond of around here."

Jonathan took the gift of time to get his men back into shape. He gained weight over the next few weeks, his body slowly adjusting to having enough food again. Writing Barbra was the perfect way to while away the hours. Jonathan wanted to hear everything he could about his new son. Her letters said he was a beautiful, bright-eyed child who smiled all the time. A son. His son. She'd named him Robert Rupert Gray. How did he get so lucky? And what did his father think of that?

Owens found Jonathan in a pensive mood as he sat outside his tent. "What's wrong, sir? You seem far away tonight."

"I feel far away. Been thinking." He pulled his new uniform coat tighter against the chilly evening.

"About?"

"About what I've done with my life so far. Or haven't done—"

Owens interrupted, "Sir, if I may, you should worry less about the past and look more to what the future holds. Like with that new wife of yours."

Jonathan shook his head. "I know I haven't turned out the way I was raised. I've done some things I'm not very proud of. Growing up, I turned against my father for no good reason. I thought he was a coward. Wanted to show him I wasn't like him at all. And now, look where we are, look at this"—he swept his arm at the destruction that surrounded them. "This is the misery war brings; this is the cost of hate and pride." He paused. "I was raised pacifist. Growing up, I never thought my father's way was right. But now…"

"Is your father a good man?"

"Yes. Yes, he is."

"Then you've turned out like him."

"Thank you, Rupert." Jonathan looked to the starry heavens. "Most of all, though, I wonder what God thinks of me."

"Well I'm pretty sure He's still in your corner."

"I'm not so sure. I don't think I'd be in my corner if I was Him."

"Now hold on a minute, Jonathan. Didn't I hear you talking about God's Grace with Sergeant Addams a while back?"

"You heard that?"

"Sure did. You know I watch over you pretty close. You said something about God not having a scale, that he welcomes everyone who believes in Him."

"Yes, you're right…of course. Thank you for reminding me. I needed to hear that."

"Seems to me He's been pretty good to both of us. He's brought you a fine wife."

Jonathan nodded. "Yes, he has. I'm just rambling on. Don't worry about me," Jonathan said, almost as if he meant it. He flexed his stump back and forth.

"Arm hurting again?"

"A little. The strangest thing is it's not even there. If it's gonna hurt, at least it ought to be there, shouldn't it? That's only fair." Jonathan shook his head with a wry smile. What would he be able to do after the war?

Who was going to want to hire a one-armed man?

Owens smiled. "What say you and me go back to Cincinnati together?"

Jonathan stared at his best friend. "You'd do that? Go back with me?"

"Sure. You're still going to need a lot of looking after."

They clinked glasses in the night.

Chapter Forty-One

As the sun peeked above the horizon, Jonathan and his men crowded makeshift docks, straining to see their ship appear out of the morning mist that hung low over the Mississippi.

The exchange captain stood next to Jonathan. "There's your ship, Captain Gray. The *SS Sultana*. It's a new ship, only two years old. It's hauled goods and people up and down the river ever since. Recently commissioned as a troop carrier."

Jonathan stared while it docked. "Looks like a good ship. But…it's not big enough to carry us all. How many are they going to take on today?"

"All of your men, and the rest of the troops here," the captain said. "The ship was designed to carry four hundred passengers, but routinely carries many more than that. It's handled the lot of you before."

While the *Sultana* was being tied down, Jonathan wondered. Could it carry two thousand men?

The first sergeant bellowed, "Men, find us a place on board where we can all stand together. There'll be no sitting as we leave behind our comrades who fell here."

The ship lumbered away from the dock. Jonathan stood at an outside rail and watched the South fade away in the distance. He didn't know how he felt. How he should feel. Numb, more than anything. As the black waters of the Mississippi slid by, the two comrades talked about what was ahead. Jonathan wanted to see Barbra and hold his son. The only things he'd been interested in for a long time. "Guess I'll try to get on with a newspaper back home, too."

"That's fine and dandy for you," Rupert said, "but I think I'd like to get into banking. I liked doing it in that cursed prison." He chuckled.

Their talk turned closer to home. "Hopefully, young Robert favors his mother."

Jonathan punched him on the shoulder. "I hope so, too." He wondered if Lizzie would let him call him Sonny.

Rupert laughed again. "I'll just call him by his middle name so 'Rupert' will live on."

Jonathan held his friend's gaze. "I don't have anyone I feel closer to, besides Barbra, than you. Thank you for all you've done for me."

Rupert blinked rapidly. "'Tweren't nothing, sir. You did all the work, growing into a fine commander we would have followed anywhere. I was just glad to be there to see it."

Jonathan stared at him, pursed his lips, and nodded, eyes filling. "Barbra and I will live at my folks' farm until we can find a place of our own. You'll come stay with us while you look for work, won't you?"

"Well, I hadn't really thought about it but that sounds awful good."

Jonathan smiled. "I'll wire my old editor at the *Inquirer* and see if he'll write a letter of recommendation for me."

Rupert nodded. "I don't suppose you know any bankers in town?"

"No, I don't, but Barbra worked for the railroad there for some time. She'd probably know someone you could talk to."

"Sounds fine, Jonathan. I might even take care of your money."

"That wouldn't take long, I've never had any." He paused. "I wonder if Barbra will still want to care for soldiers after we're back? Maybe at a hospital in town?"

"Sounds like you think she might."

"I know she might."

"Did you get that telegram off to her? About when we arrive?"

"Last thing I did before we boarded."

When the ship reached Memphis, C Company gathered together at dinner. Jonathan grinned as he listened to the often-hilarious stories that cascaded one after another, lampooning the absurdities of war. The paddle wheeler lurched as they pulled away from the dock. He could almost sense the ship struggling against a current quickened by spring rains. After saying goodnight, he smiled on the way back to his berth.

Jonathan was asleep when three of the four boilers let go. He woke to the sickening shriek of a ship in its death throes as the middle of the ship heaved up and out of the water. The explosion hurled him through debris-filled, fiery air before he smacked into the cold, hard water, stunned. The Mississippi was on fire all around him, and the ship one big firecracker against a pitch black sky. He yelled for Rupert but deafening concussions and crackling fires hid his cries. Scores of men leaped to escape the blazing ship. Burning smoke hammered his senses.

He struggled one-armed amidst the choppy water. Furious leg kicks were the only thing keeping him above water. Waves tossed him about and weariness washed over him. He'd never see his son, or Barbra again. Oh, to be this close! All the combat he'd survived and he was going to die in a flaming river at night. No—he wouldn't—couldn't. Not this close. He gasped for breath. Gagged on foul water. Something bright ahead. Another fire—or a light? What was a light doing out here? His muscles screamed as he dog-paddled toward it as best he could. A blurry image was in the light. Were those people? He couldn't tell. Swells tossed him up and down while the light disappeared and reappeared. Had to hold on. Flames circled him. He fought forward through burning wood and oil and drew near, beyond exhaustion.

Sonny! Robert! Someone else smiled faintly in the brightness behind them. Rupert? All three faded as he struggled closer. A different face—Barbra!

She stretched a hand to him from inside the light, holding his son. Smiling, motioning him closer. Energy flooded his muscles. He hollered, "Wait for me! I'm coming." Jonathan made one last surge as his strength gave way. He reached, and the light enveloped him.

Chapter Forty-Two

Three Years Later

Barbra snapped the wagon's reins as the farmhouse came into view. The family always came to Sunday supper with Tom. She bustled through the side door and into the kitchen. Belinda's kitchen—now Claire's. Sundays, she cooked Tom's favorite meal—beef stew and broccoli, with a savory brown sauce. Dessert was rhubarb pie when she could find the makings.

Peter caught a whiff while still outside. He leaned in the door, smiling. "That sure smells good, Miss Barbra. Is that cherry pie?"

"Peter Gray, you know what kind it is as well as I do," she said, with a smile herself. She'd developed a fondness for Jonathan's younger brother. Peter was fully grown now, all arms and legs. He'd take over the farm from Tom some day.

Over the last few years, they'd all worked together to build a new house on the land Tom showed Jonathan years back. Peter would live there soon with a family of his own. The two-story wood and stone home had a fine foundation and the latest in windows.

Tom crafted the doors out of the same wood he used for siding. Fashioning the floor was the most challenging part. Riding out to size up trees, he passed the lone mulberry that knocked him from his horse all those years ago. He paused for a moment, thinking back to how Jonathan rescued him. With a shake of his head, he kicked the gelding into a trot. At the Little Miami, he gazed at the big black walnut. Good wood, but leave it be. Just leave it be. He settled on a sizeable elm nearby.

The house turned out even better than hoped. As the home went up, Peter and Claire grew up in many ways as well—Claire the woman of the house now. Barbra had also forged a new closeness with Tom. A nearness she never would have imagined. The few times she'd been around him years ago he'd seemed silent, distant. Not the smiling, helpful grandfather she'd discovered underneath.

After dinner, they all sat on the front porch—Tom in his saggy wicker chair. Shadows spread like fingers over the rolling hills. The setting sun gathered the rest of daylight in and stole away. Dusk settled over the land and faint stars twinkled to life overhead.

Barbra chatted with Tom while Sonny played in the grassy yard. Out of the corner of her eye, she saw him holding something. What was it? She put a hand to her mouth. "Sweetheart, come out here, will you?"

Jonathan came out of the farmhouse, balancing glasses of lemonade one-armed on a tray. He smiled at his son standing in the yard, intent on something cupped in his hands. He patted his wife's round belly and set the tray down. Another Gray soon. A girl, he hoped. What a gift a daughter would be, and he already had a name for her. Belinda.

Barbra called out to her son, "Robert Rupert Gray, come here, please."

Sonny ran toward her with an impish grin. "Coming, Momma!" He opened his hands and showed them the firefly. It spread its wings, lighting again as it flew away into the night.

Barbra grinned. "Wouldn't Robert and Rupert have loved to see their godson?"

Jonathan smiled. "They see him, I know they do."

Barbra squeezed his hand and his eyes filled.

The End

Author's Notes

Fireflies at Dusk has an interesting genesis. It's the first story I wrote as I began my author's journey years ago. With a lifelong abiding interest in the Civil War, I set out intending to write about Major General George McClellan, one of the most notable northern commanders of that conflict. McClellan has always intrigued me because of the loyalty and devotion he inspired in his men. Even Robert E. Lee, the famous Confederate commander, didn't enjoy the admiration of his soldiers the way McClellan did. The man is a bit of a military enigma, though—both loved and castigated for his reluctance to fight.

But in order to bring the reader close to McClellan, I thought there needed to be someone else whose eyes we could "see" him through. Someone close to him. Hence, Jonathan, who became a member of his wartime staff. In order to give Jonathan depth, I wrote about his childhood years in southern Ohio. As I fleshed him out, though, he began to take the story over—and surprise, surprise—pushed McClellan into the background. But at the same time, I was pleased, as it enabled me to inject an intriguing twist of pacifism into the storyline which generated the festering conflict between Jonathan and his father that Jonathan struggled with over the years.

My research on pacifism and the Underground Railroad was fascinating, indeed. I visited the National Underground Railroad Museum in Cincinnati to get a better feel for the flow of "runaways" and how the "railroad" operated. I highly recommend visiting the museum. And yes, Quakers did help runaways, often hiding them until they could journey safely north. I was also intrigued by the homemade quilts that signaled whether it was safe to travel, and which direction to take. A fascinating historical fact I was unaware of.

My daughter, Lisa, researched many events of that era which helped me ground the narrative in historical authenticity. She was the one who uncovered information on the *USS Sultana*. In her death throes, the *Sultana* took most of her passengers down in what is still the biggest maritime disaster in US history. Between 2100 and 2400 people were aboard, nearly all of them soldiers returning from the war. Between 1200 and 1500 perished with the ship. Perhaps the main reason it's such a little-known historical footnote is because the tragedy happened within days of President Lincoln's assassination.

A delightful element of the story that sprung up from "nowhere" was the idea of Barbra's letters. They allowed me to deepen the romantic ties between her and Jonathan over time and, importantly, to reveal more of both their characters. Barbra also served nicely as Jonathan's conscience throughout much of the novel. Her letters helped start him on an arduous journey to reclaim his self respect.

I used a Gray family secret to add an underlying layer of mystery and drama to *Fireflies*. Tension and conflict are interest builders in any story. Belinda and Tom's secret also allowed me to reveal a softer side of Tom Gray that caught me by surprise and perhaps you as well. By the end of the story, it turned out Tom Gray wasn't nearly the hard case he seemed earlier.

Some of the scenes, dialogue, and descriptions came from my own military experience. What's the old saying? We write what we know? I especially enjoyed First Sergeant Rupert Owens and his irreverent ways in the midst of harsh combat. When I was a new lieutenant, I had a senior master sergeant in my office who I modeled Owens after. War is unimaginably harsh, and Rupert's manner served to lighten some of *Fireflies'* most intense scenes, another unexpected pleasure.

Along with becoming Jonathan's best friend, Parker was a bit of a symbol for what Jonathan thought he wanted after he left the farm. The change in their relationship was a metaphor for the battering Jonathan's homegrown values took after leaving home.

Barbra represented Jonathan's true love interest, and even I, as the author, was rooting for him to cast Marion off and come back to her. She was smart and pretty, with a no-nonsense attitude about her—just the type of strong woman who made a fitting partner for Jonathan. Steadfast at a time he desperately needed someone to be.

And speaking of Jonathan, I enjoyed seeing how he ultimately came full circle with his father. What started as a youthful conflict between them gnawed at him over time, and it wasn't until he came to terms with himself that he could come to terms with his father and appreciate him and his pacifism. Watching Jonathan grow and change during the war was gratifying. I haven't been in combat, but I have many close friends who have. The relationships among combat veterans are among the closest a person will ever experience. The war's harsh fighting was the cauldron where Jonathan's true nature would come to the fore. He would either prove his mettle or not, and it was satisfying to see him grow into the man he became. I particularly liked some of his speeches before battles, and the one-on-one conversations with his men at night.

Faith also played a central part in *Fireflies*. Jonathan's spiritual journey, as is true for many of us, wasn't always on an even keel, but he never turned his back on God, even when he was behaving at his worst. Life's journey is like that, isn't it, with smooth and rocky paths, sometimes straight and sometimes twisting. *Fireflies'* cast of characters experienced many of life's highest highs and lowest lows, just like we do. But ultimately, with Barbra's help, Jonathan made decisions that set his feet back on solid ground. He returned to the good person deep down we always knew he was, even if he had pushed his family and Barbra away.

Above all, *Fireflies* is a coming-of-age tale that twisted and turned in unexpected ways for me as a "seat-of-the-pants" writer. It never was about the war, although the Civil War is perhaps *the* watershed event in our history. I enjoyed so many things about writing *Fireflies*, and I hope you enjoyed reading it as well.

A word about the author...

Mike Torreano is a multi-award-winning author who is a student of American history. He first fell in love with the Old West in the fifth grade in Ohio when he read his first Zane Grey novel. From then on, he devoured every ZG novel he could get his hands on. He's also had a lifelong interest in the Civil War, which tore at the very fabric of our nation.

Mike has taught university-level English and Journalism and is a member of Pikes Peak Writers, Rocky Mountain Fiction Writers, Colorado Authors League, Western Writers of America, and several other writer groups.

He's written four traditional western mysteries, all set in the nineteenth century American West. *The Reckoning,* and its sequel, *The Renewal,* both take place in Colorado Territory, and *A Score to Settle,* and *White Sands Gold,* are set in New Mexico Territory. All are published by The Wild Rose Press. His first published work was a short story, "The Trade", which appeared in an anthology titled *Remnants and Resolutions.*

Fireflies at Dusk is his debut historical novel and was born out of his abiding interest in the Civil War, even if the story wasn't ultimately about that conflict.

He brings his readers back in time with him as he recreates life in nineteenth century America. He's appeared on a number of broadcasts, and his works have received awards from Firebird Book Awards, American Book Awards, and Literary Titan.

Mike lives in Colorado Springs with his chief brainstormer and wife, Anne.

www.miketorreano.com

Thank you for purchasing
this publication of The Wild Rose Press, Inc.

For questions or more information
contact us at
info@thewildrosepress.com.

The Wild Rose Press, Inc.
www.thewildrosepress.com

Printed in the USA
CPSIA information can be obtained
at www.ICGtesting.com
LVHW080029090124
768361LV00015B/844

9 781509 251469